Silent Partner

Brad Farrar

ISBN: 1481080237

ISBN-13: 978-1481080231

To Carole.

ACKNOWLEDGMENTS

This book would not have been possible without the love, encouragement, patience and editing skills of my wife, Carole, my parents, Ronald and Gayla Farrar, and my sister Janet Worthington, all of whom helped tremendously with substance, process and motivation throughout many rewrites. I am grateful for the love and support of our children, Elizabeth, Grace and Caroline, and also would like to thank Jean Ayre, Mark, Blair, Andy and Josh Worthington, Franny, Lucy, and Ms. Susan Kelly. Last but not least, thanks to Pete Pantsari, Professor Van Kornegay, the University of South Carolina School of Journalism, and Ashley Wells for excellent and timely cover design work.

CHAPTER 1

Bristol City Hall

Tuesday, October 6th

9:50 P.M.

The D.A. ran his fingers over the cut glass, trying to remember why he'd brought elegant crystal to this sterile government building. This was the land of plastic ware and lowest bidders, not Waterford and late night toasts. Especially ones made alone, and in defeat. Michael Pomerantz should be celebrating victory in the closest thing to a show trial Bristol had ever seen. Instead, he was drowning his sorrows, focus grouping excuses and dusting off his résumé. He'd grown to expect the irony. Somehow it didn't seem out of place to be raising the highball for a wake, not even his own.

The season changed later this year, hanging on longer than he would. Anywhere else and it would be an August heat wave. In Bristol summer hardly relented. His old friend and law school classmate was right. Autumn is for fall guys.

The sound bite dripped from that shyster's lips like a million couch cuddling promises made during a thousand free initial consultations, lapped up in a market so small the weathermen had groupies. Whenever the flamboyant Mr. Lovelace opened his mouth a press conference was sure to follow. Remington Lovelace was ahead of the D.A.'s office all the way. A mole on the grand jury guaranteed it. The spontaneous interviews he swerved into, caked in makeup with three talking points polished for punching in time for the six o'clock news. Never mind that his drug dealing client had the motive, the opportunity and the will to take another man's life over a chunk of change that wouldn't have floated either for a week. Forget that the body, the weapon, the murderer and his DNA met in the same place at the wrong time. Or the unforced confession and the retraction that dug the hole deeper. As the scientific evidence proved, there were two people in the world who could have killed local kingpin Fuzzy Shanks—the man who confessed to it after he pulled the trigger on Bristol's meanest street, and a guy who'd never left Sri Lanka.

It was a slam dunk. All Pomerantz had to do was walk into the Promised Land. Next stop attorney general, maybe even the governor's mansion. He'd run out each ground ball, planned for every contingency, stacked the prosecutor's table with the best litigators in his office, and rehearsed the case half a dozen times in front of law school moot courts at the College of Bristol. His closing argument was so engrained that on the rare nights he slept one cliché or another would rouse him, leading to a chaotic search in the dark for something to write it down on before the thought escaped him. Like a football coach who could picture every move on the field but forgot what his wife's face looked like, there was always more film to be studied. There had to be something else. The surprise witness. The glove that didn't fit. Something. What had he missed?

Jury nullification. It's just like obscenity. No one can define it but everyone knows it when he sees it.

All Lovelace cared about was that his client had issues. Society was responsible for them, along with the painful years since that hadn't healed the wounds a disadvantaged childhood had inflicted. With a more tender birth no doubt his client, Suite T. Lemon—Lovelace actually introduced a high school diploma bearing that name—would have held his temper instead of an automatic weapon. He would have reasoned with an equally unreasonable man, moved him with his words rather than intimidated him with the threat of deadly force. But that was how the privileged settled their differences, not the way the criminals he represented rolled. They stayed safe and undeterred, knowing that their guilt was irrelevant so long as Remington Lovelace could convince one holdout that the police hadn't gone about catching them the right way. Again.

Pomerantz could still hear the lawyer's affected Southern drawl, Lovelace creating his own pretrial publicity problem well enough to change the venue. Move the case to the beach, he argued, where cool breezes blow over cooler heads than they have in the heartland. *Well, members of the media, what can I say? I reckon as far as the Bristol D.A. is concerned, the wrong defendant is better than no defendant at all. The way he sees it…autumn is for fall guys.*

At the time it sent sharp pains through every part of his body. Now, Pomerantz could barely make a fist. In a week full of

Mondays, he wished he were back in the throes of the television trial, swapping ten-cent mantras with Lovelace on the courthouse steps. And without him weighing it down, City Hall could amble toward hell that much faster.

The D.A. raised his hundred-proof coffee once more for the dark side. "To you, Remy Lovelace, the highest paid used car salesman in the world."

Pomerantz let out a laugh that echoed through every corner of the City Attorney's Office. He'd been D.A. since Clinton's first term, when voters in Bristol made a straight party pull like always. He enjoyed prosecuting criminals because he understood it. You played by society's rules and people like Michael Pomerantz left you alone. You fouled the spring in this town and his kind had work. Remington Lovelace counted on it. Elected officials in these parts get more feedback than stage actors. As long as the voters were happy, the D.A. could run his office however he wanted, from wherever he wanted, and no one would touch him.

This place was different. He'd seen it coming, and he still froze. When the council chairman approached him six months earlier he should have refused the city attorney's position, handling all of Bristol's civil matters as well as its criminal docket. But they asked and he accepted—*on an interim basis, Mike, you understand. Just until we can screen all the candidates.* He was the jurisdiction's chief legal advisor until the council found someone more malleable—a cheap date among the legal profession's withered wallflowers.

The D.A. was worn thin with no energy to hide it. Maybe the dental records would show how much of a burnout he was. At forty-eight, Michael Pomerantz was still a reasonably handsome man, but the city had added ten years to his face, and taken away as many from his life expectancy. His blood pressure was high enough for two walking time bombs, as was his cholesterol count, even if rounded down to the nearest hundred. A touch of gray at the temples, the lines beneath them were well defined now, and didn't fade into smooth skin when he relaxed his face. His eyes were steelier than when he'd first asked a jury to put a man to death, and they hadn't batted much since that day. Tall and slender when he joined the D.A.'s Office, a spread was setting in, buckling his knees and destroying his tennis game. He'd hoped to grow old and distinguished in a job where that look would have been good on him. Now, he was just hoping to make old.

Pomerantz knocked off the last ounce of whiskey. He slammed the glass on the desk like he'd done something only another drunk could have appreciated. It tasted good, warming his extremities but drying his mouth with every sip. Why was he shaking?

Beneath his desk were enough unreturned messages to fill a phone book. Somehow there was still room for his gym bag. Inside was a nine-millimeter pistol stuck between a pair of basketball shoes. He usually kept the *Beretta* under his car seat, but he'd promised to shoot a few rounds with the sheriff when he made it back to the department, like the old days as a deputy before law school. There was a clip in it. From its weight he could tell the magazine held about fifteen rounds, plus the one he'd chambered. That was a dangerous way to carry the weapon, the sheriff told him, but Pomerantz insisted that prep time was for paper targets. If the real thing came, he'd be prepared, just like he was for every trial.

Pomerantz flipped through the stack of messages and found the one he wanted. He needed to hear a woman's voice, a sexy woman, but not his wife because she'd already sent her thought for the day, and not his mistress because she'd sent hers, too. He needed one who didn't want anything from him except his time and advice—an appreciative client, if it wasn't asking too much.

Selena Hall was her name, a holdover from the few private practice cases he took before the city removed "interim" from his title. Final hearing in two weeks. Divorce, naturally, but it was somebody else's so it wasn't as depressing. Beside the secretary's notes he'd scribbled a reminder to call before she left for California. There was a modeling job or a boyfriend or something there.

"Two weeks ago," he exhaled. "You're home now…or else you're never coming back."

He dialed the number and swiveled his chair toward the Bristol skyline, still and peaceful on this muggy evening. The low moon looked like a giant snowball. It threw long shadows down empty streets between shorter high-rises than they build up north. McSkyscrapers. He drifted as the speakerphone rang and rang.

A sultry voice answered, "Hell-ooohh."

"Selena," he began, not realizing. "Dammit." The machine.

"You've reached the Hall residence. We're not in right now, but if you leave your name and a brief message, we'll return your call. Thanks. *Beep…*"

The words washed over him like yesterday's weather report. He snapped to and hoped she'd listen through the long pause.

"Selena…this is…this is…Michael Pomerantz. I apologize for not getting back to you sooner. I guess you're still in California. Long shoot, huh? I'm glad your career is going well."

He stared blankly at Lovelace cupping the back of his murdering client's *not guilty* neck beneath the above-the-fold headline in the Bristol *Chronicle*.

"Uh…I've been slammed here at the city. Maybe you've been following it in the paper, the Jones trial and everything. I wanted to touch base with you about the final hearing. I'm sure you're ready to move on with your life."

His voice cracked. He forgot what he'd said, but knew he must have been speaking for himself.

"Move on," he repeated. "How 'bout give me a call when you get back from L. A.? There's still time to get ready before the final hearing. There's still time. There's always time."

He kept repeating it, never bothering to hang up the phone. "There's always time. There's always time."

CHAPTER 2

Three months earlier…

July visited its usual hardship on Bristol, baking the red clay at one end of the Lafayette River and scorching the sandy soil at the other, depriving both of the rain each desperately needed and adding another season to the deep south's decade-long drought. There was no relief from Mother Nature and no tax dollars from Washington. The small state fit within a homogenous region, its senators weren't up for re-election, and both were out of presidential favors. Such conditions debauch political capital so thoroughly that unprecedented disasters become mere local incidents.

Tucked beneath the thick canopy of kudzu, poison ivy and every weed hybrid in the ecosystem is a winding path that hugs the steep banks of the Lafayette. There is a monument, a Confederate soldier resting a long rifle on his knee, and a plaque with a quotation and the dates of his battle. The trail through Longstreet Park begins there and careens along the snake-filled water past the city limits all the way to the Saucostee Indian Reservation.

The smooth pavement is wide enough for couples to stroll side-by-side to the end of the manicured, no-mosquito zone. Roller-bladers and joggers pass by without incident. Transplanted palm trees greet them all, giving way to indigenous varieties beyond the wrought iron and lesser monuments.

Farther out, tall, shallow-rooted pine trees fight through the vegetation, stretching their thin trunks toward the sunlight like an orphan pleading for gruel. Soon the trail narrows to crushed gravel, eventually thinning to a worn dirt path. Wooden mile markers extend for a reasonable distance, ending where the casual users typically turn back. Beyond the train tracks the path is seldom traveled, but signs of municipal attention are still present, with woodchips lining the shady trail all the way to the end of the Oakdale community's cracker box houses.

Across the river bulldozers and backhoes from Dunn Construction Company sat idly in the freshly cut acres between Oakdale and the Saucostee Reservation. Bright orange government zoning notices were posted on each parcel. They advertised an upcoming meeting of some committee Michael Pomerantz should have known about. There'd been expansion along the Lafayette for years, but Bristol's riverfront project was delayed by homeowners who'd dug in their heels as more and more of their land was condemned.

The City Attorney's Office was in charge of buying up the targeted property, something else Pomerantz had to do and didn't understand the way he understood a murder trial. It was lucky for him he knew how to delegate. His best arm was warm and loose in the bullpen for a few more weeks at least, although his orders to active duty could come any day.

At the park's entrance businessmen with loosened ties and rolled-up shirtsleeves joined their families on picnic blankets for lunch on the green. A group of young men in tie-dyed shirts, cut-off khaki pants and Birkenstocks stood in a circle. They smoked clove cigarettes and kicked around a hacky-sack that was almost as dark as the soles of their feet.

Co-eds from the College of Bristol threw a Frisbee over their sunbathing friends, debating the fall line of clothes, Gap versus Abercrombie and Fitch, that type of thing. They bumped unconsciously to the distant thundering bass pulsing from a subcompact car that had gone by ten minutes ago. Its driver was a high school kid favoring the world with his musical tastes in a car he wanted everyone to call "Boom Bandit."

Sean Piper blew past a row of picnic tables like a refugee leaving Casablanca. He terrified a poodle tugging its elderly master. The old man and his dog stood aghast, waiting for the police, or a park ranger, or someone with a complaint to follow, but no one was chasing after the tall Marine. Not even Michael Pomerantz' unreasonable demands could reach him here.

Lieutenant Piper was tanned and tight-muscled, his body reshaped after last summer's pre-dawn torture on the PT fields of Quantico. Piper survived Officer Candidate School, commendably so for a lawyer, and returned to law school with the flattest stomach and shortest haircut in the third year class. He graduated the following spring and spent the summer studying for the bar exam. If he failed, he'd be shipped to the infantry instead of serving as a judge advocate. Thoroughly incentivized, he passed and took a staff attorney position with Pomerantz, cleaning up after his boss and counting the days until the Corps' little known and even less enjoyed Basic School, with its six months of infantry platoon leader training.

Without his running shoes Piper stood six and a half feet tall. He leaned hard into his stride, beating back the wind drag from his broad chest and broader shoulders. The waist belonged on a different body, one that didn't need its suit pants remade to fit a forty-six long jacket. His legs meshed like an out of control pair of scissors, and went on forever. He'd let his blond hair grow out only slightly longer than the neatly trimmed pelt he wore while on active duty. The tight hairdo showed off a pair of rounded ears, smaller and somewhat out of place on his long, well-featured face. His mouth turned up at the corners, leaving a pleasant natural smile of contentment, even one that shone through when his insides grimaced at the pavement still left to pound. It went well with his clear blue eyes that saw much but gave away precious little.

A Marine Officer at twenty-four, a lawyer at twenty-five, in the best shape of his life and engaged to the lovely Anne Wiley, Piper was nowhere near discovering why he was put on this earth. He only knew he wanted something more to show for the search than if it had taken place on the beaches of the world. He figured the ride would be bumpy at times, but knew the path of least resistance was too enticingly landscaped to be worth taking. Where he'd be until his recruiter called was at Michael Pomerantz' side, running one of the two offices the D.A. barely held on to at the city.

Piper was a good buffer between Pomerantz and the fickle council. If he could have figured out how to do it, the D.A. would have sabotaged his workhorse's impending return to military service. Both men knew that day was coming, but only one of them would be sorry to see him go.

By the start of the new year, Piper would slip back into his camouflage utilities and train in the woods with the other lieutenants, dangerous with a compass, a map, a scant few weeks on active duty and a commission from the President. Until then, Sean Piper was about the business of punishing workouts by the river, terrorizing a core group of geriatrics and urban professionals who pegged him as militia material. They didn't understand him, his haircut or the weighted backpack that ripped at his skin. But for some reason none of them would admit, they were glad his kind existed.

CHAPTER 3

Piper spotted his boss taking hits in the Mayor's conference room. He was surrounded by disgruntled looking employees from the Solid Waste Department. Pomerantz figured it was the best day of their lives.

Sean flaked out in the waiting room. He perused a wildlife magazine featuring a versatile shotgun that was perfect for shooting wildlife. Two quail articles later and the door flew open. One of the men laughed like he'd heard a good one he'd sworn not to repeat. Pomerantz met his staff lawyer and they headed toward the Legal Department.

"Sean, I should have been a farmer," he lamented. "This is no way to make a living. What's up?"

"Linda said you wanted to see me."

"She did?" It came to him at the water cooler. "Oh, yeah. I got a call today from the council chairman. He wants to know where we are on the riverfront project."

"Again? I just briefed him on that yesterday."

"Well, I guess Mr. Amsler wants to hear it from me," he said. "Politicians like to have a belly button to push. That usually means the department head."

"Oh."

"So how many parcels do you have left to acquire?"

"Fourteen," Piper said. "But we—"

"Fourteen?" Pomerantz interrupted. "I thought you said there were less than ten the other day."

"There were less than ten the other day."

"What happened?"

"Some of the landowners decided to hold out. They discovered we'd settled with their neighbors, so—"

"They lawyer'd up?" Pomerantz asked.

"They lawyer'd up."

The D.A. crumpled his paper water cup and threw it in the general direction of a metal trashcan.

"I do have some good news," Piper said.

"What?"

"I talked to an owner in Oakdale today. She said she'll sell us her house if we pay her moving expenses."

"In town move?" Pomerantz wondered.

"We didn't get that far."

"Make sure she's staying in the area. I'm not paying to move anybody to Hawaii."

"Yes, sir. I'll find out tomorrow. I have an appointment to meet her at six in the morning."

"Why so early?"

"She's having surgery."

"What kind of surgery?"

"I don't know. She said her hip was bothering her."

Pomerantz grimaced as he choked down two horse pills at the water fountain.

"God, that was a harsh," he said.

"Headache?"

"Yeah, I've got one. But those were for my blood pressure."

"Oh."

"Take care of your body, Sean. It'll last you until you die."

Pomerantz popped another one. "Listen, if this woman's getting her hip replaced, she may be in rehab for a couple months. Make sure you get her signed up tomorrow. I'm getting a lot of pressure from the council. And as much as I hate to admit it, I haven't given the riverfront project the attention it needs. So I need you to pay attention to it for me. Okay, Sean?"

"I'll do my best."

"Find out what hospital. You know, let's hope for the best, but you need to know how to get in touch with this lady. Maybe she has a lawyer already."

"You want me to ask if she has an lawyer?"

The D.A. tugged at his collar. "On second thought, don't put any ideas in her head. Just find out which hospital, and get a good number for her. And make sure she's not on any medication when she signs."

Sean did a pushup against the wall. "How am I gonna do that?"

"Ask if she understands the deed. Offer to let her look it over as long as she needs to, but don't encourage her to take you up on it. You know what I mean?"

"Kind of," Piper said.

"Good. Can she read?"

"I don't know. I suppose so. She knew where to sign for my letter."

"'Cause you can never tell. A lot of people I deal with," Pomerantz was ashamed of himself. "I've been prosecuting for too long. Most of the people in my circles…just give me an assist on this one, all right, pal?"

"Yes, sir."

The D.A. patted him on the shoulder as they reached the office.

"There's one more thing, Sean. My save-your-ass button went off about ten times last night."

"Ouch," Piper said. "That sounds painful."

"Council's going to ask me tonight where we are on the gambling ordinance."

"I didn't know that was on the agenda."

"It'll get added."

It wasn't Piper's issue. "I haven't been too involved with that."

"I know, Sean. Our outside counsel's drafting the ordinance. Calhoun and Morgan."

Piper had heard of the law firm. "Oh, so that's what all those bills are for. I've seen the invoices on Linda's desk. Looks like those guys are doing pretty well."

"We use them for lots of things. Bond work and economic development mainly. This is something I needed done fast, and I don't have time to write new laws. Ethan Morgan is the senior partner. He's handling it personally."

"Uh-huh."

"Do me a favor, Sean. Give Mr. Morgan a call and ask if he's finished with the ordinance. Jake Amsler wants to see something this week. Get me a copy of whatever he's drafted. I need to know where we are on this thing."

"Okay."

"And Sean, keep it all business with this guy. Saying hello to Ethan Morgan costs us five hundred bucks."

"Right," he said. "And he's the senior partner?"

Pomerantz smiled. "Relax. If Morgan gives you any trouble, just tell him you're calling because I didn't have time for the kids' table."

Kids' table. Piper wondered how many of those there were at the state's richest law firm. "Sure thing, boss. I'll straighten him out."

The D.A. felt better already. "Good man."

****

The sundrenched farmer set his propane tank on the sidewalk and stepped inside the convenience store. A country singer twanged on a radio from somewhere behind thick clouds of smoke obscuring a 'No Smoking' sign. Beside it a woman gummed a cigarette and balanced a gravity defying portion of her backside on a barstool as she gazed at the purple lights flashing on the video poker machine. Her wrinkled mouth made the long filter do a dance while she dumped another roll of quarters into a souvenir NASCAR cup.

"Come on, sugah," she wheezed. "Baby wanna 'nother play."

She puffed and hacked and cursed as her blackened fingertips fed the machine like a lab rat pawing the stainless steel lever for a drop of water.

The farmer stood silently at the counter as she dropped the rest of her paycheck, or whatever kind of check it had been, into the slot. She argued with the screen and reached into her pocket for anything that would spend.

"A-hem," he cleared his throat.

"Um-hmm," she said without taking her eye off of the machine.

He stood his ground.

"Skeeter," she said to a man slouching on the next stool who looked like the 'after' picture in a meth addict's life cycle. "Y'all got a customer."

Skeeter plunked quarters with the hack-mistress like a pair of dueling automatons. He drew two nines, doubled down and lost twice as much.

"'D'ya hear me?"

Skeeter spit into the wrong cup, covering his bankroll with tobacco juice. She sucked the remaining oxygen out of the room laughing at him.

"Dammit, Darlene!" he blurted as he tried to clean up the mess. It had been a healthy chew. He gave up and uttered something that had about eight syllables to it.

"Awe'iiiiiiiitte."

The farmer studied a calendar that was eight years out of date hanging on the wall behind the dusty cash register and decided it was the cleanest thing in the store.

"How much I owe ya' for the propane?" he asked.

Skeeter took four cards without going bust. He hit on nineteen and drew a queen.

"Dag' gone."

He played another hand about the same way. "Dag." And another. "Dag' gone."

The farmer gave up and reached for his wallet. He set what he thought the propane would have cost eight years ago on the counter and headed for some daylight and fresh air. Skeeter and the pantsuit ashtray kept playing while their business walked out the door all day long.

Bubba Hawkins led Remington Lovelace through the back entrance to Teal's Kountry Kitchen. They took the last booth, a vinyl-ripped job with enough rusty tacks sticking out to make an OSHA inspector take a personal day. Lovelace searched the room for anyone he might have defended along the way. The place had convict written all over it. He hung his jacket on the cleanest hook he could find.

"Am I gonna stick to anything here, Bubba?" he asked.

His client gave him the Skeeter treatment. He even managed not to spit on himself.

Darlene left her poker game long enough to plop two menus on the table.

"Wha' cha'll havin'?" she asked.

"I'll take a tetanus shot," Lovelace said.

"Uh what?"

"We're good, Darlene," Hawkins waved her away.

Bubba Hawkins owned a dozen dives like this. Before video poker they were nothing more than tax write-offs, the 'Mom n' Pop, gas n'sips that lined the highway from Bristol to his mobile home empire in Titusville.

Hawkins jumped on the games from the beginning, buying machines from out-of-state manufacturers and bootlegging them to Bristol crammed inside his fleabag mobile homes. Once they crossed the state line he set up his gaming houses in the backs of dumps like Teal's, dodging taxes and daring local officials to fine him for some business license infraction or another—a maximum of a few hundred dollars per offense, simply the cost of doing business.

Video gambling was legal so long as the owners didn't allow winners to take home cash payouts. Instead, gamblers won extra 'plays,' racking up credits until the addicts had carpal tunnel syndrome from pumping in the coins. The regulars were permitted to cash in their credits when no one was looking. These smoke-filled empires fueled an underground economy that confounded elected officials across the state and made new money for the Bubbas of Bristol.

Lovelace watched as the fat man tried to get comfortable wedged in the booth. Hawkins rubbed his hands together and twirled a soggy toothpick in his mouth as he ogled a woman about half of Darlene's size stacking cheap glasses on the bar.

"Okay, Bubba, what'd ya' want to see me about?" Lovelace asked. "I've got to be in court soon."

Hawkins leaned forward, his bottommost chin nearly touching the table. Remy's paisley tie scrambled his brain. He ran his hand through his curly hair and locked eyes with his client.

"What do you think, Remy? I wanna know why you haven't gotten my case dismissed yet."

"Dismissed? We talked about settling it, maybe, but I never told you it'd be dismissed."

"What's there to settle?"

"You sold the Wannamakers a trailer—"

"Manufactured house," Bubba corrected him.

"—that your people represented was brand new. They hooked it up and then all hell broke loose. Electrical failures, exposed wires, screwed up tie-down, leaky roof. The punch list is longer than your belt…which by the way looks good with those suspenders."

"Shut up, Remy."

"They complained loud enough to get the housing commission's attention, and unless you make it right there's going to be a hearing."

"That's a bunch of crap. It's all been denied."

"You say everything's covered under the manufacturer's warranty, and that the Wannamakers really should be suing the builder and not Bubba Hawkins' big damned super crazy RV World. Does that sum it up?"

Hawkins sat up in the booth, checking to make sure that Skeeter was minding the store.

"Well, Bubba?"

"Look. What if I told you the unit might not have come straight from the manufacturer?"

Lovelace shook his head. "Are you telling me that?"

He didn't answer.

"You are telling me that," Lovelace said. "Okay. First, you're a moron. Second, I'm not doing anything else on your case until you pay the rest of my retainer."

Hawkins buried his chubby face in his chubbier hands.

"So what, you switched the serial numbers or something? Put a new ID on a salvaged unit? Is that it?"

Hawkins' bloodshot eyes confirmed it.

"Bubba, you've got a sworn statement in the record saying you sold the Wannamakers a new mobile home? You know that, right?"

"Sworn?"

"Yeah. Your affidavit. Now you're telling me that's a lie? I can't let you testify."

"Why not?"

"You'll commit perjury, unless you want to admit you defrauded the Wannamakers. So which felony do you want to plead to?"

"Felony? Hell, I didn't know—"

"Perjury's punishable by up to five years per count. Fraud's worse. If you take the stand you could ring up a lot of years," Remy said. "You're in a crack, boy."

Lovelace held his watch up to the light. "And I've got to go defend someone who's in a bigger one. Walk me to the parking lot."

Bubba took a deep breath. The color left his face. A cold sweat formed across his brow. He struggled to make it out of the booth and Lovelace held the door for him.

"Let me ask you something, Bubba. What do you know about the Wannamakers?"

"What do you mean?"

"Are they educated?"

"I don't know. They seem pretty country to me. Where they live, this trailer may be the first indoor plumbing in that part of the state. Why?"

"No reason," Lovelace said. "Just curious."

The lawyer wiped his sunglasses. The heat from the parking lot's blacktop rose through the soles of his Cole Haans. He clicked his key fob and the Lexus began to cool its leather interior.

Remy shook hands with his nervous client and patted him on his sweaty shoulder.

"Don't worry yourself to death, Bubba. If they're like you say, maybe they won't be able to find the courtroom."

"Yeah, right." Hawkins blotted his face with a bar towel.

Lovelace stared into the distance, then straight at his client.

"Lawsuits are crazy things. You never know how one might end."

CHAPTER 4

There was at least one branch of Jake Amsler's bank along every major thoroughfare in Bristol. He used them as satellite campaign offices, littering the landscape with his college mug shot captioned by tales of the latest successes he'd presided over as city council chairman. Next to them were fliers advertising low-interest home mortgages, the kind voters could get at Southport Savings & Loan and thank him for in November. While everyone else talked about taking the money out of politics, Amsler made the two inseparable. There were convenient locations near them—a co-mingled, one-stop shopping experience giving him control of the purse strings and the ballot box in a jurisdiction he underwrote. He practiced the fiscal conservatism folks wanted in their banker, and went missing in action when the discussion turned to divisive social issues—what they'd come to expect in a career politician. He had, then, one of the safest seats in the city, tested only in elections that followed his Main Street ride in the Homecoming parade.

Amsler steered his BMW 760i into the Delano Street parking lot, drawing approving looks from the crowd at the ATM. His employees understood these impromptu visits were part of the job, and that their office would become his office during such appearances. He stayed away when things got hot, at the end of the quarter and on days when the financial industry checked its pulse. When times were slow, he was as welcome as a Bob Hope walk-on after the rest of Hollywood told Johnny 'no thanks.'

Amsler rested an expensive pair of sunglasses on his head and stood hands on hips as he took in the lobby. Three nervous tellers straightened up behind the counter. Surveillance cameras angled downward at them, capturing the S&L's founder beside a plainclothes officer every crook had made as the house detective. The old security guard almost shot himself drawing his weapon the last time the place was robbed. He needed a new job and a trigger lock until he found one.

The manager had coffee waiting for him and they walked to her office to drink it. Miss Martha was fifty-nine, healthy looking with weathered skin and windblown gray hair, as big as her boss and probably still strong enough to line up next to him in the State

College backfield. Martha was a tough manager in the toughest branch in the Southport chain. Amsler smiled, thinking how comfortable she'd look sitting next to a camp fire chopping the heads off of stunned game while waiting for the scout party to tell her if the West was worth settling.

Amsler stood an even six feet tall and stepped in at a solid buck ninety-five. He kept his dark hair short, and touched up the parts that didn't cooperate. It was councilman hair without a doubt—all barber and witch hazel, like the cuts the men he represented got for four dollars. He wore khaki pants and penny loafers, an open collared golf shirt, and a navy sport coat that would hit the back seat of his Beemer when the meeting was done.

Martha slid a jar of candy across her desk.

"Careful, Jake," she said. "Those are hard centers."

"Thanks, Martha."

"Coffee hot enough for you?" she asked.

"I think I'll wait 'til it stops bubbling."

"You're getting soft, Mr. Chairman."

Amsler smiled. "I'm getting old."

"Politics will do that to a person. You never should have left the bank. Of course, I don't know why you work at all now. Go spend time with your grandkids. You've earned your retirement."

"You may get some disagreement about that."

"From whom?"

"I don't know," Jake said as he strolled to the window. The church folks were just crossing the parking lot. "Maybe from the people on the way to see me. I need to borrow your office, Martha. I've got to do a little fence mending."

"No problem. Just say when."

"In about thirty seconds. You know, of course, Pastor Jim and Sister Hattie?" he asked, nodding toward them.

She rose to meet him at the blinds. "Sure. Jimmy Wingate's church has kept its account here for years. "They're not thinking of moving it, are they?"

"I hope not, Martha. For the moment I think they're here to see me as a politician more than a banker. It seems the congregation is going to take a public stance on video poker. Undoubtedly against it. But it's still a dicey matter," he said. "We usually don't get pressure from religious groups. Official pressure, anyway."

"I'm not sure I understand, Jake. If the church is opposed to gambling, how's that a problem for you? You're already on the record supporting the ban on video poker, aren't you?"

"Oh, it's not a matter of being on different sides of the issue. It's just that now, after this meeting anyway, I'm going to be the church's *man* in this fight. You know what I mean? If the ordinance doesn't pass, or if it withers on the vine, guess who the gambling industry will blame? From here on out there'll be a face to go along with the figure on the white horse, and you're looking at it. I'm the poster boy for Wingate's congregation. And, well, we have a lot of devout followers in this city, if you know what I mean—"

The minister's laughter startled him. "My ears are burning, Mr. Chairman," Wingate boomed as he flew open the door. The preacher towered over them. "Pardon the casual entrance."

Amsler grinned mightily and rolled with it. "Pastor Jim, good morning," Amsler greeted him, his hand disappearing in Wingate's. "And Sister Hattie, always a pleasure." Hattie wasn't interested in handshakes.

"You remember Miss Martha," he said hopefully.

"Nice to see you. Just made some coffee if you care for any," Martha pointed. "Mr. Amsler says it's too hot, but you can be the judge of that. Make yourselves at home."

She closed the door behind her, mouthed a prayer to one of the tellers and signed out for an early lunch.

They anchored down either side of Martha's couch and Amsler sat opposite in a matching chair. He leaned toward the church lady as he eyed the distinguished man who did her preaching.

"You got a good one here," he said. "I hope the session doesn't rotate him any time soon."

Sister Hattie smiled like she'd chugged a shot of lemon juice. "Yes, well, our church doesn't do that. Perhaps you have us confused with another denomination."

"Of course," Amsler nodded. "Now, what'd ya'll want to see me about?"

Wingate tapped his fingertips on the leather sofa. It sounded like 'Onward Christian Soldiers.'

"Jake, for some time now we've held our peace on this gambling thing, thinkin' that it wouldn't even be a close call, that our participation wasn't necessary."

"Hmmm," Sister Hattie confirmed.

"But it's becoming increasingly apparent that our involvement is needed," he continued.

"Oh?"

"Tell him, Pastor," she said. "Lord, give us eyes to see and ears to hear."

Amsler opened his eyes wide and listened hard.

"The city's invitin' all kinds of trouble lettin' this matter drag on," Wingate said. "We think it's time that it goes away, for the good of the community."

"I see."

"You know, if you open the door just a crack, the roaches will come in whether you want 'em to or not," Wingate promised. "And who wants a roomful of roaches, Mr. Chairman?"

"Looks like the city does," Sister Hattie observed. "What y'all need is a big 'ol can o' Raid. That'll stop 'em."

The politician twitched. "Now, let me assure you—"

"These casino houses," she interrupted, "with liquor and drugs and hoochie mommas scootin' 'round with nothing but a stitch a'clothes on!"

Wingate tried to calm her. "Hold on, Hattie. Give the man a chance. He's on our side. That's why we're here."

"Yes, yes, that's right," Amsler assured her. "I'm on your side. I'm strongly opposed to gambling in Bristol. Uh, always have been. I'm on your side. I want to be clear about that."

"Look here, " the pastor said. "We know you've got a tough job. But we can't sit by and let our community turn into a bunch of gambling addicts. Drugs is bad enough, but this video poker will eat through a paycheck even faster. Breaks up families, destroys lives. We can't sit by and let that happen."

"Yes, I suppose people will bet on anything they can get odds on," Amsler said. "That goes back to Biblical days. You know that. But as far as video poker is concerned, I think we're about to get a handle on that one."

"Oh?"

"You see, a few years ago the legislature placed restrictions on most forms of gambling in this state, except, of course, things like church bingo and such as that."

"What!" Hattie jumped to her feet. "Bingo ain't gambling!"

"What'd I say?" Amsler pleaded. "What'd I say? Let me finish—"

"Tell him, Pastor! We have that at church every week! Raffles, too! He's crazy!"

"Let me finish!"

"Bingo is bingo, and gambling is gambling!" she exclaimed. "And bingo ain't gambling!"

"These machines in those bars up and down the highway," he assured her, "That's what we're after. I'd never include bingo in that. My record is consistent on this issue. But that other mess, all that business should be outlawed for good. We don't need that in Bristol. We don't need it anywhere in the state."

"Hmmm," she sat, straightening her long skirt.

Pastor Jim remained silent. Amsler was on his own.

"I'm sorry I upset you."

She glared over the top of her glasses, correcting him, "I'm…not…upset."

"Oh. That's good."

She stared him down. "I know who I am."

Amsler was lost. "Well, sure you do."

"Okay, Jake, okay," Wingate rose. "I think we made our point. No video poker in Bristol. No gambling period." He opened the door and turned to Sister Hattie. "Except for like it's always been with bingo."

Sister Hattie chided him, too. "Bingo ain't gambling, Preacher."

"That's right," he agreed. "Got that, Jake?"

"Absolutely," the chairman promised. "We're on the same page on that one."

Sister Hattie slung her bulky purse over her shoulder, blocking the frightened men.

"We better be."

****

Piper sang along to an oldies tune while he waited for the receptionist at Calhoun and Morgan to take him off hold. A few moments later the senior partner echoed through the speakerphone.

"This is Ethan Morgan."

"Mr. Morgan?" Piper's voice cracked.

"Yes."

"My name is Sean Piper. I'm with the Bristol City Attorney's Office. Mr. Pomerantz asked me to give you a call about the video poker ordinance.

"Yes, yes," Morgan snatched the receiver from its cradle and the echo was gone. "What's the name?"

"Sean Piper."

"Glad you called, Sean. I understand the ordinance is ready for your review."

"It is?"

"Uh-huh."

"Great. I was wondering if I could come by and pick it up. I mean if it's all right. I'm downtown now. I can be at your office in a few minutes," he said as he circled Dunn Plaza looking for a parking spot. Thirty stories above Ethan Morgan gave him the Heisman pose.

"Yes, well, I'd love to meet you, Sean, but I've assigned this matter to another lawyer. Mr. Bing. His office is not in this building."

"It's not?

"No, Harvey has his own practice. I'm sure he'll be glad to e-mail you a copy of his draft."

"That's fine, Mr. Morgan."

Ethan considered it and realized Harvey Bing probably didn't even own a computer, let alone a scanner.

"On second thought, let me give you his number and the two of you can coordinate. Harvey's an old school lawyer. He isn't as technologically savvy as you and I are."

"Okay."

Morgan found Bing's dingy business card.

"Hmm. I don't see a phone number, but his address is Four Thirteen Oakdale Shopping Center."

"Oakdale?"

"Yes. About ten miles from here. Just go north on Main Street, cross the river and you'll eventually see it on your left.

Piper wrote it down. "Okay. And who is this again?"

"Harvey Bing. He's Of Counsel for the firm. He'll have everything you need."

Pomerantz had told him the senior partner was handling this one personally, although the D.A. had a lot on his mind. Morgan didn't even want him to set foot in his building. Instead, he was sending him to the worst part of town. On the way he'd have time to phone Anne and tell her they'd need to meet for dinner a little later than planned. His fiancée had gotten used to that call.

"Four Thirteen Oakdale. All right, Mr. Morgan. I'm on my way."

Morgan fed Bing's card into the shredder beside his desk and squirted a dollop of hand sanitizer on his smooth fingers.

"Goodbye, Sean." The echo was back.

CHAPTER 5

Pomerantz held the tennis racket behind his head like a lion tamer watching the sedation wear off. His limp wrist was laid back like he might try taking the pace off the rocket screaming toward him. A deftly placed drop shot that trickled over the net would impress the club pro. He'd seen someone on the tour do that before. Maybe a few hundred lessons from now. Instead he framed it into the net. *Tooook.*

The ball dribbled back to him. He stepped on it and twisted his ankle.

"Damn!"

A group of housewives playing doubles on the next court critiqued his form in between points. He glanced over and wondered if any of them recognized him from a press conference or a local news story. He didn't need any rumors started about why he wasn't at the office.

He was not out in front where he should have been, punching the ball with a short chop deep into the backcourt. His footwork was sloppy and he wasn't talented enough to overcome the poor play. The long follow-through was entirely inappropriate this close to the net. It produced an inevitable wild volley that was still rising as it flew over the instructor's head. The ball landed near the top of the windscreen, then fell unceremoniously into a pile behind the pro's basket of practice balls. He was playing muted chopsticks with the chain link fence. *Thunkkk. Thunkkk. Thunkkk.*

"Come on! Dammit! Hit the ball!"

The pro launched another round and Pomerantz muffed it even worse. *Thunkkk.* Then another and one more after that. *Thunkkk. Thunkkk.* Then a shot that missed the windscreen and went straight into the fence. *Tink.* He was a dysfunctional one-man mariachi band. *Thunkkk, thunkkk, tink, tooook, tink.*

"Come on, Mr. Potato Head! Watch the ball! Come onnnnn!" Pomerantz spun around like a top, embarrassed, disheveled, inconsolable.

"Dammit, Phil! What am I doing wrong?"

Phil The Club Pro twirled a racket that was half as wide as his student's club. He flashed the lawyer a brilliant smile and said,

"Nothing, Mike, if you're trying to knock down my fence."

"Very funny. What about my volleys?"

"Oh, they're awful," he said. "Really bad. You need some more lessons."

The pro handed him a ball hopper and started scooping up the shots that had made it to his side of the net. Pomerantz followed him around like a lost puppy.

"Okay. So how do I make 'em not so awful?" he asked.

Phil took pity on him. "It all starts with the footwork, same as every shot. Knees bent, leaning slightly forward. Be aggressive up there. Never rock back. Stay balanced. Keep your head up. Be alert. Hands in front. Volleys are punch shots. It's a punch—a short chop down the back of the ball. The underspin keeps it low. It'll skid on the court. Your shots are sitters. They sit up ready to get whacked by your opponent. Keep 'em low. Like this."

He whacked a winner that slid across the paint at the baseline. Just another day at the office.

"Unbelievable," the lawyer marveled.

"It's what I do, Mike" he said. "By the way, I never asked you…how do you have so much time to take tennis lessons? Don't you have like a real job, with a desk and a staff and everything? Most lawyers I know work six or seven days a week."

"Life's too short to spend it on someone else's problems. Tennis instructors excluded, of course." He smiled as they tidied up the court. "Besides, what makes you think I'm not working right now?"

"Huh?"

"Oh yeah. I'm surprised at you, Phil. You think I just run around the tennis court chasing after a fuzzy ball without a thought in my head?"

"Well, I know you're not thinking about the ball."

"I'll give you that one. But the practice of law is a constant. One phone call to the office and I can keep the staff busy for the rest of the day. Hell, I'm gonna start having my mail sent here soon. Then you can teach me how to hit a forehand volley."

"I'm afraid that's what it might take."

"So how long has it taken you?" he shot back at the instructor. "When did you start doing this?"

"I've been playing tennis all my life. I only played on the tour a few years. Somewhere along the line I realized I taught the game better than I played it."

Pomerantz wiped his face and laughed at the thought of it. "Really?"

"Sure."

"But you never say anything, Phil. You're a human ball machine, but you don't say a damned word. How's that teaching?" He opened the gate and led his student to the clubhouse. "How many balls did you hit this morning?"

"I don't know. Several hundred, I guess."

"And how many of those ended up in the fence?"

"Too many."

"That's teaching. If I can get you to pay me for something that makes you as frustrated as this does, I gotta be good."

Phil's next lesson started two minutes ago. The elderly student practiced her stroke while she waited.

"Now write me out another one of those soggy checks so I can go back out there and teach Mrs. Sederberg what I couldn't teach you just now."

"You're lucky I can't stand change, Phil, or I'd a switched teacher's years ago."

"Same time next week?"

"Yeah, Phil. Same time until I graduate."

****

Piper tooled up to a thirty-minute meter outside a check cashing business in Oakdale, far from the Dunn Plaza but right where Ethan Morgan told him his Of Counsel kept an office. He scrounged up enough change from the floorboard to buy a half hour and scurried along the sidewalk beneath flimsy plastic signs outside one hole in the wall after another. There was a pawnshop next to the place that cashed checks, and a guy with gold around his neck and on his teeth sitting on a bench out front. Near the end of the strip there was a chiropractic clinic. Next door was the law office of Harvey Bing. On the other side of the paper-thin wall sat the final draft of the city's gambling ordinance, the centerpiece of Jake Amsler's political career, artfully penned by a burned out lawyer who was *persona non grata* at the Dunn Plaza.

Piper mashed the bell. The light was burned out and it didn't ring. It had been a long day. He was hungry and he wanted to see

Anne. The D.A.'s little scavenger hunt had grown tiresome. He jerked the door handle and broke the knob off trying to get inside. A short, droopy geezer Piper could have curled with one arm inspected the damage.

"What the hell'd ya' do to my door, boy! Son of a bitch! Give me that!" He looked like enraged dental floss with whiskers.

Sean gave him the handle. "Sorry. I rang, but there was no answer. Your need a new doorbell."

"The hell I do!" Bing ranted.

He checked for himself but got nothing. "Hmmm. Well, that must've just happened. It worked yesterday, I'll tell you that for free. But that don't mean you can tear off my doorknob. What's wrong with you?"

"Are you Harvey Bing?"

"Who's askin'?"

"My name's Piper. I'm from the City Attorney's Office. Mr. Morgan told me to come see you."

"Ethan Morgan sent you here?"

Piper looked around the dark room. "Yeah. How else would have found this place? This isn't exactly on the beaten path."

Bing pushed the door open the rest of the way. "Come on," he said, wagging his finger like he was training a poodle who'd missed the paper.

"Not on the beaten path, huh? Well, we can't all be in the Dunn Plaza, kid. Some of us work for a living."

It was a short trip to his desk and Bing fell into a squeaky chair behind it. Piper sat on the edge of what appeared to be a backseat that was missing the rest of the taxi cab. Bing's law office consisted of a tiny room with two metal file cabinets on either side of an equally metal desk. A box fan sat in front of a window that had been painted shut. It blew smoke and the scent of a taxi driver's pine tree air freshener.

"Morgan sent you," he muttered. "For what?"

"The ban on gambling. He said you drafted it."

"I did?" He ran his blue fingers through his beard, checking out the lawyer's suit and perfect hair. "Gambling? Oh, the video poker thing. Sure. Why didn't you say so?"

"I did."

"Hey, is that crap in your way?" he pointed. "Just slide those files over. I haven't unpacked yet. You know, I used to work in local government, a million years ago. Prosecuted dog bite cases," he laughed. "They still make ya'll do that?"

"I'm afraid so." Piper moved the stack of files to the passenger's side of the bench seat.

"Well, just keep pluggin' away. You'll work your way out of that job someday."

Sean wiped the dust off his pants. "I reckon so, Mr. Bing. Out…and up, huh?"

The laughter stopped. "What? This dump? This isn't my only office, you know?"

Sean was relieved. "I was going to ask, if you're with Calhoun and Morgan, what are you doing way out here?"

"I'm the firm's Of Counsel. I only handle certain matters. I'm semi-retired. Calhoun and Morgan rent this place for me. I come in three days a week. Lucky for you this is one 'em."

Sean pointed to a large neon sign blaring through the window. "So you're not affiliated with Jacoby Chiropractic Professionals?"

"What? Oh, hell no. They're Four Thirteen-A. I'm Four Thirteen. See?" He showed him a piece of faded stationery. "Sure would be convenient, though. I do a lot of personal injury work. If some poor bastard walked in here wearing a neck brace, I'd let him sit on the couch. Ta-hee, hee, hee."

"Actually, Mr. Bing, as I understand it this is an important issue for the city, so if I could just get your draft—"

"I'm sure it is. I mean, they wouldn't send you all the way out here if it weren't."

"That's right."

"Listen, kid. Everybody knows the city's hot to outlaw gambling. That's politics. And politicians want an outcome. But you and I are lawyers. We deal in details, and details don't make news conferences. You need a wordsmith for those."

"Uh-huh." Piper set the petrified remains of a donut on top of the mountain of files beside him. "So what'd you do before you semi-retired?"

"I was a sole practitioner. Always have been. Used to work across the river in East Bristol. I'm no specialist. Took anything that came through the door. Everything 'cept domestic. I'll push around a shopping cart and live under a bridge before I'll handle another contested divorce. You can have that crap."

"I understand."

"Wreck cases were my bread and better. Still are. Do you have any idee' what county has the highest insurance rates in this state?"

"Not really, I don't do a lot of insurance work."

"You're in it, son. Hell, it's safer sleeping on a railroad track than it is to walk on the sidewalk in this county. And that's when the weather's good."

"Mr. Bing. If I could just have—"

"It's like watching an episode of Chips. You remember that old show?

"I think I may have seen it," Piper said. "California Highway Patrol or something?"

"Hell, I don't know. What's the diff? Ol' Ponch and John. Good show, wudn't it?"

"Mr. Bing—"

"But, I know you didn't come here to talk about that. Let me give you this wonderful piece of draftsmanship and you can be on your way."

"That'd be fine."

Bing handed him a tattered manila folder with one sheet of paper inside.

Piper took a look. "That's it? What were you saying about the details?"

"Not much to it, huh kid? With a stroke of the pen the city hereby outlaws all games of chance. Brevity is the soul of wit. Hope the politicians can live with some plain talk for a change."

Sean read it again. "Mr. Bing, do you have this as a Word file? You know, just in case for some reason we need to make a few changes."

"Word file? What do you think it's written in, smoke signals?"

"No, I mean the computer software program you used."

"I know what you mean," he laughed. "I tell you what, you want to make any changes, just give me a call and they'll be on the house." He scribbled something on the back of his business card. "I still have a few thousand of these left. Just call this number."

Piper took the card and nodded. Pomerantz hadn't told him what arrangement he'd made.

"Do I need to get a bill from you?" he asked.

Bing grinned like the bookkeeper had put Ethan Morgan's paycheck in the wrong envelope. He still had a few teeth left.

"You are new, ain't' cha? Don't worry about it. I 'spect you'll be hearing from Calhoun and Morgan later on this month. Their collections department will let you know they're in town. Fair enough?"

Piper took one last look around his train wreck of an office. He had to have his story straight or Anne would never believe his alibi. He shook hands with Harvey Bing and thought hard about private practice.

"Fair enough."

****

The D.A. guzzled blue Gatorade by the clubhouse phone. He rang the office and got a girl from the temp agency.

"Where's Linda?" he asked.

"Out sick," the receptionist said. "Do you want her voicemail?"

"No. Do I have any messages?"

"Mr. Amsler called," she told him. "Twice. He really wants to talk to you."

"Yeah. I know what he wants. Who else?"

"Rochelle from finance. She said you need to pick up your last four pay stubs."

"Uh-huh. Is that all?"

"No, sir. There's one more here somewhere," she said. "Here it is. Erica called, no message." His mistress never left a message. She figured he already knew he was in trouble.

"Okay. What number did Mr. Amsler leave?"

She gave it to him while he tried to remember what was on his calendar.

"Listen, when Sean gets in tomorrow morning…you know who he is, don't you? Okay, tell him I need him to cover a deposition for me in the Fulmer case. It's at the Truesdale, Blankenship firm. Find the file and give it to him. Got it?"

"Okay. Sean who?"

"Mr. Piper. His desk is about ten feet away from yours."

"Oh."

"Look, there's a phone roster laminated next to the calendar in front of you. Study it in case someone else asks to speak to one of your co-workers."

"Sorry, it's my first day, and—"

"Forget it," he softened. "I know who these people are and I still can't remember their names. I'm sorry."

"Yes, sir. Will you be needing anything else? My son's day care closes soon."

"No. That's all. You can take off. I'll let myself in when I get back."

"Thanks," she said. "I don't know if they'll send me here tomorrow, but if they do, I hope to get a chance to meet you, Mr. Pomerantz."

"Yes, well," he wondered how long he'd been gone. "Me, too. Goodbye."

The D.A. hung up and dialed the chairman's number. Amsler picked up on the first ring.

"Sorry to just now be getting back to you, Mr. Chairman."

"Mike, listen, I'm taking a beating on this video poker mess. Folks are nervous with the moratorium about to run out. Have y'all got the ordinance ironed out yet?"

"I think we're close," he said.

"We need to push this thing over the goal line. I had a meeting with a preacher in the Oakdale community this morning. He brought along a lady from his congregation who was ready to string me up."

"Sister Hattie?"

"You know her?"

"She's a frequent flyer at the city."

"Yeah, well I've got to get them a copy of the ban. Now."

"I understand. Fortunately, my deputy is picking it up this afternoon. Calhoun and Morgan's handling it. Ethan Morgan drafted it himself."

"Morgan?"

"Yes, sir."

"I want you to look it over, Mike. Go through it with a fine-toothed comb. Ethan's a good lawyer, but make sure you're comfortable with it."

"Will do. We're not talking about a long piece of legislation here. From the guidance council's given us, y'all want to outlaw all games of chance. That seems clear enough to me."

"Okay, just send it over as soon as you can. I don't want to keep these folks waiting any longer than I have to, you know what I mean?"

"Too well," Pomerantz said. "Sister Hattie only rings her dinner bell once. If you ain't at the table ready to say grace after that, watch out."

"You got that right. Thanks, Mike. I'll holler at ya' later."

Pomerantz gathered up his belongings and hobbled toward the snack bar. Every joint in his body ached. He'd ice each one with a cold beer and call in dinner on the ride home. If there was any justice in the world the pizza guy would meet him at his bachelor's pad and throw in an order of wings for free.

In the parking lot a leggy brunette leaned against the worn out hacker's car. She bopped and heel-toed it as he neared. Pomerantz admired the baggy gray College of Bristol sweatshirt, and where it fell against her tight shorts. Erica pushed the sleeves up to her elbows and tucked a long curl of hair behind her ear. She looked him up and down over the top of her sunglasses. Her eyes were clear, blue and focused on the surprised married man twice her age.

"What are you doing here?" he asked.

She bit her lower lip and rocked back and forth like a schoolgirl trading up for the prom.

"I heard Phil had an opening, so I thought he might be able to squeeze me in."

"Is that a fact?"

Erica's sleeves fell again, then her hair.

"Um-hmm. It seems some old guy he teaches passed out half way through his lesson."

"Did he now? Aren't you going to need a tennis racket?"

She slid her hands in her pockets. "Guess I must have forgotten mine. I could borrow yours…or maybe I should cancel my lesson. I'll let you make that call."

The D.A. smiled. He opened the door and Erica climbed inside.

"Guess it's door number two," she laughed.

Across the parking lot a greasy man focused his camera and snapped away from his beat up Chevy Impala. He used a whole roll of film capturing the moment. In his other hand he worked a video camera, recording the same thing in case the mosquito he was tailing survived the sledgehammer. A still photo tells a thousand words, Jenna Pomerantz' lawyer said. One that moves is a filibuster.

The D.A.'s wife would be catapulted high and to the right by what the private investigator had to show for his afternoon. But she'd reached the point in her life where not knowing how her husband spent his days was worse than blissful ignorance. The private investigator's report had begun to consume its second expandable folder. Maybe her lawyer was right. The shots across his bow hadn't worked. It was time to turn up the heat.

CHAPTER 6

The Cracker Barrel's wraparound porch was full of satisfied customers enjoying the cool breeze as interstate traffic roared beyond the tree line. Anne Wiley checked her watch as another busload of hungry tourists pulled into the parking lot. Sean running late wasn't unusual, but eighty famished seniors fighting to get their orders in would tie up the kitchen for hours.

Anne's dark hair was nowhere near as short as Piper's, but enough so that in the big comfy chair she looked like a little girl on Santa's lap, asking the old man for a handsome present with no assembly required. Maybe this was him rolling in now.

Sean wedged the battered Toyota he lovingly called the 'Lieutenant Mobile' between two SUVs. He struggled to get out and managed not to ding either one of them. He jumped to the curb and stuck his landing like a gymnast posing for a perfect ten.

Anne shook her head. "Impressive."

He smiled at her beautiful brown eyes. "Sorry I'm late."

"Yeah, yeah. What was it this time?"

"What wasn't it? Pomerantz had me running all over town tracking down the stupid gambling ordinance."

"I didn't think you were involved with that."

"I wasn't. But the city's bad about mission creep. I can get thrown into the mix at any time, and today was the day," he said.

The line was out the door. "Did you get us on the list?"

"We're just ahead of the tour bus from Florida. Have a seat, big boy."

Sean rocked and played a game the object of which was to jump golf tees in the hopes of leaving just one on a triangular board.

"So what are you doing to rid the city of video poker? Are we Bedford Falls just before Pottersville?"

"Maybe not that bad," he said. "Right now I'm just the gofer. I picked up a copy of the ordinance our outside counsel drafted. Pathetic. I've seen weightier pamphlets. And you should see the guy who wrote it. He must be a hundred years old. I don't know what he had for lunch but he was wearing it for a tie. His office was way out in Oakdale. That's why I'm so late. He has this rattrap behind a chiropractor at the end of a burnt-out shopping strip. It was classic. Go see the lawyer first so the doctor will know how bad to make your prognosis."

"How much did he charge?"

"Who knows? I'm sure it's more than I make in a year. Then after that I had to come back through downtown during rush hour so I could get a file ready for the riverfront project. We're condemning some old lady's property, and Pomerantz says I'm not doing it fast enough. I have this horrible image of me kicking this poor old woman to the curb while someone else boards her windows. Maybe it'll snow that day, too."

"You should quit," she said.

"I know. And get this. She's having surgery in the morning. Pomerantz wants me to get her signed up before she goes under. That's what he calls it, getting them 'signed up,' like I'm chasing ambulances or something. Tell me this isn't a noble profession."

"I'm sure you'll make it as painless as possible. You're always so good with people, except when you're trying to sweet talk me."

"Thanks," he said. "I think."

"Don't worry. I'm sure everything will work out. Now come on, Sean. Let's bag this place. The mall stays open until nine o'clock. We've got time for the food court, then we can check our patterns. I've got to get moving on the bridal registry."

Sean tapped her hand softly. "Patterns? Is that going to be followed by an antique show?"

"Only if you're lucky."

****

Pomerantz came to just before the alarm from hell went off. He never understood Erica's clock radio and its miniature buttons only an Oompa-Loompa could work when the chocolate was ready. He hadn't slept well. He never did before roll call. Erica thrashed all night, giggling during one lightweight dream after another. She had nothing but pleasant thoughts interrupted for no reason by a roundhouse kick or a cross punch. Cuddling with her required a helmet and a cup.

He was spending too much time working for Jake Amsler, feeding the city's obsession with economic development along the Lafayette River and neglecting crime and punishment everywhere else. Keep Bristol growing, they said, trying to reconcile its leaders' mood swings between the green movement and the even more faddish business friendly initiative. They wanted growth, but the right kind of growth, which meant no more roadside dumps like Bubba Hawkins' poker joints, even if the state was sending mixed signals about which games it intended to outlaw. *And keep the streets safe while you're at it, Mr. District Attorney.* After you've built them, make sure they stay clean.

City Council can cool it for one day, he thought. There were criminals to call by name at his other office, and assistant prosecutors who needed the only kind of advice he was qualified to give. It never ended.

Erica groaned as he crawled over her. She turned in a huff, knocking him out of bed with a knee to the kidneys. He banged his shin on some miserable damned piece of exercise equipment she never used but let take up half the room.

"Son of a bitch," he whispered.

"Mmmm," Erica moaned. "Mmmm." She hugged her pillow while he beat the hell out of his.

Erica's duplex was about what one would expect from a college kid who was wrapping up her third year as a senior. So many majors, so little direction, no husband yet. Her bedroom was an obstacle course of unfolded clothes, no distinction between clean ones and the dirties, Blu-ray discs out of their cases collecting dust, the bounty from a binge and purge Home Shopping Network spree, and magazines and catalogs overflowing wicker baskets somewhere underneath it all.

There was a kitchen at the other end of the narrow hallway. The fridge was empty except for a huge jug of milk with a spoiled teaspoonful left and fifty bottles of raspberry iced tea. There was a box of Haagen-Dazs in the freezer that would bend an ice pick.

He'd get a bagel on the way to the courthouse if he didn't skip breakfast altogether. He couldn't stomach much before court. It might set off his ulcer. Erica never understood that. *Isn't that something old people get? Like…what is that exactly?* Maybe one day she'd be nervous about something.

The hungover man stumbled toward the bathroom and found a light switch that went with the bulb Erica amazingly had replaced. Her mirror was as unkind as his. There was a film over his tongue that made his mouth taste like he'd gargled a radial tire. He dabbed shaving cream on his scratchy face and cleaned it off with a dull razor he pulled from his kit. Tiny red veins played tic-tac-toe in his bloodshot eyes to the tune his thumping heart played. He should have stopped at one margarita last night, but the Mexican dish commanded dos, or was it tres? What a mess. There was a drugstore in her bathroom, complete with everything but what he needed. This was the new practical, he thought, every lip-gloss and beauty cream in the world but no aspirin. Pomerantz wept for the future.

His head pounded, almost as loudly as the thud on the front door.

"What the hell?"

He heard it again and splashed water on his face.

"Erica," he whispered. "You gonna get that?"

She groaned something at him and pulled the sheet over her head.

"Terrific," he said. "No, really, stay put. I'll see who's at your door."

Erica's duplex was on a cul-de-sac. Hers was the only home not for sale. Except for the occasional wayward car making the loop toward the main drag, it was the quietest street in the neighborhood. Pomerantz hadn't heard any car engines, although the Space Shuttle could have flown overhead while he was weeping into her pillow.

He stopped in the living room to peek through the window. It was too dark outside to see. The old neighborhood near the campus could go either way. Two streets over, distinguished professors and Bristol's society types pushed the property tax rates through the ceiling. A block in the opposite direction and there were bars on the windows. Erica lived in the demilitarized zone.

A burglar wouldn't knock, he assured himself. On the other hand, who was it at this hour? His pistol was in a bag in the trunk of his car, doing him about as much good as his tennis racket had the evening before. He'd discretely parked two houses up like always, convinced her neighbors gave a damn that it was her house last night and not his.

The D.A. slipped on a t-shirt and walked to the front door. The peephole was dustier than Erica's treadmill. He could barely make him out, a short man in a wrinkled sport coat, no tie, pants that didn't go with the shirt or jacket, and a five o'clock shadow at six in the morning. He cracked opened the door.

"Mr. Pomerantz?" the man asked.

The lawyer was shaken. "What's that?"

"Are you Michael Pomerantz?"

"Uh, he's not here right now," he lied.

"That's okay," the P.I. said as he shoved the latest edition of the Bristol *Chronicle* into his chest. "Just give him this."

"What's this?" he asked.

"I'm from customer service. We want to make sure he's still happy with his subscription."

The headlines were in focus as he snapped a picture of the half-dressed lawyer in the college girl's doorway.

"Hey, give me that!" he lunged, missing and tripping over the door stoop.

"Sorry, pal," the P.I. said as he backed away in a hurry. And then over his shoulder, "Just closing the loop!"

Pomerantz realized who he was and what he'd done in the same moment. He'd been caught by a professional witness and there was art to prove it. The newspaper locked him into the timeframe, and eroded any plausible deniability. His wife would never believe Erica was holding him for ransom. He was there on his own.

"You son of a bitch!"

The D.A. chased him for two blocks, but the fat investigator with shoes was faster than the barefooted adulterer. Pomerantz stubbed his toe on the cracked asphalt and went down hard, scraping his hands and legs. He staggered to his feet then quickly doubled over again as he tried to bring some order to the last few seconds of his life. How had he known? When did he begin to tail him? Was he Jenna Pomerantz' P.I. at all? They'd had problems, but she hadn't even seen a lawyer yet…he thought. He straightened up and his head throbbed even harder. He stood in the middle of his mistress' dead end street, heaving like Phil The Club Pro had gotten a bigger shopping cart. There were cuts on his feet, and he was certain things would get worse before they got better. He watched helplessly as the laughing investigator made his getaway. The prosecutor hadn't even been composed enough to get the man's license plate.

He was warm from the sprint, but he still shook. "Okay," he tried to calm himself over the longest two blocks of his life. Okay."

There was nothing strong enough in Erica's bathroom to make himself look presentable. At her doorway the morning paper lay face up on the welcome mat, where he'd dropped it just after the photographer said 'cheese.' The headline read, "Gambling Ordinance on Hold as City Riverfront Project Stalls."

His career disintegrated on the front page of the hometown newspaper in words his wife's lawyer would use to pinpoint his affair. This time the D.A. didn't bother to yell. He just stood on the front porch and repeated it softly.

"You…son of a bitch."

CHAPTER 7

Calhoun & Morgan, LLC

Wednesday, 6:20 a.m.

The law firm that bore his name was hours newer than the corner office he'd called home since the doomed merger was approved. Sixty-four founding shareholders—twenty from his old personal injury shop that split office space and billboards with a bail bondsman and the rest from the ex-governor's stately corporate practice—unanimously voted to sacrifice him as Calhoun & Morgan's first managing partner. The negotiations were as awkward as the idea to join forces at all. That they produced the state's largest law firm by combining the talents of its two most disparate mid-sized ones was a triumph of tunnel-visioned persistence at the expense of each side's better interests. It took three months to agree on the ampersand between the principals' names, and five minutes to put Ethan Morgan in charge of it. The half-year since had been devoted to the slow cannibalization of an aged lawyer who deserved better, but was a fool to expect it. His judgment failed him when he needed it most, careless in a game that punishes carelessness, even for a revered man about to sit for his lobby portrait.

Public reverence became private enmity at first sight of the managing partner's back. As often as he was surrounded, it was always turned to someone. Lawyers half his age had the ears of shareholders in a position to harm him. They came with agendas. Where they saw themselves in five years, or five months unless the change they demanded was made. The only variable in the dissenters' plans was how small Morgan would be in their rearview mirror.

In shareholder meetings and in the hallways they plotted, motivating one another through the dark days with schemes and side bets gently whispered…*what if we just…imagine a firm where…wouldn't life be simpler if…*

They were confused and broke, living on Governor Calhoun's name and the credit their banker clients lent them because they were too big to fail.

They panicked and they didn't do panic well. They spoke a new language, the language invented by consultants who sell inspiration by the hour, paid for as part of an overhead that exceeded the national debt of many small countries. Calhoun & Morgan, or "C and M"—pronounced "See'n 'em" in the monosyllabic bursts the starched shirted, suspender boys spewed forth—would survive long past its founding, in spite of the shortsightedness of its founders, if men slightly less jaded would only trust their enlightened sons.

In the days after the coup there would be deliverance through something called *total quality leadership* and *best management practices*, and it would allow them to rise from the ashes through *smart growth*—they actually spoke that way—while dinosaurs like Ethan Morgan trudged off to where dinosaurs go in their grand withdrawal. Sure, Ethan was fine at the beginning, a seasoned placeholder who wouldn't mess things up unrecognizable. But eventually the real horses had to step up. *By God, Darwin and the firm's junior partners were right.*

Morgan could hear the garbage men talk now. His partners had even keener ears, and the only votes on Main Street that mattered.

Loyalty told the shareholders to circle the wagons. Their reputations were at stake, too. Maybe. He couldn't count on that. A man in his position had some chips to call home, although the blue ones were disappearing fast. They had been partners to somebody for a long time, but not to him or the ambulance chasers he'd cleaned up and brought to this merger. The Calhoun lawyers were his competitors just a few months ago, respected members of the defense bar who got paid by the hour instead of by the shakedown. The smart money had it that wounds so deep wouldn't heal simply because for the moment there were warm feelings in the outer offices.

Weston Calhoun gave his old friend a vote of confidence so timid no one believed it, least of all him. A strong one wouldn't have made much difference. The puritans he brought to the merger weren't much on second chances. Governor Calhoun had it easy, the way visionaries who marry up usually do.

The firm's loop was big, and everyone wanted to be in it, but it didn't stretch all the way to the Hillsdale Country Club. Calhoun felt obliged to spend his days there, or anywhere holding a putter or a steak sandwich, or one of those slushy drinks floating a paper umbrella in his un-calloused hands. He wouldn't be able to live with himself if he reaped these years anywhere else. The support he lent his partner from afar, nineteenth hole niceties traded with the swells, was no consolation for the firm's dwindling list of accounts receivable. The shortfall would stick to Morgan. A big picture guy like the ex-governor would remain unscathed. Although he'd make sure to feign a reasonable amount of concern for his troubled friend as he debated his club selection on Hillsdale's tricky back nine.

Calhoun was a fourth-generation glad-hander who enjoyed practicing law even less than he cared about making a difference in public office. He rode into the governor's mansion on the coattails of a popular president, and spent two of the best years of his life staying the course there. The problem was he had a four-year term, and the voters tuned out half way through it. He lost all interest in practicing law after that. It was generally conceded to have been a short trip, but no one had asked him to do anything else, and he was disinclined to work on memoirs no one wanted to read. He did manage to make it through his political career with his health and law license intact, and the bar had been more receptive in the transitioning years.

The name identification of a former governor appealed to a man who'd toiled in anonymity for as long as Morgan had. Calhoun dreamed of a firm with more lawyers and sections than any other in the state, one of the top fifty in America. Morgan could still hear him describe the newest 'Am-Fifty' law firm, right here in Bristol, the biggest in a small state still fighting its states' rights war. It would be in the largest city, where the law school was, and Calhoun would lend his name to it. His old friend, a less well-known but capable lawyer who knew his place and was obliged to stay there would run it. If it worked, both would retire after men of equal ambition judged the venture a success, and psychological needs that should have been satisfied long ago finally could be put to rest. It seemed odd to them that their impressive material achievements hadn't taken care of that by now.

Ethan had been enticed by a closing act he wanted, and hedged his bet against the legacy a one-term governor needed. The dreams they had turned into plans they made over the slowest martinis in the deepest part of the South. All were faint memories of events that hadn't happened yet in the lives of either man. It was difficult to admit they never would. Morgan was in the twilight of a good career he hoped to convince himself was a great one. There was still time, and it was fixed in his soul, undaunted by the stakes and the odds before him, for his modest cup to be half full.

The man sitting uneasily on the other side of his desk knew something about blind faith, its possibilities and its dangers. He'd walked that path all his life, just never as alone as he felt at this moment.

Thomas Crazy Bear Walker understood only a little of what the lawyer'd placed before him to read, two neatly clipped sets of documents on either side of an expensive looking pen. The fancy writing instrument was uncapped and would be presented to him after he'd signed his name, or made an "X" for all Morgan knew, or did whatever he would do to signify he agreed with all he didn't understand—a token, or would the lawyer be politically incorrect enough to suggest, perhaps the 'wampum' of their new partnership.

Crazy Bear squinted at the fine print. There were plenty of lamps in the managing partner's office, but only the one on his desk was in use. The room was almost as dark as the place Ethan was heading, barely within sight of the ethical fringes of the practice. He'd told the confused man to take his time, to ask whatever questions he wanted, that they had all morning if that's what it took, and that even though Calhoun & Morgan didn't represent the Saucostee Indian Tribe *per se*, their interests were substantially the same as those of their client. It was in all the ways that mattered a *bona fide* win-win, Morgan assured him, and all he'd have to do is sign for the tribe's profits. Even Crazy Bear didn't believe that, especially not before the sun came up in this cold man's city.

"I don't understand this," he pushed the papers away. "Lots of legal mumbo jumbo. I bet you thought I wouldn't say that, but only a proud fool pretends he knows something he doesn't when not knowing can cost him."

Crazy Bear looked more European than Native American—tall, not oppressively so, but Jimmy Stewart tall with the same professorial bearing. He had slicked-back jet-black hair, smooth olive skin that might wrinkle when he turned ninety, and strong old world features. He was like an international financier who'd come to *The States* to check on his many holdings, anything but a man who knew every third word he read and who'd raised eight kids below the poverty level. He was only a fraction Saucostee, but with enough blood for the federal government to recognize him as a full member of that sovereign nation.

Morgan would've bet a week's worth of billable hours that the words "Crazy Bear" appeared nowhere on Walker's birth certificate. Most everyone else who sat with him on the tribal council had about as distant a connection, although there were a few stronger lineages. The chief was a hundred percent Saucostee, and as Morgan found out the hard way, about as flexible as cast iron. Crazy Bear would at least listen to reason, he figured, and might even be willing to keep confidential meetings confidential.

Ethan stared at the lights in the distance, thirty stories up and miles away from his solo practice. He heard only the sound of the Indian's voice. *Hadn't he signed yet?*

"Mr. Morgan? Did you hear me?"

"I'm sorry. What?"

"Your paperwork. Pretty confusing stuff. Another white man trap. I'm not signing."

Morgan gazed into the darkness, clear and tranquil this morning, cool for late summer but that would change by daybreak. He could barely make out the airport tower beacon just beyond the city limits. He watched it revolve as he thought about which play to call next.

"First of all," he began, "they're not my documents, Mr. Walker. Those are standard forms the secretary of state's office requires—"

"More empty suits."

He smiled. "Well, you're probably right about that. But that doesn't change the fact that everyone in this state who forms a non-profit corporation has to complete the same application you have before you now."

"Non-profit?" he laughed. "That's not what your client is about. I know Warren Dunn. He doesn't get out of bed unless there's money in it."

Ethan winced. The chief had tipped him off about billionaire developer Warren Dunn. Disaster. Disaster with no crumple zone. On the other hand, the big Indian had still taken the meeting. He'd made the hour's drive from the reservation to downtown Bristol at this hour, and he knew who the client was. Either Chief Navarro had changed his mind since he'd told Morgan to pound sand, or Crazy Bear was a freer agent within the Saucostee Tribe than he held himself out to be. Or, it was too risky to consider, maybe the chief hadn't changed his mind and sent him anyway. But what did he want? Ethan didn't care as long as Walker left his signature on the pages and tucked the hundred-dollar pen in his pocket. With Warren Dunn's name on the table, the man who never met a forest he wouldn't bulldoze, the hard sell just got harder. Time for lawyer games.

"Mr. Dunn is not my client," he said. "I represent the Saucostee Preservation Coalition."

Crazy Bear's grin wrapped around his eyebrows. "That's Dunn."

"He's a member, that's true. But he doesn't act alone. There's a full board of directors that must vote on every action the coalition takes."

"Who else is on the board?"

He followed as Morgan strolled past him toward an imposing chair on the other side of a more imposing desk. The lawyer balanced a pair of reading glasses on the tip of his nose and sat down with great ceremony. Crazy Bear had punched the right button.

Ethan looked over the top of the glasses and said, "A few others who share his passion for land conservation. Mr. Dunn is just as interested in preserving the historical significance of the Saucostee Tribe as…" He was about to say, 'as you are,' but that would have ended the meeting and left him with a desk full of unsigned paper. Instead he said, "…as any other concerned citizen in Bristol."

"Un-uh," Walker said over the fine print. "Dunn wants something. This mess of paper is supposed to keep everybody from knowing what it is. Non-profit corporation?"

"Yes. This document simply lists the names of the incorporators, the business address—which is essentially a post office box—the activities the corporation will undertake, and that whatever y'all do, it's not for the purpose of making a profit."

"Uh-huh." Walker held up the second set of papers. "And what's this?"

"That's just a power of attorney form. It lets the coalition do certain things, take care of administrative matters, stuff like that, in case all the board members can't get together for a full meeting. These folks are quite busy, as you can imagine, and it's difficult to get enough of them together to conduct business. The small stuff they probably don't sweat much anyway. The power of attorney allows others to act when they can't get a quorum together."

"Quorum?" Crazy Bear rubbed the back of his neck. He loosened his tie and tugged at his shirt collar.

"Just what is this non-profit corporation going to do?"

"Mr. Dunn has purchased some land along the Lafayette River. Most of it will be developed, but the portion he's setting aside for this use is a pristine area, with beautiful first-growth timber, natural streams and wildlife. You're familiar with it, I'm sure. You probably know it better than I do, and I've lived in Bristol all my life."

"Go on."

"Mr. Dunn wants to make sure these acres stay protected. The spot is ideal for teaching young people about nature and the environment. And if we can get your cooperation, the history and traditions of the Saucostee Tribe will be passed on for generations to come. He realizes the cultural significance of that land to you people."

Morgan grimaced. As soon as it left his mouth, the unforgivable 'you people,' he knew he'd topped out the *dis-o-meter*. His body language was all back-peddle. The glasses came off, face muscles relaxed, if he'd had a cardigan he'd have slipped into it and offered Crazy Bear a cup of steaming sure-fire cocoa for bonding. Maybe he didn't hear.

"Listen, Mr. Walker. Warren Dunn knows what that land means to the Saucostees. There are artifacts everywhere. I understand members of the tribe used to hunt near that part of the river, and that there may even be some burial grounds that even the tribe has not discovered. He's sensitive to all of those concerns. The Saucostees have used that land for a long time—"

"That's because we own it."

"Of course you're aware of what the state supreme court has said about the ownership of that land. That issue has been finally decided. We've moved past that now."

Crazy Bear's dark face reddened, then it Burgundy'd. "Your law does not apply to us. We are a sovereign territory. The U. S. Supreme Court said that, and the last time I checked, they were a peg above your local judges. The state trespassed on our land, and Dunn bought up what the politicians didn't want. And you want us to go into business with him?" He dripped with indignation. "Unbelievable."

"I understand how you feel," Morgan patronized him. "Sure. That's your reaction now. It would be mine, too. But the courts have sorted things out, and the tribe received its due process every step of the way. The state won the lawsuit and it held the deeds...that is, until Mr. Dunn came along and paid fair market value for each parcel."

"It's all a little too neat if you ask me. Dunn wanted the land from the beginning. He just needed the state to help him get it. And that's exactly what they did. That's a fact and you know it."

"Okay, let's talk some other facts. Here's the main one. The bottom line is that Mr. Dunn has more land than he can use for the city's riverfront project. But he doesn't want to sell any of it either. He thinks the parcels nearest to the tribe would make an ideal green space to offset his development, and he wants the Saucostees to be involved. I can tell you this, if y'all become part of the coalition, there's no better way to guarantee that the land stays as is. If Mr. Dunn decides to sell off the pieces he doesn't develop...well, who knows what could happen to the property?" He tapped his fingers on the desk. "The burial grounds and what not."

"Is that a threat? Because if it is, let me tell you—"

"Take it easy, Mr. Walker. I'm not threatening you. I'm not threatening you, all right? You just have to think a few steps ahead, and I want to make sure you're doing that. The Saucostees have used the land for years. No one's arguing that. But they weren't the only ones. So the tribe brought a quiet title action to resolve the conflicting ownership claims. And, unfortunately, you lost. The City of Bristol stood to benefit more than any other party. If you ask me, they got the best deal since the State of New York bought Manhattan."

Walker's smooth face cracked. It was another 'you people.'

"Okay, bad example. The point is the city a windfall. Mr. Dunn's the only one who's actually paid what that land's worth. Don't punish him any more than the open market already has."

"But the Supreme Court said—"

"Oh, there's no question what the Supreme Court said. The Saucostees are a sovereign nation. No one can dispute that. And that has certain advantages."

Morgan knew only too well. He'd spent weeks researching the tax breaks the tribe had been awarded, and how his client could tap into them with the stroke of a pen.

"But that determination had nothing to do with the quiet title action," he continued. "That was entirely a matter of state law, and, of course, the state won that round. The government wanted the land for economic development, naturally. Warren Dunn is the biggest developer in the state, biggest in this part of the country. He's leasing most of the riverfront property back to the city to build a convention center. And he's got plans for further development on the other pieces, everywhere except for these few parcels we're talking about."

"Why doesn't he just put whatever he wants on them now, same as the others?" Walker asked.

"For all the reasons I just mentioned. His interest in the coalition's work, the attractiveness of the area as a buffer for the riverfront project. Lots of reasons. Besides, while this is a beautiful piece of land, there are some developmental problems. For instance, the topography is not the best, and the soil doesn't perk too well there. It's a gorgeous area, but—"

"Doesn't perk? It's next to a river? Who are you kiddin'?"

"All right, the water's not bad, but it's better downstream. It'll have that 'state park' quality to it—wet enough, but it tastes like metal. It costs too much to run pipe down that far."

Ethan was running out of reasons to account for his client's uncharacteristic generosity. Crazy Bear was ready to fall in line with his chief and walk.

"I'll ask you again, Morgan. If Dunn owns the land as you say he does, why not just build whatever he wants? Why does he need us?"

Ethan polished his glasses with a fancy cloth he kept in his desk drawer and held them up to the light. The clear lenses sparkled and the gold wire frame gleamed.

"I suppose he doesn't *need* you, as you put it, Mr. Walker. But he does want you. The piece he's talking about is good-sized, but there are still a few acres the Coalition would like to include farther up the river, within the Saucostee territory."

"Hold on," he said. "You didn't say anything about including more of our land in this deal."

Morgan reached for something under his desk. "Wait a second. Would you just wait a second, Mr. Walker? Here, I'll show you."

He unrolled a large plat and handed Crazy Bear several aerial photographs of the site.

"This big tract along here is owned by Dunn Enterprises," he pointed. "These parcels the city condemned and sold to him. Mr. Dunn intends to put this long strip of land into a trust for the benefit of the Saucostee Preservation Coalition. The property line runs along the river's edge for several miles, steadily becoming narrower as you move upstream. The Saucostee *Nation*," Ethan pandered in high gear now, "the Saucostee Nation extends to this point along the eastern portion of Bristol. This tip of land owned by the tribe is contiguous to the city. Here," he motioned, "along with Dallas County to the west. And, of course, with the federal litigation and the other lawsuits the tribe settled with the state and both counties, the Saucostees pay no property taxes. If the tribe consents to the arrangement the board members are proposing, the coalition's gift of this tract would not alter the tax-exempt status of the property. It would expand the Saucostee's ability to use this historically significant land, even if the ownership technically stays with the coalition. There's not a downside to this from your perspective as far as I can see."

"I don't get this. We owned the land, the courts gave it to the city, Dunn bought it from the city, and you're telling me he's just gonna give it back to us?"

"Not Mr. Dunn. The coalition."

"The coalition is giving us our land back?"

"In a manner of speaking, yes."

"Then what were all the lawsuits for?"

"The coalition is not transferring the property to the tribe. It's asking you to become partners so the Saucostee Nation can use the land like always, despite what the court ruled. All the coalition gets is the same tax break the tribe enjoys on its property, but since they're a non-profit, the whole thing is a wash."

Crazy Bear scratched his head while the wheels turned. "What's the catch?"

"There is no catch, Mr. Walker. All the board wants is for the Saucostee Nation to enter into a partnership—that's spelled out in more detail in these pages—a partnership with the coalition for the preservation of this property. The tribe would have representation on the board, and the board will lease the land back to you for one dollar a year, for ninety-nine years. The land becomes essentially a part of the Saucostee Nation for a century, so long as the tribe stays in the coalition."

"I don't like it. Why haven't you talked to the chief about this?"

Ethan knew his papers wouldn't be signed this morning, but there was still a chance they might not end up in the trashcan either.

"I was hoping you might do that for us, Mr. Walker. You see we tried to talk to Chief Navarro some time ago, but he wouldn't give us an audience. I thought he might have mentioned that to you."

"Continue."

"Frankly, the chief heard Warren Dunn's name and had about the same reaction you did. Reputations," the lawyer bemoaned. "How many deals have I seen die because of reputations? Such a shame. Sometimes you have to take a chance and get to know a person for yourself rather than believe what others say."

"Uh-huh. And this is one of those times?"

"Mr. Walker, you've heard me out, and I thank you for that. You're on the Tribal Council. I'm confident Chief Navarro will listen to you."

"How well do you know him?"

"Not well. But I think once he gets past Mr. Dunn's involvement, he'll see that this is a no-lose proposition."

Morgan slid the power of attorney into a folder and locked it in his desk drawer. "Here," he said, holding out the articles of incorporation. "Take this with you. We can go through the rest of these forms later."

"I don't need the power of attorney?"

"No. No. That was just a document more for convenience anyway. You can sign one of those anytime. This is all you need for now."

Crazy Bear stood. Ethan set the papers on his desk.

"If the chief knew I was meeting with you, he'd not only kick me off the council, he'd banish me from the tribe."

Ethan needed a break so he took a chance. "Why are you meeting with me, Mr. Walker?"

"It's true not everyone agrees with Chief Navarro. But he's a good leader, and he's strong. He'd never betray us. People believe in him."

"Even when he's wrong?"

"I don't know that he's wrong about this," Walker said. "I'm not sure he's right, either." He picked up the papers and left Morgan's pen on the desk. "I don't know."

"Think it over," Ethan said. "I've been authorized to hold this offer…I hesitate to call it that because that usually connotes some sort of bargain where both sides give up something—this offer open until Friday. After that, the board intends to hold a meeting, where it likely will vote to disband the coalition. If the purpose you form your group for vanishes, why have the group, you know? Then, Dunn Enterprises can do whatever it wants."

The senior partner stuffed his hands in his pockets.

"That usually means the cement mixers. You know?"

Crazy Bear nodded. "Yeah, we know about that."

"And one more thing. When you talk to the chief, be sure to tell him that the city has made some noise about annexing the same land I just showed you. They think that Dunn's project up river might lead to other commercial development. They want the taxes all of these ventures would generate. There are a lot of 'what ifs,' but if that happens, the tribe can forget about ever getting the land back. You just might want to mention that to the chief."

Walker held up Morgan's legal work. "This right here. This just—"

Ethan finished the thought. "Just gives you a say in what happens to that land. Like you used to have before the courts started meddling in everyone's business."

He offered his hand and Crazy Bear shook it. Morgan patted him on the back as they walked to the door.

"Give my best to the chief."

CHAPTER 8

Piper crept down the narrow street that separated two indistinct rows of shotgun houses in Oakdale, dodging the low-hanging Spanish moss and managing not to stall the *Lieutenant Mobile.*

At the end of River Drive catty-cornered from the rock-filled shallow part of the Lafayette, Piper rolled up the driveway. The wooden house was white with two stories, easily the nicest home in the neighborhood. There was a big front porch he couldn't miss, and a bright red swing its owner probably logged a thousand hours in with grandchildren on either side of her. There was nothing wrong with the place, not a thing real estate mogul Warren Dunn couldn't fix with a giant wrecking ball.

In a few months there would be a convention center where these mill houses stood. A major hotel chain was interested in opening a resort quality spread nearby. A mall would follow, anchored at each end by a big box chain store, and every fast food restaurant on the planet would sprout up where the Magnolias stood. Traffic lights would run in place of the Spanish moss, with cars traveling through the lawn where the elementary school's playground now sat. There was an ever-narrowing window for the progress to unfold, and just a few parcels of land to squeeze through the slit before the deal was done. City Council wanted an outcome. Harvey Bing was right about that. If it happened to be legal, so much the better. Michael Pomerantz' marching orders rang in his ears. They were government bureaucrat-proof.

Piper checked his watch. Ten 'til six. The darkest part of morning on the worst side of the most beautiful piece of Bristol and this was where he was supposed to be, carving up another defenseless citizen for his client.

He tapped softly on the old lady's door as if he were eloping with her granddaughter and had forgotten his ladder. Alma Wilson opened it all the way, no chain, no deadbolt. She wore a blue warm-up suit and slippers, a dentures smile beneath a welder's mask pair of glasses. She was short and round, and Piper knew that most days she probably bounced a grandkid on her pokey middle like he was a giant brooch. A new hip wasn't an 'if' for her, it was a 'when.' Piper wanted to hug her and ask her to tuck him in until it was light outside.

"Mrs. Wilson?"

"You must be the lawyer from the city."

"Yes ma'am. My name's Sean Piper."

"Come in, young man. I've been expecting you."

Mrs. Wilson took Piper by the arm and led him to a sofa in the front room. She sat beside him, almost on top of him, but somehow he didn't feel crowded. The ceilings were high and cracked, with several coats of white paint in various stages of yellowing that covered all but the deepest tears in the plaster. The wiring was Depression Era, with light switches and tubing running on the outside of the wall straight to the fixtures they serviced. There were hardwood floors throughout the parts of the first level Sean could see. Some appeared to sag, but the worn parts were hidden by area rugs that were almost large enough to obscure the buckling.

"Now I haven't got a lot of time," she said. "I've got to be at the hospital in a half hour."

"Yes, ma'am. I understand."

She smiled pleasantly. "Well, I guess I got a minute anyway. I'm just a little nervous. They said this is a routine operation. In fact I already had the other one done a few years ago. But I always say, anytime somebody goes to cuttin' on me, that's major surgery."

"I can't argue with you there, Mrs. Wilson."

"May I get you something to drink? The nurse told me I wasn't supposed to eat anything after midnight, but I just got to have my coffee. Would you like a cup?"

"Ah...you probably shouldn't do that, ma'am, drink coffee I mean. The anesthesia and all...I mean they tell you that for a reason, so you won't get sick. If you don't mind my saying."

"Oh, I don't mind. Maybe you're right. You want any?"

"No thanks."

"Well, that suits me fine. I 'spect you're ready to get on with business anyway."

Piper nodded that he was. He opened his leather portfolio and set her file on top. He left it there for a moment while he studied a picture of some cute young children on the mantle opposite him. Then another child, and another. They were black and white shots mostly, although the kids seemed to smile at him in living color all the way across the room.

"Those are my grandbabies." She showed him a large photograph above the fireplace. "This 'uns two now, but she was just ten weeks old in this picture. Ain't she somethin'?"

"Yeah, she's a beautiful baby. How many grandchildren do you have?"

"Eight. These two here, then my oldest daughter has four, and my middle child has the twins."

"That's a big family."

Piper held the picture in one hand, and a quitclaim deed for her property in the other.

"I guess they must like coming here to see their grandma, huh?"

"Oh, my, yes they do. I have a house full on Sundays. They like to play at that park 'cross the street."

"I bet so. I saw that the other day when I was out here. That's a pretty spot. I suppose there's all kinds of places for little kids to play around here, by the river and everywhere. This sure is a beautiful part of the city."

"Of course I have to agree with you 'bout that. I've lived here all my life. Right here in this house," she said. "Would you like to see the rest? It'll just take a minute."

"Uh. sure. If it won't make you late."

"They can't operate without me, I 'spose."

She showed him the downstairs, the long, dark hallway covered with more pictures of her family, the hardwood floors in each room and the original glass panes in the windows. It was comfortable now, but there didn't appear to be any controls for heating and air conditioning anywhere in the house. The kitchen had high cabinets with cups and saucers piled to the top, refusing to fall, although an accident could happen at any moment. There was a swinging door held open by a high chair. It led to the dining room and a boarding house length table. There was a china cabinet behind it that looked too big to fit through the door. Maybe they built the house around it. Piper wondered how she'd be able to get it out of here. No wonder she wanted help with moving expenses. He pictured her three daughters and eight grandchildren around the long table on Sundays, when the house was full and there were no government cars in her driveway.

Mrs. Wilson rinsed a coffee cup and placed it on a plastic strainer next to the kitchen sink.

"I knew you were coming, so I tried to straighten up as best I could," she said. "You can see here where I been paintin'. My arm is only so long, so I might' a missed a few spots at the top there."

He inspected her work. "You've been painting?"

"Yes, sir. And cleaning 'round the baseboards, and my vents—got 'em with some cotton balls I tore up and wet so's they'd slide in between the cracks down there. Put a good coat of black paint on 'em, too."

"You did?"

"Oh, yeah. I wanted the place to look real nice for ya'. I knew you was comin' to see me today, and I wanted everything to be just right when you came to make your offer. It was kinda tough with my hip, though. But I don't 'spect a body gets to sell her house every day. Not to the city, anyway. I want to make sure whoever gets the place next gets as good a home as I've had."

It was a punch that broke through Piper's rock-ribbed middle, came out the other side of his body, ricocheted off her half painted wall and hit him right between the eyes. The city had sent its appraiser by weeks ago, a portly man in high-water trousers whose favorite color was test-pattern plaid. He'd already low-balled her in the deed Piper kept tucked under his arm. His figure of just compensation took into account what he'd gathered by walking around the outside of the house and matching that with the other Oakdale comparables, which weren't comparable at all. Everything she'd done on the inside, the scrubbing this grandmother did on her hands and knees in the days before her second hip replacement, cleaning air conditioner vents in a house with no air conditioning, and reaching for the stars on her fragile tiptoes to paint the tops of door frames—was for nothing. She was improving a place Warren Dunn had already leveled on paper.

Sean hung his head and said nothing. She actually thought she was going to show her house to a prospective buyer, the way people in the nice parts of town get to do. There'd be small talk and sweet tea, tiny sandwiches with no crust left and *may I show you around the place?* Even if this visit weren't going to lead to a sale, she would still give him her grand tour. *Oh, you'll just love it here. The neighbors are so nice. My children grew up on this street, playing safe with no worries about riding their bicycles down the road. This place, this old wooden house across from the park by the river, between the Spanish moss and the orange sunsets, will last until your grandchildren are big enough to sit at the long dining room table. Just as mine do now. This is…this is home.*

"Well, that's fine, Mrs. Wilson," he managed. "I think your house is beautiful. Really beautiful."

She looked at him trustingly, the nice young man from the city. He held something for her to sign and then she'd get a government check. Once she took the money she'd have thirty days to move out, if the heavy equipment waited that long. Sean reckoned that even with a dozen kin folk close enough to eat with her on Sundays, she'd pack everything up herself, even if the city put a little toward the move. And from all appearances she was happy about this state of affairs. Where she'd find as nice a home on the waterfront for seventy thousand dollars, as the city's man saw it, tree-lined in the heart of Bristol, only God and a few bankruptcy trustees knew. She was happy as if this was simply what was next in her long life of supplication. It was what's next.

"Mrs. Wilson," Sean said, "let me ask you a question. Where…uh…where did you plan on moving after you sell this place?"

"Oh, I got a sister down in Pinckney. She's got a spot in that trailer park over there. She said I could stay with her until I find someplace else."

"Trailer park? Pinckney?" He studied the high, cracked ceiling. "The one off highway twenty-four?"

"Yes. That's the one. Are you familiar with it?"

"Just you and your sister?"

"Oh, no. She's got a husband and a daughter who stays with 'em. And, of course, her daughter's got kids, too."

"How many children does the daughter have?"

"She's got four kids, but only three of them stay at home."

"Uh-huh. So that's what, you, your sister, her husband, you say, and then their daughter and three of her four children, right?"

"Yes."

"So then we're talking about what, seven people in a mobile home?"

"That sounds about right."

"Is that a doublewide?"

"No. It's just a regular trailer."

"I see."

"But they say they don't mind me staying. And the rent's not so bad."

His eyes bulged. "Rent? Your sister wants you to pay rent for your spot in the single wide trailer in Pinckney?"

"Yes. My check covers it. Like I say, they's happy to have me."

Her check. He was pretty sure she wasn't talking about stock dividends. So some part, perhaps all, of Grandma Wilson's fixed monthly income would go to reserve her undivided one-seventh interest in a trailer on road-kill highway in Pinckney, a small town thirty miles south of Bristol whose largest sign read 'reduced speed ahead.'

His watch said it was time for her to go to the Medicaid hospital and swap out hips.

"I tell you what, Mrs. Wilson. I know you've got to go see your doctor. I have some other stops to make. I'll be back this way later in the week. I'll come by and check on you then."

"But I won't be here then. I'll be in the hospital or the rehab center. Besides, over the phone you said this couldn't wait. I mean, I don't have any set time that I'm supposed to be down to my sister's, but I'll be in rehab for a month or more they said. And I thought you was in a hurry is all."

He stuffed the deed inside his leather binder. It was that or tear it up. "Yeah, well, you know how government work is, lots of stops and starts. Hurry up and wait, you know?"

"Oh?"

"By the way, I don't know if anyone has asked you this yet, but have you shown this paperwork to anybody? I mean you're free to have a lawyer of your own review these documents. You know, someone you can trust."

"Oh, I trust you, Mr. Piper. You're a nice man. You come round here and visit with me. I don't get to see many men folk any more. I look forward to you comin' by and seein' me."

"What do you mean?" he asked. "This is the first time I've been by here."

"Oh, I know. I meant the others from the city."

"There've been other men from the City of Bristol to see you?"

"Why, yes. A couple."

"What did they want, if you don't mind my asking?"

"They wanted to know when I was moving out, how much I thought my house was worth. I told them I had no idea about that. They were real nice. They told me they'd help me when it was time to move. You know, with my heavy pieces and what not."

"Do you remember their names?"

"No, sorry. It's been a while ago."

"I understand," Piper said. "Can you tell me what they looked like?"

"Let's see. One was real tall, almost as tall as you. The other was short this way," she held her palm parallel to the floor, "and big this way," she said, holding out both hands like they were around the man's chubby belly. "Bless his heart."

"Anything else?"

"The tall one had a moustache, I think. Or maybe it was a beard, too. No, just a moustache. The shorter man wore glasses. They dressed real nice, you know, suits and ties, nice shoes like you wear."

"What color were they?" he asked.

"They were white."

"Do you remember when they came by?"

"Oh, it had to be 'bout a year ago at least. I think school had just let out, so maybe early summer. I guess that must've been why I thought you'd come by then. But I see you don't have any hair on your face. Ain't got much on ya' head, either. Huh, huh."

"Yes, ma'am."

"But it was hot already. They looked like they were ready to fall out. You know, I don't have air conditioning. I grew up Without it, so I don't know what I'm missing. But folks who's used to it say it's miserable without it. They were sitting on my couch there, panting like a couple big ol' Collie dogs. I remember they liked my sweet tea. I cuts it with some lemonade. You like lemonade in your tea?"

Sean checked the report on city council's directive to condemn the riverfront property. The date was March of this year. Council's motion to begin the project passed just four months ago.

"Early summer, huh?" he asked.

"Had to be. Why do you ask?"

"Oh, just curious."

He scribbled something inside the folder and clipped his pen to his shirt pocket.

"You know, Mrs. Wilson, I don't see any reason to rush into a big decision like this. Especially when I have other folks out here left to see. You just think it over, maybe take this to someone else to look at, you know, a fresh pair of eyes."

"Well, if you think that's best."

Sean looked around the room at the half-painted walls, the uneven brush strokes where Alma Wilson's arm couldn't reach any higher. The air vents sparkled and nothing came out of them. The front porch looked inviting, and a wooden bench that was older than he was creaked as a cool breeze moved it gently back and forth. Someone had tried to sweet talk this grandmother and the City Attorney knew nothing about it. Maybe they'd be back.

Later this morning there would be groans from somewhere deep inside City Hall as Michael Pomerantz heard about the one that got away. Piper didn't give a damn how his boss would spin it up the organizational chart.

He offered his hand as they walked outside.

"Yeah, Mrs. Wilson, I think that's best. Do me a favor, here's my card. As I said, my name is Sean Piper and I'm the deputy city attorney. Most of our employees have business cards like this one. Put mine some place where you can find it. If you run into either of the men you told me about, please give me a call right away. The number on the back goes to this mobile phone. I have it with me all the time. Give me a call if you see them again, would you please do that for me?"

"Okay, Mr. Piper. I'll call you."

"Thank you."

Sean bumped the swing and got a few more slow squeaks out of it. He waited until it was still again. The sun cut through the thick fog rolling off the river. It was quiet on her street, the way that part of the world had always been.

"I hope your surgery goes well," he said. "Take care, Mrs. Wilson."

CHAPTER 9

Ethan Morgan surveyed the spacious wood-paneled office, pausing to admire the more cherished pieces of framed paper on a wall devoted to his many achievements. There was a law degree from a university people had heard of, and an undergraduate one beneath it from a school no one had. The latter cost him twice as much to attend and opened half as many doors.

There were pictures of him in his Ben Matlock suit, shaking hands with politicians who called him friend at a thousand dollars a plate. There was an award from the Rotary Club for his efforts in a service fundraiser when he used to have time for good works. He'd long since forgotten the name of the charity, but still knew the amount he helped raise for something worthwhile. There was an honorable discharge from the service he'd given his country during a war when the country disliked its warriors.

They all looked better and meant more at the old homes he'd practiced law in before moving to this lonely place in the sky. Elevators and access codes at the Dunn Plaza replaced the creaky stairs and skeleton keys on the historical registry. The high rise had more security cameras than *Macy's* at Christmas. Its occupants were even more suspicious about the ones they couldn't see, but that saw them at every angle.

His office held a breathtaking view of the domed statehouse, copper beneath the same turquoise shell that settled upon the Statue of Liberty after so many years of neglect. The flags on top would be unrecognizable soon as the sun poured onto the modern, glassy eastern side of the skyscraper.

The other full length window—Calhoun & Morgan's top client producers scattered among four floors each had two—overlooked the same river Colonel Longstreet floated down two centuries ago, stopping to found the capital in a spot too humid for Sherman's March. Kudzu choked the life from anything else that might have grown on banks that hadn't changed for a thousand years. In a few weeks, and with luck, influence and decent lawyering, Morgan's biggest client would change them forever.

A pity, he thought, as he straightened his wrinkled forehead against the long, tinted glass. With major improvements, the tiny wooden houses in Oakdale might just be considered run-down.

From this height they looked like a pile of kids' blocks that had been played with and put away by a child who had better toys. Ethan wondered how many generations had called them home, and whether that would be figured into the amount the City of Bristol would pay before leveling each one for Warren Dunn's greatest development. No property can be taken from a citizen by a democratic government without 'just compensation,' and the city promised to be fair before it told the inhabitants along the Lafayette River what their land and sentiment were worth. Morgan was certain Dunn would be right there offering to help with the math.

The sun peaked around the capitol dome, and the old man squinted at the brilliant orange light. It was too early for that, and too late to think about anyone else's interests, so he closed the blinds on both, leaving the room dark and unreasonably cool. He froze his clients to death in this sweltering city. Why should their stomachs be settled when his never was here? He hated summers in Bristol, mostly because they stayed so long past their welcome each fall. On this chilly morning, amidst other things more important, the managing partner had missed the weather report.

Morgan the Rainmaker needed this career-long drought to end. He needed clients, rich ones with lots of enemies and cheating spouses, or poor ones who'd been hurt and it wasn't their fault. He needed hours on his time sheet. He needed a stream of income to feed the overhead and egos of two hundred lawyers who lived for too much because it was never enough. He needed a good lawyer and a friend, but not one old enough to know the value of separating the two. He needed a fall guy in case Crazy Bear Walker couldn't persuade Chief Navarro to preserve wildlife as a part of Warren Dunn's fictitious corporation.

The man he had in mind was young, which had to mean he was hungry and maybe even willing to take a shortcut. Everything about Peter Soard said he would be, from his off-the-rack suits to his maxed out credit cards, to the used car he still owed money on, to his young wife who could only live that way for so long before her pretty eyes started to wander.

Ethan thought he could read his promising associate, but had said the same thing about personal injury juries that stiffed him. The young man's pedigree was unimpressive for a downtown law firm where surnames meant status, and status brought clients. Soard's law school career allowed him to overcome that, and won him a job working with the state's top attorneys. They thought they were, anyway, and their hourly rates were fixed high enough to convince themselves they were right. They charged enough to keep away those who complained about high fees, and enough more to command the respect of the well-heeled clients. Any lawyer who thinks that highly of his time must be good, they reasoned. Don't be fooled by the guy down the street who gives a break because he has a passion for the law, they said. *If he's in such demand, why's he so damned affordable?*

Soard ran laps around those at the top of the firm's letterhead, many of whom were here simply because of family ties, and there was blessed freedom in success that stemmed from merit. He was smart, handsome, and beholden to no one in a way that made most envious, and the rest uncomfortable. He was fresh, energetic and saddled with student loans. Ethan Morgan was none of those things, had none of those things. That made Soard the perfect co-counsel for the client about to rescue everyone aboard this slow-motion train wreck. No one needed him more, Morgan thought, than its paralyzed conductor. *So where was he?*

Ethan twirled the expensive pen he'd tried to entice Crazy Bear Walker to sign over his birthright with a few minutes ago. He studied the secretary's notes, and his section leader's comments on Peter Soard's brilliant performance thus far at C & M. *Doesn't he want this as bad as I want it for him?*

The nervous associate skated across the exposed hardwood between deep red oriental runners that lined the firm's long hallways. By the time he rounded the corner, he was a dark-suited blur ready to blow through a roadblock.

"Morning, Caroline," Soard said. "Is he in?"

"Slow down, Pete. You're gonna set the rug on fire."

"Sorry. I'm a little late for my meeting with Mr. Morgan. That is, if he's here yet. Please tell me he isn't here yet."

Soard's mouth moved too fast. His words followed some time later. He looked like an expensive extra in a dubbed kung fu movie.

"I'm afraid he is," she said. "I'll let him know you're here." Caroline buzzed the senior partner and motioned the winded lawyer through the door. Morgan's icebox of an office was open for business, plenty of expensive chairs and no waiting.

"Good luck."

"Thanks."

Soard took a deep breath. He straightened his tie, went inside and closed the door. His eyes hurt adjusting to the light. Too dim in here for anyone to be working, he thought. All of Morgan's files were stacked neatly on a credenza that cost more that Soard's car, where they'd been the last time he was summoned to this side of the building.

"Good morning, sir," he said.

Morgan didn't move. He was a two-dimensional cutout balanced in a bulky desk chair, hands limp on either armrest with the remainder of his body hidden in the shadows. The cold silence was tough on Soard's empty stomach. The cruel man wasn't about to save him.

The new lawyer inched closer until he could see a pair of tiny holes in the snow he thought might be the senior partner's eyes.

"Sorry I'm a little late."

"Come in, Peter," a scratchy voice replied. "Sit down."

"Thank you." El Cid was alive.

There was a cumbersome royal blue leather chair across from Morgan's desk. It cost the most and sat the worst of any in the room. Soard deposited his lanky frame there. A smaller man would have been completely swallowed up by it. Maybe Ethan would send out a search party.

A neatly clipped Mont Blanc pen was visible in the 'v' created by Soard's long, crossed legs. He was breathing hard after his sprint from the ghetto parking lot, but his high-strung engine ran hot all the time, so no one could tell the difference. His hair was dark and full, the eyes, too, and fuller. They were set close to a pointy nose that didn't look wide enough to be functional. His arms and legs were interrupted at each joint by a pronounced knobby angle. There was enough daylight between Soard's thin frame and his suspenders for a fat man to sunbathe. Every stitch of clothing drooping from his body was pricey and new, but not yet paid for. He was a praying mantis in mortgaged pinstripes.

Morgan thumbed through a file, pausing every so often to grunt at what he read. Soard's back muscles tightened against the oppressively upright seat.

In most firms face time with the managing partner was coveted by the troops. Ethan's leadership problems weren't well known outside of the tight-lipped shareholders, so as far as the associates knew there was no sense avoiding him. Still, it was morning, it was first thing, Morgan needed something that was important enough to be bumped to the top of his agenda and not even Soard's section leader knew what it was. Some strange fate had made Peter Soard the man of his boss' most desperate hour. He wished he could learn all about it anywhere else but here. He was cold, arched in a chair he was convinced would lead to traction, and starving.

A little wider, a little grayer than the athletic figure who stared at Soard from all those pictures, Ethan Morgan still had a toothy smile and caring eyes that seemed to pay attention even when he wasn't. A perfect semicircular bag supported each one. The rest of his face was remarkably unlined, and provided little in the way of a personal history. His hair was almost silver, and mostly gone, with no one bald spot in particular to blame for it. Average in every way, including his Western mid-life girth, most department store suits fit him, so that's how he went, despite an income that permitted considerably more. His shoes were a peg nicer, though. Clients notice the shoes, he preached.

Morgan moved about in many circles, but had few friends in any of them. People got to know him fast, liked what they saw, then just as quickly lost interest in seeing any more. Some wanted a refund. He needed Soard to get to know him fast, and to like what he saw. After that, he didn't care what the young man did. He wanted to keep his fall guy close, but not close enough to keep him from falling.

"So, Pete, how do you like criminal defense?" he asked. His voice sounded like a wire brush dragged across a rusty barbecue grill.

Soard glanced at the liquor bottle poking its mouth over the top of the trashcan. Morgan's tie was loosened and his shirt uncharacteristically wrinkled. Soard wondered if he'd spent the night here, right here in his office, on the couch, at his desk, somewhere on the thirtieth floor pacing a hole through the hardwood with the world on his back, its problems competing for his vanishing gray matter.

"I like it fine," he said. "It's different than any other section in the firm. At least I think it is. I mean, for one thing, you get paid up front, and you know about how much, as opposed to taking a case on a contingency fee basis. I'm not sure I could play that game."

"Well that's true. It's kind of difficult to take a third of someone's freedom." He laughed. Soard laughed. The cold lawyers laughed.

"How is Mr. Lovelace treating you?"

"He's great. He gives me a lot of autonomy over my cases. At the same time, he's there for me if I have any questions. And as many notes as I took in law school, I still have lots of questions."

Morgan smiled. "We all do, Peter. That's why they call it the practice of law. If you ever got it completely right, I suppose it would be time to retire. You know, Pete, criminal defense is a good place for a young lawyer to cut his teeth. Prosecution, too. But when you're a defense counsel, you can be so much more creative. I'm sure Mr. Lovelace has told you that most of these characters you're going to represent are guilty. And all of them are lying to you. As cynical as that sounds, it's the truth," he assured him.

Ethan was happy now, more relaxed, shooting the breeze with someone who had no choice but to listen and nod at every pearl he offered.

"Yes, they lie," he continued. "Lots of clients lie. Big deal. It's just that with the criminals, you know that going into the case, so you're prepared."

"Yes, sir."

"But, of course, none of that really matters. You don't care what story the guy tells you. You just need to know what that story *is*." Morgan finished his thought like he'd completed an aria, disappointed that Soard hadn't taken a page worth of notes by now.

"Unless your client confesses to you, you can put the dumb son of a bitch on the witness stand and let him say whatever he wants. He has a right to the best defense you can give him. And Remington Lovelace can give them the best defense in Bristol. Remy knows his subject. The firm is fortunate to have him."

"Yes, sir. I completely agree."

Soard wondered just how the firm did come to have Remington Lovelace. The maverick criminal law section leader left one of the most lucrative solo practices in the state to become just another mid-level manager at the top heavy, dubiously merged firm of Calhoun & Morgan. Lovelace had turned away clients for years instead of taking on any help to handle them. Now he was working alongside lawyers he'd made a career out of disregarding, dividing his fees with full shareholders and equity partners waiting to become full shareholders in this speculative venture.

Maybe Lovelace wanted to become a judge, Soard thought, and Ethan Morgan knows some people in the legislature who could do something about that. Weston Calhoun knows even more, but you couldn't catch the *Guh' vah-nerr* unless you staked out the golf course. Whatever his motivation, and whatever deal Morgan made that brought him here, Remy Lovelace knew the law and his clients paid him well for it.

Soard squirmed in the uneasy chair to find a position he could live with for a while longer. Morgan shuffled some papers until he found a page with handwriting all over it. He studied the notes for a moment then set it on the desk.

"How's your wife?" he asked. "Laura, right?" Caroline's notes read *Laura Soard, age twenty-six. No kids. No job. Not looking.*

"Yes, sir. Laura. She's fine, thanks."

"How's she handling these long hours you've been keeping at this dreary ol' place?"

"Laura's very supportive. She knows I studied a long time to get to this point in my life, and she wants me to pursue my goals."

Ethan raised his eyes at that. "Ahhh, yes, goals." He leaned back in his chair and balanced the coffee cup on his knee. "What are those, Pete?"

Soard had a vicious flash back to the career day interviews at law school. *What kind of law do you want to practice? Give me three of your strengths, and three weaknesses. Are you a leader or a follower, and why?* No one ever asked him what kind of tree he'd like to be.

"Well, this is a nice office," he said.

Morgan thought the young associate had a point.

"You'll get there, Pete."

He read more of Caroline's notes. She'd highlighted the right things.

"Your billable hours have been excellent. And better still, it looks like you're getting your clients to pay your fees."

Soard nodded. "Thank you. I've tried to do my share."

"Pete, I called you here this morning because I need your help on a matter, something a little different from what you've been doing for Remy. I know your plate is probably full, but I've been impressed with how you've conducted yourself here and I think you can handle this collateral duty."

"Thank you, sir."

Ethan smiled. He liked his associate, although not liking him would have made things easier.

"I asked the shareholders during a meeting the other day who they'd recommend if I needed help with a special project. That's always a little risky. Some folks either shirk from the responsibility or they think you may be trying to eat out of their rice bowl.

Anyway, your name came up, and Remy Lovelace had a lot of nice things to say."

"Whatever I can do to help."

"Good." Morgan reached into his pocket for a ring of keys that would have shamed the building's janitor. He opened his desk drawer and pulled out a thin folder. Soard watched this production with interest, but his face didn't hold any more clues than the unmarked file Morgan clutched in his hand. The firm's litigation files were red. They were labeled at the top and on the side with the client's name and a five-digit code, part of the redundancies insisted upon by the compulsive office manager. The one Morgan held was an old fashioned brown expandable—the kind with a flap and a snappy string to loop around the whole thing once it got bulky and important looking. There were no labels, no codes. Soard could see only a few documents inside. Most of them were tabbed with messy yellow post-it notes that never would have passed Caroline's exacting standards. There were no signs of any staffer having *opened* the file, an event marking the inception of a client matter. Opening a file triggered everyone in the firm's chain of command from the bookkeeper to the responsible attorney to the section leader that lawyer answered to, who passed along the case essentials to the managing partner. Instead, it was simply a disorganized presentation that came from a locked center desk drawer. Morgan had put it together himself, and from the little Soard knew of his management style, the senior partner didn't order dinner without a second opinion.

"Here," Morgan handed it to him. "Read this. Study every word inside. Get to know this client, everything about him, the good, the bad, and hopefully not too much of the ugly. He's hired me, but I'm too old to do what he has in mind by myself."

Soard set the file on his knee and kept his hands at his side. He didn't look down at it, or anywhere but into the red-veined eyes of the man who'd given it to him. Cool customer, Morgan thought. Cooler than he'd been during the small talk. This may work.

"Let me know what you think after you read the file," he said. "This fella's an aggressive client."

"Right. And what's his—"

"He'll want results, soon."

"I understand. And his name—"

"With the career he's put together and the retainer he's given us, he deserves to have them. I know you're busy, and I've just handed you this, but it's not that much material and this isn't patient money. I'm just looking for your overall impression, then we'll talk more later."

"I'll do my best."

"You're gonna to be at the luncheon tomorrow, aren't you?" Morgan asked as though it were optional for an associate to pass up the firm's quarterly meeting.

"Yes, sir. I'm looking forward to it."

"I mean, you don't have any hearings scheduled or any conflicts?"

"I have docket call at general sessions this morning, so I won't know until after the judge schedules everything. I'm covering for Mr. Lovelace, too. He has a lot more cases on the roster than I do. But I don't expect any of them will be called this term. There's a murder trial that's supposed to last all week. Most everything else should be continued until at least the end of the month."

"Good. You should have some downtime at the courthouse while the D.A. calls the names. Take a look at this material while you're waitin' around."

Soard gave up on trying to get the client's name. "I'll get right on it."

"Oh, and one more thing. I'm sure it will become apparent as you read through the file, but don't discuss its contents, or this client, with anyone else. Not yet. You shouldn't need any paralegal support on this matter."

"Yes, sir."

Soard reached the door as Morgan's phone lit up like a Christmas tree. Both men were startled, as if they'd been caught doing something only one of them knew anything about. A buzz from Caroline during a closed-door meeting usually meant a call from a judge, but most of them weren't at work yet.

"Sorry to disturb you," she said. "Warren Dunn on the line."

Morgan stared at the blinking red light and then at the file folder in Peter Soard's hand. Soard knew the name, and had been around long enough to know when to excuse himself. He gave a small wave and turned the knob. The senior partner gestured palm down, and the confused associate returned to the chair he'd hoped never to see again. Then the enigmatic leader of the most secretive law firm in town put the sixth wealthiest American on the speakerphone.

CHAPTER 10

Pomerantz weaved in and out of traffic on his way to the courthouse and a murder trial he all but promised the victim's family he wouldn't lose. His legs ached from the daybreak romp down Erica's cul-de-sac as he played tag with a roly-poly private investigator. The fat man was probably doubled over on Jenna's lawyer's couch waiting for his camera to be bronzed. Maybe he'd passed out from the chase and Jenna would never see the film. On the other hand, maybe it would be on the cover of tomorrow's *Chronicle* and the D.A. could turn his license in to the bar before the ethics counsel checked his mailbox. He had a job to do, a couple of them, in fact, and no one at either office cared if he was happy at home.

The judge told him if he didn't have a jury picked before lunch he'd be trying cases every Saturday morning until he became efficient. The first trial of the week would get underway by one o'clock. Roll call would take most of the morning, and he only had a few minutes to catch Piper before he returned to Oakdale to evict more grandmothers for Warren Dunn.

Pomerantz searched for the phone number as he dodged pedestrians on Pamlico Street. He wanted Sean Piper's direct line, and maybe his office manager had been good enough to program that into the electronic memo-minder Jenna had given him when they were still speaking. The D.A.'s shirt smelled like fajitas from the Mexican joint Erica dragged him to last night—fajitas and Margaritas mixed with his mistress' schoolgirl perfume. His head throbbed and his cottony tongue felt like it should be molting. He felt like he'd been permanently fitted for a thirsty-boy suction thingy like his dentist used. He wrestled with a childproof aspirin bottle with one hand and dialed with the other.

"City Attorney's Office," Piper answered. "May I help you?"

"Sean, where is everybody?"

"Uh, let's see," he took the roll. "Linda's not in yet. Charlotte is in the file room I believe, and Linda, I'm not sure exactly where—"

"All right, never mind. Did you talk with Ethan Morgan yesterday?"

"Yeah, briefly."

Pomerantz thumbed through his copy of the trial roster. If most of the defendants took the plea bargains his assistant prosecutors dangled before them the week could be manageable. If not, he might as well pick up a new toothbrush. He wasn't going back to Erica's for his old one.

"So how does the ordinance look? Did he do a good job?"

"Mr. Morgan didn't prepare the ordinance himself. In fact, I'm not even sure he's seen it. He sent me to another lawyer way out on South Main Street. A guy by the name of Harvey Bing. He's a semi-retired—"

"Bing?"

"Yes, sir."

"Oh, God," he exhaled. "Why didn't Ethan handle it himself?"

"No idea. He said Mr. Bing is Of Counsel for the firm, and Mr. Morgan asked him to take on this specific item."

"Of Counsel? He's an ambulance chaser."

"Is that right?" Piper couldn't believe it.

"First lawyer in the state to advertise on TV."

"Is that a fact?"

"He even had a jingle…*'Got a ding? Call Harvey Bing. In a wreck? Here's your check…'* or something like that."

"Catchy."

"God. Jake Amsler's gonna love this," Pomerantz said.

"You want me to e-mail you a copy?"

"No. I won't have time to fool with it. Take a look at that for me, Sean. Unless there are any major problems, send it over to Mr. Amsler."

"Will do."

"Thanks, Sean."

Piper dropped the phone in its cradle. "No, thank you," he said.

****

The D.A. pulled into the parking garage beneath the courthouse and wondered if he had the strength to make it upstairs. He had one more call to make before show time in criminal court.

He checked his phone. The signal was faint, but it should make the connection. He said a little prayer and dialed his home number.

"Hello," a tender voice answered.

"Jenna?"

His wife said nothing, which said everything. He figured she might be buying time to see that the tape recorder was working. If her lawyer had hired a P.I., anything was possible.

"Look, Jenna, I was wondering if I could see you, today. I'd like to come by the house after court. I thought maybe you and Alex and I could go to dinner or something."

"Really?"

"Yes. We haven't done that in a long time, and I—"

"That's great, Michael. Really, that you have time for that, for your family, I mean. I know it's tough to work us in and your girlfriend, too. Will she be joining us, or is that dessert?"

"Jenna—"

"So what is this, your domestic twofer for the week? You're gonna be a husband and a father in the same evening?"

"Wait—"

"What's the matter with you? You're scheduling your visits with your son, now? You can see Alex anytime you want. I haven't changed the locks, Michael. You're the one who moved out."

"I thought that's what you wanted. I thought that's what you wanted until we had time to work things out. It was your idea for me to take that apartment. I never wanted to leave. Now, come on, Jenna. We both agreed—"

"No, you come on Michael. It's a little late to pretend you care."

"Hold on, Jenna. Correct me if I'm wrong, but we separated so we could try to work through a few things. Okay, so I've worked through some things, and what I've finally figured out is that I'm no good on my own. There's still a chance if you'll just take me back. And I don't just mean let me through the door so I can sleep on the couch. I mean take me back like we were before. Please, Jenna. I can't make it on my own."

"On your own?" she said. "Is that what you are, Michael?"

"What are you talking about?"

"I tell you what. Instead of dinner, let's see a movie. I hear there's a new release. I understand the footage may be somewhat out of focus, and the production quality is not the best. But I think we'll still be able to figure out the plot. I haven't seen it yet, but someone I know said I should. In fact, he was the cameraman."

"Oh, God."

"Yeah, it seems the main character is a tired old lawyer, a tall, hunched over guy, sort of like you, with a little beer gut and vanishing self-esteem. Probably feeling guilty about something. Whatever the case he's definitely going through a mid-life crisis. He can't keep his hands off a little Bimbette college girl about as old as his own kid. I think she's pre-law, or what's the difference? this little Bimbette attends a small, liberal arts school. You know, a lot like the College of Bristol. She could be a pre-law student. Let's hope so, anyway.

"Please, Jenna."

"How about it, dear, would you really like to take me to the movies tonight?"

This time there was silence from his end of the line.

"Oh, and sweetheart, if I were you, I'd get myself a lawyer. A good one…better than you," she said. "Have fun in the courtroom. It's not the last time you'll be in one of those."

CHAPTER 11

Bubba Hawkins sat on his hands in the silent conference room. Administrative hearings were only slightly less formal than circuit court, but perjury didn't go over well in either place. He rocked back and forth like a preschooler who'd slept through the potty break. His eyes raced from the clock above the court reporter's head, to the stone-faced commissioner, back to the clock a second later and then to his lawyer. He couldn't understand why the Manufactured Housing Commission met in a brick building, with the nearest trailer five blocks away at a construction site.

"Remy, how much longer do we have to wait?" he asked.

Lovelace didn't answer. He played scales with his fingertips on the edge of the table. It was much cleaner than Teal's Kountry Kitchen and Skeeter's video poker parlor.

"Remy, d'ya hear me?"

"You got somewhere else to be, Bubba?" Lovelace asked.

"No, but if they're not here, shouldn't he dismiss the case?"

Bubba shook his head. He let out a series of exaggerated breaths everyone in the hearing room ignored, except the court reporter who thought the fat man was hyperventilating.

"There's water in that pitcher if you need it," she said.

"Thanks, ma'am." He was now mad and embarrassed.

Another minute passed and Bubba couldn't take any more.

"Mr. Commissioner," he said, ignoring Lovelace's tap on his arm. "It's twenty after. How much longer do we have to wait?"

The silver-haired man at the other end of the long table twitched, marked where he was in the case file, looked up at him for a moment and then continued to read.

"Remy. Hey, Remy," Bubba whispered. "He ain't answering me. Do ya' think he heard me?"

"Bubba, how 'bout hush," Lovelace said loud enough for everyone to hear. "Lemme do your talkin' for ya. That's why you hired me, ain't it?"

The court reporter pretended not to notice. She played with her tape machine and memorized Remington Lovelace's business card. Bubba's face turned red.

"Don't tell me to hush, okay? It makes me look bad."

Bubba breathed hard again, only this time it wasn't for effect. He grabbed the plastic pitcher for a drink but when he tried to pour it the little white stopper popped out and he spilled water all over the table.

"Smooth," Lovelace said. He had gotten his full retainer at this point.

"Shut up, Remy," he said. "I may not be smooth as you, but I do know how to tell time. The Wannamakers ain't here. Now you better get my case dismissed. You keep messin' around and they may show up."

The court reporter slid a box of tissues their way and Lovelace offered him a handful.

"Relax," he said. "Blot yourself with these."

Bubba snatched the tissues and said, "I don't know why I let you handle my cases, Remy. You won't do what I ask, you're mean as a snake, and you charge me an arm and a leg."

"And so far I've kept you out of jail," Remy added.

"Maybe I'd be better off there, instead of all this worrying—"

The commissioner cleared his throat. He nodded to the court reporter, who turned on her machine.

"Mr. Lovelace," he began. "You got any *aye-dee* where Mr. and Mrs. Wannamaker are?"

"Somewhere between here and Dallas County, I reckon, Mr. Commissioner."

"Uh-huh."

"But since this hearing was supposed to start at nine o'clock, and the complaining party's not here, I'd ask that this case be dismissed for failure to prosecute."

The commissioner rubbed his hands together as he considered the request. He looked at Bubba Hawkins and figured he must be guilty of something.

"You talkin' about a continuance?"

"No, sir. I think this case should be dismissed entirely. These people had their chance to come before you today and they stood us up. My client has been through enough aggravation over this matter. It's cost him a lot of time and money. This case has been on the docket for over a year. I think it's only fair that we put an end to this thing once and for all."

The commissioner checked his file to make sure they'd been copied on the hearing notice.

"I don't understand this," he said. "There are several letters in this file from the homeowners. Pictures, too. It doesn't figure them not being here. I'm not inclined to dismiss the case outright, Mr. Lovelace."

"Well, we gotta do something," Lovelace said. "I still make my motion to dismiss the case, but if you don't want to do that today, then I move that this hearing be continued for a reasonable period for us to try and get up with these folks and see if we can't resolve it. Then none of us would have to come back here and bother you."

The commissioner scribbled something on the top of his file.

"No one's here to oppose you," he said. "All right, Mr. Lovelace, I'll grant your continuance request. How much time do you need to try to settle things with the petitioners?"

"Well, Judge," Lovelace promoted him, "I'm gonna be tied up in federal court on a case that's scheduled to take anywhere from two to three weeks. That'll put me behind more than usual. Of course, Mr. Hawkins has my permission to deal with the homeowners directly, but he's a busy man, too."

"Uh-huh. So how much time you lookin' at? Thirty days?"

"Can we get sixty, Judge?"

"I can live with that. Why don't you get me an order and we'll send a copy to the parties."

"Yes, sir. Thank you, Your Honor."

They grinned at each other. Even the court reporter thought it was a nice touch.

"Ya'll get this thing settled, now, you hear?"

"We're gonna try, Judge."

"Good day, gentlemen."

"Good day, Your Honor."

In the hallway Bubba nipped at his lawyer's heels. The reprieve was welcome, but Lovelace hadn't told him the reason for it.

"What do you know about this, Remy?"

"About what?"

"About the Wannamakers not showing up. They'd drive to China to talk about this mess. What's you do?"

"What do you care, Bubba? You ain't going to jail."

"Dammit, Remy. We may both be going to jail. Now tell me what you did."

"Only thing I'm trying to do is liberate your fat ass from the crevice you hurled yourself into by filing false affidavits with the commission. Five years per count, Bubba. Then you wait 'til the day before trial to tell me about it. And you want to know what I did? I stuck my neck way out to save yours. Now, here's what you're going to do for me. You're going to find their punch list and fix every damned thing on it. Or else give them the trailer you said you sold them a year ago."

"Hold on—"

"Fix it, Bubba. Offer to underpin the thing, give 'em a freezer filled with deer meat, do whatever it takes to make this case go away. It's what you should have done to begin with. Then, assuming you haven't lied to anyone else, and if you're a better repairman than you are a businessman, maybe we'll all be able to walk away from this."

Bubba stared a hole in the floor. Remy swiped his cell phone for new messages. He sent a quick text in response to one and slid it back inside his suit jacket. It was time for the next hearing.

"Now go give these country folks a decent place to live," Lovelace finished scolded him. "And stop telling your lies under oath."

CHAPTER 12

The grand jury meets in secrecy, shepherded by a politician through a civic duty its members neither bargain for nor want. Their private labors conclude in a brutally public evolution, even for a society founded upon liberty in doses. The presumption of innocence is highest at this stage, but is quickly eroded by competent stewards presenting only one side of the story. A first-year law student can make a compelling enough distinction between indictment and conviction, especially in a city where the police had caught the right guy too many times.

The D.A. leaned against the podium, still reeling from his crash-and-burn phone call to Jenna. Even his preemptive strike had been too late. She'd put together a confession-maker of a case against him. For the first time in his life he would have traded places with anyone staring back at him as he called the roll.

Pomerantz continued through the "Js," and Omar's thundering heartbeat made the perfectly read names seem indiscernible. He'd been in trouble before, and the magistrate had taken care of him, but the benches were colder and harder in general sessions. That's what the first two strikes had taught him.

'Big Court' could sting that way. The man he delivered for said as much when he posted bail for his best runner. Then the drug dealer told him to keep his mouth shut if he knew what was good for him. He'd see that Omar's trip was a smooth one, and made assurances of protection on the inside if the courier would agree to forget the things he'd seen, not talk about the things he'd done, always at the direction of a more violent man. Fuzzy Shanks got killed, Omar'd been warned. All anyone asked him to do was pretend he hadn't been there when it happened.

If their minds didn't meet on the version he'd been instructed to tell, he would be dead in a matter of hours behind the wall. Especially behind the wall. His boss' influence went a long way on the street, but there were still places a man as resourceful as Omar could hide if he decided to go that way. That would be bad for business in a business that couldn't afford bad days. The police might get to him first. The little man knew some things. Many were damaging. He might flip and tell a story that held water, or one that could be discredited through the hole-poking cross-examination of a skilled defense attorney. A lot depended on when the jury stopped listening.

Omar had two kids, and had been man enough to marry their mother, although most in his line of work abhorred such ties. They made it more difficult to do the wrong thing. And other than the tortured rationalizations that allowed him to deliver cocaine for a second-rate drug dealer, Omar Sharif Jones was obliged to do the right thing.

"Willie James. Willie James."

Pomerantz tapped the microphone. It was hot, but the man he called wasn't answering.

"Willie Reginald James."

None of the slouching twenty-somethings moved. A lot of new faces at roll call, he noticed, but just as many repeat customers. That might be useful when the time came. The reward for hard work was more of it. Clean streets are not as good as spotless streets. If Jake Amsler and the rest of the city council ever heard that someone else's shined brighter, the sheriff and Michael Pomerantz would be dealt that unfunded mandate as well.

He perused the thick packet of indictments and decided this wasn't a press conference docket. There was a murder case, but the victim was an unsympathetic career criminal who, as the street committee told it, 'needed killin.' The trial would take all week, unless the shooter agreed to accept Pomerantz' offer of manslaughter. The rest of the docket was littered with run-of-the-mill guilty pleas—'dives,' his assistant prosecutors called them. There wasn't time for another contested case this term, so he'd send most of the defendants home for the week. It would be here when he came back the next time.

Plea agreements needed to be reached, he told his staff. They were to lower the bar steadily between now and beer-thirty. Those who blinked last would walk away with sweetest deals—the kind he'd hold his nose to make and then hit the big damned delete button on the whole day, the kind he used to make before going home to Jenna. He'd tell her he'd 'done good, sweetheart,' and that she and Alex were safe. He'd lie awake at night and pray she was still that trusting.

It was days like this that made Pomerantz long for private practice, and the six figure income he would have attained by now, even in Bristol, as a sure bet for partner if he'd been able to restrain his political ambition. He laughed at the thought he'd once aspired to this. 'A stepping stone to higher offices, my boy,' the state's top prosecutor whispered in his ear all those years ago. 'No strings attached.' If he'd known the attorney general was going to live forever he might have rebuffed his mentor's overtures, leaving open more lucrative options. Pomerantz should be splitting fees with his law school classmates instead of cutting deals with them at the high end of the city pay scale. It had been rewarding in other, less material ways to wear the white hat, but those needs had been satisfied so long ago that at this point in his practice he'd welcome a tax problem. The novelty of roll call had worn off a few hundred Monday mornings ago. Now, Michael Pomerantz just did this to make a living. Defense attorneys like Peter Soard made it a hard one.

Pomerantz barely noticed as the tall lawyer slipped into the back of the courtroom, late as usual, but having missed nothing important he hadn't already heard before in the ritual.

Lawyers come and go during roll call, good-humored and giddy, secure in the knowledge that even if their clients went to jail, at the end of the day they were going home. The regulars ignored the distraction. The defendants watched more closely. There were the profilers, lawyers who styled around in Italian cut, ventless suits, with deep blue or ruby cuff links that matched their power silk ties and pressed four point handkerchiefs. Behind them tired paralegals dragged roll carts loaded with banker's boxes full of files their bosses might need by Thursday.

The profilers and their retinues passed by the solo practice 'Bubbas,' the meat and potato, street-wise lawyers who dressed and lived within their means, which weren't much greater than those of their clients.

Then there were the stealthy slinkers who weren't trying to impress anyone or to drum up any business. They looked like they'd come here to pay a parking ticket and had taken a wrong turn. They had just enough money to say 'no,' from time to time, but not enough to last them the rest of their lives, unless they intended to live until the end of the month. Maybe those styles, and the ones in between, told a tale that previewed their approaches to trial advocacy, the strength of their cases, or a desire to conceal their many weaknesses. More likely they didn't mean a thing to anyone.

Then there was Remington Lovelace, reigning king of the devil's advocates. Soard's briefcase was full of his boss' workload for the week. Lovelace told him he'd be fashionably late but to be patient. The clients wanted to talk to their attorney, not their lawyer's lawyer.

Soard nodded to the public defender and searched the house for an empty seat. He'd thumb through Lovelace's files, maybe learn enough to calm his boss' nervous clients when they found him. He thought he'd do all that, but something told him it could wait. He rifled through his briefcase and found the folder he wanted. Ethan Morgan's frail, disjointed shorthand was tough to make out, but he pieced together enough to get his attention.

'Warren Dunn,' the top sheet read, 'Riverfront project deadline approaching.' Morgan had drawn an arrow from that entry to the bottom of the page. There was a date two weeks away. Soard deciphered the writing beside it, the next scheduled meeting of the Bristol City Council. There was a name beside it and Ethan had highlighted it. It was the man propping himself up on the podium.

"Pomerantz?" Soard asked softly.

Next to that Morgan wrote, 'Jake Amsler. Go through M.P.'

Soard listened as the D.A. called the next case. He didn't know why the circuit's top prosecutor would be of interest to Warren Dunn, but Morgan had made the connection. There were no more clues in the following pages.

Roll call was surreal for all the things it said about the world. Soard wasn't sure if the words came out as he mouthed them, but if he'd been awake the bailiff beside him might have heard the young lawyer whisper to himself once more.

"Go through Michael Pomerantz."

CHAPTER 13

On the drive to the City Attorney's Office Piper phoned Jake Amsler. The chairman was on the move, too. He answered and in the background Piper heard a country singer belting out a ballad on the banker's car stereo.

"Jake Amsler," he said.

"Hello. This is Sean Piper. Mr. Pomerantz asked me to give you a call."

"Yes, Sean. I've been waiting to hear from you. So have you got the gambling ordinance for me?"

"Yes, sir. Picked it up yesterday afternoon."

"How does it look?"

Sean wasn't sure the messenger should know the answer to that.

"All right, I suppose. I'm not exactly sure of council's intent, so y'all may want to make some changes."

"You're not sure of council's intent?" Amsler mocked him.

"No, sir. Not exactly."

"Well, that makes two of us. Do you see anything you'd change?"

"It depends. I guess I'm a little like a family doctor when it comes to drafting ordinances. You tell me what you want and I'll adjust my chair."

Amsler's laughter drowned out the singer's misery.

"Adjust the chair, huh? I like that. I tell you what, Sean, are you gonna be around this afternoon?"

"I can be."

"Good. How'd you like to get out of the office for a little while? You play golf?"

"Not for a long time I'm afraid. How good do I have to be?"

"Listen, if you can make contact with the ball you're good enough to play in our foursome."

"I think I can do that," Piper said.

"Excellent. Meet me at the Hillsdale Country Club. We've got a one o'clock tee time. And bring a copy of the ordinance with you. If we have to make any changes, we can work those out right on the spot with Wes Calhoun. He's playing with us."

"Mr. Calhoun?"

"Yeah. It'll be you, me, Calhoun and an old business partner of mine."

"The governor?"

"Former governor. Now he's just another friggin' lawyer. Worst golfer you've ever seen. Don't stand anywhere near him when he swings. You might want to bring a hard hat. I'll see ya' this afternoon. So long, Sean."

He hung up before Piper learned whether the country singer got his girl and his truck back. He bopped up to the office long enough to sign himself out for the rest of the day. Linda peered at him from behind a magazine.

"Going somewhere, Sean?" the office manager asked. She watched as he wrote his destination on the board.

"Golf?" she said. "A lawyer who actually admits he's playing golf. Amazing."

"The council chairman asked me. I didn't think it would be particularly career enhancing to say 'no.'"

"You're playing with Jake Amsler?"

"Uh-huh. And Governor Calhoun."

"Good grief, Sean. You must have something on both of them."

"Yeah. Youth and inexperience," he said. "Hey, can you loan me some clubs?"

****

Remington Lovelace arrived for the nine o'clock roster meeting promptly at ten, offering no apologies for his tardiness and being asked for none. Each day he stayed away was better than the one before as far as anyone in the D.A.'s Office was concerned. Compared to the education he'd given Pomerantz' assistants through the years, a piñata on a fat kid's birthday had it better.

Lovelace filled out his red seersucker suit as well as anyone could, keeping in mind there were only three other men in the world who owned red seersucker suits. The handkerchief in his breast pocket was for show only. A row of handmade cigars poked above the natty hanky like the business end of a pipe organ. His spats must have been at the cleaners. He was missing the rest of the barbershop quartet, the Music Man *sans* boater.

Lovelace's small, upturned nose rose as he shot a Beach Boy grin to the courthouse denizens. He had one of those expensive haircuts designed to make it look like he never got his hair cut. The sandy blondness belonged on top of a much younger man. His average build was on its way to portly, and he sported a deep tan that didn't look accidental.

Remy eyeballed the swath he planned to cut through the lobby, the people he'd try like hell to avoid and the ones he couldn't sidestep with an armed security detail. He carried no briefcase, although he knew where his was and how each scar got there. His hands were free and ready to be shaken by everyone in a room he'd worked a thousand times before. He was salty and cool, saying nothing and making the loudest statement of all. This place was simply the stop he'd make as a lark before touring his vineyard.

Soard noticed him because it was his job to notice him. They both worked for Morgan, although only one of them called him 'sir.' He was pretty sure even Lovelace didn't know it was Warren Dunn the senior partner wanted help with, if that was what he wanted at all. Soard wondered if he should tell him all about what Ethan said could go no further in the darkness of his office just a few hours ago.

Remy parked it on the first row and Soard tried to make his way over but the room was too packed. He hadn't been around long enough to have a chair people steered clear of, but his usual one was taken, and the linebacker disguised as a bailiff wasn't budging. He took the seat next to him, wedging his pointy knees against the wooden rail that separated the gallery from the well of the courtroom.

The clients Remington Lovelace sent him to handhold all had names that fell in the second half of the alphabet. Except for the wrinkles and a few red marks on each page, Soard's list looked the same as Pomerantz'.

The D.A. leaned into the microphone. "Is there an Omar Sharif Jones in the courtroom? Omar Sharif Jones?"

The chiseled bailiff next to Soard came to life as he read the name again.

"Omar *Sha-reeeef* Jones."

The bailiff let out a howl from somewhere deep. It echoed down the hallway, past voter registration and the mobile home permitting counter, all the way to the tax collector's office. Between cackles you could hear a pin drop, as if the whole world were at a funeral while he watched Lucy Ricardo stomp grapes. When the uproar finally ended, a well-dressed young black male stood up behind him. It didn't take long to unfold his small frame.

"Here," he said from somewhere atop a wedding cake.

Slender and five feet even, Omar Sharif Jones had a scrunched up face with all the right parts, just condensed and cheeky. He had fast hands, faster feet, and best of all he knew how to keep his mouth shut when he was talking. In the world of drug running, then, he had everything.

Pomerantz read the man's charges. Possession with intent to distribute cocaine. There were some other offenses as well, minor ones he'd drop as part of a deal, but the distribution counts were serious.

He sure squared himself away this morning, Soard thought. Omar's suit was new and didn't come from a shopping mall kiosk like the gold-plated chains the others his age wore around their necks until they compromised their posture. His shirt and pants actually met where they were supposed to meet, and he wore them that way. Omar clashed with every other young man in the room, clad in their gravity defying, thigh-high, cinched potato sack-looking jeans, anchored at the base by untied high top tennis shoes. His head was clean-shaven, as close as his face, his eyes clear and looking straight at the man who'd called his name while a drowsy bailiff mocked. He remembered not to bring his cell phone and the three pagers his various pursuits required him to carry, and took someone's good advice to leave his earring at home. The only attitude he copped was one of respect, whether anyone believed he considered this to be a solemn occasion or not. He gave the middle-class conservatives who held his fate a reason to give him a chance. In no respect did he look like a man facing more years in jail than he'd lived.

Soard noticed him the way a maitre'd gravitates toward big tips. Omar cut against all the stereotypes that made it easy for juries to look the other way rather than to bond with the downtrodden, and for judges to punish in terms of years instead of community service. This was not his territory, and Omar had made an unrespectable living mastering the obvious. He could be himself on his own time.

"All right, Dr. Zhivaaaahh-goo," Pomerantz lived it up, "what you want, trial or plea?"

"Nice, Pomerantz," Soard mouthed. "Dr. Zhivago."

He set Morgan's messy file detailing Warren Dunn's life story on his briefcase and considered the young man for a moment before he'd forget him forever. There were no Joneses on his client list. Too bad. The kid looked like he'd do any damned thing he was told and pay good money for the privilege.

"Not guilty," Omar declared.

"I guess you want a trial then." Pomerantz looked disgusted. "Who's your lawyer?"

Omar had listened as the others offered up their attorneys' names. He'd heard of only a few of them, but hadn't retained anyone yet.

"Don't have one yet," he said.

Pomerantz turned to a lady from the Clerk's Office. "He's waiting 'til he has a problem."

She read the indictment. "Looks like."

"You want a lawyer?" he asked.

A man who could have broken in suits for Jabba the Hut sat next to the state's table. He had public defender written all over him. He uncapped an orange highlighter and waited. He looked like a dog getting fitted for a chocolate glazed flea collar.

"Yes, sir."

Pomerantz pointed to Jabba the Lawyer. "Come see Mr. Kozlowski."

Omar Sharif Jones nodded that he would, then sat down at the position of attention.

"And anybody else who wants a free lawyer line up at the table to my right during the break. I don't want to see anyone else down here except those of you who want to go with the public defender."

Soard took it all in from one of the few safe seats in the room. Every once in a while an unusual suspect ended up here. A little kid who wasn't old enough to have come by himself, and in the wrong place if he had, sat quietly on the last row of the packed courtroom. From there and to him it looked a lot like the church service he'd attended yesterday, right down to the same pesky fly he tried to catch barehanded. There were benches that resembled the pews his family sat on Wednesday nights and Sunday mornings. Every seat was filled. There were big people in them, but they'd left their good clothes at home. There was no singing. There were no robes, but there would be one later, and only one. Some man preached, or at least he stood where the preacher ought to have stood. He said nothing about love or faith. There were prayers.

Soard wondered what impact this bring-your-kid-to-work day would have on the confused boy years later or next week. Would he be better off in Warren Dunn's world? The unmarked folder he'd accepted two hours ago in the dark made it clear he would be, if success were measured by money alone. Perhaps in other ways he would be, too, but the file Morgan gave him only dealt with unspendable wealth.

"Special project," he reminded himself. Ethan's raspy voice echoed at him as it had coming from the shadows in a private meeting no one else but his body-guard secretary knew had taken place. Caroline's shorthand was distinctive, impeccable, and nowhere to be found on the stapled yellow pages. Morgan hadn't told her about Warren Dunn, which meant he didn't need her help yet or couldn't afford the risk of having it.

There was no billing code on the brown expandable. The firm didn't draft a simple will without one of those, which meant no one in the finance department was involved either. Only Soard and the man at the top of the hollow pyramid knew that the state's richest citizen wanted Calhoun & Morgan for something the senior partner was too ashamed to let through the front door.

Ethan's scrawl was everywhere, wrapping around the margins with abbreviations and symbols Soard recognized from his copious note-taking days in law school.

First million by eighteen, they began, or at least that's what Soard took the lower case 'm' to mean. *Trust fund kid. Deferment from V. Nam, possible buyout from F.* 'F' was 'father,' or *Sr.* was used just as often. Dunn, Sr., kept his boy out of harm's way during the nation's bloodiest police action and groomed him for a career in the 'son' business. He left his only child the bulk of the Dunn Trust, parceling it out in five-year increments that began when Warren turned twenty-one and ended when he reached his early forties. By then, his dad reckoned, Junior would be on his own, and could put that infallible judgment to work.

The trust was loaded and diversified. There was a textile mill in the upstate that supported the economies of ten counties, employing three thousand workers who made comfortable cotton trousers for the world. Dunn was majority stockholder in his father's express package delivery system, a video movie rental empire, and an international chain of chicken restaurants.

There was a midwestern sports team that lost money every year in the portfolio, and a few dot.com companies that went belly-up after the artificial boom created by those ventures ended.

His high-tech stocks had taken a beating lately, and there were some troubling entries in Morgan's notes dealing with recent heavy court losses, including judgments against some of his larger corporate holdings. The little triangles next to Dunn's name or the names of some corporation he had an interest in meant he or the company was a defendant in some nasty lawsuit. A few of the cases had nuisance value only, but many had teeth and the judgments were substantial. Ethan must have gotten tired of writing all those zeros and instead listed one or two digits followed by an 'M' for the million dollar verdicts.

One entry in the litigation report had a large red star beside it, and was detailed over the next several pages. It dealt with Dunn's industrial plant in the lower part of the state, Dunnex Technologies, and an E.P.A. fine of seventy-five million dollars that had been levied just last month.

"Seventy-five million equals three times cost of spill," he whispered. 'Not public yet,' the notes continued. There was a confidentiality agreement for the first six months following the settlement. Dunn got to keep his defense contract.

Dunn *settled* for seventy-five million, Soard read it again. *Gets to keep defense contract…missile defense system. Spill suggests chemical use different from government project awarded during Gulf War. Pentagon and Dunn both requested gag order. EPA agreed only after fine tripled.*

"Damn," he said softly. The sleeping bailiff beside him moaned. "What did he spill?"

The more public investments were described over the next few pages. Dunn's practice was to bull his way into a vulnerable company, depress its stock even further, set it up to be taken over by another entity he owned and reward himself as the majority stockholder in the acquiring company and as the chief executive officer of the one he'd gobbled up. He stopped there only because he hadn't figured out a way to triple dip. His silver cup runneth over until the excess diluted the next person's embarrassment of riches.

On the other side of the ledger Morgan described the real estate hit Dunn took when the tax laws changed in the mid-nineteen eighties. He landed on his feet, though, unlike so many others who weren't liquid enough to ride out the storm.

The next few documents in the packet dealt with Dunn's interests in several Las Vegas hotels and casinos, all of which made money, though he'd divested himself from the last one almost ten years ago. *Reason unclear,* Morgan wrote. *Learned casino business in Malaysia,* he noted. *Started at bottom, worked gaming floors with house detectives. Returned to U. S. in mid-eighties, Asian partners in Vegas and Reno. Immediate, heavy buy in Toby's Casino and Sierra Treasures.. SEC violations, convictions for principals in both. Asians tried in absentia. Justice Department unable to extradite. Dunn's U.S. partner found dead following a carjacking the week before trial. Indictments stopped with Asians and his dead partner. Didn't reach D. Not indicted.*

"Securities and Exchange Commission," he said. Soard had heard one of his professors discuss the Sierra Treasures case, maybe in his corporations class or it could have been criminal law.

"Didn't reach 'D.' Didn't reach Dunn. Not indicted."

The biographical entries mentioned one marriage and two daughters, both in private schools in Connecticut. The family summered at Dunn's forty-acre spread on Kiawah Island along the South Carolina coast. He commuted by plane to Bristol each day, and his international headquarters occupied the top three floors of the capital's tallest building, in fact just a little higher than his lawyers' quarters. He'd threatened the governor to move his operation to Atlanta, where there was a bigger airport and a friendlier government toward business, but he enjoyed being the biggest fish in a state that had resisted economic development since before his old man made his first fortune.

Clipped to the notes were brochures and promotional fliers from manufacturers of video poker machines. Soard had seen them but never played the games. They looked like slot machines, but apparently there was a difference. It didn't figure that Dunn would be involved in anything that pedestrian.

At the bottom of the gaming literature were copies of state statutes criminalizing such activity, along with a draft of the Bristol

City ordinance dealing with the same issue—the draft Morgan had told Sean Piper he hadn't seen yet. Ethan had highlighted several parts of each and made notes on the games Bristol had outlawed.

Soard wanted to read them more carefully a second time but Pomerantz was winding down the morning's festivities. He saw the public defender brace for the onslaught of indigents sure to come his way when the D.A. sounded the mid-morning break. There were cheerier faces in the Donner Party than the one Kozlowski wore as he prepared to meet his clients for the week. In seconds, the P.D. would be busier than a hummingbird eating for two.

Soard pumped a clinched fist at his colleague, an inaudible *'you da' man, P.D.,'* then made his way to the lobby and higher ground. The clients would come to him there. While he waited he'd dictate a tape filled with letters and motions he'd expect his secretary to have transcribed by the end of the day. He'd read more about Warren Dunn. Perhaps one day he'd actually get to meet his client. He'd seen everything but his picture. Maybe Ethan Morgan would let him know what he wanted him to do with the billionaire.

As he shoved the mess of papers into the brown expandable, he noticed one last page of Morgan's notes, the only one not stapled to the rest. It was a list of the members of the Bristol City Council. Two of the names were starred in the same red ink he'd used to highlight the Dunnex lawsuit. Soard recognized only one, Kevin Braithwaite, a newcomer to council. Their next meeting was a week away. From the agenda it appeared that the gambling ordinance was up for first reading. The last sentence in Morgan's frail handwriting was hard to make out, but he thought he'd pieced together the pigeon English as Pomerantz called the last name. He was pretty sure Ethan hadn't meant to leave it in the file.

"Soard to prep by then."

CHAPTER 14

Warren Dunn admired the view from the top floor office in the skyscraper he named after himself. He was colder and distant this morning, like he was hiding more than usual. Morgan always made him nervous, which is why he seldom summoned his lawyer to the penthouse.

A half dozen aides Dunn's schedule, but he hadn't spoken with any of them today. For all he knew he could be joining local officials in a faux scooping dirt photo op for a golden shovel grand opening, or accepting service on another search warrant from a federal agent. The possibilities were as wild as his recent mood swings.

Dunn wore a dark gray flannel suit most days, and the starched tab collar dress shirt seemed tighter than normal, pinching high blood pressure redness into his complexion which would fade to rainy-day pale by cocktail hour when he loosened the tourniquet. Short and thin, he wasn't completely bald but would be if he subjected the matching quilt patch clumps above each ear to one last haircut. They sprouted like tiny goal posts with a peachy speed bump sailing through the uprights.

He was altogether unimpressive physically, Morgan thought, especially for a billionaire, if there were enough of those to generalize. Ethan thought they should be rotund and gregarious, wearing ten gallon hats and bolo ties, or tall and sinewy in power sweaters and creased pants that ran into blinding leather dress shoes. Morgan didn't care if he wore polka dot cutoffs so long as he kept the spigot turned on at C & M.

The furrow above Dunn's dark brow deepened as he considered what this unscheduled meeting meant. Ethan's meter was running at about five bills an hour, he reminded himself, and nobody got five hundred dollars an hour in Bristol for anything that was legal. A half day's interest on his holdings could wipe out C & M's fees, but Dunn still had the first dime he ever made and he intended to hold onto it. Plus Morgan was a lawyer, and Dunn never liked paying those even when they did exactly what he wanted, and especially when they didn't.

Dunn eyed him with a mixture of amusement and disgust. Letters were bad news, phone calls good. What the hell was an unannounced visit in the highest place in the state? Was Morgan here to tell him it was the end of the line, that the riverfront project was dead, that bulldozing family homes for another tax dodge playground didn't have the votes this time?

"Say that again, Ethan," Dunn seethed.

"He didn't sign," Morgan answered. "I can't say it any plainer than that. I had Crazy Bear Walker in my office for over an hour, taking him line by line through the articles of incorporation. I used the standard forms available from the secretary of state's office. He wasn't interested."

"Did you tell him they could use the land for ninety-nine years?"

"Of course. I told him everything," Ethan assured him. "Well, not everything."

Dunn wasn't amused. "Lord, Ethan. Don't even joke about it."

"I don't know what else to say, Warren. Walker had every chance, but he didn't sign." Morgan smiled.

"What the hell you grinning at?" his client asked.

"He didn't sign, but he took the papers with him."

"He did?"

"Yes. I think he's gonna talk it over with someone," Morgan said.

"The chief? Navarro would never be my partner."

"We may not need him," Morgan said. "I checked out their council. They don't need Navarro's approval. Walker and two other elders can take an action that binds the tribe."

"Oh?"

"My bet is he's got somebody lined up ready to go for our deal. He knew the chief wouldn't agree. But he took the meeting anyway. You know what that means?"

Dunn unbuttoned his jacket, hands on hips to consider it.

"Yes. Well, that sounds like a lot of ifs. How do you know he didn't trash the agreement the minute he left your office?"

"I don't," Morgan admitted. "But I do know he's smart enough to figure out what'll happen if they pass up your offer. And more important, I think he's smart enough to know what will happen if the chief finds out we met."

Dunn strolled to the front of his desk, sat on the corner and brushed his pants leg along the crease.

"Ethan, do you have any idea how much money I was bringing in at Toby's and Sierra Treasures?"

"No, I don't."

"One million dollars a day. At the end of the nineteen eighties, a million a day, net profit. After we paid our employees, stocked the bar, staffed the restaurant, brought in a Wayne Newton or a Liza Minnelli or a Tony Bennett to sing to the drunks," Dunn said that as if there were surplus Wayne Newtons, Liza Minnellis and Tony Bennetts. "After we spent whatever it cost to keep the lights on, and paid off on thirteen percent of the slot machine plays because that's how much the state would let the house win—after all of those expenses were met, we pocketed a million bucks a day."

"Pretty sweet."

"Think of what they stand to gain." Dunn stood and paced the floor again. "How many members are there in the Saucostee Tribe?"

"About a hundred and fifty."

"And I only need three members who want to be rich?"

"Three elders."

Dunn cracked the door wide enough to see Bubba Hawkins sitting nervously in the lobby. He'd have some marching orders for him soon, but none he'd share with his lawyer. He closed the door softly and returned to the window.

"All right, then, Ethan. Do I have a partner or not?"

"Give him a couple days to think it over. Walker stands to make enough money to set up his family for the rest of their lives. Hell, everyone in the tribe could retire," Morgan continued. "And the state wouldn't be as quick to seek an injunction against the Saucostee Preservation Coalition as it would against Dunn Enterprises. Especially since they gave them a permanent Native American tax break as part of the tribal land settlement. By the time the government figures out who's really running the store the casino will be straddling two counties with an intracoastal waterway running from Bristol all the way to the beach. You'll be able to float your riverboat up the Lafayette, dock it at the Saucostee Reservation, and reap tax-free profits in perpetuity."

Dunn looked far below him. There were two men fishing from a jon boat in a part of the Lafayette that just might be deep enough.

If his lawyer could find a way to close his latest deal they'd be about where he'd dock his floating casino before the politicians knew what happened.

He turned to Morgan with a look that let him know there was more work to be done.

"Yeah. If they'll let me be their silent partner."

CHAPTER 15

Omar Sharif Jones gave the courthouse lobby the once over for the hundredth time, but this place didn't grow on anybody invited here by a summons.

There was a brown cork bulletin board that ran the length of one wall, covered with foreclosure and tax sale notices by someone who didn't staple halfway. A pudgy man in suspenders bobbed an unlit pipe in his mouth as he copied tax map numbers and the dates of each sale. He'd bid on a few at the end of the month, driving up the price for the mortgage company he worked for, or if no one else showed maybe he'd pick up some cheap property.

There were multi-colored, eye-catching forms that told injured government employees how to file a workers' compensation claim, scorned ones where to report acts of discrimination, and everybody how to beat it out of town if the second snow storm in history were to suddenly hit Bristol. Printed in bold across the top of each page was an oath upon the souls of its founding fathers that the city was an equal opportunity employer, with a twenty-four hour-a-day hot line to field complaints if that proved not to be the case.

Down the hall, high school girls with their pre-school children in tow jammed themselves into a waiting area that looked like a prison cell. They used an automated phone system to track the most recent 'deadbeat dad' payments to their accounts. The system was updated as funds allowed, and somewhere in the department somebody used to know whose job it was to do that.

Nearby, happy couples waited outside the office of the Justice of the Peace for their marriage licenses to be printed on paper suitable for a plastic frame. The women hunting child support stared longingly at them, wondering how they made it to their line without having stood in the other one.

A giant clock that was within an hour of the correct time hung next to a portrait of some judge no longer with us. An absurdly large bronze piece of modern art that must have brought about a tax hike sat unnoticed in the center of the atrium's light-colored marble floor. The dedication plaque was mid-nineteen seventies, as were the leisure suits worn by the councilmen pictured beneath it. Their ties were wider than tablecloths, and covered with what Omar thought were either food stains or the artist's signature. It was a stale place with lots of familiar faces but none of them friendly or smiling at him. He went unnoticed in a tapestry of then and now, of marble and monuments, of white-faced men with horn-rimmed glasses frozen in the nineteen forties and fifties—their decades—of presumed innocence and the protection of Lady Justice's shield, of the state's power wielded by her unsheathed sword, of acquittal and vindication, of conviction and punishment. It was the place where the governed and the agents of their sovereign forged a version of the truth that lay between pure chance and the absolute. It was where every right God and man had given would be preserved inviolate. It was where a kid like Omar Sharif Jones had no chance.

He needed for his luck to change. He said a prayer that it would. Across the concourse, visible between the card-passers and desperate souls in search of cover as the D.A.'s clock ticked, sat an acolyte with a pew all to himself, on the job, but hardly laboring in a room full of hungry lawyers.

Omar wondered which side of the street Peter Soard worked, and why it was that business looked so good there. His hair said prosecutor but his suit spoke louder than the state's pay scale. He looked too satisfied to be working in Pomerantz' litigation mill, and he cleaned up nicer than the plain-clothed detectives who hung around waiting to testify when the bailiff called their cases.

Soard folded the metro section and restored the Bristol *Chronicle* to its newsstand shape, crisp, thin, and centered on the bench ready to fetch another fifty cents. He'd get the rest of the day's news by osmosis and the man on the street. He was relaxed and still, in peaceful consideration of only contented and profitable thoughts, one gently nudging aside another beneath his coiffed impeccability. Inside he was a Picasso, only without the structure.

From somewhere on his body Soard produced a cassette recorder like it was part of a magic trick. He cradled it in his silky palm easier than a remote control on a rainy football Saturday. He had plenty of clients and was getting new ones all the time. Ethan Morgan had seen to that. He wished there weren't so many people dead set on helping him.

Omar watched him and the company he kept. He watched until he was sure the well-dressed man wasn't a prosecutor, or even a cop who would be called by one to testify. He didn't look lost either. No one that at home could. The drug runner finished his syrupy drink and tugged at his collar. The best suit he owned hung loosely on his tiny body. He didn't have time to wait until he grew into it. His game face was handy and he wore it. He said one more a prayer and shuffled through the concourse toward Soard. This was the one.

Soard rose like he was about to deliver a closing argument that mattered. Omar wasn't expecting him to be so tall. He froze and Soard spoke first.

"Good morning."

Omar was ready to march back into the courtroom and confess to anyone who'd listen.

"You doin' all right?" the young lawyer asked.

"Uh, yeah, man."

"Here for trial?"

He nodded. His voice was shakier than the one that had professed his innocence to the D.A. minutes earlier. "Are you a lawyer?"

"How'd you guess?" Soard smiled a comforting smile. "What's your name?"

"Omar Jones."

"Peter Soard," he shook his hand. "Nice to meet you."

"I need to talk to you about my case, Mr. Soard."

"Okay, step into my office."

They sat on the long wooden bench. Omar was close enough to propose. Soard took it in stride. With Warren Dunn's file contaminating his briefcase he could use a simple guilty plea.

Omar handed him a copy of his indictment. Soard quickly read the parts that mattered and returned the wrinkled paper where it belonged. Lovelace had a rule about handling paper and he made sure it stayed fresh in his associates' minds. *'Never, ever…are you listening to me, boy? Never, ever, hold on to someone else's paperwork unless he's ready to be your client.' After he hires you, then you can keep whatever he's willing to pay rent for. Until then, let him carry around his own problems. He's handing them to you so they'll become your problems. Unless that paper spends, put it right back in the poor bastard's hand. Then quote him a fee that's twice what the job is worth. That'll straighten him up good.'*

Lovelace's point was well made. Soard knew all he needed to know. The little man would leave his bench with everything he brought, and promises of nothing more.

"What do you think, Mr. Soard?"

"Possession with intent to distribute. Two hundred grams of cocaine. That's a serious charge. I'd have to check the statute to be sure, but I believe that carries a maximum punishment of twenty-five years in prison."

"Jesus."

"If the D.A. offers you a pretrial agreement, you might want to think about taking it. If he's not willing to deal, it'll take a lot of money to defend a case like this, even if you've got an alibi."

"What kind of deal?"

"It depends. Have you ever been arrested before?"

"Uh-huh."

"How many times?"

"Twice."

"What for?"

"I had a pistol—" Omar began.

"That's not a felony," Soard interrupted.

"—that I stole from a gun store."

"Oh. That's a bad fact. What else?"

"I got picked up for drugs once before. Same as this time, but not as much."

"Not as much drugs?"

"Yeah."

Omar clutched the indictment. He hung his head while Soard took a long look around the lobby. The crowd thinned as most of the defendants returned to the courtroom. With roll call over it would be the judge's show from now on, and Pomerantz would put on his murder trial while the others bought another week of freedom.

Remy Lovelace appreciated the D.A.'s predicament. He pinned him at the water fountain and the two lawyers did business. Soard watched the master at work as he tried to find a graceful way to tell Omar not to drop the soap when they sent him over. Lovelace settled more cases in five minutes than the Pomerantz would dispose of the rest of the month. To seal the deals he slipped him a Moon Pie, which the D.A. devoured, nodding contentedly with each bite. It was a long stop at the cooler, but with each nod Lovelace tidied up the D.A.'s docket. In those few moments with his old adversary shooting what's what in the hallway, Pomerantz was alive again, doing what he was here to do. He forgot about his wife, his mistress, and the private investigator he chased barefooted down the Gaza Strip while Erica dreamed of raspberry tea, guilt-free ice cream and her ridiculous sugar daddy. Soard wondered what advice Remy would have for the two bit dealer.

"Here's the problem, Omar. Ever since the legislature passed the 'three strikes' law, repeat offenders have been in a bad way. You've heard of that, right?"

"No."

"Other states have had them for years. Ours came along only recently. Every felony conviction of a particular class, including serious drug offenses, counts as a strike against you. After the third strike mandatory sentencing guidelines kick in. I say 'guidelines,' but they're really a tight range of sentences that leave trial judges little choice about what sentences they can give. And with 'Maximum' John Worthington on the bench this week, it's not a good time to roll the dice."

"Man, I can't go to jail. I've got two kids and another on the way."

"I'm sorry, Omar."

He reached into his coat pocket and pulled out a tattered billfold. "Here's my son. He just turned four last week."

"Well," Soard glanced at the child and froze in mid-sentence. He wasn't expecting the wheelchair. "Oh. Yeah, he is a good-looking kid, Omar. Good looking kid."

He slid his four hundred dollar briefcase under the bench and sat down to count his blessings.

"What's his name?"

"Tyler." Omar showed him another photograph. "Here's his baby sister. They ain't got anybody but me. My wife stays at home with the kids. I work at a warehouse loading trucks all day, but it's not enough."

Omar put away the pictures. Maybe he'd guessed wrong again.

"I'm sorry, Omar, I shouldn't have said anything. You haven't been found guilty yet, and it's not my place to judge you. But you aren't going to be much use to your family from behind bars."

"I know it. That's why I'm talkin' to you. You saw that line at the public defender's table? How hard is he gonna try for me? I might as well go ahead and plead guilty."

Soard blew out a long breath. He wondered how much it cost Omar to raise his special needs kid and who'd take care of his family once their only source of income was gone.

"All right, Omar. I'll hear you out. But understand this. I'll listen to what you've got to say, but that doesn't mean I'm going to take your case. Just because we talk, it doesn't mean I'm your lawyer. Do you understand?"

"Yes."

"Okay. Tell me what happened."

Soard listened as Jones confessed to him in the nearly empty lobby. Every so often he heard a loud voice booming from deep inside the courtroom. Maximum John Worthington had arrived. Poor Pomerantz.

Omar told him the drugs weren't his. He told him no one had read him his rights on that terrible night, but Soard said that might not matter. He asked more questions about the three strikes law, and what the lawyer could do about it. He said he earned minimum wage chucking boxes onto semis all day, but that he'd do whatever it took to upgrade from the public defender. He could get the money from somewhere. He had the clothes on his back, and the debt collectors so confused by his multiple phone numbers that they were calling each other more than him. In his line of work, caller ID was one of the world's top ten inventions.

Soard shot the young man straight. He took for granted he wasn't getting the whole truth and nothing but the truth, but from what he'd heard Omar's best move would be to turn state's evidence and sell out his boss. He could get his wife and kids pumped up about a different part of the country, assume a new identity and run for the border. Someone in the drug ring was going to jail for a long time. There was no reason Omar's little finger should be the last one in the dike.

"You should plead to a lesser offense," Soard advised. "Since you're not a first offender, you're probably going to serve some time. If you catch a break, you might get out in a few months. It beats a few years."

"Just like that?"

"No. Probably not. It's up to the government whether or not to offer you a pretrial agreement. The D.A. will want something in return for reducing the charge."

"Like what?"

"If I were him I'd want to know who you're working for. I'd want to know why you were foolish enough to try selling two hundred grams of cocaine to undercover agents, and loyal enough take the fall for the man who told you to sell them. Stuff like that."

"I can't do that."

"Why not?"

"They'd find me. They'd get me. Me and my family."

"Who?"

"Man, who do you think? I just make the deliveries. I drop off and I pick up. That's it. I never look inside. I usually don't have to count. I just take care of the packages," he said. "It's funny. I load boxes on trucks all day and nobody cares what's in them. I make a five minute run at night with a pocketful of something and everybody's after me."

"You could disappear. There are other places to live besides Bristol."

"How far am I gonna get with a pregnant wife and two kids. Tyler's in no shape to travel. You saw the wheelchair."

"Yeah. What happened?"

"A bullet hit him while he was asleep in his crib. Drive-by. There's always shootings in our neighborhood. Someone shot him, and whoever did it will never know that my boy's going to spend the rest of his life in a wheelchair."

"I'm very sorry, Omar. You shouldn't have to raise a family like that. Where do you live?"

"Oakdale."

Soard had read about that depressed community in Warren Dunn's file. Maybe he'd do those folks a favor knocking down their houses. They could move closer to a police station, or a hospital.

"The doctors say there's a chance he could walk again, but he needs an operation. I have insurance, but it's not enough. So I work a second shift," he held up his summons.

"You're running drugs for some gang to help pay for your son's operation?"

"Yeah. There ain't enough hours in the day to make it at the loading dock."

"I'm sorry, Omar, about your son, about the fact that you live in a shooting gallery of a neighborhood. It's not right. I wish I could help you."

"I know this ain't cheap. It's just that you're so young looking. I figured you wouldn't charge me as much as…"

"As the good lawyers?" Soard finished his thought.

"No. I didn't mean that. I would have asked somebody like that man over there," he motioned, "but I can't afford him. I just figured you might be starting out, maybe you could help me."

"What man?"

"Him," he pointed at Lovelace, all smiles at the water cooler with a curvy blond from the clerk's office.

"You know him?" Soard asked.

"Sure. Everybody knows Mr. Lovelace."

"Omar, I work for him. Remington Lovelace is my boss."

"Really?" he flashed his first smile of the day. "What do you think he'd say about a case like mine?"

"Probably about the same thing as me."

"I mean the money. How much would he charge me?"

Soard was wondering that himself. Remy had a rule for fees. None were too high.

"I'll let you in on a little secret, Omar. Even if you did hire Mr. Lovelace, chances are he'd have me or somebody else from the firm to work on your case. He has too many clients to handle them all by himself."

"That's okay. I mean I'd take you."

"Thanks. But what I'm getting at is there are reasons people in trouble turn to Remington Lovelace. Having him involved in a case can settle it on his reputation alone. The prosecutors respect him. Some probably fear him."

"Great. So when do I meet him?"

"What I'm telling you, Omar, is that bringing Mr. Lovelace in on a case costs money. And, he doesn't let the lawyers who work for him charge much less. To take a case like yours—third offense, possession with intent to distribute, with the facts you've described to me—to take a case like that would be a significant commitment. I'd have to devote a great deal of my time to it. The trial could take several days. Before that, I'd have to interview a number of witnesses, conduct my own investigation, the results of which might lead me to file a motion or perhaps several motions, each of which would be argued before the judge. It would take lots of time and money. There'd be a tremendous amount expected from both of us. I'd do all the work, but you'd have all the risks. To take a case like that, Omar, I couldn't do it for less than twenty-five thousand dollars."

It was a blow, but Omar took it without batting an eye. He sat next to him on the bench and stared into the distance at the bulletin board, the teenage mothers and the old judges on the wall.

"I knew it wouldn't be cheap," he said, "but I don't have that kind of money. Not even close."

"I didn't expect you to. I couldn't come up with it myself."

Omar slumped in the pew. He was running out of options.

"Do you have to have it all up front?" he asked.

"Yes, I'm afraid so. I want to be as optimistic as I can, but let's face it, people don't worry much about paying their bills from a jail cell. In criminal defense, you have to get paid at the start of the case or you may not get paid at all."

"Yeah."

"Look Omar, there's really not much more I can tell you." Soard took out a shiny business card holder engraved with his initials and ran his fingers over Calhoun & Morgan's raised lettering.

"Here, that's my direct dial," he pointed. "If you can raise the money, give me a call."

He felt sorry for Omar Sharif Jones, but not enough to add him to his growing list of *pro bono* clients. He needed to find Ethan Morgan and have a little plain talk about Warren Dunn. He left Omar on the cold bench and headed for the door, stopping long enough to give the scared defendant one more of Lovelace's rules.

"And whatever you do, don't go back in that courtroom and tell anyone I'm your lawyer. Not until you hire me. Good luck, Omar."

CHAPTER 16

Weston Calhoun wore an expensive golf glove on his bottom hand as he addressed the ball. His top hand was bare and clammy, chapped from the breeze that swept over the first tee box, slick and of no use to him in steering his drive down the narrow fairway. He rubbed it over his tan golf jacket, but the smooth leather only worsened the effect. It was a bad combination, a good feel with his power hand, gloved and in harmony with the graphite shaft, ready to lead the biggest club in his bag quickly through the hitting zone with lethal torque, and a bare top hand likely to slip off at any moment during the stroke.

The governor squeezed the driver with a precise interlocking grip, his angles and body alignment perfect in every way. He centered his skinny legs over the tiny white ball, resting the oversized club on the dew-soaked grass at the Hillsdale Country Club. A cap with a picture of a yacht he sailed covered his white hair. He adjusted it like a third base coach giving the steal sign. Then the incessant club flicking, followed by more compulsiveness with his hat. Piper watched this interminable setup, wondering if it were really as difficult as the ex-governor made it look.

There was no one waiting behind the foursome, but Calhoun wouldn't have been any more nervous if there'd been a packed gallery waiting to exhale during his exaggerated trophy-pose follow-through. First shot of the day. What if he chubbed it? What if he doinked it into the tree line, he worried, after all these years, a thousand rounds of golf with these same business associates and dozens of other distinguished old men of the course. Would they laugh at him, the way they must have laughed when the people fired him after only one term in office? Would they notice if he dropped dead of a heart attack, or would they follow his ball into the woods, shaking their heads at another tee shot sliced into the void? This time would be different. He'd never have to find out because this time would be different.

Calhoun slowly drew the club back, the way he'd been taught, but the fluid motion the teaching pro had shown him was missing. He paused at the top of his deliberate arc, then uncoiled violently, stopping short of the high-teed ball. He drilled the graphite driver into the dirt at an angle that sent his shot screaming wildly to the right. A wooden shaft would have broken and impaled him on the spot. Instead, the three hundred dollar club held together beautifully, transferring its force efficiently to the projectile now on an uncharted flight toward triple-bogeyville. At the ladies' tee forty yards down range it ripped a faded green towel from the hand-cranked ball washer and sent it skyward like a matador's cape. It continued, imperceptibly slowed by the shredded towel, on its way toward the driving range and an old man asleep at the wheel of a contraption that scoops up tattered range balls. In the instant after he picked up its flight, and once he realized the live round had acquired a new target, Calhoun let out a blood-curdling scream in the slumbering man's direction.

"Fore!"

It was not the casual, courtesy, it-would-be-bad-form-not-to-yell fairway gesture one makes to signal his lazy shot might land within a square block of another golfer, more etiquette than exigency. Instead, this was the desperate, plaintive cry of a man who hoped the sound of his voice would outpace the ball he'd set in motion, the life and death *Yawp!* one hears before he hears nothing ever again.

"FORE!!!"

There is a cage that surrounds the cab on the ball-scooping machine. It is supposed to reassure the driver as he collects bucket-loads of practice shots that even if someone on the range hooked a wicked liner toward him he'd be protected. It is about as convincing as the placebo the Russians give their soldiers to insulate them from a chemical attack because gas masks cost too much. What's more, every golfer on the firing line at one time or another has aimed for that screen with long irons and drivers trying to tag the moving target with a red-striped ball like a carnival stuffed animal was at stake. Governor Calhoun's tee shot found the only gap in the screen. His ball rattled around like an armor-piercing bullet for what seemed like an eternity to the terrified greens keeper. The poor man had a better chance ducking a Mike Tyson haymaker punch. At least he'd have known where to look when it came his way.

Calhoun's shot kicked up a dozen empty beer cans and a year's worth of dusty Hardee's take-out bags, but incredibly left the driver unscathed. He cut off the engine and shook over the steering wheel, a lucky mechanized Mr. Magoo.

Calhoun stood speechless at the first tee. The haggard man pulled back the wire screen and picked up the scuffed ball. The former Governor needed a Xanax. He waved his cap and the wobbly driver headed toward them in as straight a line as he could manage.

Amsler patted Calhoun's back with his giant hand.

"Gawd dang, Wes," he yucked. "You 'bout kill'd that summm' 'bitch. Straighten it out and you'd drive the green. Damn. That'll teach him to do his job around you."

Calhoun looked around to see if the others had taken it any more seriously. "I guess so," he said, pulling another six dollar ball out of his pocket. "How about give me a mulligan?"

"Sure thing, Wes."

Calhoun took a half-swing and dribbled one just past the ladies' tee, safely in the fairway but not in the same zip code as the first hole.

Coot Youngblood, Amsler's longtime business partner and co-founder of Southtrust Savings and Loan, hooted as the frazzled greens keeper threw Calhoun's ball into a bunker on the eighteenth.

"Thay' ya go," he said. "Thay's your ball, Guh-vah-nerr. Hee-hee-heeeee. Got a hell of an arm, don't he? Ta-hee-hee-heeeeeee."

Coot took a wild cut that sent his drive a hundred and fifty yards straight down the middle, but his follow-through caught up with it and the ball hooked another ninety yards to the left. Calhoun smirked as it stopped behind a tree, leaving him an impossible second shot. Coot pulled his cap down over his face and plopped down behind the wheel of their golf cart.

It was Piper's turn. All he had to do was not kill anybody. He found the biggest stick in the club's rental bag and made a nasty face at one of the knock-off balls he picked up at Wal-Mart on the drive to Hillsdale. He swung as hard as he could, making contact with the ball the way Amsler said he'd have to if he wanted to play with the duffers. His shot pinged no higher than his head for the first hundred yards, then took off like a jet as the sound of the contact echoed beyond the tall pine trees that lined the course. It soared majestically down the fairway, fading just in time for the dogleg some two hundred and fifty yards away. It rolled another sixty yards on the hard ground coming to rest a pitching wedge away from the green.

They watched awestruck, then Amsler started the praise.

"Gaw'd dang, boy."

"Damn, son," Coot seconded.

Piper walked off calmly, the driver on his shoulder as if he expected no less. "I'll play that one," he said.

"Did you hear that governor," Coot chuckled, "*he* don't want a mulligan. He's gonna keep that one. Ta-hee-hee."

Calhoun nodded politely at the young man, "Nice shot."

Coot and Piper sped off in the direction of their drives. Calhoun and Amsler followed them on the bumpy path. It was a quick trip to the Governor's ball. They turned ninety degrees and parked. Calhoun fished around his golf bag for a club he thought he could handle.

"How's things at the firm, Wes?" Amsler asked.

"Okay, I suppose. Ethan's running the store. Doing a pretty good job, all things considered."

"Mergers aren't easy. I've been taken over so many times I stopped getting business cards. I finally just had one printed up that read, 'Jake Amsler, Banker.'"

"I know what you mean," he said.

Calhoun's mulligan left him a mile from the green, but he wouldn't touch a low angled club the rest of the day. He pitched it safely ninety yards ahead and they were off again.

"Listen, Jake, I appreciate your willingness to extend the firm's line of credit. It'll give us more time to get back on our feet."

"Well, Governor, you've always been a pretty good risk."

"No, I mean it. Outside of the shareholders, there aren't many folks who know the full extent of our situation. You're one of the few people I've even talked to about it. But we're coming back. You can count on it."

They stopped again. Amsler chose a two iron for his long approach. He knocked a clump of dirt from his spikes and checked the wind, then ripped a huge divot but caught enough of the ball to send it just beyond the water hazard.

"Nice shot, Jake."

"Thanks."

"I'm not worried, Wes. Your word and a handshake have always been good enough for me. Besides, Ethan had a good run for so long, everyone's entitled to a little slump now and then. In my business, it's called a correction in the market. Ethan's correction has been made. I'm confident of that."

"I think you're right about that. I have a feeling some special things are about to happen at the firm, in this town, and in our state." Calhoun was back on the stump, with his arm around the poultry festival queen talking 'jobs, jobs, jobs' in a hurting rural county.

"You mean, for example, the riverfront project?"

Calhoun winked at him as they rode along the dusty path.

"We may end up with a client in the running for one of those contracts, Jake. It would be improper for me to discuss that with you until the successful bidder is announced."

"Aw' hell, Wes, I've got so many conflicts of interest on that project I'm gonna have to recuse myself. Don't worry about it."

Calhoun rolled another one down the fairway and cleaned his clubface. His partner collected him and they drove to his ball.

"That's between us by the way," Amsler added. "People are already counting up the votes. With me on the sidelines it leaves the council with an even number. That screws everything up. Too much risk of a tie. There's folks out there who'd pay a lot for that information."

"Like maybe Warren Dunn?" Calhoun asked.

"Yep. I'm not writin' off any more million dollar loans for that summm' 'bitch again. Fool me once…"

He chopped at the grass as Calhoun snickered.

"What's so funny, Wes?"

"You sure Warren Dunn's fooled you just once?"

The chairman froze in mid-swing. He bladed it and the ball flew the sand trap on the other side of the green. There was nothing in that tall grass but mosquitoes and bogeys. Coot and Piper waited for them on the green, holding putters and low scores.

"Keep practicing law, Wes," he said. "Politics and golf ain't gonna make you any money."

CHAPTER 17

Soard wheeled through the ghetto lot in the shadows of the Dunn Plaza, kissing the curb with the Audi A6's front bumper. Fifty-nine more payments and the new car was all his.

A pleasant female voice announced from somewhere that the express elevator had reached the thirtieth floor. The door opened revealing a gaudy gold 'Calhoun & Morgan, LLC' sign. Beneath it young and not-so young women wore *'do-you-want-fries-with-that?'* headphones in a semicircular bank that took up half of the lobby. Soard's secretary had drawn lunchtime phone duty.

"Got the short straw, huh Maggie?" Soard asked without breaking stride.

"Yeah, again," she said. "Hold on," Maggie culled through the messages. "This was hand delivered for you."

Soard read the heavily-taped floppy manila packet. "Shiloh Finance Company. What's this?"

Maggie covered her microphone. "No idea."

"Who delivered it?"

"Little guy about this tall," she gestured. "Kind of rapper-looking dude meets charm bracelet. He left just. I'm surprised you didn't pass him on the elevator, or step on him he was so short."

The phone lines went red across the board. Three chairs down a secretary who looked like she was working on her third Purple Heart yelled, "Incoming!"

Soard ducked into a conference room that could have fit inside a doll house. Tiny picture frames hung on the wall, a hunting series with a fox progressively in angst over the pack of dogs and sharpshooters closing in fast. Inside the finance company mailer were two smaller envelopes. The thin one contained a certified check made payable to 'Attorney Peter Soard.'

"Sixteen thousand dollars," Peter said softly. The fox on the wall looked worried. "Jesus."

He ripped open the thicker envelope and hundred dollar bills fell on the floor. He picked up handfuls of them until the table was nearly covered. On one of the bills there was a yellow sticky with a phone number and initials, 'O.S.J.,' written on it.

"Omar."

Soard stuffed it all back inside the package, said a prayer for the fox and burst into the lobby. The warmest eyes at Calhoun and Morgan met him there.

"Maggie! Get me a fee agreement."

****

Piper waited for someone to bring him his steak sandwich as the politicians recapped their round. Calhoun had lost a dozen golf balls but managed not to maim anything but his ego. Coot was drunk by the third hole. Piper convinced him he'd beaten the course record, and sent him to the pro shop to pose for the club newsletter. Amsler's play was solid and respectable, like his career in banking and politics.

Sean wondered when the chairman would ask him about the state of gambling in Bristol, but halfway through a pitcher of Samuel Adams it seemed less likely. The sunburned men sat in front of a big screen TV watching ten-year old highlights from the Masters and tossing back orange whip while Warren Dunn and Ethan Morgan plotted their Lafayette River conquest.

Forget the office Sean told himself. He'd scarf down his sandwich, turn in the bludgeoned rental clubs and fight through the cramps at Longstreet Park, this time without his backpack. He told the lady behind the counter to make his sandwich to go, stuffed a wad of napkins inside the bag and paid his respects to the head table.

"I have to head back to town, gentlemen. It was a pleasure," he said.

Amsler kicked a chair toward him. "Sit down, Sean. I'll square it with your boss. You can't tell me Mike Pomerantz hasn't played hooky before."

Piper could have told him that, but it wouldn't have been true.

"Sure," he said. "I'll stick around."

Amsler filled Calhoun's cup. "Wes, this young man not only knocks the cover off the ball, he's also a pretty good lawyer from what I hear," he winked. "Did you bring the thing we talked about?"

"Yes, sir." Piper already had it in his hand.

"Sean was nice enough to bring me a copy of the gambling ordinance," the chairman said.

"Uh-huh," Calhoun grunted.

"You know, the one your firm drafted for the City."

Calhoun turned serious. "Oh, yes, the gambling…uh-huh. Fine. Fine."

"I wonder if you could take a look at it for me, Wes. You know, make sure all this legalese don't screw us. Sean, hand that to the Governor," he waved.

Piper unfolded the page and set it before Calhoun as he bought time fiddling with his glasses. Amsler knew his old friend didn't have a clue what it was.

Calhoun scanned the title and the barebones draft, but it didn't help.

"Yes. Uh, who at the firm have you been dealing with?" he asked Piper.

"Mr. Bing."

Calhoun tried to picture the firm's letterhead but there were too many lawyers to list all of their names. He had to have been an ambulance chaser Morgan brought to the merger.

"You know it's funny," he lowered his head to speak over his reading glasses, not condescendingly, just preserving the order of succession. "At a firm our size sometimes I don't have as much day-to-day contact with all of the…"

It came to him in mid-sentence. *'Got a ding? Call Harvey Bing. In a wreck? Here's your check…Oh, my God.'*

"Harvey wrote this?" he asked.

"Yes, sir."

"Well, uh, does it address your concerns?"

"We were hoping you could answer that, Wes," Amsler said."

Calhoun studied the draft more carefully, the way he used to when the legislature sent him a bill to sign into law.

"Jake, where are ya'll going with this?"

"What do you mean?" Amsler asked.

"I mean what's victory look like? What's your policy objective?"

"Mine or council's?" Amsler smiled.

"That answers one question," he said for Sean's benefit. "Jake, y'all got the votes for this?"

"I guess we'll find out," Amsler chuckled as he buried his face in a plastic beer cup.

"This ordinance is vague, which may or may not be what you want. If you're trying to outlaw gambling, you may want to spell out which games are prohibited," Calhoun said. "Then again, there could be some reason to leave it open. I'm sure Harvey Bing did what he was told to do," he lied.

"So would you suggest I take this to committee and let them sort it out?"

"Might not be a bad idea," he said. "As it stands now, if I was on the council I might have some real concerns about this. In its present form this law could be exploited easily. But like I say, that may be what some folks want. I don't know. I have to admit, I haven't been terribly involved with this matter. Ethan should be able to tell you more. Maybe you'd want to talk to him. If you do let me know and I'll set something up."

Amsler owed Reverend Wingate and Sister Hattie a call. This wasn't the news they were waiting to hear. He was in charge of the city and he had nowhere to lead it.

He needed a lifeline and Coot, giggling into the beer pitcher, wasn't it. He turned to Piper instead.

"Sean, what's your opinion?"

"Mr. Calhoun has a point, sir."

The Governor had no idea what it was, but he developed an immediate man crush on Piper.

"I mean, you definitely should consider spelling out which games you want to outlaw, maybe even add an attachment that lists them all by name. Otherwise, it may be too vague to be effective. But I also agree that it doesn't make much sense to dissect this draft if there's no clear direction from council. At least this gets something on the table, if you're looking for a point of departure. I don't know."

"Uh-huh," Amsler said.

"But there again," Sean continued, "it may not be the most attractive place to start. And, of course, the press will report this version to the public and that may take on a life of its own."

Calhoun agreed. "Jake, this is a smart man you've got working for you. He's not just giving you his legal opinion, he's got some sage political advice as well."

"Make 'em all legal," Coot chimed in. "What'ch'all care if folks wanna play video poker in this state? They can go to Vegas or Atlantic City and play slots all they want. Hell, they can go to Tunica, Mississippi and do the same thing." He drank directly from the pitcher as the rest of the foursome ignored him.

"You raise some good points, Sean," Amsler said. "And I appreciate you rearranging your schedule to come out with us today. You drive the hell out of the ball. I'd stay with this game if I were you."

"Thanks. I'll try."

Calhoun toasted him, "Nice to meet you, Sean."

They shook hands and Piper left as fast as he could. By the time he reached the parking lot he'd polished off half of his cold sandwich and dialed Anne's number. He wasn't worried about a thing. He'd just left the world's problems with men who knew they could solve them better.

CHAPTER 18

Calhoun & Morgan, LLC

9:50 p.m.

Soard's office was indistinguishable from every other associate's at C & M—small, windowless, life-draining broom closets they referred to as glorified cubicles until they remembered where their secretaries worked. He wanted to lie down on the floor and blow bubbles at the ceiling but there wasn't room. The old lamp on his wooden barrister bookcase might look retro in a few years. Now it was just junky. It shined on the law school textbooks he was too scared to sell back to the used bookstore in case one of his professors found out about it.

Soard rubbed his tired eyes, too worn out to look at another file. He massaged his forehead and tried to make sense out of the fine print on the aspirin bottle. The childproof lid was kicking him hard.

"Dammit," he said.

A voice outside his door, that lazy twang he heard in his sleep, said, "Lord, it's started already."

Lovelace leaned against the doorframe, sporting a different suit than the one he came to work in this morning, and a shiny silk tie that looked like it would glow in the dark. He carried a bag of take-out food in one hand and jiggled a set of keys in the other. The fobs could remote start either of his foreign cars. One of them would have been enough to pay off Soard's student loans. Lovelace was drunk. Either that or the take-out bag was filled with Jack Daniels.

"You ain't supposed to be talking to yourself 'til seven years of marriage…or three years of practicing law. What's wrong with you, boy?"

"How long have you been standing there?" Pete asked.

Lovelace showed himself to the only other chair in the room.

"Long enough to hear you cuss those pain pills. What are you still doing here?"

"I was just asking myself that. I'm tired, my head hurts and I'm hungry enough to bite a hole through my desk. Do you think the termites would care?"

Lovelace opened the bag. "How 'bout this instead?" he asked.

"DuBose Steakhouse?"

"Prime Rib sandwich and fries. You may want to nuke the fries."

"How much?"

Lovelace wadded up the receipt and hooked in into the trashcan.

"How much for what?"

"Thanks."

"No, thank you. I heard you made me a lot of money today," he said. "So what the hell, Pete, why are you still here? Why are you eating cold take-out food alone? You should be out on the town with your wife, celebrating the rising legal star of Peter Soard, defense counsel extraordinaire."

"I'm not alone," he said. "Besides, I haven't earned any of the fee, yet."

"As long as it's in the trust account," Remy smiled. "You did get him signed up, didn't you?"

"No, not yet. Jones took off before I got back from lunch. But he's coming by in the morning to sign his fee agreement."

"I wouldn't worry about it. Anyone who gives you that much money will sign anything you stick in front of him. If he gives you any problems, call me. I'll be here all day."

Lovelace handed him a small envelope with his initials in raised ink on the flap. Inside was a thick stock note card with a check drawn on his personal account clipped to it. Soard read the card.

"Just a small token of my appreciation? Remy, this is a thousand dollars."

"A thousand? Hmm. Guess I got carried away with my zeros. Oh well, you earned it."

"I don't know what to say."

"'Thank you' always works for me."

"Thank you. Thank you very much."

"Now, Pete, if you really want to thank me log off your computer and go home."

"Don't worry. As soon as I finish my time sheet I'm outta here."

"Ah, yes. The time sheets. The lifeblood of the firm. Ethan is a stickler about the time sheets. I probably should turn in one of those things in myself someday. I find that if I wait long enough to complete one, I forget what I actually did for my clients, so it's easier just to guess. I can't imagine Calhoun and Morgan would let an associate get away with something that radical."

"Not a chance."

"Well, at least you don't have to worry about this month."

Lovelace strolled to the bookcase to check Pete's library.

"So how'd he pay?"

"What?"

"How'd Jones pay his fee?"

"Oh. Actually, it was kind of weird. He dropped off a package with a certified check for sixteen thousand, and the rest was in cash. Nine grand. The check was made out to me. I had to sign it over to the firm—"

"What d'you do with the cash?"

"Uh, I gave it to Jeanine in Finance.

Lovelace stumbled back to his seat. He needed a cab and someone to dial the number for him.

"Listen, Pete, I haven't had a chance to spend as much time with you as I should have. I've been a solo practitioner for too long. Every lawyer in the section is my responsibility. I want you to know you can come to me when you need help with anything, including help with the business end of your practice."

"Thanks." Soard hoped Remy would remember making the offer.

"The biggest thing is the fee, Pete. You've got to get the money up front. There's no other way it can work. I don't care how pathetic the guy's story is. The fella behind him's got it even worse. There'll be more fees like the one you got today. If you were by yourself you'd get to keep all of them."

"Then again, I probably wouldn't have any clients if I was by myself. I'd rather have a third of something than a hundred percent of nothing."

"This firm has every creature comfort Governor Calhoun could dream of, but you only get to keep a small percentage of what you bring in. You don't even get to eat what you kill. You only get the leftovers. That's the bargain prestigious law firms make with assembly line guys like you and me."

Soard wasn't buying it.

"Okay, so maybe I'm a foreman. But how can two hundred lawyers stand each other, indulge each other's egos, with only a few slots at the top? Because it's profitable. As long as the water's flowing they'll tolerate each other. Watch what happens when the well starts to run dry."

The conversation was above Soard's pay grade. Was it a test to see if he was a company man? Lovelace jingled his pocket change. Some of it fell on the floor but he didn't notice.

"Are you a high-minded person?" he asked.

"What do you mean?"

"Things move fast in this business. We have a job to do, and there's no time to get bogged down in the details. Landing clients, arraignments, motions, witnesses to track down, cases to try and others to settle. The list is endless. The last thing you want to deal with is a bunch of pain-in-the-ass office managers. Especially when you bring in as much money to the firm as we do. You know what I mean?"

"Kind of."

"Do you think the other sections are pulling the wagon any harder than we are? I don't see any lights on in real estate section, or workers' comp. Have you seen the parking lot? It's just you and me. Even the cleaning crew's gone home. Look at yourself. It's ten o'clock. In eight hours you'll be back in the same chair, banging your head against that damned air conditioner shaft and trying to remember the last time you took your wife out on a date."

"That's depressing."

"Go home, Pete. You've made your hours this month. It's not all about the time sheets anyway, despite what the shareholders tell you," Lovelace assured him. "You know who sees your billable hours?"

"Everyone, I thought."

"Un-uh. Your section head, and the managing partner. That's me and Morgan. If I show them to anybody else, it's simply a courtesy."

"I didn't realize that," Pete said as he stuffed the rest of his cold sandwich in the bag.

Lovelace made it to his feet without losing any more money.

"One more thing," he said. "Don't shy away from the cash fees. Unless your client is charged with counterfeiting, take all you can get. These guys will pay you in cash. There's no credit rating in the drug trade. Yes, take the checks to the ladies in finance. But the cash fees you can leave with me. I'm the one responsible for this section's receipts. We can take a draw on our net proceeds right here, whenever we want, without having to go through the bookkeepers for every dime we bring in. We could all use some walking around, money, am I right?"

Soard wasn't sure what expression had crossed his face as Remy gave the marching orders. His boss needed a designated driver and an ethics refresher. He was pretty sure he hadn't said a word as Lovelace told him to skim off the top.

"Anyway, don't turn the cash fees in to Jeanine. Bring them to me. Nice job today, pal."

CHAPTER 19

The waitress hit her stride every night midway through the graveyard shift. She fired water glasses across the counter like a bowler picking up spares, leaving each one within reach of a laminated menu stained with every condiment in the truck stop. A thirsty driver a country mile away downed his and eyed her like a stray pup. Menus were for newbies.

"Be with 'ya in a sec', hon," she said on the way to the kitchen to kick a little tail.

A burly man who'd been busy at the jukebox walked past a row of empty stools and sat down next to the trucker. The music lover was on the job, but it wasn't hauling stuff across country.

"Good evening," Nick Luciano leaned in and said.

The man nodded.

"Your name Damke?"

Kenny Damke figured he was at least six four, but Luciano was so solid and square-shouldered on the stool it was hard to tell. He wore a gray checked jacket, an open collared blue button down and brown shoes, dressy enough to get him a table at a nice restaurant and with good enough traction for him to leave the not-so-nice ones in a hurry. Damke knew he was a cop.

"Who wants to know?"

Luciano showed him the federal badge. Somewhere behind that strong chin he must have had a neck, or maybe his beer keg of a chest just kept going all the way up. His powerful looking biceps made the Jim Rockford sport coat ride halfway to his elbows. Luciano was in shape, not the aerobics, meat market, mirror watching, nuevo in-shape, like he was looking for a date and the rest of the time he sat behind a desk. He was put together as though he came into this world, got spanked and bench-pressed the doctor who'd delivered him.

"Special Agent Luke-e-ah-no," Damke butchered it.

"Luciano. I'd like to talk with you."

"What for? I ain't done nothing wrong."

"Who said you did?" Luciano managed what for him passed as a smile. "That booth in the corner's open," he said. They all were. "Come on. I promise she'll bring you your breakfast."

Damke left his bone-dry water glass and followed him to the corner booth. Luciano sat against the wall. He grabbed a stack of sugar packets and shuffled them with one hand as he stared out the window.

"You come here often, Mr. Damke?"

"Damn key."

"What?"

"My name. It's pronounced 'Damn key.' You know, like when you're locked out of your car and you say, 'where's my *damn key*?'"

"That's easy to remember. So how's the food in this place, Mr. Damn Key?"

"It's alright. Flo' usually has it out by now. Whatch'oo want to talk about?"

"I want some information."

"Call four one one."

"No, this is more of a recommendation. I need a good lawyer. You know any?"

"I've known a few lawyers in my life. None of 'em any good."

"Ever heard of one named Remington Lovelace?"

Damke stared at the floor. It was where he looked to find his lies.

"Doesn't ring a bell."

Luciano took a notepad out of his jacket pocket and flipped to the page he wanted.

"Didn't he represent you at your most recent court appearance? Drug charge, wasn't it?"

"Keep it down. That stuff gets around."

Luciano look around the restaurant. There was a scruffy man passed out at the counter, Flo wiping down tables and a cook mumbling to himself in the kitchen. Through the glass double doors that led to a fish and tackle shop he saw a clerk getting ready to open.

"Gets around to whom?" he asked. "It's four o'clock in the morning. We're the only people in here not buying bait."

"What do you want? Tell me or get back in your flippin' federal cop car and leave me alone."

Luciano grabbed both ends of the table like it was a giant tray and he wanted seconds.

"Was Lovelace your lawyer or not?"

"Alright, alright. I know him."

"What happened at trial?"

"My case never went to trial.?

"Yeah? And why not?"

"Remy got me a deal, same as everybody else."

"Same as everybody else? Come on, Kenny. Possession with intent to distribute. Four counts. And you get all of 'em dropped but one."

"Alright, so I know at least one good lawyer."

"Uh-huh. And then the one count left gets changed to simple possession. You're a pretty lucky guy. How does somebody get a deal like that?"

"Ask Lovelace."

"How do you know I haven't already?"

Damke turned whiter than the sugar packets Luciano was using for card tricks.

"We'll come back to that one," Luciano continued. "The D.A. said the case against you was airtight. Then the week before trial somebody broke into the evidence locker. They tampered with some things. You know, tried to make it look like it could have been anybody. But all that was missing were the drugs they found on you. Your dope goes bye-bye, and so does the state's case."

"That's a shame," Damke said. "Even the sheriff's department gets broken into these days. What's the world coming to?"

"Funny thing was the lock was intact. There was no forced entry. Somebody used a key and walked right in. All they left was your 'get out of jail free' card. That's some coincidence. Now how do you suppose that happened?"

Damke didn't answer. Luciano was unflappable. In an hour he'd meet Mason, his man working the inside as they built their case against Lovelace. They'd compare notes as they'd done most days of the sting, methodically amassing enough evidence to take it to a federal grand jury. Lovelace had pushed the envelope for too long. This time he'd crossed the wrong prosecutor.

Luciano exchanged his notepad for a tiny lab bottle.

"Okay, Mr. *Damn Key*, when's the last time you filled up one of these?"

"What?"

"Don't tell me you've never seen one before," he set the jar on the table. "You know as I was sitting in my *flippin' federal cop* car reading through your file, I noticed that it says here you're supposed to be drug tested every month as part of your probation."

"That's right. I took it at the clinic last week. Clean as a whistle."

"That's good, Kenny. But it also says in your release order that you're subject to random testing. And the test can be administered by any authorized law enforcement officer. Even a fed."

"Now, wait a second—"

"We're running a drug test this morning down at our field office. We're nearing the end of the fiscal year, and if we don't use up all the specimen bottles we won't get any new ones. That's the government for you. Use it or lose it. How 'bout fill one of these up for me. The lab's open two-four-seven."

"You're crazy."

"Now, my guess is that a few days before your regular tests you clean yourself of all those impurities. Or maybe you sneak somebody else's pea into the john and pour it into the specimen bottle when no one's looking. That's why every once in a while you need a random test to see what's going on. You know, to separate the contenders from the pretenders. Come on, Kenny *Damn Key*, let's step into the can and take a whiz."

Luciano stood over him holding the bottle.

"Alright. Sit down."

"What?"

"I said sit down. I may know a little something about it."

The special agent rocked back against the booth again.

"Go on."

Damke leaned across the table and said softly, "When I got busted this last time it was my third offense. I figured the public defender could only do so much. My ex-wife knew this lawyer at a big firm, but he only handled bankruptcy cases. He referred me to Lovelace. He said it would cost a lot, but it would be worth it."

"How much is a lot?"

"Thirty grand."

Luciano shook his head at the thought of it. He'd spent countless early mornings in dives like this, talking to losers who'd say whatever the highest bidder wanted to hear.

The waitress returned with Kenny's breakfast.

"Y'all want anything else?" she asked.

"Nothing for me," Luciano said.

He waited as she topped off Kenny's water, dropped the check on the table and disappeared.

"How'd you pay him?"

"What do you mean?"

"Was it all at once?"

"Yeah. He said he had to have the full amount up front."

"Was it in cash?"

Damke nodded.

"You came up with thirty grand in cash just like that?"

"I borrowed from everyone I know. Still paying it off," he said. "Lovelace told me once he had the money he'd take care of everything. I remember him saying, 'Kenny, you get my fee together and then go drive your truck. Don't worry about a thing. I'll let you know how it turns out.'"

"Is that so?" Lovelace leaned back. "And how do you suppose things turned out so well for you?"

"I don't know what happened for sure. I was on the road six days a week. If I don't drive I don't get paid. He made it sound like it would take a while, but they dropped all but one charge a few days after I gave him the money."

"Did he ever say why?"

Damke sopped up a runny egg with a flimsy toast wedge.

"I'm not sure I should answer that."

"Relax, Kenny. I'm not here to arrest you. Your case is over."

"Well, he said there was a problem with the stuff they found on me. Somebody messed with the drugs," he said. "But you already know that. Hey, do you think thirty grand was too much?"

"Who did Lovelace deal with, the D.A. or the cop who arrested you?"

"I never heard him talk about the D.A."

"Pomerantz?"

"Yeah, that's the guy."

"So as far as you're aware Lovelace didn't have anything worked out with Pomerantz before the drugs disappeared?"

"Not that I know of. The cop who busted me said I'd do twenty years, easy. He didn't even try very hard to get me to confess. He said he didn't need it. They had the evidence and a witness, he told me. They knew I wouldn't talk so they didn't even bother."

"Go on."

"That was it. I got the money together and a few days later Remy's secretary called and told me to meet him at the courthouse. I freaked out. I didn't know if I was ever coming back. When I got there, Remy was waitin' for me. I remember he had a big smile on his face. An assistant D.A. stuck a plea agreement in my face and said, 'Merry Christmas.' There was a fine, but no jail time. Just probation. I couldn't believe it. Lovelace said he was going to walk me in, and that's what he did. Then he walked me right out."

"Just like that?"

"Just like that."

"Did you ever have a fee agreement with Lovelace, or a receipt for the money you paid him?"

Damke thought about it for a minute. "I'm not sure. To tell you the truth, I don't think he did."

Luciano stacked the sugar packets neatly in the holder.

"Did you ever talk to anyone else at Calhoun and Morgan besides Lovelace and his secretary?"

"I can't remember. It's been so long ago."

"Try."

"Let's see," he said as he scooped a mound of grits into his mouth. "I wanna say it seems like the day after I paid him Lovelace had me talk to somebody. You know, one of his assistants. I gave my story to him, witnesses and what not."

"Another lawyer?"

"I think so. He dressed like it. Tall, skinny kid."

"Do you remember his name?"

"No. It was short. You know, boom. One syllable. Powell or Howell? Something like that. Sowell, maybe."

"Soard?"

"Yeah. That's it. Soard. You gonna bust him, too?"

"Did you talk money with Soard?"

"No."

"Was there anyone else?"

"That was it."

"And within a week of hiring Lovelace, your airtight case fell apart. You walked?"

"I walked. Still got the debt to prove it."

Luciano stood and buttoned his jacket. "Kenny, there may come a day when you'll need to remember the things we've discussed. I'll let you know if that day comes. But until then, you just forget about this little conversation, and I'll postpone your drug test. Maybe until after your probation runs. Otherwise…"

Kenny inhaled another soaked piece of toast and kept his head down.

"What conversation?"

Luciano left the empty specimen bottle on the table.

"Be careful on the highway," he said. "See you later, Mr. Damn Key."

CHAPTER 20

Piper waited in line as the crowd filed through the metal detector outside the courtroom. An old man carrying a wooden cane he could have clubbed the judge to death with strolled past the security guards without even drawing a glance. They turned into the KGB when a punk behind him set a miniature Swiss Army Knife on the conveyor belt. Piper's suit and haircut didn't fit their profile, and he had nothing to declare. A deputy whose mind was on anything but keeping sharp objects away from the courthouse cleared him. The hoops people had to jump through to enter a place no one wanted to be.

Pomerantz was scarcer than usual, and his third trial of the week was about to resume. If Sean needed to see him, this was his best chance. Once the jury arrived, the D.A. would be on Maximum John Worthington's time.

Piper scurried past a group of young men waiting to talk to their appointed counsel, their 'fifteen minutes of *shame*,' Pomerantz called it. The D.A. sat on the rail separating the parties from the gallery. He was cutting up with the public defender about something, probably the death penalty or whose turn it was to pop for lunch. He waved Piper to the jury box.

"How's it going, Sean?" he asked.

"Okay." Piper flaked out in the foreman's chair. "Is it always like this crowded?"

"When there's murder trial, yeah."

The court reporter opened a box of blank cassette tapes, setting in for the long haul.

"I know you're busy," he said. "I talked with Mrs. Wilson."

It meant nothing to Pomerantz.

"The lady I was telling you about with the property in Oakdale. The one having surgery."

"Oh, right. Did you get her signed up?"

"I didn't have a chance—"

"Why not?"

"She's wants to show the papers to someone else."

Pomerantz straightened his tie, the redness coming back to his face.

"Terrific. I thought this was a done deal. Is she going south on us or what?"

"Not necessarily," Piper hedged. "I think she just wants to hear it from someone else."

"Uh-huh."

"I did find out one thing you may be interested in, though."

"What's that?"

"I talked with her quite a bit yesterday, about her house, how long she'd lived there, her family and what not—"

"Aw', Sean. I told you not to bond with the other side. You can't get a good deal if you put a face with the name. You'll end up giving her the store."

"Let me finish. Mrs. Wilson told me she'd been approached by someone from the city more than a year ago about the riverfront project."

"So?"

"Council didn't authorize the condemnations until this year. Nobody would've known to approach anyone in Oakdale about buying up their property until it was approved. Right? So there wouldn't have been any reason to contact her until then."

"No," Pomerantz said. "I suppose there wouldn't."

"So I was kind of wondering, you know, what the hell's going on? And the men she said came to see her, wearing suits and ties in the middle of the summer. That doesn't sound like anyone from the public works department."

"Huh?"

"Those guys were blue shirts with 'Mel' or 'Buck' written on them, not suits," Sean continued. "I'm not sure what we've got. Should I have her file a report with the sheriff? Because impersonating a city employee is probably not a good thing. I mean I can't quote you the chapter and verse, but I'd imagine the state sort of frowns on that kind of thing."

"Well—"

"And you prosecute cases for the state."

"Yeah. When I'm not developing land for the city. Look, Sean, from what you've described it could have been a couple of Mormons dropping by to visit."

"Mormons don't ask to buy your house."

"No," he said. "I guess they don't at that." Pomerantz

instinctively turned his back to him. The bailiff stood straight as six o'clock. He knocked twice on the rail. The door opened and he bellowed.

"All rise! All rise as the Honorable Judge Jonathan Worthington enters the courtroom. The Bristol Circuit Court is now in session!"

"That's my cue. Look, Sean, I don't know what to tell you. It sounds messed up."

Piper thought for a moment he'd convinced his boss that a conspiracy was afoot in Oakdale. Alma Wilson would get some answers and maybe a chance to keep her house a while longer. Pomerantz was concerned with bigger things.

"All I know is we need her to sign the deed. Yesterday. Stay on this one for me, buddy," he said. Sean was dismayed but the D.A. was too busy to notice.

"Council's losing patience," he said in his courtroom voice as he strolled to the state's table. "We need those river deeds."

****

Morgan sat alone in Fagan's Bookstore café, sipping coffee hot enough while he edited the third draft of his speech. In a few hours he'd address the troops at *See'n 'em,* and do his best to calm the shareholders' fears at the firm's quarterly luncheon. He looked for magic in the Espresso. Maybe in the next cup.

A pale woman dressed in black with dark lipstick, darker fingernail polish and John Lennon glasses waifed her way toward him. She set a blueberry bagel and a healthy butter substitute on the table.

"Can I get you anything else?" she asked.

"No thanks," he said. "This should hold me for now."

Soard stopped long enough to grab a muffin and a cold bottle of designer water. He set a fiver on the counter and joined the senior partner.

"Good morning, Pete. Thanks for coming over."

"No problem." Soard eyeballed the room and saw only

strangers. Every table was full, but no one was talking. They read national editions of big city newspapers and glossy magazines with foreign titles.

"Have any trouble finding this place?"

"No, sir. I've been here before, although never this time of day. We usually stumble in here around two in the morning. Laura likes to do the coffee thing after a late movie."

"Uh-huh," Morgan grunted as he read another passage in his speech. He crossed it out and scribbled a line in the margin that made him smile instead.

"So, Pete, did you get a chance to review the file?"

"Yes, sir. It was pretty slow at roll call yesterday."

"Slow?" Morgan raised his eyebrows and kept writing. "That's not what I heard. Unless you call a twenty-five thousand dollar retainer slow for one day. Is that an off day for you, Peter Soard?"

"No. Actually, that's the biggest fee I've had. I didn't know you'd heard."

"There's not much that goes on at Calhoun and Morgan I don't know about, sooner or later. Big fees I hear about sooner. I'm sure Remy Lovelace was quite pleased."

Soard remembered his drunken section leader's 'high-minded' talk last night.

"I guess so," he said.

"Of course he was. So other than a record payday there wasn't much happening at the courthouse, huh?"

"There's plenty happening, just not with my cases. There's a murder trial this week. And somehow Mr. Lovelace is not involved."

"That is unusual."

"The judge continued the rest of my cases."

"It's all right to catch your breath, Pete. I know you'll find other things to occupy your time. Got to keep billing those hours, right?"

Soard didn't answer.

"Did you prorate?"

"Sir?"

"While you were at the courthouse. Did you prorate your time over a number of files?"

"Oh. Yes, sir. Remy told me about that the day I joined the firm."

"I bet he did," Ethan chuckled. "You don't want the clock ticking that long without getting paid for it. But that doesn't mean you can't be equitable. It's good to spread the pain around, not tag any one client while you're there, you know?"

Morgan set his pen down and spread fake butter over his bagel.

"So tell me all you know about Warren Dunn," he said.

"Well, I know I'm impressed with him. I've never seen a portfolio like that. I've handled a few white-collar cases, but most of my clients are in their line of work precisely because they need the money, not because they have money."

"Uh-huh."

"It looks like he's been on the board of directors for half of the Fortune Five Hundred companies."

"Warren does get around."

"The only boards my clients see are at their parole hearings."

"No doubt," Morgan said. "Warren's done well for himself, there's no doubt about that. It's true his father set him up nicely, but our client's not just a trust fund kid. You saw the material on the trust, right?"

"Yes, sir. I must confess it would've helped if I were a CPA. I'm not used to the spread sheets."

"You don't need to be an accountant to tell the difference between red numbers and black ones. The trust is in good shape, I can assure you of that."

"Oh, he definitely looks solvent," Soard agreed.

Morgan wiped a spot from his glasses and held them to the light. Soard sipped about a dollar's worth of his upscale well water.

"Some people are born lucky, others just make their own breaks," the senior partner said. "Old Man Dunn had both. His son picked up right where his father left off, only more so. Warren's aggressive with his developments. Mostly in the southeast, but he's got properties everywhere. His latest conquest is the Lafayette River. You've seen the signs in the Oakdale community?"

"Yes, sir."

"Dunn's got all the land worth having. When the city cleans up the rest he'll have enough contiguous property to proceed with the next phase of his development."

"What's the city's role?" Soard asked.

"They own the roads. Once construction begins traffic will be diverted to a new main access point that cuts across several residential blocks. The houses belong to individual property owners. They're small lots, dinky houses. Old family homes, minority-owned mostly. They've been there since before the Civil War. Some were even used to house slaves, that's how far back they go."

"So are any of them historic properties?"

"Maybe they should be protected," Morgan admitted. "But no one's gotten enough political clout behind the idea to get the proper designations. They're so run down. People would rather see anything else go up there. City council voted to condemn enough land to build a convention center. The project was put out for bid, and the contract was awarded to a developer. As part of the winning bid, the developer wanted the city help him acquire more land beyond the original condemnation."

"I see."

"For years Bristol has been losing tourist revenue to the beach and the mountains. We're in between two more attractive places. Why visit a flat eyesore when you can see the ocean or the hills in either direction? So there's a big push for economic development. The problem is 'Old Bristol'—the old money crowd in this town—are slow to change. The folks who graduated from Longstreet High School, then went to the College of Bristol and never truly graduated. The council's full of people like that," he joked. "They talk a good game, but they really could care less if any new jobs come to town. They got theirs, so why should anyone else?"

"This can be a clique-ish town," Pete said.

"So once the City Attorney's Office signs up the holdouts, Dunn will be in business, provided a couple of things happen."

"What things?"

"Dunn owns a nice strip of waterfront property. He can bulldoze all but a few of those rattrap houses tomorrow, if he wants. Of course, the land is still zoned residential. Unless that classification is changed to commercial, all he can build are nicer houses than the ones he's planning to demolish."

He lost Soard. The defense attorney knew little about land use or construction law.

"Who determines whether to change it to commercial?"

"The city," Morgan said, not at all unhappy that his fall guy was clueless about how it all worked. "His request goes before the planning board next week. Given that the city initiated the condemnations, and since they've sold most of the land to our client, it's likely they'll approve the zoning change. But there's no guarantee. Dunn's a polarizing figure. Some members of council can't stand him, and they're pretty open about it. Others tolerate him because he makes a lot of money—mostly for himself, but the trickle down is attractive to a town that needs jobs."

"Yes, sir."

"But even the ones who think the project has merit still have to feign a little outrage when they hear his name. Warren's publicity problem keeps getting worse. He's moving all of the minorities out of Oakdale."

"I thought the city was doing that."

"Technically, it is. But this is politics, Pete. They're not gonna take the blame for uprooting a community. They'll just sit back and act surprised that the developer is actually developing consistent with his plans. Warren Dunn is the perfect scapegoat. The council gets the tax base it needs so it can live high on the hog, and Dunn catches the hell. That's how the game is played."

Soard nibbled on the dry muffin. He turned Morgan's fake butter bottle and read the label. "That stuff any good?"

"It spreads. If you want movie popcorn butter, this won't do it for you."

"Gotcha," he passed. "So, who's on the planning board? Is it a committee of the council?"

"No. It's an independent body. Well, let me rephrase that. It's supposed to be independent. Council appoints the board members, so I suppose they indirectly control them through the threat of not renewing their appointments."

"Okay."

"Although why anybody would want to serve on that board I don't know. It's not a paid appointment. They don't even get reimbursed for their mileage when the drive around to look at all of the properties they have to vote on. And half of the people who come before them end up going away mad. But, apparently there are a few misguided individuals who want to serve anyway. The threat of being kicked off usually is enough of a hammer to make them a rubber stamp for the council."

"But they can vote however they want, in theory anyway, right?" Soard asked.

"In theory, and sometimes even in practice."

"I mean if they're supposed to be independent, wouldn't it be against the rules for anyone to lobby them before they meet?"

"You mean can you have an *ex parte* communication with the board?" Morgan asked wryly. "Sometime when you're having trouble falling asleep, take a look at their by-laws. It's a big no-no to communicate with the board members other than at a public meeting. But let's face it, Pete, City Council's not teeming with parliamentarians."

"So it's possible a councilman's position on a given issue would be known to the board before it votes?"

"Not just possible, probably a certainty. In this case, for example, I guarantee you somebody's gotten to them with whatever Dunn has in mind. So it may not be a problem…for us."

Morgan thought of something clever to tell the troops and wrote as fast as his hand could move. Soard tried to read it upside down. The handwriting matched the notes all over the file he'd given him on Dunn. The senior partner finished and seemed proud of whatever it was.

"Now, assuming you get through this hurdle next week, there are a couple other things I need to brief you on."

"I'm sorry," Soard choked on his muffin. "Assuming *I* get through this hurdle?"

"Mr. Dunn would like you to represent him at the board."

"He would? But I've never met him."

"I've mentioned you to him. I've told him how impressed Remy Lovelace is with your work. He feels…we feel, Warren and I, that you'd be perfect for the job."

"You do?"

"Absolutely. It's important, but it's also a low-key proceeding. There shouldn't be many people in attendance. And if there are, they'll probably be just waiting around until the board gets to their case. Ours is only one of many they'll hear."

"Well, I don't know."

"Look, Pete. This is a tremendous opportunity to get your face out there representing the biggest player in this state. Do you know how many lawyers would jump at the chance to be in your shoes? It'll be a turkey shoot. Ten minutes, tops. I'm sure your shortest closing argument was longer than that. Besides, the board probably won't ask more than a couple questions."

"Will I know how to answer them?"

Morgan committed the revised speech to memory and stuffed it in his pocket. From somewhere deep inside he felt for the young lawyer. He'd thrown him overboard holding a cinderblock. He didn't even have the decency to tell him that their client had paid off two of the five board members, and before the hearing number three would be in his pocket. Instead he'd keep Soard in the choppy water, maybe even encourage him when it looked like he couldn't tread any longer.

"Pete, I don't want to say that it's a lay down, but let's just leave it at this. Council wants this zoning change. They can't say it publicly, but they want it. The right people, you understand, want Dunn to win."

"And I'll know when I'm speaking to the right people?"

"Don't worry," he said. "You'll be fine."

"I'm much better at criminal defense."

"This is easier. If you lose, your client isn't going to jail."

"No," Pete said. "He'll just lose millions of dollars."

"Millions?" Morgan laughed. "Sure, Pete. So what do you say? Are you my man on this?"

Soard wanted to rip one of those foreign magazines out of somebody's hand, roll it tight and whack Ethan in the mouth with it. Instead, he said, "Yes, sir. I'm your man."

"Excellent. Caroline has a copy of the board's agenda and a summary of Dunn's proposal. Everything you need should be in the file."

"Okay," he said as he downed the last of his water. "I guess I'll go find Caroline, then."

"Hold on. There's something else I need you to do first."

"What's that?"

"A little errand. It seems our client is getting anxious to wrap things up. You see the zoning change is only part of Warren's problem. You'll knock the board out of the park next week. I'm confident of that. But we have further business with the city."

Soard's caseload was falling apart fast. A reluctant drug runner's freedom was at stake. Omar Sharif Jones had given him a bundle for his best defense. His case would be back on the docket next term of court. He needed to hear more about what happened the night his client was stung by the cops, track down witnesses and decide whether to put on a case or argue reasonable doubt to the jury. He couldn't count on Maximum Worthington dismissing the charges even if he had enough to make a motion. Morgan was loading up his 'Petey-do' list and the end was out of sight.

"What is it?" he asked.

"Not what, Pete. Where. I need you to fly to Washington this morning."

"D.C.?"

"That's the one."

"But I have to—"

"Don't worry about packing. You'll be back this afternoon. I want you to pay a visit on Dunn's lobbyist. He's got his own firm in Georgetown. Guy's name is Mitchell."

Ethan handed him a copy of the man's brochure. "Caroline's got your flight information. She'll have a cab waiting to take you to the airport when you get back to the firm."

Soard studied the flier. "Joseph Daniel Mitchell." 'Joe Dan' was in quotes beneath his name in case his customers couldn't make the moniker conceptual leap.

"That's three first names," he said. "Joe. Dan. Mitchell."

Morgan nodded. "Yeah. I guess it is at that. You won't need to remember any of them. Everybody calls him Peaches."

"Peaches?"

"Joe Dan loves 'em. He comes back here once a month just to get a couple of large baskets full. In fact, why don't you run out to Minah Farms before you go to the airport? They're the best."

"Minah Farms."

"Yeah," Ethan pulled a large bill from his wallet. "Here, take this. Get him a great big bag. He'll be eating out of your hand."

"That's what I'm afraid of," Pete said. "Although I'd hate to get on Peaches' bad side."

"Bad side. That's funny. Now listen, I know this is short notice, so if anybody else wants you to do something today, let me know. Even Lovelace. This is our biggest client. I'm pulling rank in this case, understand?"

"Yes, sir."

"And remember, Mitchell works for Dunn, same as us. But I wouldn't tell him any more than is necessary. Let him do most of the talking. Just pick up whatever information he has and come home. You can wave to the monuments if you want."

"All right."

Ethan smiled contentedly over another gem of a one-liner Soard wouldn't get to hear at the luncheon. Maybe the peanuts on the plane would be better than the spread Calhoun and Morgan had laid on for its staff. The company sure would be. There wasn't even time to call Laura before he got on the plane.

He stood to leave and wondered if the senior partner noticed.

"Oh, and one more thing, Pete. At the hearing next week, be sure not to mention Dunn's name."

"What?"

"Keep him out of it. The case is listed under the name of the development company. There will be a representative present if you need him."

"The development company?"

"Yeah," Morgan said. "Saucostee Enterprises. It's in the file."

CHAPTER 21

Lovelace puffed a cigar as he strolled through Longstreet Park. The man beside him was adamant about something.

"Wish I could hear what they're saying," an agent named Frank Taggart said as he watched from a distance in a government sedan.

"You don't have to," Luciano replied. "That they're together tells you all you need to know. Lovelace represents the biggest drug dealer in town. He's offering to dime out his competitors right now. The local cops will make the busts and grab all the headlines. His client walks. The law of supply and demand."

"You're sure that's Nelson?" Taggart asked.

"That's his car. Everybody knows the Chief of Narcotics' unmarked Beemer. He might as well drive a blue light."

"Yeah. So Lovelace has a mole in the sheriff's department. That would explain a few things."

"Like his astronomical dismissal rate? Like acquittals he gets when evidence disappears? Stories that change and investigators who get short-term amnesia? Yeah, Frank, that explains a few things."

"We gotta tell Mason."

"Yeah." Luciano smiled.

Taggart had all the pictures they needed. He'd catch their good side on the return trip.

"You know," he said, "I still can't believe the number two man in the sheriff's department would let himself be seen with Lovelace in broad daylight. Maybe they're just friends and this is how they spend their lunch hour."

"Sure, Frank. That's probably it. Lovelace berates the cops for years in public, and now he wants to patch things up. Good theory."

"All right. But I don't see why they'd want the small-timers instead of Lovelace's client."

"It's simple. As simple as the Cold War."

"How's that?"

"Come on. When it was just us against the Commies, we knew who the enemy was. You didn't have as many assessments and profiles as we do today. When we bankrupted them, everybody said we'd won. Then someone realized that the nukes were still there. But instead of one huge government controlling them, we've got a bunch of factions with nobody in charge."

"Right, Luc'. And how does that translate to a crack dealer?"

"Easy. The sheriff wants one kingpin. So he sends his narcotics chief to make nice with Lovelace. If he deals with him, he can keep all the pretenders down and Lovelace's guy from doing anything too crazy. It's détente at street level."

"Détente? What's that?"

"It's when people agree to disagree."

"Well, whatever. We still better tell Mason about this."

"We will when we see him tomorrow."

"You don't think this is worth calling him now."

"It may be worth it, but I don't want to put him in any more danger than he's already in. Let's stick with the regular schedule."

"Yeah. I guess you're right. But if this thing goes all the way to the sheriff—"

"We weren't sent here to bust the sheriff. We're here because of Lovelace. Besides, I'm not folding our tent without talking it over with Mason first."

"He doesn't share your confidence, huh Luc'?"

"Mason's a cautious fellow. I can't fault him for that. Maybe I wish I had his temperament for these long operations. But I tell you, Frank, I've about had it with this town. I'm getting tired of watching rich lawyers and cops on the take through my binoculars. Tired of interviewing his dumb-ass clients, knowing that any one of them could run to Lovelace without us knowing it. And then we'd put our own people at risk."

Lovelace fired up another cigar and climbed into his Lexus. He sent smoke signals to the head of narcotics as he rolled quietly away.

"What now, boss?"

Luciano checked the schedule. "Lovelace has court this afternoon. He can't get into too much trouble there. I'll try to reach Mason tonight. Maybe you're right."

"Okay. What 'til then?"

"I don't know, Frank. Looks like we've got the afternoon off. Got any ideas?"

"Getting out of this hot car for starters. How about a movie? Air conditioning and a big box of buttered popcorn might be just the ticket. If they put something on the screen, that'll be a bonus."

Luciano closed the file. He checked his wallet and it didn't take long.

"I'll buy," Taggart said.

"Frank, I like your police work on that."

****

Maggie threw together a smart-looking binder for Soard, complete with his itinerary, plane tickets and parts of the Dunn file Morgan's secretary had given her under seal. She even printed directions to Minah Farms. There was everything but a sack of sandwiches for the trip and the market price of peaches.

"Thanks, Maggie," Pete said. "I'll call you from the airport."

"Okay." She pretended to scratch her face and pointed in the direction of the business types in the waiting room. He'd spotted them and thought they were here to see one of the Calhoun corporate lawyers.

"There here for me?" he asked.

"Um-hmm."

"I thought I didn't have any appointments today."

"You don't. There walk-ins."

"And they want?"

"No idea," she whispered.

"Terrific."

He tucked the binder under his arm and walked across the lobby. Soard's clients wore gang colors and pants that wouldn't fit Bozo. The man's suit was too conservative for an undertaker. The woman dressed like his twin. She wore tiny studs in her ears and a scowl that would run off an Amway salesman. Her hair was pulled back tight like she'd been prepped for radical scalp therapy. Soard figured they were white-collar criminals or he'd inherited a fortune and they wanted to show him how to spend it. Soard spoke first.

"Good morning."

"Mr. Soard?"

"Yes, ma'am," his voice cracked like she was holding a ruler.

"I'm Megan Van Arsdale. This is Robert Nuessle. We're from the State Bar, Standards of Conduct Division."

She handed him a card that said the same. The man dared him to ask to see his. He towered over Soard, his chest puffed out like he was only using half a lung.

"Division? They have a division for that?"

They didn't smile. They'd done that for the year.

"Is there someplace we can talk in private, Mr. Soard?" she asked.

There was, but he didn't have time for a closed-door meeting. On the other hand, for all he knew they were the division.

"Actually, I was just on my way to the airport. Can you tell me what it's about?"

"We're conducting an investigation," she said. "But if you're too busy to speak with us."

"Investigation into what?" Soard asked.

"We'd prefer not to go into that in the hallway," she said. "It's just that we don't like to meet our witnesses for the first time on the record, so we thought we'd give you a chance to discuss things with us before the hearing."

"Witnesses? What hearing?"

"Before the disciplinary counsel," Nuessle said. "It's in your interest to cooperate with us." Coming from him it made sense.

"I'm cooperative," Soard promised. "I'm Mr. Cooperative." He peered down the hallway. "Come on," he said.

Soard led them, slowly for a man in a hurry. They followed close behind. His office was out of the question. They might take pity on him in that broom closet, but if he was the target of their investigation, he figured why put them in the crime scene.

"This room's usually empty," he pointed. "Please have a seat." Nuessle took up one side of the table, content to let Van Arsdale loose while he picked the young man out of a lineup. He pretended he was too afraid of his partner to open his mouth. Soard knew better. Nuessle had ten years on her easy. Soard tried to place him. He'd seen his name somewhere before. Maybe it was at the top of the bar's disciplinary rulings. He ran the show while Van Arsdale did all his lifting, but when it was time to lower the boom, Nuessle lowered it.

"Mr. Soard, we investigate complaints made against attorneys licensed, and in some cases unlicensed, in this state," Van Arsdale said. "Have you ever dealt with anyone from the division before?"

"No, ma'am. I can't say that I have."

Nuessle stared through Soard like he was taking a polygraph.

"How long have you been with Calhoun and Morgan?" she continued.

"Just a few months. I came here straight from law school."

"Uh-huh. What's the firm's structure?"

"Structure?"

"Describe your organization. The hierarchy, the chain of command. Things like that."

"Oh. Well, the firm's divided into sections. You know, commercial law, bankruptcy, trusts and estate planning, domestic, workers comp, criminal law. There are eight or nine sections, depending on who claims foreclosures each month. There's one section leader and any number of associates in each specialty."

"How many partners are there?"

"About thirty. I suppose I should know the exact number, but the truth is, most of the associates don't really know how many there are. There's a senior partner, Mr. Morgan. He's also the managing partner. All the section leaders are shareholders."

"And which section do you work in?"

"Criminal defense."

"So you for Remington Lovelace, correct?"

"Yes."

Nuessle folded his arms. Soard could swear he felt a breeze from it.

"Explain how the criminal section works. What's the basis—"

"Ma'am, is there something specific I can help you with? I'm really not sure where you're headed."

"How does Lovelace run his section? How do you get your cases?"

"Lots of ways," Soard said. "Referrals. Friends of friends. I have clients who call me because they like our ad in the phone book. It's understated, but with so many lawyers listed we seem to draw a good deal of interest. And we have some well-known attorneys. Mr. Lovelace brings in a lot of business. Mr. Morgan. And it doesn't hurt having the former governor."

"And does Mr. Lovelace ever make case assignments?" Van Arsdale asked.

"Sure. Lots of times. It's his section. Mr. Lovelace is one of the best defense attorneys in the state. People ask for him all the time, but he can only handle so many cases, so he spreads around the rest to us. Especially the run of the mill cases. Most times he stays involved and we help out. You know, we second chair them."

"I understand. Did you ever second chair him on a matter involving a man by the name of Juan Mezzariego?"

"I don't recognize the name. I've got about a hundred open files right now, and twice as many in storage," he said. "What was the case about?"

"Mr. Mezzariego helped a woman blow up her ex-boyfriend's car. He stood lookout while another man threw a Molotov cocktail on the engine. They were all charged with domestic terrorism, among other things."

"Oh. I have had a few destroy-the-car cases. But most of those were people who'd gotten behind on their payments, or they were trying to cash in on the insurance or something. Allegedly."

"Uh-huh."

"But that doesn't sound like the motive in the case you're describing."

"This would have been about a year ago. Oh, and Mr. Mezzariego doesn't speak a word of English. Does that help?"

"Wait a second," it came to him. "There's a chance I could have done his bond hearing."

"A chance?" Nuessle asked. "You don't remember?"

"I cover tons of bond hearings, not just my own but for others in the office. We rotate unless there's already an attorney-client relationship formed, or if one of us is requested. They run bail proceedings every other day at the jail. Most of them take less than five minutes. Unless they're a flight risk or charged with a violent crime, usually they make bail. I've done a few hearings for illegal aliens, migrant workers and folks like that. Bond court usually provides an interpreter. It's possible the man you're asking about could have been one of those detainees."

"All right. So it's possible you did meet him?"

"Sure. Anything's possible at the detention center."

"How'd you know it was at the detention center?" Van Arsdale asked.

"Most bond hearings are," Soard said coolly. "You don't do any criminal work, do you, Ms. Van Arsdale?"

Nuessle exhaled like a dragon. His partner could handle herself.

"Not at the local level," she put him back in his place. "All our prosecutions are in the supreme court."

"Right."

"So you're positive you didn't represent him at trial?" she asked.

"Not a chance. What's the problem? Is he making a complaint against me or something?"

"I suppose you have a right to ask that, Mr. Soard. No. He's not making a complaint against you. He just gave us your name as someone he may have dealt with in his case."

"Then what does he want?"

"Mr. Mezzariego was convicted and sentenced to fifteen years in prison for his part in the attack. Remington Lovelace was his lawyer."

"Why didn't you tell me that to begin with?"

"Mr. Mezzariego alleges that Lovelace charged him twenty thousand dollars, and he never heard from him until the day of the trial. He said Lovelace promised to fight the charge, then he entered a guilty plea for him on a deal that wasn't any better than he would've gotten if he'd gone in unprotected. Mezzariego says Lovelace never even told him about it."

"Never told him?" Soard asked. "That's unlikely. The defendant has to approve a pretrial agreement. How'd the judge let that go through?"

"I don't know, Mr. Soard. That's a matter for the appellate courts. What we want to know is why Mr. Lovelace took so much of this man's money for essentially pleading him straight up after he said he was pulling out all the stops."

"I couldn't tell you, ma'am. I don't know what Mr. Lovelace did or didn't do for this fellow. And I don't set his rates."

"You didn't discuss the case with him at all?"

"Not that I can recall. I'm sure I would've told him what happened at the bond hearing if I'm the one who handled it. But that would have been it."

"I see. What is the firm's policy with respect to the payment of fees, Mr. Soard?"

"We're all for it."

Nuessle piped up, "No. What Ms. Van Arsdale is asking you is this. What happens to the money? Do you divide the fees up at the section level, or does everything go through one accounting department? How do you process the money through the firm?"

"All I can tell you is how I do it. What's supposed to happen is that the client signs a fee agreement, no matter how small the matter is. Sometimes it's a one-pager, other times they can be quite detailed. It all depends on the case, and, I suppose in some cases, the client."

"And the money goes where?"

"Everything goes to the finance department after that."

"Why did you say that's 'what's supposed to happen'?" Nuessle asked.

"Because I don't know how anyone else does it. I mean the bookkeepers look busy, so I assume I'm not the only one using them. But I don't supervise diddly squat in this place."

"We appreciate your candor, Mr. Soard," she said. "Are there ever cash fees?"

"Sure. The firm gets cash all the time. Usually it's for modest services. Simple wills, stuff like that."

"How about your section?"

"It depends. We prefer certified funds, as you can imagine. I even had a guy once who wanted to let me hold the deed to his house. We can accept property for payment, but that's pushing it as far as I'm concerned. They don't want to go to jail, and sometimes that's all they have."

"Uh-huh. And Lovelace supports this policy as far as you know?" she asked

Soard felt himself pause too long. Lovelace would axe the finance department if it weren't so good about honoring his travel claims. He'd balance the budget with what remained of their 'walking around money.'

"Like I said, I only know the way I handle it. I'm sure Mr. Lovelace has the same expectation of the other lawyers in his section."

It could have been close to the truth. Soard wondered if he'd be willing to swear to what he'd just said informally to these officers of the court twenty-four hours a day.

"That's interesting. Mr. Mezzariego says he paid Lovelace's fee in cash. Twenty thousand dollars. Where a migrant worker got that kind of money I don't know. But that's what he says. Is that a common practice at the firm, Mr. Soard? Do you routinely get thousands of dollars in cash from illegal immigrants?"

"Most of my clients can't rub two dimes together. But I don't know of any reason why we can't take cash."

"So long as there's a record of it," she said. "I'm sure the firm has records of every client transaction. Certainly one of that magnitude. Perhaps we should see the bookkeeper."

Soard nodded. "That'd be the floor below us. They know a lot more about what goes on at this place than most of the lawyers. If it's not divisible by three, I don't think any of us can do the math."

They sat there stone-faced. They were paid by the state twice a month. Contingency fees were not of their world.

"I'm sorry, but I really do need to get to the airport. Is there anything else I can help you with?"

"No, Mr. Soard," Nuessle said, offering his business card. "That's all we want for now. If you recall any more about Mezzariego, give us a call."

"Okay."

"Oh, and by the way, all conversations with the division are confidential. We won't share your comments with anyone."

"Thank you."

"And you're prohibited from discussing this matter with anyone either. Do you understand that?"

"Yes, sir."

Van Arsdale shot her arm out and rang his hand like she was bringing up oil. "Thank you for giving us so much of your time," she said. "Have fun in Washington."

Soard was in more trouble than he thought. "How did you know I'm going to Washington?"

"D.C. plane tickets," she said. "Peeking over the top of your binder."

"Oh."

"You don't do any ethics work, do you?" she got him back. "Have a safe trip, Mr. Soard."

CHAPTER 22

Morgan did laps around the thirtieth floor. The staff parted like the Red Sea during his morning constitutional. He turned the corner and nearly ran over Lovelace. Remy did an about-face and followed the senior partner down the hall. If you joined Morgan during these power walks it meant you had clout, or you'd screwed up and he wanted to chew you out before he forgot about it. No one chewed out Remy Lovelace.

"What the hell, Ethan. Trying to break the four-minute mile?"

"Trying to keep up with the old man, huh Remy?"

"Sure. You just go from zero to sixty a little faster than most."

They rounded the bend. Morgan waved to the new copy guy.

"When did he start?" he asked.

Lovelace didn't recognize him. "You got me. A place this big ought to come with a revolving door."

"Hmm."

"No reflection on you," Remy added.

Morgan made the loop to the long straightaway and opened up the throttle.

"I want to thank you for recommending Peter Soard to me. He's rather a bright young man."

"Good. I thought you two might hit it off. I'm glad to hear he's working out for you."

"You know, Remy," his voice lowered, "apart from you he's the only person at the firm I've told about Warren Dunn."

"Except for the governor, right?"

"No. I haven't even mentioned him to Calhoun."

"Really?"

"Orders from the client. Dunn likes his privacy."

"I see. Well, I'm sure with the dough he's laid out the shareholders won't mind."

"We'll see soon enough. I was planning to make the announcement today. Of course, I'd like to tell Wes Calhoun first...if he comes in. You'll be at the luncheon, won't you?"

"Sure. I'd like to see how the other sections are doing this quarter. Everybody's so secretive these days about the bottom line."

Lovelace fell behind for a moment. He kicked it up a notch.

"How long," he panted, "…how long do you do this, Ethan?"

"Twenty-four times around. There's sixteen laps to the mile, so that's right at a mile and a half."

"Well how 'bout I just go with you for another lap?"

"Suit yourself," Morgan said. "By the way, how'd your hearing with Bubba go the other day?"

Lovelace forgot he'd told the boss about it.

"You did have that hearing, didn't you?"

"It was continued. The other side didn't show. I moved for a dismissal, but the commissioner was cautious. He postponed it until next month."

"The reason I ask is because Bubba works for Dunn. You knew that, didn't you?"

"No, I didn't," Remy said.

"That's another thing Dunn wants kept quiet," Morgan smiled. "He's not overly proud of his association with Bubba. Mobile home dealer rubbing elbows with the richest commercial developer in the state."

"I never thought much about it."

"You've seen his sign haven't you?" Morgan asked.

"Whose?"

"Bubba's. Ever driven down I-30 toward the beach?"

"Yeah."

"There's a great big billboard with this guy standing on his mobile home lot, holding his finger way up in the air, you know, 'we're number one,' that kind of thing."

"That's Bubba?"

"Yep. That's your client."

"Holding up one finger, huh? Sure he wasn't announcing his IQ?"

"Probably that, too. But he may be smarter than all of us. He's going to be a very wealthy man soon. We'll be hicks to him after Dunn gets what he wants."

"You may be right."

"Listen, Remy. If Bubba has any other business, like loan closings or contracts or something, see if you can bring it to the firm."

"I'll put the bite on him. If his problem with the manufactured housing commission goes away, he may just name me in his will."

"I'd make sure that it does then."

Lovelace slowed down as they reached his section.

"This is as far as I go, boss."

"Wimp!" Morgan said loud enough for the staff to hear.

"I'll put Soard on you next time," Lovelace said in the distance.

Ethan rounded the corner and said under his breath, "Once is enough."

****

Joe Dan Mitchell's office was a rustic three-story house within a stone's throw of Dupont Circle. It was surrounded by elm trees and empty park benches. Soard rang the bell and someone buzzed open the sturdy wooden door. The glass one behind it was unlocked so he went inside.

A middle-aged woman who smoked a long-tipped cigarette smiled at him. She slid on a pair of flats she kept under her desk and said, "Lookin' for Peaches?"

"Yes, ma'am. I have an eleven thirty appointment. My name's Peter Soard."

"Okay, sugar. You just wait right here. I'll tell him."

She turned and yelled at the top of her lungs, "Hey, Peaches! Your eleven thirty's here!" It was some intercom system.

When the yelling stopped Soard heard a low thud that grew louder with each step. He wondered if someone was dragging a bowling ball down the stairs, or perhaps a mallet to whack the town crier in the head. He figured no one with any sense would come downstairs with her in the house unless it was part of the fire escape route.

The lobbyist tapped the rail with a silver-tipped cane each step of the way. At the bottom of the staircase he reached for the young man's hand and said, "I'm Dan Mitchell. You must be Soard."

"Yes, sir."

"Okay, Darla, bring us a couple Co-Colas," he said to his vocal receptionist. "Right this way, young man."

Peaches hobbled ahead of him, pausing every few steps to catch his breath. Soard waited a step behind of him. Even there Peaches came to just below the lawyer's shirt pocket. He wiped the back of his neck with a wrinkled handkerchief, panting as if it was sweltering, although Soard thought it was drafty in the old home.

Peaches wore clunky black shoes that might have been lifts, or maybe he had a problem with his legs. He moved like he did. His face was as smooth as an Englishman's, like the clouds protected his skin wherever he went. If he'd had a mustache to go with his little round head Soard could've seen him as the *Monopoly* guy. He'd sport a top hat to go with his cane and hide somewhere in Community Chest.

In the library Peaches steadied himself as he rolled onto a cushiony chair where he read all day waiting for business to find him. The room had twelve-foot ceilings, built-in bookcases overflowing with journals and historical biographies, hardwood floors covered with huge, finely detailed Indian rugs, and pictures of campaigns won and lost during a half century in politics. Soard looked at the faces. He read the autographs and spotted Mitchell in most of them.

"You must know everybody in Washington," Pete said.

"Oh, I guess if you live long enough you get to meet a few folks."

"What's this one here?"

Peaches struggled to his feet.

"I'm sorry. I didn't mean for you to get up."

"Now that little item there I'm especially proud of. That's a rare picture of the four living Presidents."

Soard scratched his head. "Aren't there five?"

"Well, yeah…now. But when this was taken there were only four. I got this from President Reagan himself. He gave it to me in the Oval Office."

"No kidding?"

"Sure did. He invited me there after I helped him get elected to his first term. I was his regional campaign manager, down in your neck of the woods as a matter of fact. We covered Bristol like a blanket. Of course, that was like preachin' to the choir. We could've run a corpse against Carter after the recession and carried that state by twenty points. But anyway, ol' Dutch was grateful just the same. You'll notice it's signed by all the Presidents," he pointed. "See that? Nixon, Ford and Carter…and, of course, Dutch. After he sent me this picture, as a token of my appreciation, you know what I did?"

"No, I don't."

"I sent him four pounds of quail that I puh'sonally kill'd."

"Four pounds? Wow," Soard marveled. "One for each President, huh?"

"Oh. Well, I never thought about it like that. That's just what we shot that day. But still, I thought that was one hell of a gesture on his part sending me this picture, so I reciprocated. I know how to return a favor."

Soard considered the swap. Peaches got an autographed, limited edition color photograph of the living Presidents, and Reagan got four pounds of rotting bird carcass that the Secret Service probably pitched before the commander-in-chief got botulism. Some deal.

"Yeah. Well that's quite a story, sir."

They took their places across from one another, Peaches in his cushiony chair and Soard on the other side of the small table where the lobbyist kept his daytime reading.

He leaned in and whispered, "All right, then. Where are my peaches?"

"Oh. I completely forgot. Here you go. Hope you like 'em."

Soard handed him the bag, and Peaches inspected his namesake.

"Great Gosh a'mighty. You got Minahs. Bless your heart."

"Yes. Mr. Morgan said Minah Farms. These are the right kind, aren't they?"

"Right kind. They're better than gold dipped in melted butter. Better than spring water in the desert. I take back everything I ever said about Ethan Morgan. He did me a solid this time. No doubt. Minah peaches. Doggone. My favorite. I like you, son."

"Thanks."

"You're a pleasant and considerate young man."

"I appreciate it."

"Now, what can I do for ya'? I know you can't stay long. You just want the board member stuff, right?"

"Board member? I'm not sure."

"Planning Board. Or does Dunn want the council files, too?"

"I don't know. Mr. Morgan just said for me to bring back whatever you had for Mr. Dunn."

"All right then, that'd be the council files, too."

Mitchell pulled his briefcase forward with the cane. There were two envelopes inside.

"So how long you been workin' for Dunn?" he asked.

"I don't work for him directly. I'm just helping out Mr. Morgan."

"Uh-huh. Well, you just do a good job for Warren Dunn and he'll throw lots of business your way. That's one good thing about Warren, he knows how to reward success. On the other hand, if you screw the pooch just once, he'll fire you faster than you can say Saucostee Indians."

"Why would I say that?"

"Oh," he covered his mouth. "Did that slip out?"

"What slip out?"

"Right. Come on, kid. You don't have to play dumb with me. I know you're working on the tribe business."

"Tribe business? I'm not following you."

"The Saucostees. You think Dunn's gonna tackle the state head on? He knows what that'll get him. He's got the business community on his side, but they're outnumbered by the Bible thumpers and the limousine liberals shuffling back and forth to the capital. He needs to push those undecideds over to his side, and he ain't gonna do it alone."

"He's not?"

"No. He's got to tug at their heartstrings a little. You know, make the casinos about something more than just money."

"Casinos? I'm not working on anything like that. Mr. Dunn's just developing some property for the city."

"Of course he is. But as part of the deal the city's agreed to sell him the rest of the land they don't want. They don't need any more than a few acres for their pitiful little convention center. So he gets some free legal work out of Bristol, and they sell him whatever's left at bargain prices 'cause he bid the development so low."

"Oh?"

"So the question is, what's Dunn gonna put there? A few houses nicer than the ones he's tearing down? Some condos? He's got plenty of those. What then?"

"I don't know."

"Think about it. He wants revenue, not rent money. What better way to do that than to guilt-up on all those hypocrites in the legislature? Understand?"

"Umm..."

"Well, don't you see? If they think they're just helping out rich ol' Warren Dunn, they ain't gonna do it. But, if they believe, or, more to the point, if they can act as if they believe that land's gonna be go to help out an Indian tribe they screwed over in all those lawsuits...well, hell's bells, boy, everybody comes out smellin' like a rose."

"I see."

Soard learned more about his client with a bag of fruit and five minutes with the kingmaker than he'd gotten from Morgan in a week. He was glad Mitchell's nickname wasn't 'Watermelons.'

"Okay, now here's the file on Nickels. He's the board chairman."

Peaches spread out a series of surveillance photographs.

"Now these were taken down at the beach last spring. Not bad, huh kid? She's a little homely, face-wise...but hell, when you turn out the light who cares? Am I right or am I right or am I right? Huh-huh-huh."

"What is this?"

Peaches smiled like he'd swallowed a coat hanger. He laughed to the top of the high ceiling.

"Boy, didn't they tell you anything?"

"Who?"

"Morgan and Dunn? The men ya' workin' for?"

"Mr. Morgan just told me to collect what you had that would help with this client. And I've never met Mr. Dunn."

"Never met him?" He ran his hand over the smooth walking stick. "Son, let me ask you a question. Just what do you know about his plans?"

Morgan had warned him not to make it a two-way street with Peaches. All that did was make him more convinced that he should level with him.

"Not much. In fact, you've told me more than anyone else has."

Peaches' face lost all color. He wheezed like he was back on the steps.

"Okay," he said. "Now right there…we're gonna have to have us an understanding about this here meeting. You're not gonna repeat anything I tell you, you got me? It's just like you're talking to your lawyer, or a priest or something."

"Priest?"

"This here is confidential. Right down the line. You got me? You don't repeat what I tell you."

"Tell me about what?"

"Why…"

His eyebrows raised and he smiled. "Oh. I get it. Huh-huh-huh. That's good, kid. You just keep your mouth shut, ya hear? You keep your mouth shut and we can do all the business Dunn wants to pay for."

"Fair enough."

"But let me tell you this. If Ethan's kept you in the dark, and you've never even met the client, you just better watch your back. That's all I'm saying. Ethan sent you up here to get the dirt on a local politician that's giving y'all some problems, and you don't know nothin' about it? Man, oh, man. I should've known. It never changes. Watch your back, kid."

"Yeah. I've been doing a lot of that lately. This isn't the kind of work I usually do. I've never handled a land deal, or dealt with city politicians or convention centers. If this doesn't turn out for our client, I may be the last to know. By then it'll be too late. I'm in a bad spot."

"Like David was against Goliath," Peaches said. "Although, that turned out all right, I suppose. Maybe this will, too."

"David and Goliath," Soard repeated. "That's how I feel about it all right. So I reckon as long as I just put my faith in God I'll be okay."

"David had faith in God, too," Peaches said. "But he brought along his slingshot just the same."

Soard thought about that for a moment. "That's true."

He slouched in his chair and felt himself slipping deeper and deeper into a lonely place. A wicker fan spun overhead. Its chain tapped against the motor, reminding him of a peaceful front porch and lazy summer afternoons. He could've fallen asleep if his stomach would permit it. Peaches had only shown him part of what he could fit inside one envelope, a set of photographs he was supposed to bribe a city official with if Dunn didn't get his way. He didn't want to know what was inside the other package, the same way Omar Sharif Jones told himself to stay in the dark about his deliveries. Bring home the goods was the only direction he'd given. Morgan could deny he ever knew what those were. Soard didn't have that privilege. He'd been kept from their client, and Peaches would be out of the picture as soon as he took the brown envelopes from him.

Peaches had given him all the warning he could. Morgan had told his secretary to book an early flight back to Bristol. Soard now understood why.

"David brought along his slingshot," he said. The fan ticked away and Peter Soard felt the tall ceiling start to cave in on him.

"I don't have one of those."

CHAPTER 23

Piper showed the lady the flowers he'd bought at the hospital's gift shop. He told her the patient's name and she gave him the room number. At the end of the corridor someone had written Alma Wilson's name beside the door. He looked inside, but her chart was gone and both beds were empty.

He returned to the nurse's station and said, "You sure that's the right room? I checked and no one was there."

"Wilson?" the lady said. "Yep. Three Thirteen."

The head nurse overheard and said, "Mrs. Wilson has been moved." Her face told him the change wasn't for the better.

"Where?"

"Intensive care."

"Oh?"

The nurse told the clerk to update her records. She pulled him aside and said, "Are you a friend of hers?"

"Not exactly. But I am concerned about her. My name's Sean Piper. I'm a lawyer. Mrs. Wilson and I are working on something together."

"I'm afraid we can't discuss a patient's condition without her consent. Especially since you're not a relative."

"I see. Is there someone from her family I can talk to?"

"There was a young woman in the ICU waiting room a little while ago. I believe she's Mrs. Wilson's niece. She may be able to give you more information."

"Thanks."

She told him the floor. It took Piper three elevator rides to find it. The waiting room outside intensive care was empty except for some folks Piper learned had carried in their fishing buddy after an accident. A tired girl in a plaid jumper sat on the other side of the room, resting her head against the wall but too worried to sleep. She had niece written all over her.

Piper introduced himself. She told him her name but it went past him. She thanked him for the flowers and set them beside an overnight bag she'd packed in a hurry.

"I work for the city," he said. "I've been dealing with your aunt on a project we're trying to complete."

"She's my great aunt."

"Sorry. I understand there's been a complication. Can you tell me what happened?"

"I don't really know. She came in for a hip replacement. Now they say she's got a blood clot in her leg."

"Oh. I'm very sorry. Have you seen her doctor?"

"She's got a bunch of doctors. The last one came out about an hour ago."

"Did he say how she was?"

"About the same. Which means she stays here. He said they wouldn't know anything else for a while. There's some medicine she can try, but they don't know if she's strong enough to take it."

Piper told her his business wasn't important, and that he'd check on her later. He gave her a card and told her he wasn't looking for any new clients. She was to call if she needed a friend. He wished he told the nurse that's what he was.

Sean asked if there was anything he could do. She asked him to pray and he said he would. He would pray for Alma Wilson, pray that she'd pull through to rip up Warren Dunn's insulting deed and see her big family sitting around the dining table again.

****

The dessert tray made its second pass through the main dining hall at the Piedmont Hotel. It was picked clean by the time it reached the head table. Morgan didn't notice. He was too busy fighting off a sycophant who'd switched nametags so he could sit across from the managing partner at *See'n 'em's* forced fun luncheon. The ambitious associate babbled something about client development and emerging markets and wouldn't he be the perfect point man for it all. Clark, the senior partner thought his name was, or Tompkins. He was on his short list to fire when the time came to downsize.

Morgan cleaned his glasses with a fine cotton cloth and tried to remember who'd hired the guy. He knew he hadn't done the interview. He nodded every so often, occasionally smiling like he did at the dentist's office before the lady who zapped his x-ray buried herself under a lead blanket.

Ethan left the young lawyer in mid-ramble and moved to the podium. He set his watch beside the speech, gently massaged his wrist, and then filled a glass with water as he looked out over the packed house. The troops needed a shot of motivation. He remembered an Army commander who warned him not to be the kind of officer whose men follow him only out of curiosity. The lawyers, paralegals, secretaries, clerks and even the errand runners at Calhoun & Morgan all had that suspicious look in their eyes. The former governor was there, along with every lawyer he'd brought with him to the merger. Morgan wondered what he'd shot in his morning round at the country club. He might have the time to play with him soon, but he wasn't sure they'd be able to find anyone else to round out the foursome. Calhoun might not even let him play once he hears about Dunn. He'd meant to give him notice before now, but the governor had been missing in action so often the custodians stopped emptying his trashcan.

Caroline smiled at her old boss reassuringly. She could always calm him that way, although there was enough schoolteacher left in her that when their eyes met he found himself checking his posture. Remington Lovelace tiptoed to the back of the gathering like he was leaving a motel room he'd rented an hour earlier. He sat beside an impish law clerk at the kiddie table. That was as close as he ever got to the partners unless they were talking about reducing his share.

Except for a few girls catching the phones, the firm's quarters were deserted. Morgan felt something he hadn't experienced in a long time. He'd addressed a couple hundred juries in his career, but in each one there were only twelve sets of eyes to plead with. He hadn't seen so much of the firm together in the same place before. There'd been other luncheons, but the no-show rate for them was high. It looked like everyone was here today. Someone had even commented that Peter Soard must be deathly ill to not be present. Even with court he'd get a lunch break. Had he quit?

Morgan took a drink of mostly ice and set the glass next to his speech. He needed a miracle. Warren Dunn was as close to one as he would ever get.

"Good afternoon," he began. "I'd like to welcome everyone to our quarterly luncheon, especially the newest members of Calhoun & Morgan. I'll have more to say about them in a moment. First, though, let's have a big round of applause for the great staff here at the Piedmont."

Ethan waved the headwaiter over. "Cecil, how 'bout bring your folks out so we can say thanks."

The servers appeared from every corner. They smiled, acknowledging their guests' polite applause with Queen Elizabeth waves before they scattered. A drenched cook made his way from the kitchen to see what the commotion was. He turned around in disgust that he'd been disturbed for this. He fixed lunch for three hundred people five days a week. They all ate the same way.

Morgan offered some more niceties about the accommodations before returning to his prepared remarks. He recapped the firm's achievements since the last meeting. It didn't take long. He made a passing reference to their production goals for the quarter, but promised not to bore everyone with them. The details would come in the shareholder meeting that followed immediately after he told everyone else not to focus on the details.

He introduced the new employees, many of whom Morgan was catching his first glimpse of, botched all the names capable of botchery, and read aloud a few of the better mini-bios of the firm's hot young associates. Each stood and smiled at his co-workers. The lawyers snickered at the turnover rate among the secretaries. A few of the boys prided themselves on running off as many as possible. And then there were the young ladies at the crossroads of life, hard workers who'd gone out on maternity leave and just said to hell with it at the thought of coming back. They liked the men they worked for, but whatever appeal private practice had for them faded at the prospect of raising a family. At home they would only have to deal with one or two crybabies. Here there were two floors' worth of those.

The good will was running out fast. Out of the corner of his eye Morgan saw his top client skulking beyond the doorway with at least two others from his retinue. Warren Dunn couldn't believe he'd agreed to take part in this public display of affection, but if things were as bad as Morgan had said they were, his lawyer needed a boost. It wasn't that he hated to see him grovel, but if Ethan got the boot before he sewed up the riverfront project, the repercussions could be unacceptable. He might loosen his lips on the way out the door, and Dunn couldn't chance it. So he'd oblige him for a few seconds of fist pumping at the podium. He could be adored for that long.

"Now," Morgan continued, "I realize we've had some setbacks over the past few months. I often tell the shareholders that with as many lawyers as there are in this town, we're lucky to have any clients at all. This is the most saturated legal market in the state. Even so, we've done all right for ourselves. And, as many of you know, I'm an eternal optimist—not a pie in the sky dreamer, but a positive person who looks to a new day, a better day than the one before. In that regard, I have a little announcement to make. I haven't completely finalized things, and I'm not exactly sure of the scope of our representation, but since we're all here together, this is the perfect opportunity for me to tell you about our newest client. Many of you know him as a pioneer in industry, a real estate developer of unequalled magnitude and a loyal supporter of economic growth in our state. I simply know him as Calhoun & Morgan's biggest client. Ladies and gentlemen, would you please help me welcome Mr. Warren Dunn?"

A hush fell over the room. It lasted longer than Ethan could stand.

"Warren, if you would, please join me at the microphone."

His name spread through the hall like wildfire. The Morgan lawyers began a round of timid applause that gained steam when one of the shareholders goosed them to a crescendo. Someone stood and others followed. For all the associates knew the deal had been in the works for months. They cheered like they'd been in on it from the beginning. Most of Calhoun's people joined in, unaware that the partners had no clue Morgan had been courting him.

Dunn made his way between the round tables to the podium. He grinned beside Morgan as his lawyer showed him off, grinned like he would wring his neck when the show was over.

"As we all know," the senior partner needled them, "Mr. Dunn's development company is one of the largest and most respected in the country. As I speak to you this afternoon he has projects underway in twenty-seven states, Canada, Mexico, South America, Great Britain, Australia, South Africa and a several more in Europe. He's been awarded a number of contracts by the state and the county, and has bid on the ambitious Lafayette Riverfront Project. Mr. Dunn has retained our firm to play an integral part in his real estate acquisitions and construction plans, contracting issues, and the inevitable, but we hope, minimal litigation that may flow from these activities."

More applause. *Yes, litigation unfortunate, but necessary.* The young guns whispered their best guesses on how big the retainer must have been for Morgan to parade him around like a number-one draft pick. They wondered if any of it would come their way. Everything else rolled downhill, why shouldn't the fees?

They shook hands as if a peace treaty were riding on it. A photographer told them to smile until he realized they already were. Morgan adjourned them and told the shareholders to reconvene in five minutes for the business portion of the meeting. Item one was more good news about Dunn. With him on board, they could throw out the latest numbers and rewrite history with Morgan this time as the protagonist.

Calhoun's old managing partner, Lawrence Bridwell, was the most visibly shaken, and one of the few who didn't stand during Dunn's 'perp walk.' There were others, stodgy members of the firm's high society wing who were just as indignant over the slighting, the impropriety of it all, grandstanding at the expense of every lawyer who owned a piece of the machine Morgan seemed to be flying solo.

"Did you know about this?" one of them whispered to Bridwell.

"Hardly," he replied.

"Outrageous," someone said.

"He's lost his mind," another echoed.

Where the hell was the 'heads up,' they demanded. Was Calhoun in on it? If he was, then he'd ambushed them right along with Morgan. If the answer was 'no,' then that meant Ethan didn't trust him either. He'd shown up every shareholder in the firm for a lifetime worth of payback in five minutes. They'd plotted their coup for months while he did what managing partners are supposed to do, pick the sweetest fruit from the tree so everyone can eat. They had a madman all right, a madman every associate in the firm would follow while the shareholders mumbled sour nothings to one another.

"Weston," Bridwell said, the fawning 'Guh-vah-nerr' decidedly missing as he was called. "I wonder if we might have a word."

CHAPTER 24

They were the world's best-dressed construction crew. The Calhoun lawyers sacrificed thousand dollar suits as they negotiated exposed wiring, fiberglass insulation, steel beams, sawdust, nails, and iron filings that covered the twenty-eighth floor of the Dunn Plaza. *See'n'em* was to have outgrown its two stories by now. Where they gathered should have been a finished conference room in the expansion. Instead, it was an idle work site immediately beneath the firm, the last place anyone would ever look for them. They were used to sitting, but the dust covered crates and boxes were off-putting. No one considered the floor.

Bridwell found a snake light and looped it around an I-beam. Someone plugged it in, and there was light. They stood in a circle as if someone had forgotten to start the campfire. One of them, Stanek, heard rustling near the place where the door might go. He put his fingers to his lips and went to check it out before they started. It was Clark, the brown-noser who'd talked Morgan's ear off at lunch. He'd seen which way the wind was blowing and transferred his situational loyalty to the Calhoun faction. He'd found a girly magazine one of the workers left behind and was seeing things he'd only heard about. He saw the shareholder coming and stuffed it in a folder he'd brought in case they wanted him to take notes. Hereafter it would be known as his *porno-folio.*

"Take a wrong turn, Dennis?" Stanek busted him.

"I…I was just—"

"What are you doing here?"

"I wanted to see what was going on. Maybe there'd be something I could do."

"Sorry, Dennis. This is just for the partners."

"I figured I could just…sure, I understand."

He turned and retraced his steps through the debris, leaving the scorned lawyers in peace.

"And Dennis," Stanek told him, "Don't tell anyone where we are. Understand?"

He dusted himself off and said that he did.

Calhoun passed the party crasher on his way out, and the partner welcomed him to the Star Chamber.

"Who was that?" the governor asked.

"Clark. He's an eager associate," Stanek said, as if that distinguished him from the others.

"Careless," Calhoun scolded. "Now the whole damned firm's gonna know where we are."

"I'll take care of him," he promised. "Clark will keep quiet, believe me."

They reached the others, and Calhoun said, "All right, I'm here. What do you want?"

"Sorry about the accommodations, Weston," Bridwell said. "But maybe it's appropriate that we all stand. We've been sitting on our backsides for too long in this merger, if I may be so bold."

"You may, Lawrence. But let's stick to what we know, shall we?"

"Fine," Bridwell continued. "What we know is that Ethan made an executive committee level decision without talking to anyone at the firm. I sure as hell didn't know he was soliciting Dunn." He pointed to the others, "John, Nathan, did you have any idea this was going to happen?"

The old lawyers shook their heads.

"Robert?" Bridwell continued. "Hollis?"

Neither had been informed.

"Unless he told you, Weston, then he went down this road alone."

Calhoun said nothing.

"Well," Bridwell pressed him.

"Watch your tone, Lawrence," one of the older men cautioned.

"My tone? You know, I'm getting a little tired of hearing about my tone? We don't have time for that crap. We need answers. We've got responsibilities to each other, to everyone in this firm. All I want to know is whether our leader has any idea what Morgan is doing. And I haven't heard his answer yet."

No one came to the governor's rescue this time. Something rattled in the ventilator shaft. It was the air conditioner kicking in on a floor no one used. Bridwell figured Morgan had signed off on that expense, too.

"No," Calhoun said simply. "Ethan didn't tell me about Dunn."

Suddenly the angry lawyer had no more questions.

"I know Ethan's always recruiting new clients," Calhoun said. "That's kind of his job, don't you think, Lawrence?" his voice grew louder. "But I hadn't discussed this one with him."

Bridwell held his tongue while he considered the matter. There was a loose cannon on deck and a semi-might-as-well-be-fulltime-retired politician sipping a fruity drink on the shore. Bridwell stood in the middle with the others who didn't have the luxury of either vantage point.

They heard more rattling and this time it wasn't wasted caused by cooled air. The shuffling grew louder. No one moved until they saw the man's face. It was Lovelace.

"Hi, fellas," Remy said. "I was getting lonely upstairs. With all the revelry above us I guess I'm the only one who realized half the firm's missing."

No one wanted to be the first to answer. Only a few of them were willing to make eye contact.

"You know," he said, "the last time I was in a place this gloomy my sadistic fraternity held some ritual sacrifice. So, what the hell guys? Anybody want to get something off his chest?"

They stared at the floor. Lovelace dealt with it the only way he knew how.

"Hey, there's the governor. Don't tell me you're Deep Throat," he laughed.

"No, Remy," Calhoun put a stop to it. "I'm not Deep Throat. I'm just a lawyer, like you. We're all just lawyers having a little chat about how we practice law together."

"Oh. Well, that's nice. I think it's great when we can get this many of us in one place and no hand grenades go off. I thought our earlier meeting went well," he joked. "Especially the part where the managing partner added a billionaire to our client list. The cheesecake was good, too, but I thought the billionaire thing was the real highlight. Of course, I suppose there may be some self-absorbed, shallow and pathetic a-holes who might feel like the founding member of the firm should have asked their permission to make us all rich. I don't know," he said. "So what were you guys talking about?"

Lovelace made them dizzy as he slung them around by their dusty lapels. They weren't through with the issue, but Calhoun knew they'd never get to it now. A junior associate had already busted them, and Lovelace had one to tell the boys about well into his retirement, how he shamed the governor and his partners caked in asbestos while they debated what to do about prosperity.

"You make a good point, Remy," Calhoun spun it. "Ethan's busier than anyone else in this place. He's brought in something quite lucrative, and we should all be thankful."

Bridwell nodded until Lovelace saw him. It sounded good to the others, too. Some even smiled like cruising the construction site was part of their mental health day. Lovelace grinned just to show he could do it as well as they could. He didn't buy a thing, but he was certainly delighted at how giddy they all seemed.

"After all," Calhoun ended the sideshow, "our biggest problem is how to divvy up the retainer."

****

There were two envelopes filled with political capital inside Soard's carry-on bag where the sack of peaches had been a few hours ago on his flight north. They were loaded with embarrassing soft-core memories for one man, immeasurable financial benefit for another. The action photos were grainy and out of focus, but it looked enough like a member of the city's planning board to get the man's attention when it came time to vote. He'd been caught in the act with a beachside bimbette, and it would be worth something to him for the package to stay sealed.

The other envelope was larger, twice as heavy, and Peaches hadn't told him a thing about what made it that way. *Just give it to Dunn, he said.* Come to think of it, the lobbyist hadn't told him to discuss anything with Morgan. Deal directly with Dunn, he warned him as he slurped a Minah special. He couldn't question a man who'd personally killed four pounds of quail for the President.

Soard bypassed the luggage carousel and found his car in the short-term lot. He drove one-handed toward the firm while he worked the phone checking his messages. Omar had called with some new information on his case. Soard had read some encouraging appellate court opinions on unreasonable searches and seizures during the plane ride and wondered if Omar's latest revelations would be necessary. He decided to swing by the courthouse to see if Pomerantz could do two things at once. He reminded himself that his criminal defense practice still paid the bills even if collecting blackmail chips for Dunn might be better than a parallel move.

Soard shot up the courthouse steps. He heard a buzzing sound and wondered if he were back on the shuttle flight. Giant box fans blew at top speed and all the windows were open. Inside he questioned a man at the metal detector. The guard told him the AC had conked out, but court was still in session.

Soard ducked inside to see for himself. Maximum Worthington's robe was unzipped, his tie loosened and he looked like a wet noodle with a migraine. He kept his eye on the jury, but it was the public defender who succumbed first. Kozlowski collapsed early on in the defense's case. He'd been too nervous to eat lunch, and had forgotten to administer his midday shot of insulin. There was a nurse's station in the public health building across the street. They'd checked his dog tags and did all they could for the diabetic. Someone was to call the judge in a few minutes with his prognosis.

Pomerantz zoned out at the state's table. He draped his jacket on the chair next to his and buried his face in his hands. He was still in recovery from Erica's tough love. He drank all the water at his desk and swiped Kozlowski's pitcher. He figured the defense attorney was flat on his back next door with a tube in his arm. He wasn't about to join him there. Soard tapped him on the shoulder.

"Go away," the D.A.'s muffled voice said. He lifted his head and saw the lawyer he was twenty years ago. "Ahh, Peter Soard. What do you want?"

"You're an animal. Are you waiting for it to get hot or what?"

"It's not me. Talk to the judge. He thinks this is mild. He keeps telling us about how it was when he practiced law in the low country. No air conditioning. He thinks I'm Atticus Finch."

"Where's Boo Radley?" Soard asked.

"Take your pick," he gestured to the gallery.

"So does the jury have the case already?"

"No. We're waiting for the medical report on the public defender."

"What?"

"Kozlowski fell out. His diabetes flared up. I wonder if Worthington's thought about the liability if he croaks. I suppose that's the city's problem."

"Isn't that you?"

Pomerantz thought it over. "Oh, yeah. I guess it is. Damn."

"Well, since you've got this recess, how 'bout we do some business?"

"Might as well," he said. "Let's go outside."

Pomerantz left word with the bailiff, and they stepped outside. The breeze felt good on his face. He leaned against the white marble and said, "Feels nice. Maybe he'll let us finish the trial out here."

"Don't count on it."

"Okay, Pete, what can I do for you?"

"Omar Sharif Jones."

It seemed like years since he'd read the name. "So you represent Dr. Zhivago?" Pomerantz laughed. "That's great."

"Careful. If you continue to invalidate his personhood like that I'll have to ask the court to order counseling for both of you."

"Invalidate his personhood?"

"Sure. Name-calling can cut a guy. Deep. Emotional scarring is as painful as a physical injury, you know?"

"Is that right? I always wondered what they taught you guys in the defense bar. So what do you want to do with the case?"

"I want you to dismiss the charges. Didn't you get my letter?"

"You're kidding, right?"

"Only some. But your undercover man blew the arrest."

"Oh, yeah? Just how did he do that?"

"There was no probable cause. My client was seen walking away from another man in an alley. That's not grounds to stop him."

"Yeah, but it wasn't just any alley. It was downtown in drug pan alley. The corner of Crack and Whore, wasn't it?"

"Uh…that would be Fifth and Rose," Pete said.

"Same difference. That's as bad a part of town as there is. The sheriff won't even put a substation there."

"Uh-huh. And what were the specific, objective facts that lead him to believe my client was involved in criminal activity?"

"Oh, God. 'Specific, objective facts?' That sounds like it's straight from an opinion. What case is that?"

"The language comes from *Brown vs. Texas.* Supreme Court decision. Nineteen seventy-nine," he told him. "*U.S.* Supreme Court."

"I've heard of it."

"You've got to have more than just one person walking away from another to make a stop, even in a high drug traffic part of town."

"So what are you telling me? You want the whole thing dropped?"

"I'm at least obligated to file the motion to suppress. And without the drugs, my guy's confession won't do you any good, even if it came in as evidence. It won't do you any good because there's no corroboration without the alleged little plastic baggie."

Pomerantz smiled at him. Soard had read the state's file.

"I heard they found one near my client," Pete confirmed. "Let's face it, the department profiled my guy. Even if he fits it, that's not the proper way to do things."

"A judge might see it that way, that's true. But Worthington's gonna be here three more months. And last time I checked he wasn't scoring too high on the ACLU composite, you know what I mean?"

"He's an iron ass," Soard agreed. "I'll give you that. But he's just as hard on cops who don't catch bad guys the right way."

"Smoke and mirrors," Pomerantz lamented. "You're good, Pete, I've got to hand it to you."

"Smoke and mirrors? Try Fourth Amendment and Supreme Court precedent. I know the folks around here have never had much regard for federal law, but this judge isn't in the business of getting reversed. If he lets the evidence in it'll be plain error. Besides, my client didn't sell anything. Somebody else did that, and now he's on the lam. That's who you really should be after."

"All right, all right. I'll admit the case has some fleas. And I really don't have time right now to draft a response to the phone book of a motion I know you've already got on your computer. But if I recall, your guy has some serious priors on his sheet. One more and he's mine for life."

"Why do you think I've got the phone book motion?"

"Uh-huh."

"So what do you say?" Pete asked.

Look, the best I can offer you is to knock it down to…God, I can't believe I'm doing this…simple possession."

"Simple possession. Less than one ounce? That's the felony-B one, right?"

"Yeah, counselor. That's felony-B. I suppose you want probation, too."

"I'd appreciate your making that recommendation. My client has two young children. One of them is paralyzed, cute little boy who got hit by a stray bullet while he was asleep."

"Jesus."

"He moved drugs to pay for an operation that might help him walk again," Soard told him. "Off the record."

"Is he married?"

"Yeah. I don't know her, but he does have a wife."

"Does she work?" Pomerantz asked.

"No. She's at home with the children. He's the meal ticket."

"And—" he raised his finger.

"And we've already talked about him going on a diet. Don't worry."

An ambulance rolled up, and Kozlowski walked out under his own power.

"Damn," Pomerantz said. "I mean I'm glad he's all right, but I thought we were through for the day."

"Yeah. Looks like you could use an easy one."

"I don't know. I still don't like it. Jones is a three-time loser. When's he gonna turn it around. I don't see a lot of rehabilitative potential."

"Let me put it this way," Soard said. "This is the last time I'm representing Dr. Zhivago. He knows he's close to going away forever. And after Worthington gets through with him, I'm sure he won't want to go near his side of the campus ever again. Sometimes one of his butt-chewings is the best thing that can happen to a defendant."

Pomerantz wiped his forehead with a sticky paper towel. "I can't believe I'm even considering it."

"Come on. Give the kid a break."

"Can you get him ready to go first thing in the morning?"

"Tomorrow?"

"Why not? Are you holding out for a better deal? 'Cause you can forget about that."

"You'll support probation? Give him all the community hours you want, but you'll support probation, right?"

"Ah, what the hell? If somebody shot my kid I might sell drugs so he could walk again, too," Pomerantz said. "All right. You've got a deal."

"Okay. We walk him in tomorrow morning."

They shook hands on it. "You know," Pomerantz said, "I'm glad to see somebody in your firm still practices law."

Soard rubbed his neck from the bumpy flight. "What do you mean?"

"You're still at Calhoun and Morgan, aren't ya'?"

"Yeah. As far as I know. Have you heard something?" Soard joked.

"So how do you like it?"

"Compared to what?" he asked. "Yeah. It's not bad. I can't say I want to stay at the bottom of the letterhead forever. I'm getting tired of looking up."

"Your boss is quite successful. A little unorthodox, but effective just the same."

"What do you mean?"

"Well, take this case, for example. Remington Lovelace would've just pleaded the guy out. Or better yet, maybe my evidence would disappear right before trial. Or the arresting officer suddenly moves half way across country with no forwarding address."

"Huh?"

"Sure. It's been a while, but those things used to happen all the time. Probably before you got here. Oh, yeah. Ask anybody. Your boss is one lucky guy. Things just always seem to go his way. I'd like to tag along with him next time he goes to Vegas. I could retire early."

"I haven't seen that side of him," Soard lied.

"Don't keep your head buried in the sand forever, Pete," Pomerantz gritted his teeth. "Anyway, it's nice to see a young lawyer who gets his client off with legal theories, instead of old ones who create legal mysteries."

"I'll take that as a compliment."

"For part of your firm, anyway."

Soard held his tongue. Lovelace was a scoundrel, but dammit, he was *his* scoundrel. Pomerantz had no business running him down that way, even if he had given his client the deal of a lifetime.

The D.A. said, "Forget it, Pete. I've sparred with him for years. He's gotten his licks in, and maybe I'm a little more bruised than he is."

"Consider it forgotten."

The bailiff waddled to the door and mouthed something through the glass. Pomerantz gave him a thumbs-up. The public defender was alive and ready to try the rest of his case.

"I'll see you and the good doctor in the morning, Pete," he said. "Can't wait to see what little Jones-y has on this time. You sure know how to clean 'em up."

CHAPTER 25

Piper made it to the canteen before the kitchen help at City Hall knocked off for the day. He set a Dr. Pepper on the counter and went back for something to munch on while he considered suing Michael Pomerantz for abandonment. He found a package of cheese crackers with a freshness date he could live with and settled up with the checkout girl.

His office manager, Linda Jaffe, spotted him and came over.

"Hey, Sean," she said.

"Hello, Linda."

"Mind if I join you?"

He slid out a chair for her.

"I haven't seen you around much the past few days."

"I know," he said. "I don't like to be gone when Mr. Pomerantz is in court, but I'm getting a lot of heat on this riverfront thing."

"I'm sure," she said. "Oh, by the way, he called this afternoon and said his trial is spilling over to tomorrow. He wants you to sit in on the planning board meeting in the morning."

Piper chuckled. "There's a shock. I saw that one coming last week when he told me about the murder case."

"Maybe it won't be that bad," Linda said. "I saw the agenda and it looks like a few cases have already fallen out. The major item I saw was the Oakdale rezoning."

"Oh, swell. More condemnations."

"I don't know. There's some Indian group listed as the applicant. Maybe it's not the same issue."

"Indians?" Piper was too tired to think. He'd planned on a backpack run after work, but his heart and legs weren't in it. "Then I guess I don't know what that is."

"Sure you do. It's Chief Warren Dunn and all the honorary members of the Saucostee Tribe."

"What are you talking about, Linda?"

"It's not enough that he's stacked the planning board. He had to hide behind a group of Native Americans rather than come forward with his plans."

"Stacked the board?"

"Of course. He's got a least one member of city council in his hip pocket. Council appoints the board members. You do the math."

"Are you serious?"

"Does this look like my happy face?" she asked. "I do have one, just so you know. But this isn't it."

"I wish you hadn't said that. I'm afraid to ask, but who is it from the council that he has in his hip pocket?"

Linda frowned at him with her unhappy face of a thousand dimples.

"Who do you think?" she asked. "Who loves to hear her own voice more than life itself? Who makes council meetings run two hours over just so she can say whatever's on her mind at the time? Who bases her beliefs on what the last constituent she spoke to wants?"

"I'm not much at handicapping politicians these days."

"I'll give you a hint. There are only two women on city council, and the other one is so quiet sometimes the clerk forgets to record her vote."

"You mean Trish McDaniel?" he asked.

"Bingo! Of course I mean Trish."

"Well, when you say he has her in his hip pocket, what do you mean? Are you talking about politically, philosophically, ideologically?"

"No, Sean. I'm talking about monetarily. He contributed more to her campaign last year than every other donor combined."

"I didn't think you could do that. Aren't there limits on how much you can give."

"Of course. But Warren Dunn's got enough shell corporations to start his own beach. He funnels money through straw men. It's not hard if you know how."

"That explains some things."

"Just be careful around her, Sean. You may want to come back to this town when you get done with the Marines."

It was the best laugh Piper'd had in a long time. "Come back to this? Yeah, Linda. I might do that. I might want to do that if I can't catch on as a crash test dummy."

****

The Saucostee tribal chambers looked like any other governing body's meeting room, complete with shiny, high-backed imitation leather chairs where the elders sat, a podium for witnesses to give their testimony, modern video equipment for high-speed presentations, a recording device in case the real time transcription backed up, an official flag and seal, everything one associates with sovereignty.

The session had gone smoothly tonight. Chief Navarro, the tribe's titular leader, awarded proclamations honoring recent Saucostee achievements. A group of school children had placed well in a national science competition. One of their members worked as a policeman in town. He'd broken up a carjacking and taken a round in the shoulder for his trouble. On disability now, his award confirmed he'd be back on the beat as soon as he could pull his weapon again.

Following the presentations the chief took a report from their budget director. The coffers had been depleted by the lawsuits they lost to the state, or broke even with at best. They'd need a major influx of cash to keep from defaulting on their loans. Navarro asked him to come back next month with a sharper pencil. He liked the man's company but told him that short visits make good business.

The chief adjourned the meeting and worked the crowd from the dais. He asked Crazy Bear Walker to stay for a moment, and invited two others to join them. Crazy Bear felt the hair on the back of his neck stand as Navarro closed in on him. Someone had tipped him off about his meeting with Ethan Morgan, someone from the tribe with an agenda, and that narrowed it down to about two hundred people.

Navarro waited until they were alone.

"I wanted to tell you gentlemen that a disturbing development has been brought to my attention," he said. "As you'll recall, I was approached by a lawyer from Bristol not long ago concerning a proposed use for the land we lost to the state. It sounded a little too good to be true. The lawyer's client was a man named Warren Dunn. I think you all know how I feel about him. He's the reason we have two thousand fewer acres than we used to. Now he wants to let us use what he spent millions to take from us. I have my suspicions."

"As do I," Councilman Agra said. "Like the chief, I have my doubts about this man. He's a snake."

"I know you feel that way," Navarro told him, "but I disclosed this offer to you all so we could conduct our business in the open as much as possible. Now I understand this same lawyer is attempting to circumvent our normal process by approaching individual members of our council with the same proposal."

Agra and the other man sat still and listened. Crazy Bear ran a marathon in place.

"What is it, Thomas?" the chief asked. "You seem a little jumpy all of a sudden."

"I wasn't sure when I first heard of this, but I guess it's the same man who contacted you. Someone has asked me about Dunn as well. His name is Morgan. Is he the lawyer you mean?"

"Yes, Thomas. I believe I told everyone that when it happened."

"I must have forgotten. I don't know anything about lawyers."

"And what did he want with you?" the chief said, rubbing the smooth ends of his gavel.

"He said Dunn's formed a group called the Saucostee Preservation Coalition."

"They're using our name?" Agra asked.

"I guess. Morgan told me they're a group of environmentalists who want to keep down development along the river. They want us to join them. We'd have a long-term lease. Morgan said they were a non-profit corporation."

"Non-profit?" the other elder said. "We've heard that before."

"And did they say what our end would cost?" Navarro asked.

"Nothing, except out support. We get to use the land like before, but we won't own it. We'd work it like we used to, hunting, fishing, whatever we wanted. School kids could travel there to see how we used to live. You know, it would be an environmental preserve for Saucostee Nation."

"Who's in this coalition?"

"They have a seven member board. I checked them out. Two are professors at the College of Bristol. One's in history and the other's an anthropologist. Two others work for an environmental consulting firm, Earth In Action—"

"Inaction?" Agra said.

"No. *In action.* Two words."

"Oh."

"Another man works at a bank. I don't think that's why he's involved. The rest I don't know about."

"Except for Dunn, right?" Navarro said.

"I don't know that he's on the board."

The chief kept his cool. There was a headdress in the chair next to him. He wore it for ceremonies only these days. He considered sliding it on his head and telling Crazy Bear to stand down.

"You no doubt told this man, Morgan, that he was wasting his time talking with you, right?"

"I didn't say anything. I listened."

"When did you speak with him?"

"One day last week."

"And why are we just now hearing about it?" Navarro asked.

"We didn't meet until tonight. I didn't want to bother you all with it. It's just an offer. We get those all the time."

"You met with Dunn?" Agra asked.

"No. Just his lawyer."

"Where?"

"At his office in Bristol."

"I see. So you met Warren Dunn's lawyer in Bristol last week to discuss a matter that would affect the entire tribe, and you didn't think we'd be interested in that?"

"Well—"

"Yes, Thomas. That's quite enough," Navarro scolded him. "Gentlemen, it seems to me that we need to make a decision about this matter, whether to take it to the whole council or dispose of it before our next meeting. I'm not scheduling a special session to deal with this."

"Mr. Morgan did say there was a time factor," Crazy Bear cautioned. "He said the coalition's board is meeting soon, and that if we're not interested in joining them, they will most likely vote to disband. That would leave the land open for whatever the developer wants."

"Wait a minute," Agra said. "I thought the city owned everything beyond our property line."

"It did. But Morgan says they've agreed to sell most of it to Dunn."

The revelation caught Navarro by surprise. An old enemy had beaten him again, and one of his own had betrayed him.

"This man caused all the problems that led to the lawsuits," Navarro said. "Now I see it. It was Dunn behind the city's actions. He was the one all along—"

"Hold on," Crazy Bear did his best to calm him. "We filed the quiet title action. Remember?"

"So you're making his case now, huh, Thomas? Very well." Navarro stood. "This is not a dictatorship. You may do as you wish. As for me, I will not support anything that links us with Dunn. I'll go back to court before that happens. Now, if you'll excuse me, I promised my granddaughter I'd tell her a story before she went to sleep. I'm sure she's picked out a fairy tale. One more believable than this."

The elders stayed put after Navarro was gone. Crazy Bear expected the tongue lashing to continue, but they sat in silence instead. They respected the chief, but didn't always share his views on where to take the tribe.

"Without the chief's vote, I can't see the council passing a resolution for us to go along with this offer," Agra said.

In Crazy Bear's follow-up conversations with Morgan, the ones the chief didn't know about, the lawyer had explained how it could work. "This is not an economic development issue," Crazy Bear paraphrased Morgan. "It's a non-profit. Our by-laws allow for three head men to take an action that binds the tribe. If it doesn't impact on our finances, the council is not required to act. We can agree by affirmation."

"Go behind his back, Thomas?" Agra asked. "Is that what you propose we do?"

"What's behind his back? You just heard him. He told us to vote as we feel. It's up to us to act."

They knew he was right. Their by-laws did allow it. But it would hurt their leader badly, and he'd earned better than that.

"I'm still not sure," the other man said.

"In the long run the chief will see that this is the best way," Crazy Bear promised.

Agra said, "I don't know either."

"Well, make up your mind. I have to tell Morgan something right away."

"All right. We'll meet back here tomorrow night and decide.

It must be unanimous, right?" Agra asked.

"Yes," Crazy Bear said. If we do it this way, all three of us must agree."

"Should we tell the chief we'd like to discuss this again?" the other elder asked.

Crazy Bear shook his head. "Did he look like he wanted to be asked?"

"No, Thomas. I guess he didn't at that," Agra said.

"Tomorrow night then. I'll let Morgan know our decision after we meet. Remember, if we don't join with Dunn, our land is gone forever."

Agra reached over to the chief's place. He picked up the gavel and tapped it lightly on the convoluted budget report the tribe's financial officer had laid at their feet. From what he'd heard they needed something exciting to happen soon. He knew no matter how things worked out Dunn would prosper. There was a fortune to be made in the non-profit business. Maybe they could get in on it for once.

"So you said, Thomas. So you said."

****

Soard dialed Omar's cell phone. There was no answer, but Jones called back right away after he confirmed his lawyer's number. He understood he'd have to plead to something. Soard gave him a range of punishment he could live with, anything from community service to a few months behind bars, if he behaved himself. With the D.A.'s recommendation, even Maximum Worthington might go along with probation. He would read him the riot act from the bench no matter what, but at least Omar might get to tuck his kids in to bed again before they stopped being kids.

Soard drove upstream against the rush hour traffic to Calhoun and Morgan. The firm had shut down for the day, which meant the real work was just beginning. Caroline was gone, but her boss's door was open like it used to be before he started to circle the wagons. It was high times again with Dunn headlining the bookkeeper's list.

He stuck his head in, but Ethan was missing. He found a pad and scribbled, 'Sorry I missed you,' on it. Below that he simply wrote, 'From today's meeting.' Pete stuck the note to the package and left it on his desk. If the old man wanted to talk about it, he knew where to find him. He'd be at home reading the giant book of baby names to Mrs. Soard, on time while it was still daylight outside. And there wasn't a thing *See'n 'em* could do about it.

CHAPTER 26

Lovelace set his cell phone down long enough to give the waitress their drink orders. It was humid on the deck at Mercado's Seafood Company, like a storm was blowing in, but he figured they'd get served faster outside this time of day in the warehouse district. So what if his date's hair went flat?

"Put that thing down," the natural blonde told him.

"Sorry, Camille. I've got an antsy client. This won't take a minute."

His girlfriend could hear Bubba Hawkins booming all the way from his mobile home lot.

"Yeah, Bubba," Lovelace assured him. "I got the fax. Now, is this the entire punch list?"

"Hell yes it is," Hawkins snapped. "It cost me ten grand to fix everything on it."

"It's money well spent. If you're sure this is all they want."

"I don't know what else there could be. I ain't putting a gold-plated toilet in that trailer." They were manufactured homes when he tried to sell them.

"Okay, Bubba. I'll get an order together and tell the commissioner we've resolved the case. Do you think you can get them to sign it?"

"Me?"

"Yes. I would, but I don't want to raise this to a level they're not comfortable with. If they see a lawyer coming, they may want to think it over first. We don't need that at this point, do we?"

"No. I just thought you'd handle that for me."

"I can. But like I say, why stir the pot now? There's no better time to approach them than right after you've given them everything they've asked for."

"All right. I'll see if they'll sign."

A droopy kid with pageboy bangs and a baggy t-shirt came by with two glasses of water and a basket of hushpuppies. Lovelace tried buttering them one-handed.

"Good man. I'll draft the order first thing tomorrow."

"I tell you what, Remy. I'm gonna be in the building in the morning. I'm having lunch with my business partner. I'll stop by after that."

"Lunch with your business partner? So it's no longer a secret, then, about you and Dunn."

"Oh, we have a private room in his club. But I did hear that your law firm is finally willing to claim him."

"Yeah. Ethan Morgan made the announcement to the firm the other day. I guess he's saving you for later," he kidded.

"I don't think Calhoun and Morgan is gonna hold a luncheon for me. I'm a little out of their class."

"Not at all, Bubba. I'm expecting big things from you. And don't forget me when you reach the top, okay?"

"Forget you? I don't think I'll ever forget you, Remy. You're the man who almost sent me to jail."

"Un-uh. I'm the guy who kept you out of jail. You know, when you throw a Hail Mary when you should be running up the middle…if the guy drops the pass everyone wants to fire the coach. If he catches it they offer to extend his contract. Knowing when to take that chance separates the two," he said. "When I drop the ball, Bubba, you let me know."

There was a long pause at the other end. Lovelace checked his phone and the signal was still strong. Before he could hang up he heard Bubba say, "I will. See you tomorrow, Remy."

The waitress set a slushy Daiquiri next to the girl and a whiskey sour in front of him. She asked if they were ready to order dinner. His date called out a special and Lovelace said, "Make it two."

"You're talking about football?" Camille made from his end of the conversation.

"What?"

"You said 'catches the ball.' If he catches the ball they keep the coach."

"Oh. I was trying to make a point with my client. He does better with analogies."

"Uh-huh." She covered her face with the menu.

"Want something else?" he asked. "I'll call for the waitress."

"Remy," she whispered. "Who's that guy sitting over there?"

"What guy?"

"There's a man at that table behind you. By the door."

Remy started to turn.

"Don't look. He'll see you."

"Hey, I don't have eyes in the back of my head. Do you want me to tell you if I know him or not?"

"Wait a second. He's still facing this way. He looks like that guy who kept watching us the other night at wherever we were."

"Where's that?"

"I don't know. Hudson's, I think. Somewhere by the river."

Lovelace sipped his drink. The bartender hadn't stirred up the sour flavoring, if he put any in at all. "All guys stare at you," he said as he brushed her hand. "That's what I did when I first saw you. You're delicious."

"Not me. He keeps looking at you," she said.

"I'm spoken for."

"Okay, he's gone now. See, he saw you turn your head and he took off. He didn't eat a bite of his food. Look."

"I don't know, sweetheart. Maybe he wasn't hungry. Who knows? The best thing at this restaurant is the bar. I bet that's where he went."

In the parking lot Luciano lit into his partner, "Dammit, Frank, if Lovelace saw you I'm gonna pinch your head off."

The agent's heart pounded from the rush of nearly getting made and his boss's exasperation at the careless way it happened.

"I don't know if he did or not," Taggart said. "The girl may have spotted me. Son of a bitch."

Luciano sped off before anyone could get their license plate. He checked the rearview mirror all the way down Pamlico Street until he was sure no one had followed. He pulled into an empty parking lot and put it in neutral.

"You did that on purpose," Luciano scolded him. "You want me to fold the investigation, don't you?"

"Take it easy, Nick. You're the one who said you're tired of watching Lovelace live it up. You want him as much as I do."

"All right, knock it off."

Luciano threw it in gear and headed back downtown.

"Where are we going?" Taggart asked.

"To see a loan shark."

"The financials? Now? They'll tip him off for sure."

"Yeah. I know," Nick said. "Give me the phone, Frank."

"Who are you calling?"

"Mason," Luciano said. Their insider had prayed for this day. "Maybe we do have enough after all."

****

Jenna Pomerantz confirmed the faces with a single nod at each picture. The private investigator had assembled quite a scrapbook since she'd seen her lawyer last.

"Yeah, that's Michael," she struggled to get the words out. "That's the Bristol District Attorney. And I suppose that's the little tramp you caught him with at his love nest."

"Actually, the house is rented in her name," the lawyer said. "Erica Lee."

"Figures. What is she, a stripper?"

"She has no job as far as we know. She attends college full time. Or at least she's enrolled as if she does."

Helen Grodecki slid a box of tissues to her client. "You're not the first, Jenna. Don't hold back. These walls are pretty thick."

Jenna Pomerantz let the tears flow in earnest. Mascara bled down her pallid cheeks. The crow's feet that bracketed her eyes grew as her face throbbed. Her nose was red and swollen, like she was a professional drunk, or she'd cried herself to sleep every night since she'd found out for sure—alone, no cuddle, no caress, and most important to her lawyer, no condoning.

"I don't know why I'm crying now," Jenna said. "This has been going on for so long."

"It's not easy."

The divorce attorney wondered how long her old acquaintance had been stepping out on her. She knew Michael Pomerantz years before Jenna met him, but not well enough to present a conflict of interest worth turning down the case. This was what she'd been rushed by Calhoun & Morgan to do, file and defend high-end divorces while making the firm 'look like America.' The Calhoun lawyers counted two women among their midst. Morgan had been slightly more open-minded, but none of them had made partner before the old boys ran them off, none except Helen. She insisted on the instant tenure as part of the deal or there was no deal at all. Grodecki joined along with Lovelace when Ethan was building his empire. Unlike Remy, however, none of the shareholders blackballed her. She might have found out about it and there'd have been fury unmatched.

"Most of my clients don't get so lucky, if that's what you call it. For a man to let himself be found out this easy...well, I'd like to say I have the best P.I. in the business, but Rodney is nothing special. You've got a slam dunk of a case with these," she put away the photos. "That's the upside. The downside is your husband has given you so much to work with."

"Yeah," Jenna whimpered. "It looks that way."

"This may not the best time to discuss this, but with the hours Rodney put in over the past few days and with the temporary hearing to prepare for, you've used up most of the money you deposited with the firm."

"What? It's time for more money?" Jenna thought she heard herself say.

"It would help move the case along."

It was a cruel irony that one so skilled at dissolving the bonds of matrimony was so attractive. Grodecki was five years older than her client, but looked fifteen years younger. Jenna's face was pruned up from considering her future, Helen's smooth and beautiful as she smiled confidently upon reflection of her own. Pomerantz would do a double-take when he got a look at her, twenty pounds lighter than when he flirted with Helen at the bar meeting last year. Jenna didn't know about that or maybe she'd have had the P.I. follow her, too.

"There's a strong chance the judge will order your husband to pay most of your fees." She took one more look at the gumshoe's latest round of photos. "A very strong chance."

"Uh-huh."

"But I'm afraid I'm going to have to ask you to add to your account before I gear up for the temporary hearing. That's one of the biggest expenses in the case."

"I understand. Michael's told me how it works before. I'll have to move some money from one place to another so he doesn't notice. Can you give me a day or two to do that?"

"Certainly. We're in control of this case. His hands aren't clean. He won't want to go anywhere near divorce court. We can file whenever you want."

Jenna reached across the table for one more peek at the investigator's file. She read his report. The dates and times went on for several pages. He referred to pictures after each one, exhibits he called them. Her husband seemed so much younger in them, probably because the girl beside him could have been his daughter. The smile was real. If this was what made him happy, so be it. She didn't feel the same emotion. It was time for him to pay for that.

"That won't be necessary, Helen," her voice came back strong. "I'll have the money tomorrow."

CHAPTER 27

A clerk from the zoning department scurried through the hallway juggling sign-up sheets and directing attendees to the city council chambers. She heard the chairman's gavel and went into hyper-speed.

"This meeting of the Bristol City Planning Board is now in session," he announced. "At this time I'd like to recognize the city attorney, Mr. Pomerantz, who has a brief introduction for you."

Someone nudged him and the chairman revised and extended his remarks. "I'm sorry. Mr. Pomerantz is not here today. Mr. Piper, will you please deliver the opening remarks?"

Sean was already at the podium. He turned the microphone around and said, "Good afternoon. I'm Sean Piper from the legal department. I'm going to explain the process used by the board and make a couple of corrections to today's agenda. If you'd like to speak to a case this afternoon, please make sure you're signed up on the witness list," he pointed to an empty chair as the staffer hustled to her seat. "Please see Miss Neary if you haven't already put your name down."

Sean reviewed the order of presentation, the types of evidence the board could consider, and the time limits for each speaker, encouraging them to elect a spokesperson, and of course the appeal avenue if they lost. He admonished those who might lose to please wait until they reached the hall to curse the board. They seemed agreeable enough for him to move forward.

Piper settled in with the rest of the staff, his work through unless the board wanted a legal opinion. The zoning director would run the show from here. The director briefed the cases and the city's position on each one. Ethan Morgan had someone make a call and the right person bumped Dunn's request to the middle of the agenda. No one made a fuss.

Trish McDaniel had listened as Piper told the folks how to act. She slipped out the back as the first case was announced. Sister Hattie followed her into the hallway where they could talk about the riverfront project in private. She'd given the councilwoman an earful about the gambling ordinance, but today she was interested in other business.

"Now I'm not saying that community doesn't need some help," Hattie said, "but the way ya'll did those people down there ain't right."

Trish held her ground. "Wait a second, I voted for the river development, but I didn't tell anybody to kick those people out of their homes. The city's supposed to pay those folks and help them find another place to live." She was right about half of it.

"Well, ain't nothing like that happening," Sister Hattie assured her. "I think you need to get up there and say something."

Trish strolled over to the agenda posted outside of the auditorium. "Which one is it, Hattie? This case here?" she pointed.

Hattie put on her reading glasses. "Residential to commercial zoning? Yes. That's it. I don't know who these people are, but this is the property I'm talking about."

"Saucostee Preservation Coalition?" McDaniel asked. "I've never heard of them either. All right, I'll talk to the board for you."

"Good. You think I've got time to run up to the mayor's office?" Hattie asked said. "I've got to see him on the gambling ordinance."

Trish cracked the door and the lights were still low. She heard an old lady discussing the negative effects of electrical power poles on migratory waterfowl. She was sure her child's hyperactivity was caused by them.

"Yeah, Hattie. This lady'll be up there a while."

****

Warren Dunn sat behind the wheel of the cheapest car in his motor pool. The engine was off and there was enough time on the meter to keep the attendant away for hours. The man next to him played incessantly on his phone.

"What the hell's that, Ethan?"

"Angry Birds," he said proudly. "My wife gave me this for my birthday. Got all kinds of games."

Something in the rearview mirror caught Dunn's eye, a TV news van that had slowed down at the corner and eased onto the sidewalk.

"Oh, hell. What are they doing here?"

Morgan put his phone away. "I don't know. The press comes to a lot of city meetings. Half the time they don't even get a story out of it. Probably just a beat reporter doing his job."

A perky media babe with a bright pantsuit and dark hair bounced out of the van. She wielded a microphone like she was in the middle of a sound check.

Morgan admired her from the passenger seat. "Doing *her* job," he corrected himself.

The van's driver unhooked something on the roof and a giant antenna rose high above the council chambers. Dunn wagged his finger at his lawyer.

"Your boy better not screw this up, Ethan. I'm telling you right now, if he loses I'm gonna hang him from the Channel Five news tower."

"Relax. Pete will handle it. Trust me. He's Lovelace's boy."

"Why isn't Remy handling it himself?" Dunn wondered.

Morgan shook his head. "Too much baggage. Remy would've killed the project for sure. But his protégé's perfect. No one knows him. He's got Lovelace's backing without his image trouble. It's a win-win."

"Protégé?"

"Remy personally recommended Soard to me. He's been in court more in the past six months than anybody else at the firm."

"Has he won anything?"

Omar Sharif Jones' payment was fresh on the senior partner's mind. "He's making me some money, yeah."

Morgan checked the time. "The first case should be about over. I'm gonna go see how the kid does."

Dunn cracked open the window. "Call me when you know something," he said.

Morgan held up his phone. "You're on my speed dial, Warren. First preset."

****

The zoning director briefed the next case and Soard eased toward the microphone.

"Good afternoon, ladies and gentlemen," Pete began. "My presentation won't be nearly as polished as some you'll see today. I don't have a slide show or a videotape. I'm not gonna knock your socks off with any fancy graphics. I'm here on a straightforward request for a zoning change. It's an important one, but it's simple. I represent an organization that is interested in preserving the cultural and historical significance of the Saucostee Indian Tribe. As an offshoot of that preservation, my client, the coalition, has entered into a business partnership to develop several acres along the Lafayette River. The area is now zoned residential. The coalition wants to establish a commercial node as set forth in your agenda packets that will include restaurants, shops, an inn and conference center, and related services. The city has condemned more land than it will need for its convention center, and has agreed to sell the excess to us provided we build a development suitable to the planning officials. The tax revenue generated by this development will be substantial. The numbers are set forth in your material. I won't go through them all, but I do believe that if it yields anywhere near the five-year projected figures it would be highly attractive for Bristol."

The two votes Dunn had bought were ready to approve it without further discussion. Piper watched their eyes to see if he could pick out the plants. He recognized Soard from his many trips to the courthouse to track down Pomerantz. He'd seen him with the D.A., settling cases in the bush leagues compared to Lovelace. Piper thought Soard did strictly criminal defense work. Maybe that was drying up for him and he was moving into something new. He seemed prepared enough for this matter.

Sean read the nameplates from where he stood. Nickels was on the far end, trying his best to blend into the wall. Soard couldn't look in his direction without thinking of the shapely bimbette he snuck to the beach with for some extramarital romp. He wondered who Dunn used to break the bad news to the nervous board member. Whoever it was, Nickels looked like he'd seen the light.

"Are there any questions for Mr. Soard?" the chairman asked. "Hearing none we'll move to the other witnesses."

Two Oakdale residents spoke in support of the economic revitalization the development promised, but asked the board to impose restrictions that would keep the coalition from clear cutting the land. They asked for assurances from the developer. Soard agreed to nothing but promised the Board he'd relay the concerns.

"Now," Nickels said, "I see that we have a request by Councilwoman McDaniel to speak to this issue."

Piper quickly made his way to the staff table. The zoning director nudged him. "What's the matter?" he whispered.

"Nothing, yet," Sean said softly. "It all depends on what she says. Council members can't testify before the board in their official capacity. They appoint the members. It's a direct conflict of interest." Piper thought about calling for an executive session to discuss the matter in private.

"On the other hand," he continued, "if she's testifying in her personal capacity, there's no problem. She's got a right to have her say if the issue directly affects her. So I can't tell her…ask her…to be quiet until she says something she shouldn't. I hate this job."

Trish McDaniel yanked the microphone from the stand like she was in a town hall meeting where every eye that wasn't on her should be put out with a red-hot poker.

"Good afternoon, members of the board," she said. "This development is in my district. I supported the city's convention center and the related construction originally referred to as the riverfront project. However, I think we've had a little spillover as things have gone along. What we have now is a private developer getting a free ride on the condemnation program with no city oversight. I don't believe that's right. We've got to study the plans, see what the developer submits in the way of an agreement, and run it through committee before we can bring it to council for consideration. In my opinion we're moving way too fast here. I'm not even sure the community knows what's happening. We've only heard from a few witnesses. It would help all concerned if we scheduled a neighborhood meeting so the citizens can know what's going on."

Nickels thanked her for her testimony and asked Soard to respond. Pete returned to the podium and said, "Well, I certainly could understand that concern in other cases. But with all due respect to Mrs. McDaniel, there is no community left to meet with—the city has acquired nearly all the properties, as I understand it. The residents had a chance to challenge the lawfulness of the development, but my understanding is that almost all of the homeowners have taken the city's offer of just compensation. So

I'm not sure what good it would do to hold a meeting at this point. This project has been advertised. It was in the paper for months. Each lot was posted according to law. There have been inspections, appraisals and site visits. The city has tendered offers and the homeowners have accepted them in virtually every case. How can anyone say they haven't been informed? Besides, I believe Mrs. McDaniel was arguing the other way during the council meetings where this was discussed. In fact, I think it was she who insisted that the developer be required to put in additional services to ensure the projected tax revenue."

McDaniel did a slow boil from her seat in the audience. Soard had her in the box and wasn't nearly through running her.

"I don't know what happened between those meetings and today that would have made her change sides. We've done everything the council has requested, including the specifics she personally demanded. I have copies of the minutes of those meetings if the chair feels it's necessary to enter them in the record."

Trish twitched as he delivered his rebuttal. The high and mighty young lawyer was right. She had supported the project, and the money it would bring to her district. There was a transcript where she'd said as much, and Soard was prepared to offer it for public consumption. It was true. There'd been no cries from the landowners as they took the city's bids. The crowd Sister Hattie thought had come to protest the riverfront project was instead there to fight the cell tower request. They were more interested in the old lady's kid who couldn't pay attention because they lived near a power pole than in what Trish McDaniel was railing against. She'd gone to bat for Sister Hattie. Now the church lady sat quietly somewhere beyond the bright lights that ringed the podium. Soard had made her look uninformed about the biggest economic development issue in the city and impeached her credibility as a witness at the same time. It was almost enough to impeach her credibility as a politician.

None of it added up to Piper. Peter Soard was either the bravest lawyer in the world, or the dumbest, or he'd won the lottery and this was his last case before moving to the Seychelles, or he had his nervous breakdown earlier than most members of the bar. Or there was another possibility, one Sean would never think of this early in his career. It was just what Trish had wanted.

The chairman offered her a chance for rebuttal but McDaniel quietly declined. She glared at Soard as he took his seat and made sure to avoid all eye contact with Sister Hattie.

Nickels closed the hearing. "There are no other witnesses. The chair will entertain a motion."

The two men Dunn had put on the board looked at one another to see whose turn it was. Neither wanted to claim it.

"Hearing none, the Chair will make a motion. I move that 'Case B, Riverfront Development by the Saucostee Preservation Coalition, Zoning Change from Residential to Commercial,' be approved.

Someone offered a timid 'second' and they all raised their hands.

"Mr. Soard, your request has been approved."

Pete returned to the microphone long enough to say 'thanks' and then he was gone. He'd been in practice long enough to know that once you've gotten exactly what you've asked for, it's time to get out of the room. He zoomed by McDaniel before she could give him both barrels. They'd need her more than ever to pass the gambling ordinance, but Soard had no clue about that. If he had, it wouldn't have made sense that Morgan told him to fillet her.

In the hallway the senior partner patted him on the back like he'd made the varsity. "Great work, Pete," Ethan said. "She hates you."

"Thanks," he said, more confused than ever.

Back in council chambers Piper breathed a sigh of relief at the thought that the worst was over. He excused himself as the next case was briefed and took the stairs to the top floor. Maybe someone from the sheriff's office would give him five minutes to discuss the Oakdale conspiracy and corruption within their government. He was surprised to see Pomerantz standing by the elevator, looking like a man with all the time in the world.

"Why the long face, Sean?" the D.A. asked.

"It goes with my upset stomach," Piper said. "I just came from the planning board. Trish McDaniel is fit to be tied."

"Why?"

"She just got pummeled by a hot shot attorney on the Oakdale rezoning."

"Uh-huh."

"You know, the condemnations you're always asking me about?"

"Right. Any permanent damage?"

"Nothing Trish can't fix. I'm sure she'll last longer than any lawyer who crosses her," Sean said. "What are you doing here? Is your trial over?"

"No. One of the jurors had a death in the family. Worthington slipped up and had a fleeting moment of compassion. He's giving her some time to sort things out before he puts the alternate on the panel. Since we're almost finished I don't think he wants to rock the boat too much," Pomerantz surmised. "So who was the lawyer?"

"The one who made McDaniel look like a fool? Guy's name is Peter Soard. I think he works for a big firm in town."

"Yeah. Calhoun and Morgan."

"You know him?"

"Sure. He's a defense attorney. Pretty good one, too. What's he doing at a planning meeting?"

"Other than embarrassing our elected officials, I couldn't say."

There was something else he was supposed to tell his boss, but Piper couldn't remember what it was. Anne had said it was important.

"That's some law firm," Piper said instead.

"What?"

"Calhoun & Morgan. They did our gambling ordinance, and now this guy, Soard, comes in here and kicks Trish's teeth in. They must think they're invincible."

Pomerantz had forgotten all about Harvey Bing. "That's right, they did do the ordinance, didn't they?"

Piper told him he had to return to the meeting before he was missed. Pomerantz knew the feeling. Halfway down the hall Sean thought of what Anne had told him.

"Mr. Pomerantz," he said. "I can still go to the beach, right? You remember I mentioned it to you last week? I'll just be gone for a few days."

Pomerantz couldn't think of any reason why not. The council meeting would be over by then. They'd have an answer on the gambling issue. Trish would be on to something else and Jake Amsler could take up banking again. There was light at the end of the election cycle, and it would burn brighter once their biggest issue was behind them.

"Okay, Sean," he nodded. "You've earned a few days off. Just give your leave slip to Linda. She'll take care of it."

Sean smiled at the thought of the peaceful ocean breeze, crashing boogie board waves and fried scallop sandwiches at Howard's Pub. He'd be in Ocracoke this time next week, and it'd be cool enough for two.

"Okie-Doke."

****

Morgan knocked on the car window. Dunn rolled it down far enough to see his lawyer's smiling eyes.

"I thought you were going to call," he said.

"I can if you want," Ethan hunched over the door. "But since I'm here I thought you'd like to know you got your zoning change."

Dunn held open the door and Morgan climbed inside. It sunk in and he could have sworn he saw what passed for a grin creep onto his client's face. He waited for Dunn to trash him for something anyway, but it never happened.

"That's good, Ethan. I don't want to think about what I might have done if…"

"If what?" Morgan shamed him.

"Nothing."

The celebration was short-lived. Unless the council passed Harvey Bing's gambling ordinance he'd be just another top bracket taxpayer with a few more acres he couldn't use.

"That's good news about the zoning, Ethan. But it won't help me much if I can't turn the hotel conference room into a casino. Your boy had an easy time with the board. I don't have the same pull on council. I need some help."

"I'm working on it."

"We're running out of time. You better talk to Trish. Or were you planning on having the kid do that, too?"

Morgan laughed. "It's probably a good idea you didn't sit in on the meeting. Pete chopped her up pretty good. I think he's the last person she'll want to see."

"All right," he said. "You then."

"I'd rather not," Ethan said. "My partners are mad enough that I kept you from them. If my name comes out of her mouth at the council meeting, I'm finished. God knows she'll say anything."

"Somebody's got to talk to her. It sure as hell can't be me."

"What about Bubba Hawkins?"

Dunn mulled it over. "Believe it or not, I did consider him."

"Why not? She responded well to him last time."

"Trish responds well to anyone who fills her war chest," Warren remembered. "I still can't believe I'm gonna buy her again."

"You don't have to buy her, Warren. You just need to rent her for the evening."

"It's the same."

"You think Bubba would do it?"

"Oh, he'll do it all right. He'll deliver the message, Ethan, but you'll have to tell him what to say."

"I figured that. Okay, Warren. Have him meet me tonight at D'Amici's. I'll be waiting for him in the bar around seven o'clock."

"He'll be there." Dunn started the car. Ethan took the hint.

"I'm very pleased with how you've handled things, Ethan. I know I'm probably not the most appreciative client you've ever had, but in case you're wondering, you've done all right so far."

"Why thank you very much, Warren," Morgan said, genuinely touched. "That means a lot coming from you."

"But I still need a partner," Dunn said. "And I can't pass for Saucostee."

CHAPTER 28

It was one of those rare, wonderful, why-I chose-this-life moments in the career of Michael Pomerantz. At the end of a complex murder trial where the victim and his killer were interchangeable, the alibi witness fell into the ultimate perjury trap just before he was fitted with concrete flippers. The D.A. put the man in a place so remote from where he needed to be to support the murderer's story that Superman couldn't have gotten back in time. He drew him in, lulled him into a false sense of security, slackened the noose with a few innocent sounding questions, cornered him, pigeon-holed him, and put him in a box so tight that when it was all over Maximum Worthington leaned across the bench and told Pomerantz to read the witness his rights.

During the recess the man confessed to every bad act he'd committed in his life and all the sins he hadn't. Kozlowski drifted in and out of consciousness as his client struggled to understand where it had all gone wrong. When they reconvened the D.A. had an announcement for the court. The professional liar had decided to become a witness for the prosecution in exchange for leniency when Pomerantz decided what to do about his seventeen counts of perjury.

Kozlowski pleaded for a recess. The judge reluctantly granted rather than create an issue on appeal. The public defender asked that his client's handcuffs be put on before he explained what had happened. The defendant's wrists turned red as he tried to break free long enough to get to the traitor sitting behind Pomerantz. His lawyer assured him he could impeach the turncoat so thoroughly that the jury would have to figure out whether he was lying then or now. The client amplified every one of his thoughts with all the expletives he knew and the various tenses of each.

Worthington asked him his pleasure. Kozlowski told him he'd been fired, but that if he understood the substance of his client's sentiments when parsed through the profanity, he was ready to talk with the state about its manslaughter deal. Pomerantz said his door was always open, but warned him not to trip over the crowd waiting to low-crawl through it.

Soard pitied his colleague's crash-and-burn defense. No time to corroborate the man's story, he figured. It's tough to find two people who can remember the nuances of the same lie. It took half the sheriff's department to escort Kozlowski's client from the courtroom. When the crowd thinned Soard found the D.A. and congratulated him.

"Nicely done, Mr. Pomerantz. You don't get many like that."

"Thanks, Pete. I knew that guy's story was an undiluted pile of crap, but I didn't think he'd step in it that much."

"So he's gonna plead to manslaughter?"

"Yeah. Looks that way. I wish he'd done it when I offered it to him last month. Damned guy shot my whole week. I guess as long as we get to the right place, that's all that matters"

"It's a good deal," Soard assured him. "The victim lost his life. This lowlife goes to jail for the rest of his. And you've got a big case off of your plate."

"Yeah. A good deal."

"It was a pleasure to see a cross like that. And I'm not just saying that so you'll take it easy on my client."

Omar sat straight as a rail on the front row.

"Right," the D.A. smiled. "I see you've got him all gussied up. He's got a helluva wardrobe, I'll give him that. Are those lapels or spinnakers?"

"Are you still willing to offer probation?" Soard asked.

"Yeah, Pete. Against my better judgment."

"Then he's ready to go. Let's find the judge."

Worthington took Omar's plea and assured himself the little man understood what he'd admitted. He answered every question in a full, confident voice, ending every sentence with 'sir.' When it came time for sentencing the judge seemed dismayed by the prosecution's lenient recommendation.

"Well, I can't say I understand it, Mr. Pomerantz, but if that's what the state believes is appropriate in this case, I'll grant it." He turned to Soard and said, "Counsel, I'd like to see you and your client for a moment please."

The D.A. joined them for the sidebar. Worthington unzipped his robe. He scooted toward them and continued in a low voice, "Listen, Mr. Jones. I want to tell you something. This is your third offense, and the second time you've been in here for the same crime. I don't like trends. Selling drugs is not the way to a meaningful retirement. And selling drugs to undercover cops suggests a profound lack of proficiency in your chosen profession. I was reviewing your rap sheet before I took your plea. You've got an illustrious history, son. You need to transition to another line of work. You're not competent in your field. Have you noticed how you keep getting caught? I don't know how much the man pays you to run for him, but whatever it is, I bet it's not worth going to jail for the rest of your life. Do you understand me?"

Omar shook his head that he did.

"Now, for some reason only God knows, the district attorney has agreed to accept this lesser included offense I just found you guilty of. And he went on to recommend probation, which in my opinion is reserved for people with rehabilitative potential. I'm not sure I see that in you."

"Your Honor I swear—"

"Now, if you don't turn yourself around, I'm convinced as sure as I'm sitting here that you'll end up living in a dumpster or standing on the street corner holding a cup. I'm going to grant the state's request that you be given probation. But I'm gonna order about ten thousand hours of community service so you won't even have time to deliver groceries. And if I ever see you in my courtroom again you better bring your toothbrush. I've got a whole wing at the state prison named after me. I'll see that you get a corner cell. Do you hear me, son?"

Omar's body quaked. Beads of sweat he couldn't have wiped away with sandpaper covered his forehead. He thought he'd answered him but he wasn't sure.

"Yes, sir," he repeated until every man in the room felt respected. "Yes, sir. I swear I won't be back. I swear it, Your Honor."

Soard patted him on the back. He gave him the number for his probation officer and said, "Call him today. Don't miss any appointments, all right?"

Omar would have gargled pepper spray if it meant he could step down from the judge's bench.

"Come on," Soard took his arm. "It's over." He tipped his cap to the D.A. and whisked him away before the judge reconsidered.

Pomerantz found himself alone in the well of the courtroom. Worthington looked down his nose at him, but he didn't care. It was the only expression the judge had ever given him. With his trial over and the walk-in guilty plea out of the way, Pomerantz' afternoon opened up like a magnificent flower. He was ready to surprise Erica. It was a good day for tennis and a chance to show her his college form. He'd always wanted to impress Phil the Club Pro. If he couldn't do it with his game, maybe he could with his playing partner. Erica wouldn't mind if he used her like that. It was what she was made for.

****

The waitress left the hungry men in peace, alone in the private room at D'Amici's except for a plate of stuffed mushrooms Soard could eat by himself until the next course arrived. Morgan was winded from his mad dash down Main Street after meeting with Dunn's bagman. Bubba Hawkins was quick on the uptake. Morgan convinced him that behind closed doors he and Trish McDaniel spoke the same language, even if neither could be seen with the other in the light of day. The lawyer said nothing he thought could come back to bite him. It was an entirely conceptual discussion, the kind where the mastermind says to his foot soldier something along the lines of, *'Wouldn't it be nice if she voted a certain way on a random issue like the gambling laws of the city…and wouldn't it be an equally happy event if you got civic minded around the time Trish's campaign fundraising drive needed a boost?'* Bubba agreed that such a coincidence would make the world a better place.

Morgan played with the light switch until they were dimmed the way he wanted. The view was almost as good as his client's penthouse vista one story above, although Dunn hadn't rigged a fireplace in this private dining room.

"You like what you see?" Ethan asked.

"I guess Mr. Dunn can afford it," Crazy Bear said.

"You'll be able to afford a view like this yourself soon."

"Uh-huh. Look, I don't have much time. I'm sure the food here's great but I have to get back home. Let's get this over with."

Soard passed him the hors d'oeuvres. "Try one of these. They're delicious."

"No thanks. I'm not hungry."

"All right, Mr. Walker. If you're feeling bad we won't keep you," Morgan said. "Pete, may I have the papers?"

Ethan had told Soard little about Thomas Walker. He was a forward-thinking member of the Saucostee Tribe, as Morgan spun it. Walker had managed to convince two other headmen to join their client's business venture by the Lafayette River, the property Soard had made considerably more valuable with his performance before the planning board. Beyond that, there was nothing more he should be concerned about—not Chief Navarro, nor the long-term lease Dunn tried to entice him with, and certainly not that the non-profit corporation's mission would radically change once Crazy Bear became a member.

Caroline had put the package together cleanly as always. There were tabs by each exhibit, and where they should sign. Morgan valued her efficiency, except for now. She'd even filled in the dates on everything, even the power of attorney her boss said could wait. Today's date.

"Damn," he whispered under his breath. It startled Soard, but he said nothing.

Crazy Bear hadn't noticed. He was too ashamed of himself to think clearly. He'd sold the chief out, in the name of something too good to be true, mind you, but whatever it meant to the tribe if Dunn kept his word paled in comparison to this act of disloyalty. There were four courses left in the dinner. He could walk away during any of them, but his legs didn't move.

"What?" Walker asked.

"Oh, nothing, Thomas. I just noticed something on these. I need to get another copy so you'll have one."

"Oh, I can do that afterwards," Soard blundered.

"No, no, Pete. Stay and eat. I'll take care of it."

Crazy Bear was beaten. "What now?" he asked.

"I'll be right back," Morgan promised. "You two enjoy your dinner."

Soard did his best to do just that. He wasn't detained by conversation. For someone about to enter a partnership with the easy money, Crazy Bear looked like he'd given everything to the blood bank.

"You sure you don't want to try one of these, Mr. Walker? They're quite tasty."

"No thanks."

Soard popped a mushroom and hummed a little tune. "I guess you must be excited about the hotel? I saw the plans. It looks awesome."

Walker stared at the lights far below. The days were growing shorter, but he could still see the reservation clearly enough in the distance.

"What hotel?"

Oh, God, Soard kicked himself. He doesn't know about the hotel. *How can he not know about that?*

"Oh, nothing."

"Nothing? You just said I must be excited about the hotel. What hotel are you talking about?"

"I don't know. I must have your project confused with another one. Mr. Dunn has so many."

"Uh-huh. That must be why he's becoming such a nature lover, if he keeps the land pristine like he says. I'll believe it when I see it."

Soard saw the sketches at the board meeting and there was nothing pristine about them. It was a change to commercial, or hadn't Morgan told Crazy Bear about that either?

"Right," Pete said. "If you'll excuse me, I've gotta run to the men's room. Four glasses of sweet tea is plenty. Am I right?"

Soard was gone before the man could answer. In the hall he saw Morgan fumbling with the clean copy he'd printed for Walker to sign.

"Everything all right?" Ethan asked.

"No. This guy doesn't even know about Dunn's hotel. He hasn't heard of the convention center. Nothing. He said he's looking forward to the land staying pristine."

"Oh?" Morgan was shaken by the associate's confrontational stance. He wondered what else they'd talked about while he was gone. "I see. How did that come up?"

Soard was just as shaken. "Very awkwardly," he said.

"Yes. Well, Pete, that's not really our concern. Our client has asked us to bring another party to this relationship. We don't represent Mr. Walker. If he has a problem with what we're asking him to sign he can consult a lawyer. There are a few of those in this town, you know?"

Soard didn't answer. Ethan feared he was losing him.

"I appreciate your sense of fairness, Pete. But Mr. Walker is a big boy. Don't let his demeanor fool you. He's all business. He drives a hard bargain. Dunn made a lot of concessions to bring him to the table," he lied.

"Really?"

"Sure. A lot happened before I brought you into the picture. There was no need for help until we got a framework we could flesh out. I didn't want to get the firm's hopes up before I knew we'd landed Dunn as a client. Without the Saucostees this project wouldn't work. That's why I waited until the firm luncheon to introduce him to everyone."

"I wasn't there for that, remember?"

"Oh, yeah. You were with Peaches. I forgot to tell you. I brought Dunn up to the podium with me. It was a big hit. Everybody's excited again, like right after the merger. Everything's fine."

Soard didn't understand any of it. He thought Dunn was still a secret, but apparently now even the mail clerk knew. Maybe he was legitimate after all. Maybe Morgan has lousy timing and he puts a wicked slant on things, but that's what lawyers do all the time. Even ones the bar honors while it tells its newest members about virtue.

Morgan held his antique wristwatch to his ear. "Still ticking," he said. "My, my, it's late. I tell you what, Pete, I'm about finished here. This fella's ready to go home and I don't think the club's too keen on doggy bags. I'm gonna leave as soon as he signs. Why don't you go now? I'm sure Laura's ready to see you."

Soard was surprised he remembered his wife's name without Caroline's cheat sheet."

"You're sure you don't need me?"

"Oh, no. You've done plenty for tonight." He wondered if Lovelace had made the right call after all. The young man was developing a bad case of Boy Scout. "But I would appreciate it if you'd stop by to see me in the morning."

"Okay. What time?"

"Whenever you have a minute. I'll be in all day. You did such a good job with the board, I'd like to talk to you about the council meeting next week. You keep it up and Lovelace is never getting you back."

CHAPTER 29

Trish McDaniel watched as her granddaughter tried to tame a vibrant plastic horse on the Tryon Mall carousel. The councilwoman wondered if the little girl was as dizzy as she was.

"Hold on!" she encouraged her.

A voice she recognized called to her from behind. She turned to see who belonged to it.

"Bubba Hawkins. What are you doing here?"

"I thought I might take a spin," Bubba said. "Looks like fun."

Trish waved to the little girl and her mother as they whizzed past again. "Yeah. Right, Bubba. Let's get on together. That elephant ought a hold us. You wanna ride on my lap?"

"Okay. Maybe I'm here about something else."

"Uh-huh. You always are, Bubba."

The music stopped and the kids scrambled to their parents for another handful of tokens. Trish's daughter collapsed on a bench. Three round trips were enough.

"Got a minute?" he asked. They'd done business before. This place would do, good and public, with lots of screaming kids and parents too blurry-eyed to notice the lobbyist and the politician he lobbied.

Trish smiled as her grandkid climbed aboard for another go.

"Sure, Bubba. You don't live in my district, but fortunately for you I consider everyone in the city to be in my district."

They took a seat in the food court. Bubba cruised the Japanese restaurant for free samples.

"What's on your mind?" Trish asked him.

"I was looking over my expenses for the year. Business and what not. And I noticed that I had a little extra money come in last month. I wasn't expecting it."

"That's a nice problem to have."

"Yeah, it is. So anyway, I decided it might be a good time for me to give back a little to the community. I've been blessed. I like to donate to different causes, especially if I know the money will go for what I want."

"You say that like you've been disappointed before."

"Maybe. Some contributions have worked out just fine. Other times…well, let's just say I miscalculated the intentions of the donee. So I got to thinkin' this might be a good time to exercise my right to free speech by contributing to some deserving local politicians. Know any?"

"My campaign office is on Pamlico Street. You can drop all you want off there."

"Oh, I know where it is. But before I go there I thought I'd share with you my concerns on an issue I've been following. It's important to the city."

"We're not outlawing mobile homes, Bubba. Don't worry."

"No. I'm not here as a representative of that industry. I wouldn't want to put you in that kind of a box."

"That's nice. What sort of box do you want to put me in?"

"Come on now, Trish. I'm serious about helping out with your campaign."

"Really? Are you going to carry a sign around for me? In Oakdale, maybe?"

Bubba twirled a piece of spicy chicken on a toothpick and licked his considerable chops. "I don't know about carrying a sign, ma'am, but I might be able to help pay for it. If I felt comfortable with your position on something."

"Fair enough. What's the issue?"

"Video poker."

It was all she needed to know he was here on behalf of someone with deeper pockets than his own. Bubba sold salvaged trailers to folks who taped episodes of *Cops* to see who'd made the big time from high school.

"You want to know my position on gambling?"

"Yes."

"Tell me yours first."

"I'm against it."

"Since when? You've got more machines than IBM."

"That's different. My games don't give payouts."

"Like hell," she said.

Bubba kept as straight a face as he could manage.

"All right, why don't you want to see jackpots legalized?" she asked.

"I think they'll hurt people, minorities especially. Folks in your district would suffer if the ban fails."

Even in the noisy food court Trish's laughter rang out. "That's great, Bubba. I had no idea you were so offended by the thought of folks in my district suffering."

"It's true."

"You know, it's interesting you say that. I've had a number of calls from folks who want the games legalized. They say it would give them hope. They know the only chance they have to make it out of Oakdale is if they hit the jackpot. They may not have much, but they can still dream."

"Sure they can," Bubba said. "But when they wake up they're nothing but losers and addicts. Only a handful will ever win enough to make it worthwhile. The rest pour their paychecks down the drain."

It was an argument she'd heard before, although he had no business making it if he wanted anyone to believe him. Her district was split down the middle. There were the government dependents who considered the games to be time passers in between handouts. The recreation would be just another entitlement. That's how the contract worked. They voted for her every few years, and she voted for them all the days in between elections. At the other extreme were Sister Hattie and the evangelicals, who saw no separation between church and state on this issue. They could be real inconvenient from a public relations standpoint. Trish wanted to punt on the issue but hadn't figured out how to without paying a price. Bubba had clouded her calculations, although he'd at least had the decency to do it under the pretenses of a bribe.

"To tell you the truth, Bubba, I haven't decided which way I'm gonna vote on the ordinance."

He believed that as much as she believed the games had led him to moral outrage.

"Yeah? Well, that's your prerogative. I was looking to part with my donation money pretty soon. It's kind of burning a hole in my pocket. Of course, I suppose one of the other campaigns could use it just as much."

"That's up to you," she called him on it.

"Okay. Suppose that ordinance was to come before the council next week—"

"What ordinance? I haven't seen anything yet."

"I'm talking about the one y'all got from Calhoun & Morgan."

"What?"

"I did some checking. I know y'all farmed that out to them."

"And you've seen it?" she asked.

"Yeah. Haven't you?"

"No, Bubba. I haven't."

"Oh. Well, I'm sure you've got a copy waiting for you at your office. Don't y'all get updates from the city attorney?"

"Go on."

"The ordinance outlaws all games of chance in Bristol. Now when that comes up for a vote, if you supported that, it'd pass easy, right?"

"If I supported it? Yeah, I guess so."

"Because Kitchings will vote the same way you do. She always does."

"Not necessarily."

"Come on, Trish. I pulled her voting record. It's the same as yours. She don't ever put her hand up until she sees where yours is."

"So?"

"And what's that other woman's name? Dot Randall? She's right in there with y'all, too."

"So you're saying if I go along with what you want, you're gonna get three votes for the price of one. Is that it?"

"Something like that."

"Uh-huh. But I'm not sure I'm going to support the ban."

"Okay, then. Would you consider not opposing it?"

"Don't oppose it?"

"Yes. There'll be enough votes to pass it if you don't put up a fight, because, like you said, that'll be three for one."

She buried the hook deeper into his mouth. "Then I suppose you'll have no problem making three times your normal campaign contribution."

"What? I can't do that. I can't do that even if I wanted to. You know the limits better than I do."

"You can get around those, Bubba. Don't sell yourself short."

"Three times?"

"That's the going rate for righteousness these days, Bubba. If you weren't so committed to your principles you'd get to keep more of that extra money you came into."

"Look. Between us, there's a reason I know why the ordinance came from Calhoun & Morgan. There's a lawyer from that firm who's going to brief it to y'all next week. I think you may know him. His name is Peter Soard."

It did nothing for her. "Never heard of him."

"Yes you have. He was the one who crossed you at the planning meeting the other day."

The whites of her eyes swallowed up her pupils. "Oh, no," she said. "Not that boy. Un-uh. I ain't listening to him again. Forget it, Bubba."

"Listen to me, now. He's gonna brief the ordinance. I just need for you not to oppose it. It has to pass in exactly the form it's in now. No amendments. Understand?"

"No way, Bubba. No one embarrasses me twice. Not without paying for it."

"Hell, Trish. I'm cutting you a check that'll pay your campaign expenses for the next three elections. I'd call that paying for it."

"No, Bubba. If I have to listen to that boy again…it's gonna cost you more than that. I want five times your usual contribution."

"Five times!"

"Listen, that smart ass ran me down in front of my constituents. He made me look bad before the board and the city staff. I have to work with those people. Forget it. It's five times or you can give your money to the Confederate States of America. I ain't putting up with no more of your bull crap."

"But—"

"Now if you'll excuse me, I have to pull my granddaughter off of Flipper."

CHAPTER 30

Jake Amsler swallowed a chalky handful of *Tums* like he was shelling peanuts at the ball game. The air was thick and none of it circulated in the crowded city council chambers. He'd seen it packed this full only once before, when they honored the women's tennis team from the College of Bristol. Most of the players were from Sweden, and you didn't need their passports to tell it. Someone from the mayor's office called for the fire marshal and he stepped up to the dais.

"It's tight, Mr. Amsler. But we should be all right. I'll cut the air on full blast and see if she holds."

"Don't push it too hard, Chief. If we lose the air conditioning we'll have to call the meeting off." The fireman smiled at him. "On second thought…"

The Chairman counted his colleagues to see who was missing. Trish McDaniel strolled in, not as late as usual, but fashionably enough so that she'd be noticed in time to draw whispers all the way to her chair. She made it eight of the nine members. Councilman Utley had been called away on a family emergency. He left word by proxy of his preferences for the agenda, but they were routine issues and for the real show he'd have no say.

Trish pressed a few palms and gave her respects to the dignitaries assembled at her end of the hall. Amsler recognized one of them, a clergyman who asked them to bow their heads for the invocation. It was a moving violation of the establishment clause of the U.S. Constitution, concluding with a chorus of "Amen" that left no one feeling any less American than before.

Amsler recited the Pledge of Allegiance and the audience punched it at the 'Under God' part, the way the drunks on the infield at Churchill Downs come alive for a line or two of *My Old Kentucky Home.* They outdid each other sticking pins in political correctness, and the right-thinking assembly was in session.

Several members exercised points of personal privilege to honor every non-basket case member in their districts for one achievement or another. Then Amsler called for unanimous consent and proudly declared it 'Tree Week' in Bristol. He asked everyone to do something special for his favorite tree, and other than prune it no one could think what that might be.

Next came citizens' input, an opportunity of unspecified duration where anyone could speak on any subject—he could read from a cookbook, favor them with a musical selection, compose a Haiku, anything but insult politicians, which was instantly gaveled off in contempt.

The first speaker claimed to own an elderly nursing facility. He wanted the city to reduce his property line setbacks so he could move his driveway closer to the main road. When his patients die off, he argued, it was important for motorists to notice the ambulances outside the home. He could pick up a lot of street trade if they only knew about the vacancies.

A woman made an impassioned plea for her husband's good name after he'd been wrongly convicted of sodomizing inattentive livestock. She said the negative publicity was hurting his business, and him personally, and felt the best way to remedy it was to ask for a pardon at the busiest public meeting of the year. Amsler thanked her for her testimony, but was sad to inform her that the city doesn't issue pardons. She might try the governor.

After the open forum a councilman moved to bump the main item to the top of the agenda. It was seconded and Amsler read the law's caption.

"An ordinance prohibiting games of chance in the City of Bristol," he said. "We have a number of folks signed up to speak to this issue. I understand the main brief in support of the ordinance will be given by an attorney…" he searched for the young man's name, "an attorney from the law firm of Calhoun and Morgan, Peter Soard. Would you come to the microphone, please, sir?"

Trish McDaniel straightened up at the mention of his name. She looked like she was in oral surgery and Novocain wasn't covered under the city's dental plan. This was the skinny punk who'd dismantled her testimony in the same room just a few days ago. He was the bastard with all of the answers and no respect. He was the man who'd cost Bubba Hawkins five times the going rate for her tolerance. The clock was ticking.

"Good evening, Mr. Chairman, members of council. As Mr. Amsler said, our law firm prepared the ordinance that's in your agenda packet. Now, as you can see from the language in this draft, the ordinance proscribes the playing of all games of chance in Bristol."

The Chairman held his breath as Soard pitched it. Sister Hattie was somewhere in the audience. His sense of self-preservation told him that. He stared at Pomerantz who sat beside the city manager. The D.A. was oblivious to it all but still floating after having unloaded a turkey of a homicide case and with the cleanest docket in years. Pomerantz finally saw him. Amsler nodded confidently that it would work out fine.

"With the exception of bingo," Soard continued, "and those couple other activities listed in the exemptions section."

"Yes," Amsler said in the direction of every churchgoer. "Expand upon that, would you please?"

Soard repeated the news until the law might as well have been named for the church bingo exception. Then he rested his case.

The politicians were stunned at the brevity of the presentation. The issue was critical to their survivability. It should be talked to death, or at least until they were hypnotized. They'd do it if he didn't, but that's not how they preferred it. The opposition found a voice in an unlikely source. Councilman Fred Burkholder, a staunch conservative who never met a tax he didn't cut, suddenly became enamored with the windfall they'd get if the games were legalized.

"I'm not convinced we should outlaw everything," Burkholder said. "We're losing millions of dollars to our neighboring states. They've got lotteries and we don't. And they've also got new schools, high-tech equipment, everything they need. Education is the most critical issue facing our state, and I believe the decisions we make today will dictate whether or not we go from second to last in education to rock bottom, or whether we can turn things around and be competitive with our neighbors. Our schools are in critical need of repair and upgrading. Our infrastructure crumbling thanks to years of neglect at the highest levels of our government. We've avoided the issue, failed to engage the state in the debate, and there's no communication with the school boards."

"That's fine," Amsler said, "but we're not voting on the lottery. That's the state's concern. Isn't that right, Mr. Pomerantz?"

Someone nudged the D.A. "Yes," he said reflexively. "Well stated, Mr. Chairman. That's my understanding all right. You're right about that." Then he added, "You got that right."

Burkholder wasn't sure. "But what about economic development in the city? Not all of that money has to go for the schools. They'll be enough left over for other things. What direction are we heading? I can't remember the last time we had a ribbon cutting around here, Mr. Chairman. And I'm not talking about for private business. I haven't seen anyone put up new construction for months, except for Warren Dunn."

"Thank you, Councilman Burkholder." Amsler peered down the dais to see who else wanted to weigh in. He was surprised to see Mr. Goodson's hand raised. He never spoke unless it was to make a motion to adjourn the meeting. Goodson was a farmer from the other side of the Lafayette River. He hated meetings, couldn't remember anyone's name, and didn't care for public policy. But someone had convinced him the council needed a healthy dose of common sense, so he agreed to take one for the team.

"Mr. Goodson?"

"Thank-ee, Jake," he said. "Now, as an abstract proposition, I don't have any problem with the folks in this state wantin' to throw away their money on slot machines and video poker. Because I think that's really what we're talking about here, let's just cut out the horse pucky. This lottery business is just so they can get a foot in the door. Everybody knows that the gambling industry has spread enough money around so we'll end up with a casino on every street 'fore it's done with. But as to the concrete proposition of a lottery, the whole debate is *dis-in-gen-yous.* If you want to have a lottery, just come out and say so. Why wrap it in a sacred issue like education? That tells you right there the folks proposing' it know there's something wrong. They're admittin' it'd never stand on its own merits. But tie it to education, and, boom, everybody wants a lottery. And then they stick a catchy name to it, like the 'Learning Lottery.' Give me a break. What are they gonna propose next, the 'Education Whore House?'"

The proper citizens broke the tension with a round of laughter that Amsler tried to gavel off, but nobody believed him.

"Or the 'Research and Development Three Card Monte?' he continued. "You know, what the heck is that?" They roared so loud some didn't hear him, so Goodson said it again. He was cooking with gas. Three more councilmen raised their hands to pile on the issue.

"Mr. Amsler," one of them pleaded. "I'd like to associate myself with Mr. Goodson's comments. I think his point is well made."

"Me, too," said another.

"Ditto," the third testified.

"So if you'll consider passing the ordinance…" Soard rode the momentum, "we can nip such things in the bud."

Morgan stood in the doorway, waiting for the magic words.

"As drafted," his lawyer implored them. "Pass it as drafted, without amendment. We feel that would give you the best opportunity to put a stop to all forms of gambling in Bristol."

It sounded good to most of them, but Burkholder still had his doubts. He called for an executive session to discuss a legal issue. Pomerantz hated those. He couldn't hide as easily in the smaller chamber. He scrambled at the staff table for a codebook. Sean Piper usually lent him his. The motion got a second and they headed for the cramped back room to hear the city attorney's best advice.

Amsler sat at the head of the table. "Okay, Fred, what's the problem?"

The staff had outdone itself tonight. The buffet had everything. Burkholder helped himself to a ladle full of mashed potatoes and a pile of chicken wings.

"I missed dinner," he said.

There was a cauldron of sweet tea. He spilled enough of it into a plastic cup to wash everything down.

A few others joined him. Some disappeared into the restrooms. Trish got on her phone because it had been a while since she'd done that.

"We've got a packed house and a long agenda, Fred. Let's keep it moving. Now what do you want to talk about?"

"All right. Who's this kid briefing us? Didn't he say he worked for Calhoun and Morgan?" Burkholder asked.

"Soard. Yes. He's one of their lawyers."

"I've never seen him before. Any idea why they didn't send over one of their government affairs people? Is he a registered lobbyist or something?"

"Pete?" the D.A. said. "I don't know."

"Maybe we should ask him."

"Why?" Goodson said. "He doesn't have to be registered to

appear before us."

"Well, I don't know about this," Burkholder griped. "I'd feel better if we had the full council here. Did Utley say where he was, Jake?"

"His father passed away Monday. He's at the funeral. I think it's in Michigan."

"Oh."

"We sent flowers," the city manager said. "On behalf of the council."

"I'm sorry about his father," Burkholder said, "but I still think on something as critical as this we need to have everyone."

"Fred's right," Trish put the phone down long enough to say. "Can't we wait 'til Utley gets back?"

"No. This is the public hearing," the manager said. "Third reading's tonight. If we postpone, there's not another meeting scheduled for three weeks. It's up to you, but if you defer, we may not be able to bring it back before the election. It'd have to be a special called meeting."

"Oh, hell no," Goodson said. "You wanna go through this twice? Did you see that mob out there? They want it done tonight."

"I'm afraid he's right, Fred," Amsler agreed. "Too many problems if we postpone. Besides, we have plenty of folks to vote. Right, Mike?"

"That's right," Pomerantz nodded. "You've got a quorum. You can take action."

Burkholder took his own poll. There were more chicken wings on his plate than votes on his side. He told the others dinner was satisfactory, even if the executive session hadn't been.

They reconvened and Amsler called the assembly to order. "We're back in session. If there's no more discussion, the Chair will entertain a motion."

They sat quietly waiting to see who'd flinch. Amsler prayed for it to end, to have Sister Hattie off his back until the next crusade. No one noticed that Trish McDaniel had stayed behind. Amsler heard her bellow into the phone through the thin wall of the executive session room. He'd have bet his interest in the savings and loan that she was talking to a dial tone. He was sure it sounded better than Sister Hattie enraged.

"I move to approve the gambling ban as drafted," Goodson

said. "If it'll do what this young man says it will."

Soard nodded to him from his seat on the front row.

"Second," someone said before Amsler could do anything about it. What was the difference, he figured. The votes were there. Besides, you never question a colleague's strategy when it comes time to vote. Trish had her reasons for abstaining, and it didn't cost him one way or the other.

"All those in favor please raise your hand."

The clerk called the names. There were five for the motion, two against. Councilwoman McDaniel was absent.

"Motion passes," she declared.

The crowd burst into loud applause that Amsler didn't even acknowledge with his gavel. Some raised homemade signs that read, 'Education Yes, Gambling No!'

Soard beat it to the hallway. Morgan was waiting for him. He gave the young man an awkward high five. They'd call Dunn from the car. Bubba would be sitting next to him. There'd be a victory toast in their client's penthouse within the hour. Morgan might even let Soard see it.

The chairman called for order. There was none. Burkholder excused himself for more wings and sweet tea.

Trish emerged from her inner sanctum. "What'd I miss?" she asked.

Linda Jaffe jumped from her seat behind Pomerantz. She whispered into his ear but it didn't take. She colored his codebook until the highlighter bled through to the index. The D.A. shooed her away as if she were a bloated horse fly. She was hot enough to call the fire marshal over.

Amsler slowly exhaled as the happy voters left his meeting. He'd take them through the rest of the agenda without incident. They had their city back.

After the meeting Pomerantz relaxed with a plate of leftovers and his own version of sweet tea, fully leaded. Someone had left an old sports section from the *Chronicle*. He read the box scores until he realized the games had been played a month ago. There were a few answers missing in the crossword puzzle. He found a pen in his codebook. It fell open to the page Linda had brightly colored.

"God," he said. "Give me strength." The D.A. laughed at what she worked herself up over, details, distinctions without differences. He inhaled cold chicken as he worked the puzzle.

"Linda," he chuckled. "Take a pill that chills."

What was she so upset about, he wondered. A passage she'd marked caught his eye. "Voting requirements," he read the code section aloud. "Two-thirds needed to pass an ordinance. Okay. What's the problem? There were seven members present and five voted for it. That's two-thirds. Get a grip."

He slowed down on the crossword. "Seven letter word for…begins with an…"

Pomerantz read the law one more time. Linda was obsessive, compulsive, neurotic, lonely and agitated by misaligned sock drawers. It didn't take much. But she was so insistent, and dammit, the old girl knew the code better than he did.

"Two-thirds to pass an ordinance." He read it again and again, and then it clicked. "Two-thirds…of the whole *council*." There was nothing about whether a member was present of not.

"Damn. The whole stinking council. That's six votes. Who voted against it? Burkholder and one other member. Everyone else was in favor. That should be six."

He did the math over and over. Utley was out of town and that left six votes for the ban.

"Son of a bitch," he proclaimed. "That sorry…She would be the type to…Just had to get on the phone right then. Just had to run her mouth one more time. Damn."

Pomerantz needed a five-letter word for sabotage. He'd found it.

"Trish."

****

Soard left Dunn's hundred-year old Scotch to the men who would understand why they were toasting him. Laura was the only one he wanted to share the moment with, and all the others he'd denied her, playing dumb for men who coveted that. Morgan understood. He had to extend the invitation after Soard's performance tonight. He was relieved when the young lawyer turned it down. There was enough conscience still in him to feel that emotion.

Dunn cringed as Bubba guzzled the expensive whiskey. What a waste, he thought. He would have been happy with ripple.

"So can we bring the machines in now?" Hawkins asked. "What's the deal?"

Dunn and Morgan looked at each other, both wondering who was going to tell the poor boy.

"Well? I mean I can read the ordinance, fellas. It says all games of chance. All games, Ethan. I mean, I'm dumb, but I'm not stupid. How does this help us?"

"That's right, Bubba," Dunn nodded. "All of those kind of games."

"So we're screwed, then."

"Ethan, would you please explain it to him?"

"I'd be delighted. Bubba, have you ever played video poker? Blackjack, perhaps?"

"Is he kidding me, Warren?"

"Well?"

"Sure I have."

"Um-hmm. And when you played, did you ever have to make a decision about whether to hit, or stand? Don't you have to do that?"

"Of course you do. That's how you play poker."

"And those are decisions every player would have to make. Is it fair to say that the better the decision, the greater chance you have of winning the game?"

"That's brilliant, Ethan. So what?"

"Well, don't you see? The players make those decisions. The machines don't control what they do. They're dealt a hand. There's no discretion in what they get. But from there they can choose any course of action they want. Hit in this game, stand in the next one, and so on."

"I'm not following you, counselor."

"The better adept you are at the game, the longer you get to play, and the more money you could win, if there were payouts."

He threw his hands up in disgust. "So you are telling me we can't have the machines. No payouts."

"On the contrary, Bubba. Bristol has outlawed all games of chance. Poker, as I have just illustrated, with all the careful decisions an experienced player must make during the course of each hand, is a game of *skill.* There's really very little chance to it.

In fact, when you get down to it, they're really all games of skill. So in answer to your question, you can bring in your machines."

Hawkins threw back Scotch like he had his own barrel. Fifty members of the Saucostee Nation would split the share he'd get when the casino doors opened. Dunn would even let him keep it for a while.

"Games of skill," Bubba yucked. "Damn, Warren, I love this guy."

CHAPTER 31

Linda Jaffe paced in front of the long windows outside Pomerantz' office, annoyed, ignored as always, waiting for her boss to say there was an empty townhouse that missed her, and *watch yourself in the garage.* She wondered if he thought she was still enticing enough to have that problem. Linda used to wear tight sweaters for their tightness. Now Linda bought sundresses by the yard, light colored ones with flowery patterns so they wouldn't be mistaken for choir robes. Three kids, a husband who vanished when things went from health to sickness, and twenty years of ghost writing great ideas for ungrateful politicians will do that to a girl.

Pomerantz wasn't in court. Linda called the clerk's office and the lady there said they'd had enough of him for a while. The judges were in chambers preparing for next week's docket, so the D.A. couldn't use that excuse to hide his absence.

Linda was still steamed over the farce last night. Council passed a law that was void on its face, and her boss let them do it. She needed a backup. Piper would have to pick this week to take his first vacation. He'd be helpful in shaming Pomerantz. It would be a real confrontation. You needed a heavy for that. Vain men listened to other vain men, or at least they seemed to pay attention to each other if for no other reason than to figure out why each was so proud. Piper wasn't conceited, but the men consumed by their own egos he dealt with wouldn't know the difference.

Linda was mad at herself that Pomerantz had made her this way. Babysitting the staff without her boss was old hat. But Piper'd been around to listen, which was ninety percent of what Linda needed anyway. Only this time there was substance to her outrage, a quantifiable screw-up only the man in charge could remedy. That took two things, his presence and his interest. Then he'd have to do something about it. Three things.

****

Bubba met the semi as it rolled into the parking lot of Hawkins' RV World. Texas plates. The machines were from the far side of the state. He'd smuggled them in the pre-fab homes' living rooms. It was like all the other runs the bootlegger had made over the last few months, nothing to hide, nothing to get nervous about at the weigh stations. The driver was tired and dusty. He'd eat well off his tip tonight.

Bubba signed the manifest himself. The trucker gave the signal and a group of immigrants piled out of the back of his rig. They paired up, every other man pushing a dolly.

"That's all ten?" Bubba held up as many fingers. The man nodded. "Good. Do you know where the next stop is?"

"Sí, señor."

He handed him a wad of twenties. "Take this. You and your men get something to eat when you're done. Skeeter will take you to the motel."

"Gracias, señor." The driver stuffed the cash in his pocket before the others noticed. "Vamanos!" he yelled. "Let's go. Adiós, señor."

Bubba waved as they drove off. His was the engine that fueled an underground economy. Soon, his smoke-filled dives would be packed with eager players instead of vacant but for a few burnouts. Skeeter would give tutorials. 'This is a jackpot,' he'd tell them. 'You get to keep it. No more plays for wins. The training wheels are off. You keep what you win. The rest belongs to the house. We have change for your dollar.'

It was a license to steal. A license which meant it was legal. There'd be protests from the local government, confusion in its legal department, the mandatory injunctions, and the hand-slapping court orders that vindicate the slime-ball operators while judges tell the city what the definition of 'is' is. Games of chance. Bubba was right. Morgan was brilliant. Just look at those hacking rednecks too stupid to buy home computers with every game package on the market. Nothing would suck up a paycheck faster. They couldn't snort it up their noses, or pour it down their throats, but in a couple hours they'd flush the family rent money down the slot without breaking a sweat. When their heads stopped spinning they'd stagger to their cars and think of what to say when they got home. By the time the politicians figure out how to regulate it, the addicts will have financed an upwardly mobile school system. The students would have enough sense to talk their parents into rehab. In God's country.

The sun warmed Bubba's puffy face, still powerful enough for that at sunset. A cheer went up behind him as the bar's regulars heard the good news. He watched the eighteen-wheeler disappear over the horizon. It was calm on the highway. The sun dipped behind a hilltop at the Saucostee reservation. He wondered what the newest members of the coalition were doing. They were the non-profits he'd fought so hard to join. They did such good work.

"Adiós, amigo."

****

The phone rang and Anne wondered who had their number at North Carolina's Outer Banks. It wasn't her mom, because she was on the couch beside her shelling boiled peanuts as she chaperoned. Sean told them the pizza man had read his mind. He answered and before he could say 'thin crust' Linda Jaffe had disparaged the D.A. three times.

"Hello to you, too," Piper said.

"I'm sorry to bother you, Sean, but I have to talk to someone. Your boss is out of control."

"Hmm. Well, thanks for calling, Linda."

"I'm serious."

"What is it now?" Sean covered the phone and told Anne to pack for the beach without him. He'd be there after peak tanning hours.

Linda told him about the council meeting, the gambling law debacle, who was absent and who didn't raise her hand at all. She read the code section to him long distance and made her case that the vote never happened at all.

"I don't know what to say, Linda. I didn't bring my codebook with me to Ocracoke. I'll have to take your word for it."

"But I'm right, though. Aren't I? You've got to have two-thirds of the entire council, not just of those members present."

"Why don't you ask Mr. Pomerantz?"

"I have."

"And?"

"Have you ever tried to talk to Michael when he's got his mind on something else?"

"Is it ever in another condition?" Sean asked.

"No. That's the problem. I'm in there rattling off the law verbatim and he says, 'Uh-huh. Um-hmm…right, Linda. Good job. Put it in a memo.'"

Piper knew that conversation. "I can't tell you how nice it is not being there."

Sean took the cordless to the screened-in porch. He watched a ferry sail past the lighthouse toward Cedar Island. He wanted to leave the phone on the wicker chair and go inside. Maybe the tree frogs would listen to his office manager.

"Michael just sat there like a potted plant when they announced that the ordinance had passed. I called him on it, but it was like I was talking to the wall. If you ask me I think he was a little embarrassed. I don't think he even spotted the issue. But he played it cool like he had. He said he'd talk to Mr. Amsler about it tomorrow, but he won't. Something else will come up and he'll forget. He always does."

"I don't know, Linda. If he said he'd talk to the chairman, I'm sure he will."

"Huh. He probably won't even remember we talked. I think he'd had a couple when I came by to see him. He had that coffee cup on his desk. You know, the one he tries to fool people into thinking there's coffee in it."

"I know the one."

"I think she finally did it," Linda said as if Sean knew what she was talking about.

"Oh?"

"His wife. I think she's trying to serve him with divorce papers."

"Really? How do you know that?"

"Well, for one thing I ran into the process server."

"Uh-huh. Linda, we work in the legal department. How do you know he wasn't serving a lawsuit on the city?"

"Because I talked with him. He said he needed to serve the papers on Michael personally. She's about to drop the big one on him. Thank God the guy missed him. Michael was a wreck when I left. I thought he was on the phone when I walked in, but it turns out the poor guy was talking to himself."

"I do that sometimes, Linda. When I start answering, then I'll know I have a problem."

"Yeah, well I think he was doing just that. I tried to get him focused but it was no use. He finally told me what I wanted to hear so I'd shut up and leave him alone."

At that moment Sean considered the D.A. to be the smartest man in the world.

"Look, I wouldn't worry about it if I were you, Linda. If he says he's going to talk to Jake Amsler, that's all he can do. There's only so far we can go to point out our clients' shortcomings. I'm sure he'll lay everything out and the council can make its own decision. They had to have been elected for something."

"Hmm. The council," she sighed. "I just wish you were here, Sean. Michael listens to you. He only patronizes me."

"Come on now. That's not true. He values your opinion."

"You're a good man, Sean. You're loyal, even to someone who doesn't rate it."

"Linda."

"I know, that was a mean thing to say. I'm tired. I'm frustrated. And you're on vacation," she remembered. "What am I thinking?"

"Forget it. Besides, I'll be home tomorrow. Now you just relax and unwind. You should take a vacation. It's great here. I thought about going for a run, but the ceiling fans and that feather bed are making a better case."

"Sounds wonderful. I'm sorry for bothering you, Sean. Have a safe trip home, and I promise I won't call you again."

Even from the Outer Banks he knew her fingers were crossed.

"Take care, Sean. And thanks for listening."

CHAPTER 32

Buck DeWeese muscled open the door and made for the elevator, mission accomplished, only one day late. Not bad as process servers go. Linda rounded the corner and stopped short of the human roadblock.

"I guess you must have found him," she said.

"Yes, ma'am," he nodded. "I always do."

Linda told DeWeese she didn't envy his job, but it seemed he did it well, and she was glad he looked like the kind of man who could take care of himself when the drop-offs weren't so civilized. Inside she found her boss' door closed. He never stayed long enough for it to be shut. She decided he needed his space and tiptoed to her office.

Pomerantz trembled. His stomach felt like it did when he introduced himself to the jury for the first time. He was still wet from the shower at Erica's and the cold sweat she gave him when she called in her marker. She threatened to chop him off at the knees if he didn't walk out on his wife for good. Too late. His wife had beaten him to it.

He reached into his desk drawer and came out with a bottle. It poured easily into a clean enough mug. He practiced his aim a couple more times before he could bring himself to look at what the tough process server had delivered. Jenna was running quite a tab. Private investigators can be a big help in pinpointing the truth, but they cost, and the expense can take away from the lawyer's share. Jenna's attorney knew her way around the domestic code. He recognized Calhoun & Morgan's letterhead from all those bills their bond counsel had sent to the city. They work both sides of the street, he thought. After all the business he'd thrown their way, the firm had no qualms about returning bad for good. Morgan should have sent out a big memo about that. 'Let's endeavor not to screw our client, shall we?' If he had, Jenna's lawyer hadn't gotten the message.

The D.A. felt his arteries constrict. He was convinced they'd open only with another belt. If one was good, two would be better. He felt lonely, but not alone. He heard something in the hall that confirmed it. He mumbled to himself. Lately, he'd found it easier to organize his thoughts if they came to him aloud. It felt like late afternoon, but Pomerantz wasn't sure. He wondered if Morgan still kept such hours. At that firm he'd better live in his office. It was the kind that got filled when it was empty too long.

Pomerantz had memorized Morgan's direct number.

"Hello," he answered.

"Ethan, this is Mike Pomerantz."

"Good afternoon, Mike. How are you, sir?"

"I've been better, Ethan. I've been a lot better."

"Oh. I'm sorry. Is there anything I can—"

"I didn't know Helen Grodecki worked for you."

Morgan figured no one brings up a divorce lawyer's name to talk about anything but which ring of hell she's going to occupy. Lots of folks get married. Over half of them get unmarried. Helen didn't need permission to take on another client, although it would have been nice if she'd told the senior partner she was suing the D.A. That had to be it. Pomerantz wasn't calling to update his phonebook.

"Why, yes. Helen joined us a few months ago. She's heading up our family law section."

"No kidding."

"Look, Michael—"

"That's not why I called," Pomerantz slurred the words. "I'm afraid I've got some bad news."

"Oh?"

"It concerns the gambling ordinance. Not the substance, of course. The council adopted your version. But there's a procedural issue that's come to my attention. We need to discuss it."

"Procedural?"

"The effect is still the same. If the process is flawed, we don't have a good law."

"I don't understand. What part of the process are you talking about?"

"The vote, Ethan. There was a problem with the vote. I'm afraid it may be a showstopper. I don't know what the chairman wants to do about it. I'm going to call him tomorrow, but I wanted to let you know about it first in case you have to gear up for another public hearing. Or, I guess you'll send your man Soard over here again. I don't know."

"Hold on. I don't understand, Mike. The vote was five to two. It passed easily."

"Oh, it was a clear majority all right. The problem is that under our code it takes two-thirds of the council to pass an ordinance. That's six votes. A simple majority won't cut it for a code change. We had five in favor, not six. We're one shy. I thought Trish McDaniel would support the ban but she was absent when they voted."

"She was? But I spoke to her right before the meeting started. She was there."

"She was at the meeting but she stepped out of the room when the vote on the ordinance was cast. It's funny. I thought she'd want to be on the record on this issue for sure. I guess she figured it didn't matter since her side had a majority."

There was a pause while Morgan took down every word.

"I see. I didn't realize her vote wasn't counted."

"It kind of puts me in a box. I want a good law, and I know you do, too. If it's challenged now…hell, Ethan, I think the thing's void on its face. Without that sixth vote, it's like it never happened."

"That's a problem, Mike. For a lot of people."

"Yes, it is."

"Well, let me ask you this. You said you wanted to tell me first. I'm assuming you haven't gotten any complaints about from anyone else, have you?" Morgan asked.

"What?"

"Do you think anyone else is aware of the discrepancy? You know if I'm asked about it I'd like to know who all's interested."

"I couldn't say, Ethan. It just happened yesterday. The minutes won't be ready until next week. I'm sure if the right person does any digging it'll come out."

There was more silence at the other end. It was working better than he could have imagined. Pomerantz just wanted to screw with Morgan because one of his lawyers had done the same to him. The old man was acting as if he had a stake in the outcome.

"I see. I certainly appreciate the heads up. Let me know if there's anything I can do to help. I don't want to see *you* get hurt by any of this."

"Uh-huh." Pomerantz rolled his wife's divorce papers tight enough to pound nails. "I'll keep that in mind."

"Please do. Goodbye, Michael."

****

There's a phone number Warren Dunn answers when his appointments secretary or Dunn Enterprises' chief operating officer calls in case of an emergency. He added Ethan Morgan to that list when he hired him to double cross the city. His lawyer rang it with news so troubling it had to be delivered at once and in person.

Bubba was waiting in his partner's penthouse when Morgan arrived. He was moving much too quickly for a man of his stature with rich clients.

"Say that again," Dunn commanded. "We got three more votes than the other side did and that's not a win?"

"Not according to the city attorney, it's not. Pomerantz says you need two-thirds of the council to pass an ordinance. That's six out of nine. There were only five votes in favor."

"Who was missing?"

"One of the councilmen was out of town. Utley. But we weren't counting on his vote anyway."

"And the other?"

"The other was Trish McDaniel. She didn't vote."

"She didn't vote? I thought we had that worked out, Bubba."

"We did," Hawkins said.

Morgan shook his head. "She wasn't against us, Warren. She just didn't vote. Period. Pomerantz says she was out of the room when they took it up. By the time she made it back to her seat they'd finished with the issue. She probably saw that the thing would pass and decided not to bother recording her vote for the record. I doubt she even knows about the two-thirds rule."

Dunn whirled his chair around in disgust. Bubba looked like a bloated tuna holding its breath. Morgan waited while his clients shook Magic Eight Balls deciding what to do.

"She screwed us all right," Bubba said with a curious smile.

Dunn saw no humor in it. "I'm glad you're enjoying yourself."

"Trish told me she wouldn't vote against the ordinance, and she didn't. Not voting at all...now that part I didn't count on."

"Well, you sure as hell should have. Dammit, Bubba—"

"It's the smart play," Morgan interrupted. "A vote for the ban would have ticked off anyone looking to get rich in her district, and that's everyone. A vote against it and there goes the church crowd.

She still has the support of both groups because she didn't go on the record. Smart lady."

"Damn right she is," Bubba nodded.

Dunn couldn't hold it any longer. His eyes shifted from side to side and his arms flailed as he tried to figure out which one of them to bludgeon first.

"I'm so glad you individual and collective dumb asses are ecstatic about this. Now, if you're finished congratulating Trish McDaniel on her skills as a politician, will somebody kindly tell me what the hell we're gonna do now? We've got a big friggin' problem. There's a fleet of semis hauling video poker machines from west Texas to your lot, Bubba. I told you I had commitments to the dealers. You knew the deadlines. Both of you! I told you when, and where, and what things had to fall into place…and you said, 'relax…trust me…everything will work out fine.' You said we've got the law we need, Ethan, and now you're telling me we don't. What happened? What happened and how are you going to fix it?"

Morgan had heard about his client's darker side for years. He had a temper, but until now it had peaked at frustration. He'd never seen Dunn so flustered. There was a harder edge this time, a rage almost. He wanted what he'd been promised, and he expected it on a spoiled kid's timetable. Dunn had been outmaneuvered by a high school dropout who ruled her district more effectively than he led his international conglomerate. She'd whipped his lawyer, too.

"What the hell, Warren? That's Trish for ya," Bubba said. "She just don't stay bought."

Dunn ignored him. He wanted to hear it from Morgan.

"I don't know that she's the problem now," the lawyer said. "She's just happy it passed and she didn't get any on her. No. The problem is we're exposed. We're exposed if…"

"If what?" Dunn asked.

"If the wrong person finds out about it."

"And who might that be?"

"Could be all sorts of folks. That's up to the city attorney."

"So, let me make sure I understand. You're telling me that Pomerantz is the only one who knows about this?"

"About the vote? Yeah, Warren. I think that's right. He called to give me a heads up before he told anyone on the council.

I'm sure he'll let them know tomorrow. My guess is he'll tell Amsler first. What he'll do with it, I really couldn't say."

"Well, since I cost him several million dollars the last time I did business with his bank, what do you think he'll do?" Dunn asked.

"That thought had occurred to me."

"Tomorrow, huh?" Bubba asked.

"If not sooner," Ethan answered.

Dunn straightened his tie. His shirttail had come out during the tirade, so he tidied that up, too. The scowl was gone, as was the outward rage. He needed his lawyer to follow them.

"Yes, Ethan. Very good. Let me reflect on this new development. I want you to keep a close eye on things for me at the city. I wouldn't want our business venture to get derailed when we're this close to the goal line. That would be bad," he nodded toward Bubba. "For all of us."

"I understand," Ethan said. "I'm sorry it had to come to this, gentlemen. Trish ran for cover and we still won by three votes. For some reason the law requires a bigger landslide than what we got. I felt I had to tell you about it right away. I hope I did the right thing."

Bubba started to answer but Dunn cut him off. "I would have been more concerned if you hadn't told me about it, Ethan."

Bubba turned his back on them as they walked to the door.

"I would never do that."

"I know you wouldn't, Ethan. That's why I trust you." He shook his hand to prove it. "Don't worry. You did the right thing."

****

Soard reached the criminal law section as his paralegal was closing up for the evening, or so he thought. On the other hand, Maggie didn't wear wingtips.

"Dennis?"

It was Dennis Clark, the sycophant who tried to crash the Star Chamber meeting of the Calhoun lawyers when Ethan Morgan ambushed them with the Dunn announcement at the firm's luncheon. Clark sat in Maggie's cubicle shaking like a dog chewing peach pits. He had the look. Soard knew it well. It was the way all first year associates looked when Lovelace dumped a case on them just before trial.

"Dennis? What in the world—"

"Pete," Clark jumped to his feet. "Man, am I glad you're here? We gotta talk."

"What is it?"

He led him past Soard's office and kept going all the way to the exit sign.

"Dennis, where are you taking me?"

Clark held the door and they walked into the stuffy fire escape. There they'd have all the privacy the haggard lawyer needed. A cold sweat covered his ashen face. He didn't know where to begin.

"Why are we in the stairwell, Dennis?" Soard asked.

"I've got a big problem, Pete. I don't know what to do.

"Take it easy. Just tell me what it is and we'll work through it."

"This has got to be between us, okay?"

"Okay," Soard nodded.

"It's Lovelace."

"What'd he do?"

"It's not what he did," Clark said. "It's what he wants me to do."

"Oh?"

"Look. Everybody knows I've been handling mostly but dives so far, which I understand. I'm sure you did the same your first few months here."

"Right."

"But lately things have been picking up. You heard about that manslaughter case I got last week?"

"Yeah. I meant to congratulate you."

"Don't bother. I wish I'd never met the client."

"Why's that?" Soard asked.

"When I landed the guy I was so excited. I couldn't wait to find Remy. I almost got creamed racing back here to tell him. Serves me right for wanting to brag on myself."

"So he was pleased, right?"

"At first, sure he was. He asked what I charged the guy. I told him and he said he was real disappointed in me. He told me I should go meet with him again and quote him a fee of twenty grand."

"Well, that is a serious charge. I don't know the facts, but I could see a fee that high."

"Oh, I had no problem going back and asking for that much. I thought the guy would punch my lights out, but he said he could come up with the rest. When we met yesterday, he gave me a check for the whole amount. I was upset with how Remy'd treated me, but it hurt a lot less when the guy paid the full fee. So I took the money down to finance. Everybody was gone. I think they went to happy hour for one of the girls who just got engaged. Anyway, no one was there so I threw the check in my briefcase to take home. I stopped by to tell Lovelace on the way out. He was a different man when I showed him the check. He pulled me into his office and offered me a drink. I didn't know he had a bar."

"Yeah. I think all the corner offices have them."

"Oh. I haven't been in many of them. Anyway, I told him the bookkeepers were gone for the day, but that I'd make sure to deposit the money first thing in this morning."

"Okay."

"Remy said it could wait. He said they'd just escrow the fee, and since I hadn't done much for the client yet, there was no hurry. He asked if I thought the client would mind cashing it. He said if there was a fee for doing that I could offer to chop off a couple hundred for it."

"It's not his fee to reduce, Dennis," Pete said. "That money belongs to the firm. I'm sure he gets a cut at some point, but the deposit stays with finance. Hell, I don't know how that all works. Somehow it trickles down."

Soard leaned over the rail and followed the dusty staircase to the basement. The fall would have been long enough to kill Remy's ego.

"So what'd you do with the check?" Pete asked. "Did you give it back to the client like Remy said?"

"Yeah. I took it to him this morning. What else could I do? My boss says give it back, so I gave it back."

"What happened? Did he come up with the cash?"

"No."

"So you lost a twenty thousand dollar fee because Remy wouldn't take a check?"

"No. When I told the client what my boss wanted, he said he'd have to make some phone calls, then he'd get back to me. I think he wanted to find out what the deal was. He called me this afternoon and said he could get me fifteen grand in cash, and he'd come up with the other five thousand later. I know you've got to get the fee up front, especially from a criminal, but what could I do? I'd already returned the guy's check."

"Did you tell Lovelace that?"

"I haven't told him yet. I just got the cash this afternoon. Remy was with a client, and I didn't want to see him anyway. I've been hiding out since then," Clark said. "I don't know what to do. Pete, he told me not to give the fee to the bookkeepers. What the hell is that? You know how tight they watch the money around this place. I'm not even sure I'm gonna get credit on the books for what came in. He's screwing up my numbers big time."

"I know."

"But that's the least of my worries right now. You know, we're supposed to report everything over ten grand to the bank. It's not an excuse that I gave the money to my boss. There's supposed to be a record of it. I think Lovelace is ripping off the firm, Pete, and now he's got me mixed up in it," he said.

"Easy, Dennis."

"So, no, I haven't given him the money. I shouldn't have returned the guy's check in the first place. If he settles for fifteen grand in cash instead of his percentage of twenty after finance divvies it up…I mean what do you think he's going to do when I tell him?"

"Somehow I don't see him escorting you down to the bookkeeper," Soard said.

"I don't either. Look, Pete, I didn't mean to drag you into this, but I don't know what to do. If I tell one of the shareholders this thing will explode. I don't know Morgan well enough to take something like this to him. Maybe there's not a problem with what Lovelace wants me to do. I don't know. But they were real specific about how we're supposed to route the fees when they hired me. Like I say, maybe it's not a problem."

"No, Dennis, it is a problem. It's a very big problem. Have you told anyone else about this?"

"Are you crazy? I just told you the shareholders would—"

"No. I mean anyone, not just the shareholders. Does anybody else know?"

"Un-uh. It just happened. I wanted to talk to you first. You know Remy's not stupid. He watches the stats each month. He knows I'm bringing up the rear. They're probably ready to can me anyway. I've been trying as hard as I can, but it's been tough. This hasn't been my year. Nobody's going to go to bat for me. Especially not against a section leader. What would you do? If I tell anybody Lovelace will just deny it and fire me. It's my word against his. On the other hand, if I quit without telling anyone and the whole thing blows up, he'll point the finger at me and go straight to the cops. I won't be able to defend myself to the firm. They'll be glad I'm gone and I won't even get a call back if I try to explain what happened. They'll just take Remy's word for it and I'm done."

Soard nodded and told him that was a real possibility.

"So you got any ideas?" Clark asked.

"Yeah, Dennis. A couple. If I were you I'd tear up your fee agreement, unless you didn't have one. Get him to sign a new one for the fifteen thousand. Then I'd put it in an envelope and have your secretary hand deliver it to Remy with a memo that says something like, 'here's the full retainer…please route to finance, making special note of the reporting requirement in connection with a cash payment of this kind.' I'd send it by e-mail and attach the hard copy to the envelope. Tell your secretary what you're doing. Make sure she understands the money's going from you to your boss at his direction. Tell her how excited you are to get such a big fee, and you know Mr. Lovelace will be, too. You know he'll want to share the good news with his partners, something like that. Then sometime tomorrow I'd ask one of the computer guys to come by your office and show you how the long term memory works on the local network. Show him your e-mail account. Tell him you want to be able to archive important messages. Tell him about your case, and that you want to make sure you can save such an important e-mail. Let him read it. Make about a dozen copies for yourself and hide them all over the place. You should be all right as far as that goes."

"Slow down, Pete. I don't want to miss anything. Okay, so I give it to Remy and let him do what he has to do. I should be okay after that, right? I mean at least I'll have a couple witnesses. He won't lie if we all tell the same story. Right?"

"It may not be that simple, Dennis. If he's gone this far I wouldn't be surprised if he doesn't try to keep you close by."

"What do you mean?"

"He might offer you some money, a bonus or something. If he does, make sure it's legitimate."

"How can I do that?"

"You may not be able to," Pete said. "Oh, and I left out the most important thing. If I were you, I'd dust off my résumé and look for a new firm. I doubt this'll be the last time he comes to you."

Clark buried his face in his hands. "What a nightmare," his voice echoed down the stairwell. "I need this job."

"Do you need it enough to get in trouble for Lovelace? There are plenty of jobs for lawyers in this town, Dennis. Even honest ones. Not everyone's like him."

Clark told him he was grateful and shook his hand. Soard said it might look a little strange if they both came in from the fire escape at the same time, and besides, he could use the exercise. Clark thanked him again and said goodbye.

Lovelace had crossed a line he'd chipped away at his whole career. That's why this all started. Soard could see that clearly now, or as his mentor would say, beyond a reasonable doubt. It was time to go home. He dialed the preset number and a woman's voice answered after one ring.

"Go," she said plainly.

"This is Mason," Peter Soard announced.

"Go ahead, Mason."

The man who'd worked the inside all these months breathed deeply as his brief legal career came to a close. It happened calmly as he gave the signal.

"Diamond Dog."

The code name was all the operator needed. Soard started the long walk from the thirtieth floor. He told himself he'd never ride that gold-plated elevator ever again. By the time he reached the bottom Luciano's team would have Calhoun & Morgan covered in yellow tape, the most expensive crime scene in the state. Remy had been in his office when Soard joined Clark on the stairs. He'd be confused at first, but Lovelace would figure out who betrayed him soon enough.

The agents would carefully pack their belongings and deliver them to his destination of choice. By late tonight Soard figured he'd give the director a full debriefing, maybe even Attorney General Gallman. It'd be a feather in his cap as he delivered on his pledge to take a bite out of white-collar crime.

Laura Soard had learned how to pick up and go in a hurry. He told her that would be part of their life on day one at the FBI Academy. She'd load the van herself if it meant saying goodbye to Calhoun & Morgan. Soard called himself a first class son of a bitch that he'd made her wait so long to do it.

CHAPTER 33

Anne slept on the ferry all the way home from Ocracoke. Her skin was brown from a week in the sun, her hair turning lighter just in time for the wedding. She was so relaxed she couldn't make a fist. Sean kissed her goodbye, hugged Anne's mother and then drove home to crash in his lonely apartment. He needed to do some serious running, not the sightseeing kind he did on the Island. His pitiful refrigerator was covered with pictures of his fiancée and so many sticky notes they'd lost their effectiveness. He threw away all but the one about the meeting with the city manager in the morning. Pomerantz wanted him to give a brief on the riverfront project. The file was on his desk. Good thing, he thought. It would be an excuse to drag his sorry body down to the office. Night runs were best after a break in training. He hadn't timed himself in days. His watch disappeared somewhere on the trip. Come to think of it, he didn't even take it with him. The Outer Banks had served their purpose.

****

At first Lovelace thought it was an elaborate practical joke, a few of the Calhoun shareholders getting back at him for crashing their coup plotting over Morgan's freelancing on Dunn, but not even that collection of malcontents could pull off something like this. Someone read him his rights and he corrected them when they misspoke. Even that would be held against him.

Lovelace was booked, printed, photographed and tossed into a makeshift holding cell built for one in the rented quarters Luciano had sweated in for the past year. It was real. This was happening. He'd been busted and it was federal. He was alone now, waiting for a chance to call someone. Remy needed information. It was what allowed him to stay free for so long. He pressed his ears against the door but his captors weren't talking. They snickered plenty, relaxed now that they'd gotten their man.

"Damn," Remy whispered. They were packing. Whatever this is, he told himself, it's over. "They're going home."

He tapped on the door. "Hey, you out there. How 'bout a phone call?"

A scruffy-faced detective closed in on him. Lovelace thought he looked familiar. He couldn't place him for sure.

"I'm gonna give you a chance to talk all you want," Luciano said. He pointed to the lawyer and a guard let him out. Lovelace nodded his appreciation for the gesture. They led him to 'the box,' where it was colder than ever.

"Do you know who I am?" Luciano asked.

"No."

"Special Agent Luciano. Welcome to my world."

Lovelace inspected it from his chair. "Hope you make it out someday."

"Oh, I will. Don't worry. In fact, we'll all be gone soon. But you…well, let's just say this may be the nicest place you see for a long time."

"Swell," Remy said. "Would it be too much to ask what I did?"

"Two years, Lovelace. That's how long I've been on your tail. At times I thought you knew I was there. I thought you'd made me as an undercover cop, that you were simply throwing me a bone every once in a while just to keep it interesting."

"I wish I had known you were around. Truly. I would have told you to go chase criminals."

"Make no mistake," Luciano said, "the trail was dry for a long time. No one wanted to talk to me. Can you imagine that? A guy with as bubbly a personality as I've got, and nobody wanted to give me the time of day."

"You can't mean it."

"But then one day we caught a break. And then another. Soon the witnesses started to fall like dominoes. It's amazing how many dissatisfied clients you've had over the years. They all said one thing, though. Remington Lovelace was worth every penny. All that cash they put in your palm. Now why would a lawyer who works in the biggest firm in the state, with over two thousand square feet devoted to the bookkeepers…why would that lawyer have such an aversion to accountants? Why all the cash, I wondered. No reason, unless you never report it. The clients didn't mind. Your cash rate was much more reasonable. You still got paid well, but you came off your fee enough to make it worthwhile for your clients to keep quiet about it. They got your services for less, and you pocketed the money without reporting it. All you had to do was make sure enough passed through to keep your partners from getting too nosy. But from what you skimmed—you and the lawyers in your section—well, let's just say you were able to keep your lady friends in the life they've grown accustomed to."

Lovelace wanted to slug him for being so right. "It's lucky for you I'm a public figure or I'd sue you for slander as well as false arrest."

"Truth's a defense, Remy."

"Yeah. Truth is."

Luciano let it pass. "So why'd you join Calhoun and Morgan anyway? What the hell d'you want with them? You had it all to yourself in your solo practice. Why become just another lawyer at a big firm?"

"I like people."

"Good. Me, too. I like you, Remy. I want to be your friend. And I know you want to be my friend. You see we're not in circuit court anymore. You're going before a federal grand jury tomorrow morning."

"On what charges?"

"I reckon we'll put on at least the first twenty or so counts of obstruction of justice. Witness tampering and what not. Then we'll let the IRS have a crack at you. See if your records match your clients' accounts, and the firm's. I'm sure your partners won't object to the demise of Remington Lovelace. They'll pile on if it's the difference between them and you. That sounds reasonable, doesn't it?"

"You're pretty proud of yourself, aren't you?"

"No. I just lived up to my expectations."

"I doubt that's possible."

"You believe whatever you want. But I can make it a smoother ride if you like. I can't take all the pain away, but I can sure as hell make it sting a lot less."

"Uh-huh."

"But only if you help me."

"Like hell. I want to speak to my lawyer."

"Sure. You know your rights better than we do. Who'd you like to call?"

Lovelace thought it over. Who does a criminal's lawyer call for help? The cop was right. The only thing that'd make the shareholders laugh harder than the thought of him in jail would be his call for help from deep within it.

"I'm listening," Luciano prodded.

Soard would know the most. He could tell him what happened today, and how far the destruction went. He was the only one at the firm he could trust. He'd covered his back since he came aboard, and he'd be here for him now. But what if they'd pinched him, too? They didn't rent out a building this size just so they could cast a small net. He needed to find out how wide it was. He gave him the number and Luciano recognized it.

"Calhoun and Morgan? You got any friends there?"

"Ask for a lawyer named Peter Soard."

A marshal who'd been listening grinned from ear to ear. Luciano smiled at the two-way mirror like he'd made it to retirement. He might as well put it for it now. He had nothing left to prove.

"Peter Soard?" Luciano chuckled. "Sure thing, Remy."

"What's so funny?"

"Nothing. Is there anyone else you'd like to call? You know, in case Soard's not available?"

****

Morgan left messages all over town for his client but Dunn wasn't taking any more calls, not even on the hot line. He needed to tell him about Lovelace and how far the sting at his firm went before he heard it on the late news. If he did have a temper like everyone said, this wouldn't be the time to act on it. The senior partner panicked when Bubba didn't answer either, not even the private line Lovelace had given him. He was cut off and it wasn't random. Something was about to happen, something worse than a posse of federal marshals inventorying *See'n 'em's* files. He was prepared to look everywhere for it, but somehow he knew he'd never see it coming.

Across town the D.A. made circles with his syrupy bourbon and Coke, made them right over his wife's pretentious lawyer's signature. The rings smeared the nasty cover letter paper-clipped to the divorce papers. How much does Calhoun & Morgan get an hour for ruining the lives of strangers, he wondered, for publicizing private indiscretions, for shining its spotlight on the darkest corners of a marriage—for painting him as he probably was, he admitted to an empty chair, but that still didn't make it right.

The swallows came harder as his insides began to resist the liquor. He considered the breadth of what Jenna'd alleged, and war-gamed what might be left when the dust settled. The personal consequences were obvious, and too painful to consider. As for his career, clearly the judgeship was gone. Womanizing might have enhanced his chances with the politicians he lobbied. Skirt chasing is a college tie to that crowd, even in a state this conservative. But nobody trusts a drunk—not with their money, not to look after their children, and not with their secrets.

"Jesus."

A swinger and a lush. It was too much to fit on his business card. His body was racked with guilt, enough to allow some miserable contrition to seep into his conscience. What was he forgetting? He thought for a moment, replaying all the trouble they'd had in just the past six months. Only one of their fights had led to…

The chair pitched him forward and Pomerantz struck the desk with the force of a car crash. He needed an air bag but all he got was a face full of mahogany. His hand jerked away and the mug shattered into a thousand pieces. Bourbon sloshed from the bottle and splattered the messages he hadn't played hoops with yet. He lay on the floor clutching the complaint, not sure what had happened.

"Oh my God," he whispered. He sounded like Citizen Kane calling for his sled. *Haahhh…Rosebudddd.* "Oh my God. No. You didn't. Please, God, don't let that be in here. Not the beach. I said I was sorry. It was an accident and you know that, Jenna! You know that! Not the beach! No!"

Pomerantz scanned the pages, racing through each line in search of anything that sounded like that weekend—that lost weekend he'd only been able to consider in the months since as 'the unfortunate incident.' He ripped out every staple. Large parts of the complaint hit the floor. His head throbbed harder and harder, almost as violently as his chest pounded. Only her lawyer's meter moved faster than his eyes and fingers did as he flew through the lines.

"Think, Pomerantz, think!" *What had she actually remembered about that night, anyway? Not much, right? I mean that would have been on page one. Would've trumped adultery. Would've dropkicked it to the back of the complaint.*

His breathing quickened, shallow and forced like he'd become fatally allergic to whiskey and divorce lawyers. His throat closed up and his cheeks turned numb. He could have blotted the Great Lakes with his tongue. The drunken lawyer's head swam as he turned the last page, not sure where he was in the room, only that it was spinning wildly there.

"Maybe…she didn't…remember," he slurred. "Didn't *rememmer.* It's not here. Not here. Maybe it's not…"

When he opened his eyes the room was still out of focus, but he'd grounded himself somewhere. Somehow he'd managed to climb back into the chair during all the commotion. He thought he might have cut his hand on shards from the coffee cup, but didn't care if it had to be amputated. The D.A. played connect-the-dots with the pockmarked tiles in the ceiling. He'd fired pencils into them as a diversion during tiresome phone calls while he tried to remember why he'd taken the job. His insides were scrambled but still with him. He looked like a candidate about to deliver his concession speech, with the posture of a jellyfish. He let out a long, steady, strangely contented exhale. *"Wheeeeeeeeeeew."*

It wasn't there. No physical abuse. No mention of how one night after their wretched tropical excess his wife savagely attacked his open hand with her beautiful face. No beach. There was still hope.

He smiled the smile of a man whose good news is that it's not the electric chair, just life in prison. There was no third prize, only an unconfirmed rumor that the hangman had taken a long lunch. Still, on this night in the abyss it passed for something.

"I'm not a wife beater," he convinced himself. *Not reduced to writing. She didn't allege it and it never happened.* To a man who rationalized for a living, it was vindication by omission.

This called for a drink. The D.A. rummaged through his desk in search of anything he hadn't broken. He found a reasonably clean glass and poured another round. It wasn't orphaned. Not as good as the rum at sunset, *right Jenna?* Okay, so maybe on that sweltering night in the Keys he did have a drinking problem.

"She was just as drunk," Pomerantz said. "Hah!"

He pictured her auburn hair reaching toward the sky, suspended there like a string-less marionette while the rest of her body whirled around, arms flailing at the air, her legs limp and out from under her, a heap of tanned beauty on the cabana's hardwood floor. He remembered the sound the pearls made as her necklace shattered, free at last, bouncing toward every corner of the room. *Pop, pop, pop, pop.* He looked like a neutered bulldog on all fours chasing the little suckers down. The strand was harder to put back together than his alibi.

The next day Jenna thought she'd fallen face first into the bed and breakfast's fruity bed frame. She was curious about how the finger-shaped welts on her cheek were about the same size as her husband's outstretched hand. It was an open-fisted smack, so there were no broken facial bones, just an unsightly blemish, darkly bruised where his palm had landed. There were five beat red marks where his fingers caught her flush across the cheek—the painful tributaries of unconditional love turned conditional.

"Not alleged," he consoled himself.

After the demonization was complete Jenna's lawyer listed all the things Mrs. Pomerantz should get. She wanted the house, their best car, all the stuff she'd brought to the marriage and most of what she hadn't, half of his retirement, even though it hadn't vested yet, and her maiden name back.

He wanted a hot shower, a half pound of *Vicodin,* a voodoo doll with 'Calhoun & Morgan' written all over it and a big damned mulligan on the last ten years of his life.

The D.A. massaged his temples until his sideburns bristled like sandpaper in his ears. The ice had melted but the glass still felt cool against his forehead. Through it the lawyer could just make out the councilman's name written in his secretary's grade school block print across the top of a phone message. It was Jake Amsler. He wants to know if the gambling ordinance was sent to the publisher yet, she wrote. *You can reach him at home. Be sure to call back today.* Had Linda seen this? The call came in at four o'clock.

"Jake Amsler. Six hours ago," he crumpled it in disgust. He'd given standing orders for the staff to corral him anytime an A-lister phoned. He'd told Linda as much and it was her job to shepherd the staff through ominous duties like that.

"Call Jake tomorrow, stupid. Apologize for your office one more time."

There were other messages, older ones piled high on the desk, organized in some fashion only he understood. Erica'd called, three times in fact since her ultimatum at lunch. No last name given. None needed. Everyone in the office knew the D.A.'s shack-up. His wife's lawyer knew her name. Why shouldn't The Help?

Then there were messages from his private clients. So long as they didn't conflict with city business his employer let it slide. Selena Hall's divorce was days away. His notes said she was in L.A. But if it went like most of her other jobs the magazine probably folded before the shoot began, or the photographer ran out of film, or Selena'd ticked somebody off and they canned her. All she needed was fame and fortune. Selena had a star's attitude down pat already.

Pomerantz lost his place halfway through the voice mail message. He told Selena Hall not to worry about the final hearing. He had it under control. It would be smooth, in fact, much smoother than anything he was facing. The hours and the bourbon hadn't made any of it sink in, although he knew something bad had come from his wife's law firm. He reminded himself to punch Ethan Morgan in the mouth the next time he came to city hall.

"You can't pick your clients, Pomerantz," he heard himself utter. "The hell you can't."

He heard noises but was sure it couldn't be Linda. He'd put her on the elevator and stayed on his side of the door until she drove away from the parking garage. The squeaking was the familiar janitor's cart, but it made no rounds this late. A huge man, almost as big as the bastard who'd served him with Calhoun & Morgan's calling card stood in the hallway, his biceps bigger than canned hams as he hoisted the heavy trash can. He seemed amiable enough for someone policing government refuse on the third shift. But Pomerantz had never seen the man or heard of the company he claimed to work for.

"Good evening," the lawyer said.

The custodian nodded.

"New here?" he asked.

"I'm from the temp agency," the man said.

"Oh."

He wondered why the janitor wore surgical gloves. Maybe the brute was afraid of a paper cut. The risk manager had sent a notice about tainted mail. It could be that. They looked brand new. That figured.

"Temp agency?" Pomerantz said.

The man dumped the day's futility into the mobile bin and bid him a pleasant evening. The D.A. felt his mouth move and figured he must have said the same. He poured one last drink but got more whiskey on his floor than in the stained coffee cup. Was he finished talking to his client's answering machine? It didn't ask him any questions so he must have been.

The room seemed darker than before, fuzzier somehow. The light from the hallway dimmed like something was blocking the way to where his secretary sat when she came to work. He thought it might be the janitor again. The bull had forgotten to turn his desk upside down and dust the bottom with a white glove.

Dunn's man inside the sheriff's department was good. He even knew what kind of gun the D.A. shot with, and where to look for it if his workout bag were here. Pomerantz struggled to his feet, but the man from the temp agency knocked him back with his fingertips.

"What're you doing? Ohhh. Jesus," he felt the liquor make its return trip. "I'm gonna be sick."

"Keep still," the janitor said softly. He bent over for something but Pomerantz couldn't see what it was. "Everything will be all right."

"What? Who are you? What are you still do-ooh-ing here?" he slurred.

The man was deliberate in his work. There was precision in what he did, made simpler by his target's self-imposed disability. He was glad to see Pomerantz so drunk. He wouldn't feel a thing. It would be a peaceful end to his broken life.

"Be still," he said one more time as he slowly squeezed the trigger. The bang echoed even louder than he'd imagined. Even the guards five floors below couldn't sleep through that. There was blood everywhere, even on the socks tucked inside the killer's work boots. He unloaded and grinded the dead lawyer's index finger into the trigger. He ran the full magazine through his hand, popped it home and wrapped the D.A.'s bloody hand around the pistol grip. He grabbed the gun in Pomerantz' gym bag and ran to the fire exit. He thought he heard the front door open before his closed all the way. If the guards were behind him they had a choice, they could chase his shadow or try to put their old friend back together until the ambulance arrived. The guards knew him. He was the man who tried the arrests they made. They'd stay by his side. They'd stay right by his side until someone told them what Michael Pomerantz had to live for.

Outside, Sean Piper shuffled the last quarter mile to the Administration Building, an abbreviated cool down to a fast three-miler he banged out in just a shade over fifteen minutes. The lights in the Legal Department shined brightly. There were shadows dancing on his boss' wall like the old man had court in the morning and he wasn't ready for it.

Piper reached for a key tucked inside his wet sock, surprising himself that he remembered the building's security code. The sixth floor was a thirty second elevator ride away, but Piper felt like doing some stairs to get back the pump his cool down had robbed him of, so he hoofed it, a flight every fourth step.

The stairwell was an all-concrete job located directly behind the elevators, the steps painted an institutional gray. Halfway to the top, Piper heard a sharp noise, a piece of scrap iron falling down the elevator shaft, he thought, smacking hard against the basement floor and echoing throughout the vacant building. *Crack!* It was that sound exactly—either that or the noise a gun makes when filtered through several feet of concrete. Probably loose metal in the elevator shaft.

Sean sprinted to the legal department, his heart racing from the climb and the loud noises that came from a locked building. He flew down the hallway and threw open the door to the City Attorney's Office. Inside he heard a muffled click near the back staircase. That door led to a fire escape that was covered with cobwebs. It stayed closed except for the yearly fire drill, unless the real thing came. It was dark and calm there now, no motion and no smoke. The fire escape and the door Piper stood in front of were the only two ways in and out of the room.

The lights from Pomerantz' office beamed a few feet away. There was someone at the desk. Piper could see a hand quivering beside what looked like an empty bottle of sipping whiskey. It stopped for a second, then another spasm, then still. There were a few more spasms, then it went limp for good.

"Mr. Pomerantz?" he said. "Michael?" It was the first time Piper'd called him that since the D.A. had taken over as city attorney. His boss had nothing to say. He ran to his side to see why.

"Michael!"

There was blood spattered on the desk. Pomerantz' head lay flat against the smooth wood, his body slumped over a pile of papers. A pool of dark blood stained the ones on top. There was blood on the D.A.'s hand and on the pistol it held. It was everywhere, even on the last page of his wife's divorce papers.

Sean propped him against the chair. He tore off his soaked t-shirt and wiped the lawyer's pierced temple but the crimson flow gushed even more. He wrapped the shirt around Pomerantz' head, ran to the door and yelled down the open-air middle of the building, startling a uniformed guard asleep in front of ten television screens.

"Help! Security, help!" Piper's heart pounded. There was a faint noise from the guard shack far beneath him. He propped open the heavy door and barked out more orders. Two figures scurried five stories below.

"Up here!" he cried. "Get an ambulance! Hurry!"

Pomerantz fell forward, knocking his lamp onto the floor. His head bounced off the desk. The young lawyer's bloody shirt was still wrapped around it. Piper gasped for air between desperate cries to the frightened night shift. If he hadn't been so busy rallying the slowest troops in Bristol Sean might have heard the high-pitched sounds coming from the D.A.'s grainy speakerphone.

"Beep, beep, beep, beep, beep..."

The red light shined, but there was no one at the other end of the line. Somewhere in California a middle-aged photographer ogled his subject, clicking away. He begged her in a cockney accent to, "Work it, baby, work it."

The wannabe supermodel posed indifferently in front of hot lights and a white background. The South of France would be morphed all around her during post-production. Her mind was on home and her final divorce hearing in a few days—the one her lawyer would have her ready for, even if he hadn't returned any of her calls. Three thousand miles across country and in the stillness of Bristol, Michael Pomerantz lay still through the beeps from his client's answering machine. Selena Hall's voice mailbox was full.

CHAPTER 34

The cleanup continued through the early morning hours. A rookie sheriff's investigator needed an airsick bag to make it through his first death scene.

"God, what a mess," he said. "Every see anything like it, sir?"

Lieutenant Tobias worked the rubber gloves down each finger. He took a pencil from his pocket.

"Use this," the rookie offered a pen as if his partner needed it to take notes.

Tobias ignored him. He went about his business with the pencil, carefully lifting the victim's hand far enough to move the pistol.

"Beretta. That's his gun all right," Tobias said. "I used to shoot with him. The sheriff, too. That was a long time ago. Any luck on the pictures?"

"I was just going to check on that."

The young man disappeared while Tobias inspected the D.A.'s phone. The screen showed an out-going call. He took down the number and the time it was made.

"It's been flashing the whole time," a lady he knew from forensics said.

"Did you get the time of death, Kate?" Tobias asked.

She found it on the report. "Says here the victim expired at approximately ten-thirty last night. Found by witness Sean Piper."

"Uh-huh."

"It's sad. I don't think I could kill myself," Kate said.

"What makes you think he did?"

"You said it's his gun, didn't you? I just pried his finger off the trigger. There's no sign of forced entry. And look at this," she pointed. "That's his name. His wife just filed for divorce."

"Hmm. I hadn't seen that," Tobias said.

"Look, I didn't know the D.A. like you knew him, but from what I heard the guy was a walking time bomb. He was in over his head at the city and everybody knew it. Then his wife slaps papers on him the day he turns up dead. Let's face it, he couldn't take any more. Can you blame him? So he downs a fifth of whiskey and plays Russian Roulette until he loses. Makes sense, doesn't it?"

"Too much, Kate."

"At least it makes for a clean investigation," she said.

"I like clean," Tobias agreed. "Clean's good. Makes our job easy. But I'm always curious when the decedent didn't die from old age."

"You've got a point there."

"And then there's motive. There's motive everywhere. Pomerantz put some of the worst people in this state behind bars. If his marriage is falling apart, that could be something, too."

"You think his wife did this? Why file for divorce then?"

"I'm not saying she killed him. But someone did."

"Why so sure?"

He tapped the gun with his pencil. "You said you just pried his finger off this." He held up his right hand.

"Yeah."

"Pomerantz was left-handed."

"He was?"

"Look at the magazine release," Tobias pointed. "It's on the right side, where his left thumb could reach it easily."

Kate saw for herself. "You're right. Guess that's why I don't work motive."

A deputy Tobias knew and didn't care for bulled his way into the office. He was always showing up uninvited, offering to help but not doing more harm than good.

"Need any help?" the lawman asked.

Tobias shook his head no. "Thanks anyway, Deputy Jennings. We were just about to clear out. The boys from the lab need this room."

Tobias collected his partner and said, "Wait 'til we're outside. I want to tell you something about him," he whispered.

Jennings hung around the D.A.'s desk where Tobias had spent so much time. He leaned over the telephone but couldn't make any sense out of the elaborate call screen.

"You, too, Jennings," Tobias said.

The deputy whirled around like he'd been busted. "Oh, right. I ain't never seen a system like that before."

"Uh-huh," Tobias didn't buy it. "The station only got theirs about two years ago. I guess you don't pull much phone watch, huh Jennings?"

****

The agent held the phone at arm's length until the Attorney General's strongman finished his diatribe.

"Yes, Mr. Tanner. I understand. I'll give him the message."

Luciano appeared with two cups of coffee just as the tongue-lashing was about to end.

"Wait a second, sir. He just walked in," the man pleaded. "Mr. Tanner?"

"Hung up on you, hey Frank? Who was that, your landlord?"

"No. The Attorney General's Office. It was Mr. Tanner."

"Wanted to congratulate us, huh?" Luciano asked.

"Not exactly."

"Well, what did he want?"

"He said you're to come up there. ASAP. The Attorney General wants to meet with you personally."

"Me? What for?" Luciano asked. "Soard's who they really want to see."

"Un-uh. He said this concerned the local D.A. They want to know who killed Pomerantz."

"How the hell should I know?" Luciano said. "He wants me at this hour? We can't get a pilot this time of night. Besides, I haven't been tailing the D.A. all this time. They wanted Lovelace and he's down the hall on ice. Let somebody else crack that case. Maybe he killed himself like the news says."

"Come on Luc'. You said yourself it was a hit."

"I said I suspected it was a hit."

"Right, right," Frank said. "Well, whatever your suspicions, headquarters wants to hear them from you in person."

"Damn," Luciano said as he walked away slowly. "Ah, what the hell? I could use a trip home. Okay, get the jet ready."

"Where you going?"

"To scrounge up a toothbrush. Tanner's a tougher bastard than I am. For all I know I won't be coming back."

Lovelace tried to make out their conversation from his jail cell. It was drowned out by CNN. The story made the national news. *District attorney found dead on eve of the FBI's sting on the state's biggest law firm.* Maybe it was a coincidence. The medical examiner's report might tell them something, but he wasn't holding any press conferences.

"Jesus," Lovelace said. "What's happening?"

He'd seen Pomerantz just yesterday at the courthouse. He seemed the same as always, stressed, but it was nothing a *Moon Pie* and a few settled cases couldn't handle. The D.A. was unopposed for reelection, his caseload was lighter than it had been in months, and his son had made the varsity basketball team. They'd stopped asking about each other's wives a long time ago.

Lovelace wondered if there was a connection with the firm. His partners could be real bastards, but as far as he knew they weren't violent men. They had plenty of clients. Maybe the bust scared one of them into saying something stupid.

"Dunn," Remy whispered to himself. "That son of a bitch." Where was Bubba in all this? Did they dime him out together? Was Morgan in the next room, he wondered. Or maybe he'd set him up right along with Soard. There was no way to be sure. All he knew was that his old friend was dead, and even though they stood on opposite sides of the courtroom, they respected each other no matter whose tail got kicked. Pomerantz was good to go. He was a trial lawyer, like Remy, and they were supposed to look out for each other because it was lonely in their business without someone to fight. They rested at the end of each battle. The war never did. It wasn't supposed to.

Lovelace was in jail and his friend was dead. Somebody knew why on both counts. Somebody at the firm. He heard his lawyer's voice as he reached the basement floor. He wondered who'd get that beat up briefcase when the old man finally kicked. No one at Calhoun & Morgan.

"I'm here to see Remington Lovelace?" the man said. "Name's Harvey Bing."

The marshal stapled Bing's business card to the file.

"Over here, Harv'," Lovelace called.

"Shut up, you," the guard said. "He's over there."

Lovelace gritted his teeth. With the split TV screens the networks were able to give viewers the weather, last night's ballgame scores, the stock market's ups and downs, and regional news stories like the one about the D.A. lying dead on top of his divorce papers. Something clicked, and Remy remembered the welcome aboard party the Calhoun & Morgan threw for him and another lawyer the firm touted. Helen Grodecki. Morgan was just arrogant enough to turn her loose on the D.A.

"Hey, Luciano," Lovelace yelled. "Don't go anywhere."

Bing waited on the other side of the bars for the lead agent to return.

"Oh, yeah," Nick hollered. "And why not?"

They waited until Luciano was close enough to discuss things in private.

"Why not?"

"Okay, hard nose," Lovelace answered. "I'm ready to deal."

****

Jennings found a digital camera he could impress the folks from forensics with. He pretended to sharpen the image while he made sure they saw his badge.

"About finished?" he asked one of them.

"You kiddin'?" the woman said. "This job takes time, if you do it right."

"Sure it does," Jennings said. "Mind if I take some more pictures?"

"No," she said, not sure he'd taken any at all. "I don't mind."

"Thanks." Jennings worked his way to the D.A.'s desk, snapping once or twice for show. He shielded the phone with his body and lowered the volume control. He pressed the redial button and scribbled down the last number Pomerantz ever dialed before anyone at Selena Hall's residence could answer. He'd worked the crime scene all he wanted.

Through a contact in police identification Jennings was able to match the number to a local address with one call. The clerk told him off the record he'd just researched it for someone else on the force. Jennings knew the man. He had to find Selena Hall before Tobias did.

CHAPTER 35

Luciano put another hole in his scuffed penny loafers pacing the hallway while Lovelace decided how much of the truth he was prepared to tell. He knocked twice and let himself into the conference room.

"I thought you wanted to talk to me," he said to Harvey Bing.

"We're almost done here, Mr. Luciano."

"Look, I've got a jet burning the U.S. Attorney's fuel budget on the runway," Nick said. "I can't wait any longer."

"Please, sir. I'm old. It takes a while. I don't hear so good no more."

Luciano didn't know whether to throw him out of his office or get him a warm glass of milk.

"This better be good, Lovelace. You got five more minutes." He held up as many fingers and left them alone again.

Bing had told his client most of what he knew. Calhoun & Morgan had been turned upside down, mostly the criminal defense section and the finance department. They wanted to hear what Morgan knew, too. He'd been pinched, informally, as Bing understood it, but he wasn't in custody and no one had mentioned his name in connection with the indictments.

"How much does Ethan know, Harvey?"

"About what? I don't think he knew a damned thing about you skimming off the top. None of us did, you dumb ass."

"I never took anything out of your pocket, Harvey. Your deal with the firm is a strict percentage, a third of what you bring in. I checked that out myself."

"No. I mean I never got a cut of what you skimmed, you bastard. You should have thrown a little my way. It might have helped your sorry butt now."

"Oh," Lovelace said. "I'll try to remember that next time."

"Of course, what good is my information? They've got me working practically in the next county. I lost my inside track a long time ago. Calhoun's so ashamed of me he won't even invite me to the Christmas party, the bastard."

"Any idea what they shook out of Ethan?" Lovelace asked.

"No. He's not talking. I'm sure he'll address the shareholders soon, but like you say, I've got my own deal with the firm. I don't sit in on those meetings anymore."

"Too bad," Remy said. "I need to know whether he's gonna back me. I thought he was all right, for a while. Now I'm not sure who to trust. The best lawyer in my section turns out to be a federal agent. If I couldn't see what Soard was all this time who's to say that whole firm's not crawling with cops and informants. I've lost whatever ability I had to read people, Harvey. And I'll tell you something. It's worse than riding a roller coaster blind. I don't know which end is up any more."

"I know the feeling, Remy. But we've got to tell this fella something. Normally I'd say he was pulling your leg about having to go, but I heard them talking about it when I came up. I think this guy really does have a plane waiting for him," Bing said.

"Oh, I'm sure. He's big time. I wish I were half as important as he thinks he is."

"So what have you got?" Harvey asked.

Lovelace came at it from every angle. He could give up plenty, but not without it costing him. He pit the evils against one another and the answer kept coming out the same. He was down but not out. He could liberate himself from that condition, but someone would have to trade places with him.

"What about Pomerantz? Do you think Ethan had anything to do with that?"

"Ethan Morgan?" Bing laughed. "A murderer? Ethan couldn't kill a pint of Shirley Temples."

"I didn't say he killed him. But he's got clients. Some of them are vindictive as hell."

"And?"

"Harvey, what if I told you I've got a client who committed perjury."

"I'd believe you," Bing said. "But how does that help?"

"Because I'm a witness to it. This fellow lied under oath about a dozen times if you add up everything he put in his affidavits. And, oh yeah, he happens to be in business with one of Ethan's clients. You may have heard of him," his voice lowered. "Warren Dunn."

"How close are they?" Bing asked.

"Dunn can't stand him. But he is his partner in the casino they plan now that they passed that law you wrote."

"You talkin' about Bubba Hawkins?"

"Uh-huh. How'd you know—"

"I may be hard of hearing," Bing said, "but ain't nothing wrong with my eyes."

"I need to talk to him, Harvey," Remy said. "It won't help me to give them a guy who perjured himself in an administrative hearing. But if his partner had something to do with what happened to Pomerantz, he may know about it. He's worth something. How much I won't know until I talk to Bubba."

"Remy, how long we been knowin' one another?"

"A long time."

"I gotta tell ya', buddy. That's pretty thin. You're gonna violate your duties to your client, give him up for something that can't possibly help you in the hopes he'll do the same thing to someone else. And you don't even know if he's got anything."

"Hell, Harvey. I know it's thin. But in case you hadn't noticed this is uncharted territory for me. I didn't plan on having my mid-life crisis in D block. It's worth a shot, especially since it's the only one I've got."

Bing had taken worse to a jury before. The other side blinked often enough to make him believe in small miracles. He hadn't lost anything on Ethan Morgan and his bloated legacy law firm. Lovelace did owe something to him, though.

"Harvey," he said. "There is one thing, however. I'm prepared to let the chips fall where they may as far as Ethan's concerned. Him and that whole damned bunch at that firm. I never liked them anyway. And as far as my client goes, he deserves what he gets. I can live with the ethics problems. Besides, if he knows what I think he does, perjury's the least of his worries. And I didn't counsel him to commit murder. If he had anything to do with Pomerantz' death, he's gonna have to answer for that. Screw him."

"So what's your problem then?"

"You."

"How am I your problem? I'm the only one without a badge who wants to get near you."

"All right. Let me ask you this. Did you know," he mouthed Dunn's name again, "was Morgan's client when you drafted the gambling ordinance?"

"No. I didn't hear about that until Ethan told everybody at the luncheon…which I didn't get invited to, by the way."

"So as far as you knew you were just doing what you'd been told when you drafted that law?" Remy asked.

Bing was slow to answer, but Lovelace saw what he wanted to see in his eyes.

"Remy, I'm comfortable with that characterization. I can live with it."

Lovelace patted him on the shoulder. "You're quite a man, Harvey."

"Yeah. But you need quite a lawyer."

Bing opened the door and waved to the guard. "Hey, young fella, where's the man in charge?"

Luciano rounded the corner. "Time's up," he said. "What ch'a got for me?"

"Agent Luciano, did your people seize any videotapes from my client's office when they violated his Fourth Amendment rights?"

"Something wrong with the warrant?" Nick asked.

"Well, did they?"

"Sorry, but I don't have the inventory on me, Mr. Bing."

"Find it," he said. "There should be an unlabeled tape in a clear plastic holder. Bring it to me and I'll show you what's on it…and what it means to you."

Luciano snapped and a girl came over.

"Ellen, run down to the evidence locker and see if you can locate the inventory on Mr. Lovelace's office. Bring me any videotapes you find."

She nodded and was on her way.

"Okay, Mr. Bing. Anything else you want to tell me before I leave."

"Yeah. Have your men pick up a guy named Bubba Hawkins. Here's his work address." He tore off a corner of the chicken scratch notes he'd made while talking to Lovelace. "Home's on there, too."

"Round up your own witnesses," Luciano said. "I already did my investigation."

"A good detective is never done looking. My client's prepared to make a proffer that could prove invaluable in solving a major crime that was committed right under your nose. It might just be worth your while to nab Mr. Hawkins, before the locals grab all the glory."

"On what grounds?"

"Conspiracy to murder the district attorney, for starters," Bing said. "If you're interested."

****

Linda heard the news from the A.M. shock jock as she rolled her hair the next morning. To him it was simply another name he mispronounced from the wire in between traffic and weather.

"Repeating our top story," the announcer said, "District Attorney Michael Pomerantz found dead at city hall. Coroner says cause of death single gunshot wound to the head. Possible suicide. Investigators are on the scene now. More details as they become available."

Linda burned her forehead with the curling iron. She left it plugged in on the sopping wet bathroom counter and collapsed on the floor. The fall and poor circulation put a strain on her system that left her short of breath and her heart needing shallow coughs to keep it going. She pulled it together long enough to find the phone. She couldn't remember when Piper was coming back. If Sean was still on vacation there would be no one in the legal department she could call for the details. She dialed a few numbers in the city manager's office but only got the answering service. She'd promised not to bother Sean again, but neither contemplated their boss' death when she made that pledge.

Piper was unconscious on the sofa when the cell phone rang. He stumbled to the kitchen and yanked it from its charger.

"Yeah," he moaned.

"Sean? Sean, it's Linda."

He thought she was crying. He'd been asleep for less than an hour. The investigators were still combing the D.A.'s office when he finished giving his statement.

"Linda?"

"Yeah. Sorry to bother you. I know I said I wouldn't call anymore while you were on vacation, but something's happened."

"I'm not on vacation," he said. "At least I don't think I am…oooh, what time is it?"

"Six-thirty."

"Oh, God."

"What do you mean you're not on vacation?"

"I'm back, Linda. Remember I told you—"

"Michael's dead!" she blurted.

"I know. I was going to call you first thing this morning."

"It's horrible! They found him in the office. He was shot in the head, Sean. Right in our office."

"I know, Linda. I'm the one who found him."

"What?" What were you doing there last night?"

"We got back yesterday afternoon. I forgot a file I needed for a meeting I was supposed to have this morning. I ran down to the city and he was there when I walked in. It must have happened right before I got there."

Linda sobbed hysterically.

"Look, I don't know what's going to happen today," Sean continued. "It's certainly not going to be business as usual. The police have got the whole floor roped off. I'm going back there in a couple of hours. I was with the investigators until just a little while ago."

"So…was it," she cried, "a suicide?"

"I don't know, Linda. There's all kinds of stories going around. You knew him as well as anyone. Do you think he'd take his own life?"

"Oh, Sean. I don't know what to believe. He was so distant these past few weeks. Even more than usual. He totally lost it when his wife filed for divorce. I don't think he ever believed she'd do it."

"Yeah. That was brutal," Piper agreed.

"You know," Linda whimpered, "he looked different when I saw him last night. He'd had a couple of drinks, but that's nothing new. He had this blank stare. Then he'd think of something else and he seemed fine."

"Linda," Sean said, "the police may want to talk with you, too."

"Oh, God! I can't handle this, Sean. I mean this is really out of control."

"Why don't you stay home today?" he suggested. "If they need you I'm sure they'll be in touch. Like I say, I don't see us getting much done for a while. I would like to see what he was working on, though. Maybe it would tell me something. I don't know. I want to help, but I know the sheriff's department is doing all it can. It's a sick feeling being this helpless."

"Yeah," Linda said. "I may do that, Sean. I may stay home today. I don't feel well."

"Do you need me to do anything?" Sean asked. "I really will be in trouble if you're not all right."

"No, Sean. I'll be okay. It's just a shock. I'll be all right," she assured him.

"I'll have my phone with me all day," he said. "Give me a call if you need anything."

"Thanks, Sean," she started to cry again. "It's comforting having you back. Goodbye."

"Take care, Linda."

Piper rolled off the sofa and landed on the living room floor. His head pounded and his vision was blurred. He'd forgotten to take out his contact lenses when he came home and now they were fried to his eyeballs. Sean staggered into the kitchen and poured a tall glass of something cold. He held it to his forehead, then downed it in one long gulp.

He punched in Anne's number and counted the rings until she woke up. She wasn't as upset as Linda, but still shaken. He told her the details were sketchy, but the main thing was he was all right and the police were on the case. He'd help clean up the mess. It was a time for troopers and he wasn't letting anyone down. Anne told him she loved him and to be careful. She wanted to hear his voice every hour. If he didn't call she'd come down there and embarrass him in front of the cops. He whispered something into the phone and said goodbye. Piper threw cold water on his face, slipped into his wrinkled pants and crawled on the floor in search of his car keys. He found them under a cushion. He put the big one in what he thought was the ignition and tried to start the couch. It wouldn't crank, so he fell into a deep sleep instead.

CHAPTER 36

Mary Goolsby pushed the noisy vacuum cleaner through the living room. She piled her great-grandson's toys halfway to the ceiling with the clunky sweeper throughout Selena Hall's starter home in the transition neighborhood between Oakdale and where it's too nice for Warren Dunn to have condemned. She'd set the newspapers and mail on the harvest table while they were away, but the house needed some attention before Selena and Little Eddie returned from California. She'd pick them up at the airport in a couple of hours. It was exciting, her granddaughter's first magazine cover. Little Eddie would have some stories, too, although none would be about his father. The divorce would be hardest on him, although there'd be enough women in his life to see he grew up the right way whether he stayed close to his father or not. The exposure from this job might allow Selena to support them even if the judge cut Eddie a break on alimony.

Mary finished one room and started on the kitchen's bare floor. A red light on the counter caught her eye. She cut off the vacuum and said, "Oh, dear. I forgot to check the phone."

Selena asked her to screen messages every couple of days. With none culled so far it might take a while for the tape to run. She was to get in touch right away if her lawyer had any news. Mary couldn't remember his name.

"Goodness. How does this thing work?"

She pushed every button until there were voices. She dusted while they played, pausing every so often to write down the names her granddaughter might need. Near the end of the tape a tired sounding man said, "This is…this is Michael Pomerantz."

"That's it," Mary threw down her rag. "That's the man. Attorney Pomerantz."

The lawyer apologized for not having called sooner.

"That's all right," Mary said as if he were sitting across the table. "You talkin' now."

Pomerantz told her what she could expect at her final hearing.

"Get them records in order," she paraphrased. "You got that right. Eddie's sitting on a gold mine with that ball career of his."

The D.A. paused after he said they'd need to get together before the trial, but he never bothered to hang up the phone. Mary wrote a long note at Selena's place around the kitchen table. She wondered if it was for the best. People in her day didn't get divorced. They stuck it out, although she wasn't sure that made any more sense.

"It's her life," Mary said. "Let the girl live it."

The table needed some polish. The living room furniture, too. She'd do that next, then drive to the airport to see how much Little Eddie had grown in two weeks.

The sound of a man's voice startled her. It came from the answering machine but there hadn't been any beeps since Selena's divorce attorney had finished. She couldn't make out what he was saying at first. Then it was too loud, like someone was circling the phone and every so often needed to fill his lungs.

"Don't move," she heard the man say after one orbit. "Keep your hands where I can see them. Don't do anything that…" he faded in and out, "…upset me—"

Another man cut him off. It was Pomerantz. He didn't sound tired this time, just confused.

"Who are you?" he asked.

"Relax," the other man said. "This'll just take…" his voice cut out again, "…few seconds…I won't disturb you long…then I'll leave…in peace."

"What's happening?" Pomerantz asked softly.

"Where' on… -un…sends…'is best…" the first man said, or he might have asked it. Mary couldn't tell.

"Where' on sends 'is best?" she repeated. "What's he saying?"

There were creaky sounds, a desk drawer opening perhaps, then a thud as it closed. A struggle ensued. Someone gasped and she braced herself for a yell, or a scream, or whatever men let out when terror reigns. There was silence instead, a pause where she thought they'd been cut off, and finally a crack of gunfire as real as what she heard in the neighborhood when there was discord in the drug trade.

"Oh, Jesus!" she cried. "Jesus, Lord, they done killed that man!"

She steadied herself in Selena's kitchen chair and waited for the next burst from the machine.

"Done killed him!" she yelled as she listened.

Seconds later another door opened. A man's voice called out desperately, "Mr. Pomerantz! Michael!"

There were bangs and thuds everywhere. Someone raced from room to room, it sounded like, yelling frantically for help and an ambulance.

"Great God A'mighty!" Mary cried.

The tape caught everything, even the knocks the dying man's hand made as it struck the desk in spasms close to the speakerphone, until suddenly she heard it whine and click as the commotion ended.

Mary was woozy at the table, mouth agape and trembling. She was too still, she feared, like her heart needed something else on her body to move with all the blood it pumped. She leaned over the counter, disturbing the pile from two weeks' worth of Selena's unpaid bills and rejection letters.

"The sheriff," she wheezed. "Got to call the sheriff."

Beneath the mail were back issues of the Bristol *Chronicle*. Today's copy was on top. She popped the rubber band and read the caption beneath the file photo of Michael Pomerantz.

"District Attorney?" she said. "He's a divorce lawyer."

The beat writer only had time to note the vital information before the edition went to press. Deputy City Attorney Sean Piper found him slumped over his desk. Dead at the scene from a single gunshot wound to the head. Preliminary indications were that it was suicide.

"Suicide my foot," she said. "That wudn't no suicide. They shot him. That man was murdered."

There was a knock on the door. This time is wasn't Pomerantz' answering machine. Mary leaned far enough to make out the silhouette of a long sedan parked on the street. It might have been a government car, but she couldn't see the plates through the lace curtains. She quickly removed the cassette tape and replaced it with a fresh one hiding behind some of Little Eddie's toys in Selena's junk drawer. She figured whoever it was had come to retrieve the outtakes of the lawyer's last moments on Earth, and to catch whoever'd made them that.

"Just a minute," she said when they knocked a second time. Through the peephole Mary saw two well-dressed men, official types, clean-shaven and fit looking even beneath their sport coats. The shorter man carried a thin binder. He looked through the narrow window beside the door, shielding the sun from his eyes as he peeped into the house. The taller man sized up the neighborhood. The streets were deserted, as was the tot lot across the way. The modest homes were well maintained.

Jennings whispered something and his partner nodded. This was the address that matched the number he'd taken from the D.A.'s call memory screen before Lieutenant Tobias could chase him out a second time.

Mary pulled back the curtain and got a closer look at their ride. It was a dark blue Town Car, brand new she thought, with no City of Bristol markings and no police emblems. Maybe the councilmen had shiny Lincolns, but the troops drove beat-up Tauruses and Crown Vics. The sheriff promoted community policing, like the beat cops who worked city blocks. Mary hadn't seen either of these men at the meetings. She slid the tape beneath her apron, took a deep breath and opened the door.

"Afternoon, ma'am," Jennings said.

She forced a smile and said quietly, "Good afternoon. May I help you?"

"I'm Investigator Morris," Jennings called himself. "This is Lieutenant Sorensen. We're from the Sheriff's Department." He held out his badge. Mary studied it longer than he'd expected her to. The man with the binder shifted his weight from one foot to the other. Jennings wanted to smack him. There was nothing wrong with the badge.

"We're looking for Ms. Selena Hall," Jennings told her. "We understand this is her residence. Is she home?"

"You'll have to forgive me," Mary exaggerated her age only slightly. "I don't see well without my glasses."

Jennings shot her a closed-mouth smile and held up his credentials one more time.

Sorensen was perplexed. "Um. You're wearing glasses right now, ma'am."

"No," she said. "I mean my reading glasses. These are what I use when I'm driving. I have two pair. It's like that when you're old."

"Yes, ma'am," Sorensen said, stopping short of noting it on his clipboard.

"Sheriff?" she said. "Well, what's the matter, officer?"

"Are you Ms. Hall?" Jennings asked.

"No. I'm her grandmother. Mary Goolsby's my name."

"Pleased to meet you," he nodded. "So, your granddaughter's away?"

"Yes."

The car parked in the driveway matched Selena's. If the old lady was covering for her, she was doing it in broad daylight.

"Do you have any idea when she'll be back?" he asked.

"I really couldn't say. I'm just watching the house for her."

"How long's she been gone?" Sorensen asked.

"About a week," she answered.

"I see," Jennings said. "Well, we were hoping to speak with Ms. Hall, but since she's not here, I wonder if we might have a word with you instead."

"Is Selena is any trouble?"

"No," Jennings assured here. "But we would like to talk with her as soon as possible…to apprise her of a situation that's come up. If we can leave the message with you, maybe if she calls you could let her know."

"Of course," she said. "Won't you please come in?"

Mary showed them to the living room. She sat across from them, concerned but smiling pleasantly. She forgot about the tape. It rattled as she ran her hands up and down her pants leg. She thought they might have heard it.

"Can I offer you something to drink?" she tried to cover up.

"No, thank you," Jennings said. "We won't keep you long."

"All right."

"A man was killed last night, a lawyer at the Bristol City Attorney's Office."

"Oh, my."

"Have you heard about that?"

Mary couldn't remember if she'd left the *Chronicle* face up on the table or not. They couldn't see the kitchen from where they sat. She said, "Why, no. What happened?"

"He was shot in the head."

"Heavens."

"We found him still sitting at his desk," Sorensen said. "It may be a suicide, but we're not sure yet."

"Gracious." She listened carefully as they spoke, not for what they said but how it sounded. Neither man matched the voices she heard with Pomerantz. "Who would do such a thing?"

"That's what we're trying to find out," Jennings said. "We believe Pomerantz—that's the man's name—we believe Pomerantz might have called your granddaughter shortly before he was killed. In fact, from his telephone it appears that he may have called her very near the time of death."

"Oh?"

"Yes. Was your granddaughter a client of his, Mrs. Goolsby?"

"I really couldn't say," she answered. "I suppose it's possible. You see, Selena…well, I guess it's okay to tell you…Selena's going through a tough time right now. Her marriage isn't good. The divorce hearing is coming up soon. I don't know when. It's not easy for her to discuss those things with me, with anyone, I'd imagine. You can understand that."

Jennings' shadow did a dance on the carpet. She wondered if their car had to be back by five o'clock.

"Of course I can," he said. "That would be hard to discuss with anyone, especially your grandmother."

"That's right."

"I don't suppose you were here last night, were you?" Sorensen asked.

"Oh, no. I come during the day to collect the mail. I water the plants if they need it. I don't go out much at night anymore."

"Uh-huh," Jennings understood. "Does your granddaughter have an answering machine?"

"Why, yes," she hesitated.

"Maybe he left a message," Jennings said. "From the call history it appears he was on the line to this number for several minutes."

"Really? Hmm."

"Do you mind if we check?" he asked.

"No," Mary said. "I don't mind." Then she added a nice touch. "I believe it's in the kitchen. Follow me."

She moved fast for a lady with two pairs of glasses.

"There," she pointed, "under the cabinet." She scooped up the newspaper and folded it so they couldn't see what she'd been reading.

Jennings alerted on it like a drug dog chained outside a crack house. "There it is, Jimmy."

Sorensen reached to cue up the tape and Jennings stopped him. "Not here," he whispered.

"Ma'am, would you mind if we took this tape down to the station?" Jennings asked. "We'd like our technicians to listen to it. It might give us a clue about what happened to Mr. Pomerantz."

"That tape?" she asked. "No. I don't mind. If you think it will help."

"We won't know until we listen to it," Sorensen promised.

"Yes. Well, I hope you gentlemen find whoever did this. I don't want a murderer running around town. Dear Lord," she said. "Do you think whoever did this would harm Selena?"

"No way to tell, Mrs. Goolsby," Sorensen said. "We're not even sure it was a murder."

"Oh."

"I wouldn't worry, ma'am," Jennnigs said. "It's just something to be aware of. We would appreciate it if you'd let your granddaughter know when she comes home. She can call me at this number," he handed her a card.

"Thanks, officer."

They told her goodbye and climbed back in the Lincoln. Mary waited until they turned the corner and then grabbed the newspaper, locked the house, got in her car and sped off to the courthouse to find the young lawyer mentioned in the *Chronicle*. Someone there could direct her to the City Administration building a few blocks over.

The man who'd called himself Investigator Morris, complete with a newly printed business card that confirmed it, rewound the tape as they drove toward downtown Bristol.

"It's on here," he said. "This thing is full."

Sorensen took the corner on two wheels. "We'll know in a second."

As they passed the Delano Street branch of Jake Amsler's savings and loan the messages began to play. There were some unintelligible noises at first, then the sound of a small child carrying on about something—anything but what had played out in Michael Pomerantz' office the night before. Warren Dunn's men on the take in the sheriff's office did a slow burn as the tape Mary Goolsby switched kicked into high gear. It was his musical debut, Little Eddie Hall and his rapped ode to a very special treat.

Doot, doot, doot, doot…

I like ice cream, that's what's up,

I like it in a cone, I like it in a cup.

My name is Eddie, my best friend's Freddie,

His favorite food's spaghetti.

Did I tell that already?

I like ice cream, I really, really do,

Gonna have a scoop, or maybe two…

I-i-i-i-i-i-c-e cream! I-i-i-i-i-i-c-e cream!

Doot, doot, doot, doot…

I-i-i-i-i-i-c-e cream! I-i-i-i-i-i-c-e cream!

CHAPTER 37

Piper woke up not knowing where he was and with a crick in his neck that looked like Amen Corner at Augusta National. He made right turns all the way to the administration building. The blue lights guided him to the parking garage. Everyone was there, the city cops as well as the sheriff. Pomerantz prosecuted cases for both forces. Everyone who word a badge knew the D.A. His killing was personal. They'd catch whoever did it if it ate up every dime in the budget. God help the usual suspects.

The legal department was open in name only. Linda watched the crime scene investigators like they were part of an interactive TV show. They combed the office for anything that might help them learn what happened to their boss. Piper flashed his ID to prove he belonged there. The deputies recognized him from the chaos earlier that morning and waved him through. That was as far as they were willing to go for him. Sean made his case to one of them who seemed more in charge than the others.

"But I need to see what Mr. Pomerantz was working on. This office is open for business," Piper stated confidently, despite telling Linda they were in hyperspace. "We've got active case files in there, and court deadlines. I'm probably the only one around here who'd be able to make any sense out of that stuff."

"I feel your pain, buddy," the deputy said. "But they're still gathering fingerprints. You get yours all over everything and we'll never know who was in that office."

"I understand," Sean nodded. He wanted to hear someone tell him it wasn't a suicide. By the looks of the crowd in the D.A.'s office it seemed they already knew that.

Tobias walked in and the deputy snapped to attention. "Piper?" he asked to the lawyer.

"Yes, sir."

"I read your statement. That's a helluva note, finding your law partner shot to death. I'm sorry."

"Thank you, sir."

"Drop the sir," Tobias said. "I'm not that much older than you, although if I look like I feel I may have to take that back," he said. "You're in the Marines?"

"Yes."

"I heard you were on vacation. D'ya cut it short?"

"Yeah, I did sort of. I was at the Outer Banks. I wanted to stay longer but things are too busy here. But now all my meetings are canceled. I wanted to see if there was anything I could do to help. Do y'all have any leads?"

"Leads?" Tobias asked as if he'd never heard of such things. "The newspaper says it's a suicide. Isn't that good enough for you?"

"Well, I—"

"Relax, Sean. I don't buy it either. Tell me something, was Mike working on anything unusual recently?"

The whirlwind trip had made Sean a little disoriented. He should be lying on the beach planning his honeymoon instead of talking to a cop about his boss's murder.

"I guess the biggest thing is the gambling ordinance. The council passed a ban on video poker earlier this week. Mr. Pomerantz had been involved with that."

"Uh-huh. Anything else?"

"No," Sean said. "I can't think of anything. I've been working on the riverfront project, wrapping up the condemnations. But Mr. Pomerantz didn't have much direct involvement with them. They're straightforward. Lots of paperwork, but nothing complicated. I'd be interested to know what he was doing in the D.A.'s Office."

"Uh-huh. Okay, Sean."

"I don't suppose you have any idea who did this, do you?"

"If I did it would be confidential," Tobias said.

"Oh."

"But I guess you can keep a secret. For the record we're still gathering evidence. Between you and me it looks like a professional job. Very clean," he pointed to the corner office. "We're not finding much in there."

"Maybe it was a suicide," Piper speculated.

"No. I used to know Pomerantz. He feared death almost as much as he feared growing old. He wanted to be frozen when his time came. That guy didn't take his own life. He planned on living forever."

"Yeah," Sean said. "I agree."

"You look like you could use some rest," Tobias said. "Check with me later, Sean. Maybe I'll have something for you. Go home and get some sleep."

"I'm all right," Sean insisted. He pulled the detective aside. "Any chance I could take a look at the files in there? I don't want to see anything you haven't inventoried yet, but I do need to get some idea what my boss was working on. I'm sure folks will start asking me questions, and if I can't get a peek at that mess I won't know what to tell them."

"Hmm. I hadn't thought of that."

"I don't want to interfere with your investigation. I could set up out of the way. There's a room down the hall. It's secure. They could let me have a few files at a time."

He nodded. "I suppose I could make that happen. Let me check with them and I'll see what I can do."

Tobias worked his men through the imposition. Piper showed them the room he had in mind, and a custodian toted the D.A.'s law practice to him one box at a time. The deputy stood watch outside the door for good measure. Sean dumped the contents on the table and they expanded like a roll of biscuits. Entire portions of key files were missing. He figured some had been labeled and taken into evidence. He understood that, and would be happy to repeat the excuse if anyone asked about a piece of business. It would scare the hell out of whoever wanted Legal to step on it.

Sean sorted what was left, made a sketchy inventory and prioritized the piles. There were phone messages that dated back to his first year of law school. How the D.A. had managed that in just a few months in his new office Sean didn't know. He found three personal checks Pomerantz hadn't bothered to cash, various amounts long since voided, a half dozen subpoenas and as many unanswered complaints where Pomerantz had let the city go into default. Piper wondered why he hadn't just lobbed the cases on his desk like he'd lightened the rest of his load. Sean hadn't cried 'uncle' over anything else.

There'd been recent calls from prominent lawyers in town. Sean recognized most of their names. Ethan Morgan stuck in his mind for some reason. Peter Soard had logged time behind the council podium lately. Maybe that was it. Morgan called several times this week, twice on the day Pomerantz turned up dead. No doubt he wanted to remind him about Calhoun & Morgan's latest bill. From what Piper had seen of their ordinance drafting that deal should have been comped. He knew Harvey Bing wasn't getting much of a cut, and if he did it wouldn't go toward his office furniture.

Sean made his own timeline of how he thought the D.A. spent his last week, his last day, his last hours. The divorce papers were missing. Linda said they landed with a thud on his desk around quitting time that day. He assigned a time to that unpleasant event and plugged it into the equation. He was having trouble connecting the dots, finding a motive that wasn't stuck behind iron bars where Pomerantz had put so many. He knew one thing, though. Tobias was right. It wasn't a suicide. It looked too much like one.

Somewhere after lunch Sean felt his head snap as he bobbed himself to consciousness, not sure whether he'd read the last file three times or not seen it at all. There was a commotion outside the door. He heard the guard's dulcet tones as the disagreement neared them.

Piper stepped into the hall to see what Linda wanted now. The receptionist was flanked by Sylvia Conger, the city's chief troubleshooter Sean affectionately called the Ombuds-person, and an old lady who looked like every other woman he'd defrauded in Oakdale. He ducked too late.

"Sean!" the Ombuds-person nailed him. "In here, Miss Mary," Sylvia led her. She locked them inside and Sean ran out of room in the small office. Sylvia came with her own tape player.

"Listen to this," she said.

The long message confused him. "What's this?" Piper asked. "Are you getting divorced, ma'am?" he asked Mary Goolsby.

"Shhh,' Sylvia hushed him. "Keep listening."

Piper gulped as the D.A.'s voice cracked. They stared at the cassette player as if it was an old radio chapter play. They leaned closer as the struggle faded in and out. The gunshot startled them all, even Mary who'd heard it several times now. Piper was surprised by the sound of his own voice as he desperately tried to revive the D.A. His heart pounded like it had when it happened just a few hours before.

When it was over they sat in stunned silence. The *Chronicle* had it wrong again. Someone had murdered Michael Pomerantz and he'd been kind enough to leave the whole thing on someone's answering machine.

Sylvia made the introductions after the fact. Sean had a million questions for her, but there was time for just a few.

"The men you talked to today, Mrs. Goolsby," he said. "Describe them for me."

"Well…there were two men. Nice looking suits. One short little fellow, stocky though. The other man was tall, almost as big as you. He did most of the talkin'. He had dark hair, and his face was kind of pock-marked like he had a skin condition or something."

"What were their names?"

"I can't remember the little fella's name. The larger man was Investigator Morris. He showed me his badge. It looked real to me, but I've never seen either of them in our neighborhood before, so I wasn't sure I should give them this."

"Uh-huh." Sean looked in the stack of junk on the table. "I wonder. The sheriff has a book he puts out every couple of years. What am I trying to say?" The adrenalin was working against thirty-six hours of no sleep. "God…a directory," he said. "Sylvia, do you have a copy in your office?"

"Sure do," she said. She relayed the request to the troops and in no time they were turning the pages in search of Deputy Morris.

"This the guy?" Sean pointed.

"Him? No. He doesn't look a thing like the man I saw," she said.

"I don't understand. This is the only Morris in the department. Sylvia, how current is this?"

"Came out last month, Sean."

"Maybe he didn't sit for his picture," Mary said.

"Oh, no, if you work for the sheriff, your face is in here," Sylvia assured her.

"Keep looking," Piper said. "He's got to be here somewhere."

Mary studied the officers closely, reaching the end with no luck.

"Flip to the front," he said.

"Okay."

"You sure about his name?" Sylvia asked.

"Yes. Like I said, I got to look at his badge and…here he is!"

Sean matched the name with his mug shot. "Investigator Jennings, Randall K."

"Jennings?" Mary asked. "He said Morris."

Piper turned the page. "Does he look like Morris?"

"Sure don't," she admitted.

"Did you see the other man in here?" he asked.

"No."

Sylvia was used to working the problem quickly. She'd have had it assigned to someone now and moved on to the next unsolved murder.

"So what should Miss Mary do, Sean? Stay away from her granddaughter's house?"

"Absolutely. They'll be back for sure when they find out you gave them the wrong tape. If I were you I'd—"

"Oh, Lordy!" Mary exclaimed.

"What Miss Mary?"

"Selena! I was supposed to pick her up at the airport. Her plane's probably here already. She told me she'd take a cab and not to bother, but I wanted to surprise her."

"What time?" Piper asked.

"Three o'clock."

Piper held out his watch. "Twenty 'til," he said. "We've run out of time. Come on!"

"Sean! What are you doing?" Sylvia said.

"If the plane's late we may have a chance."

"We?"

"Yes. You go to the airport," he told her. "Look for a beautiful model and a little boy. If you find them, don't come back here. And don't take her home. Call me on my cell phone and we'll meet up later."

"But I—"

"You're coming with me," he grabbed Mary by the arm.

"Sean! Where are you going?"

"I need her. I don't know where Selena lives."

"And I don't know what she looks like!" Sylvia said. "Let's get the police."

"Who are you going to tell, Sylvia? Investigator Randall K. Jennings? You tell me who we can trust at this anymore."

They knew he was right. They couldn't tell administration either. All they'd do is hold a press conference announcing what's on that tape, and then take bids from consultants on what to do about it.

Piper wrapped the cassette in heavy paper and stuffed it in his backpack. Mary lagged behind him. She'd never make it to the stairs.

"Wait here," he said as he summoned the elevator. "Meet me in the parking garage, second floor."

"Okay." She was winded, but amazed at how much action she'd gotten from her public official. Piper stopped and Mary asked, "What's the matter?"

"Uhh. You'll never be able to climb into my convertible. Sylvia!" he hollered. "I need a car!"

"What?"

"From the motor pool! You know what I drive!"

She did indeed. "You got it!"

CHAPTER 38

By the time Little Eddie finished the second chorus of 'I like ice cream' Jennings had doubled back to Oakdale. They jimmied the back door, pried open the bathroom window and let themselves in like cat burglars. Jennings waited in the living room. Sorensen covered the den across the hall. They peeked through the curtains, but there were no cars coming in either direction along Riverfront Drive.

"You sure this chick's coming in today?" the little man asked.

"Yeah, Tommy," Jennings whispered. "That's what they told me."

"Okay. It's ten 'til four now. Let's say her plane got here on time. She's been to the baggage carousel by now. She made her way to the parking lot and found her car."

"Her car's parked out back," Jennings said.

"Okay, she takes a cab then. Traffic shouldn't be a problem this time of day. She should be pulling in any minute."

"Uh-huh."

"So where is she?"

Jennings didn't answer.

"Huh, Randall. She oughta be here by now."

"Shut up. Here comes somebody," Jennings said softly. "Stop those curtains from swinging."

The muscle car had tinted windows, wheels that shined like a new dime and a stereo that couldn't sneak up on a dead man.

"That's no taxi," Sorensen whispered.

Eddie Hall, Selena's soon-to-be ex-husband, unfolded his six foot four frame and started toward his old house. "And that's no chick," he said. "Damn, he's built like a linebacker."

Eddie rang the bell.

"Get back," Jennings whispered. "He'll see you."

Hall tried again. "Open up, Selena! I know you're in there. I see your car. I know you can hear me. Open up!"

"What do we do?" Sorensen asked.

"Shut up."

Eddie pressed his face against the glass but saw nothing through the white lace curtain. When no one answered after the third ring he went to the driveway and felt the hood of Selena's

Nissan. The engine was cold. He walked the grounds, finding nothing but an overgrown backyard and the football he gave Little Eddie last Christmas. He returned to the front porch and decided to wait on the steps.

Inside the dirty cops kept an eye on him.

"Who the hell is this guy?" Jennings asked.

"Beats me. Sure wants in, though."

"How long do you think he'll stay?"

"Why don't you go ask him that, Tommy?"

They stayed that way for a while, two strangers waiting for Selena Hall on the sofa she bought when they were newlyweds, while her husband was locked out of his own house.

"This screws up everything, Randall. This guy ain't going away. We may have to—"

"She's here," Jennings whispered.

"What?"

"I think this is her, Tommy."

The yellow cab turned the corner, slowing as it neared her house. Little Eddie stuck his head out of the window as they pulled into the driveway.

"Dad! Hey, Dad's home!" he shouted.

Selena got out slowly. She stayed by the car as her son tugged on her sleeve. Eddie stood up but didn't leave the porch.

"What are you doing here?" she asked.

"It's my house too, remember?"

The curtains behind him swung from side to side. She didn't notice if the windows were open.

"Selena, I want to talk to you. I think we should try to—"

"Who's in the house, Eddie?"

"—work things out. I think we should…what?"

"Who's in the living room? Look at the curtains."

Piper screeched the tires as the government sedan roared down Riverfront Drive. Mary Goolsby gestured wildly toward her granddaughter. He swerved to miss the taxi, spinning out on the driveway as he gave the Halls a vicious yard job.

Jennings came out first, followed closely by Sorensen. Eddie turned in time to see the butt end of the revolver coming his way, but couldn't react fast enough to dodge the pistol whip. He dropped to one knee. The sun blinded him as he tried to see their faces.

"Eddie!" Selena screamed. He rolled down the steps, coming to rest on the tall grass.

Mary cried for her granddaughter, but Selena didn't know what time zone it was. Piper wrapped his long arm around her tiny waist and heaved her like a sack of potatoes to the back seat. He corralled her son and tossed him the same way, slamming the door as Little Eddie yelled, "Daddy! Daddy!"

Sean threw it in reverse and spun the wheels across the lawn. Sorensen ran next door to where he'd hidden their car. Jennings caught half of the license plate. He repeated it in his head as the car disappeared.

Jennings towered over Eddie Hall. The big man wasn't moving. He kicked him in the stomach until blood trickled out of Eddie's mouth. His partner cut a new road to the Hall residence. He gave Eddie one more boot for good measure, leaving him motionless on the front yard, but still breathing. They sped after Piper through the streets of Oakdale.

"Did you get the tag?" Sorensen asked.

"Enough of it. He's driving a city car," Jennings said. "Same as ours."

****

Luciano put his size twelve wide through the door to Skeeter's Video Palace and grabbed the first nappy head he saw.

"Three seconds," he said as he twisted Skeeter's quarter-plunking arm off. "Where's Bubba Hawkins?"

"Ow! Damn, you breakin' my arm, boy!"

"One, two—"

"Upstairs! All right? He's upstairs!"

Bubba heard the ruckus below and peered over the banister at them.

"Cops," he told the stock boy. "They think they can shut me down. Well, I got news for them. All this crap's legal now, courtesy of the City of Bristol."

Luciano reached the top of the stairs then rolled downhill all the way from there.

"Y'all can't come barging in here like this," Bubba declared. "You think you're gonna get an injunction or something, huh? Well, you just try to find a court that'll let you—"

"Shut up!" Luciano cradled him at the base of his fat skull. He drove his head into the flimsy wood paneling, leaving a hole big enough to run with the bulls through. He made a matching one beside it, and Bubba let out a noise that was the vocal equivalent of a white flag.

"What the hell are you doing?" he said as his backside inched to the chair.

"Frank," Luciano said. "What d'you see?"

"I saw him throw several punches at you and make other aggressive movements in your direction. Fortunately, you were too fast and they all missed. Then he slipped and hit his head on the wall…twice."

"I'll sign that statement," Luciano said.

"You guys cops?"

Luciano's eyes crossed. "What do you think, scumbag?"

"Then what are you hitting me for? You can't do that. I've got rights."

"Sure you do, pal. You have the right to an orthopedic shirt. You have the right to radical reconstructive surgery. You have the right to give someone a high five with two fingers. Frank, ask him if he understands his rights."

"Understands them. I think he's ready to waive every one."

"Give me the phone," Bubba begged. "I wanna talk to my lawyer."

Luciano smiled like he was chewing a coat hanger. "Isn't that wonderful? You want to see your lawyer, and your lawyer wants to see you. In fact, he wants to see you so bad he told us where to find you."

"What?"

"Remington Lovelace is your attorney, isn't he?"

"How'd you know that?"

Luciano stood him up and fit him for a set of matching cuffs. He changed his mind and used the humiliating plastic twisty the professional protesters get once they've made their point.

"Oh, I reckon there's not much I don't know about you, Mr. Hawkins," Luciano said. "But we're gonna chat awhile anyway.

Frank, you wanna look downstairs and see if there's anyone we can bring along to keep him company?"

"You got it, boss."

"I mean as long as Lovelace is giving out names."

****

Piper nestled the beat up *Ford* in the cradle between two slow moving eighteen-wheelers heading south of Bristol. After the screaming stopped there was silence as what could sink in did. It was awkward trying to make the introductions with his eyes glued to the dusty semi and his passengers sobbing in the back seat.

Mary did her best to explain the message Pomerantz left on Selena's machine. Sean wanted to ask her who would have motive to kill her lawyer, but he was afraid she'd say, 'Who wouldn't?' He couldn't discuss it with her son slumped across her lap.

Thirty miles out he pulled off the highway. They found a gas station that was half unleaded and half McDonald's. Sean gave Grandma Goolsby enough money to buy Eddie a Happy Meal. He asked if she'd stay with him while he talked to Selena.

"Do you think they killed him?" she asked.

"Those men? I don't know, someone did. The tape proves it."

"Tape? No, I mean Eddie."

"Oh."

She wiped her eyes with a recycled napkin. It was the first time he'd gotten a good look at her angelic features. The rearview mirror during their escape hadn't done it justice. Her long, creamy legs brushed against his under the table. She thought it was a support for the booth. He wasn't about to tell her different. Even with tears running down her face, she still was worth burning a roll of film on and making each one of the prints a billboard. She batted her moist eyes and he managed to get out of the way before her lashes struck him from across the booth. Selena Hall was enough to make a monk dispute the fine print.

"I don't know," Sean said. "I didn't hear any shots. They followed us so fast they may not have had time even if they wanted to. We were lucky to lose them. It may not have been necessary for us to drive this far, but I don't want to take any chances."

"My son wouldn't be able to handle it. If they killed him, he wouldn't be able…"

The tears choked out the rest of it.

"There were too many witnesses," Piper consoled her. "You, me, your son, your grandmother, the cab driver, and whoever else came out when they heard me screeching down the street. It was broad daylight. They wouldn't risk it."

Selena smiled faintly. It led to another recycled napkin across her million dollar eyes. "I hope you're right."

He had more questions. She was a wreck, the best looking one on the lot.

"Are you…do you want something to eat? You can order by the numbers here."

"I'm not hungry," she said.

"I know," Piper said, his Marine training coming through. "But it may be awhile before we get the chance again."

She let it go.

"So you don't have any idea who might have wanted to kill Mr. Pomerantz."

She stared past him to her son lying on a pallet of rubber balls on the playground. "No."

"When was the last time you talked to him?"

"Couple of weeks ago. Before we left for L.A. In his office."

"How'd he seem?" Sean asked.

"Same as always. We talked about my case. He thought it looked good for me, as good as a divorce can be. He wanted to get together when I got back," she said. "What's going to happen to us?"

"You can't go home," Piper said. "I doubt those guys expect you to come back any time soon, but they may still be watching. Your grandmother's place is out of the question, too. I haven't told her that yet. I'd take you to my apartment, but there's a chance they know who I am."

"God," Selena shook across from him, "I can't believe it. I never should have filed for divorce. Maybe none of this would have happened."

Sean couldn't stop looking at her. He wanted eye contact to see if any of it was registering, but she wouldn't have it. Pomerantz dialed her number late at night, his guard down over the divorce and more whiskey than usual. She was who he thought of when he was sad and lonely, unattainable even in his wildest dreams. She crept into the D.A.'s fevered mind at the lowest point in his life. She was the one. Sean understood why.

"We should go," he said. "I have to see someone in the sheriff's office."

"I thought you said it was the cops we're running from."

"Not everyone in the sheriff's department is on the take. It's a good office. How Jennings went bad I don't know. Someone must have paid a pretty price to turn him."

"I don't feel like talking to anyone else right now."

"I wasn't planning on taking you with me," Sean said.

"Why not if we have nothing to fear from the sheriff?" Selena asked.

"I didn't say that. I said not everyone in his department is crooked. Trouble is I don't have a program of all the good players."

"So what are we supposed to do while you're gone?"

"I'm not sure, exactly."

"Not sure exactly? Terrific."

"Come on," he said. "Let's get back to the car. On the way home I'll think of something."

She stayed in the booth. It was the safest place since her plane had landed.

"Come on. You can trust me. You can trust me if nobody else. Do I look like a guy who wants to see a young girl cry? It'll be all right, Selena. But we've got to get going."

She dried her eyes and followed him slowly to the door. Mary and Little Eddie were waiting for them. Piper took a circuitous route to Bristol, changing lanes enough so that if anyone had been following him they'd be seasick. He pulled into a Hampton Inn not far from downtown. Piper rented a double in a fictitious name, no luggage.

They snuck in through the back and drew the curtains. Piper had a man-to-man talk with Little Eddie. He didn't understand what had happened at their house, and why he couldn't see his dad. He smiled for the first time when Sean told him his theory about what must have happened.

"I can't promise you he's all right, Eddie. But I think there's a good chance. All we can do is pray that God will take care of him. Okay?"

"Okay," he said hopefully.

Mary had her arm around Selena as they watched the closest thing the boy had had to a father-son talk in a long time.

"I'll be back with best news I can as soon as possible," Sean said. "Lock the door behind me and don't go out. If anyone knocks besides me, call the front desk and tell them the room's on fire."

"Fire?" her son said.

"Never mind, Eddie. Just tell your mom."

He turned the knob. Someone touched his back and he stopped.

"Be careful, Sean," Selena whispered. "I'll never be able to thank you for what you did for us today."

"Right," he exhaled. "I'll see you soon."

He took the stairs down two flights and rode the elevator the rest of the way. The parking lot was half full, about right for middle of the week with an away football game scheduled.

Sean guided the hard-driven Ford down Main Street. Every so often he zigzagged to a parallel road to see if anyone was following. He couldn't tell much. All the headlights looked the same. A bright pair closed on him steadily. Piper sped up and they stayed at the same interval. He changed lanes, slowed almost to a stop and made a sweeping turn onto Pamlico Street. His shadow turned with him. Sean saw a tinge of yellow in a row of stoplights ahead. They were all about to change and the sea would part for him if he timed it right. He crawled along with the tail content to keep his distance. There was a rolling stop to the first light. Piper floored it as the sequence unfolded. His heart raced as whoever was behind him followed suit. They reached sixty miles an hour on a street made for parades.

Piper slammed on the brakes and turned too late. He was headed the wrong direction on the one-way street. A little later in the evening and he might have gotten away with it. A city crew getting in a night street sweep pulled into his path. He was blocked in. Sean cut across the sidewalk to a narrow alley he didn't know was there. Bright lights shined in his mirrors. A rusty yellow sign that had been knocked over leaned against a dumpster.

"Dead end!" he exclaimed.

Sean ran out of room a few yards past it. There was a chain link fence in front of him, and several stories of brick building on either side. Behind him high beams drew near. He found reverse and put the pedal through the floorboard. The collision shot the back end of his car four feet in the air. He checked the damage. It worked. Their late model car had airbags everywhere. Its passengers looked like they were trying to rip off straight jackets.

Piper bailed. He made it over the fence and sprinted toward Confederate Park. He heard the chain-links rattle as his pursuers struggled to clear the fence. He could outrun all of them. He turned to see who was closest. A car slowed to see what was wrong. Piper considered flagging it down, but the driver was one step ahead of him.

Someone crawled out of the back seat and dove for his legs. Piper sidestepped him. The other man leaped into action, and before Sean could slip by he felt his knees buckle. He didn't recognize any of them, not the driver, nobody from the car that had tailed him since the hotel and not the acrobat who made the shoestring tackle.

Another car screeched its tires, and the skid mark ended a few feet from the pileup. Someone yelled at them. He wanted to see Piper's hands, or he'd let him have it right there.

"Hands!" he cried. "Lemme see 'em!"

He heard someone chamber a round in a serious looking revolver. *Cha-ching!* Then a chorus of guns made ready. *Cha-cha-cha-ching!* Sean thought this was it.

The man closest to him shined a light in his eyes.

"Get that flashlight off his face," a winded voice said.

They rolled him on his back, and Piper was afraid to look.

"Your name Piper?" the man said.

Sean wondered which answer would keep him alive.

"Well?"

"Yes," he said.

The man helped him to his knees. "We want to talk to you about Michael Pomerantz."

"We?"

Piper's eyes said 'thank God,' and his mouth formed a smile that tried to swallow his forehead.

"Special Agent Luciano. Is this a good time?"

CHAPTER 39

Harvey Bing made an unusual request on behalf of his client, but it was way above the guard's pay grade.

"I don't know," the federal officer said. "I've never heard of that before. But it's not up to me. I'll pass it along. I wouldn't count on him going for it."

"Thank you, son," Bing said as the young man excused himself to find the agent in charge. Luciano laughed out loud until he realized the kid was serious. He stormed down the hall and Harvey assumed crash position.

"You want what?"

"We need to speak with Mr. Hawkins. You did arrange to have him picked up, didn't you?"

"Yeah. I arranged it."

"Excellent. We'll be waiting in your office."

"Look, crazy old man. I'm not letting you talk to my prisoner."

"Agent *Lucy-ahh-no,* what in the hell do you want with Bubba? What do you care about some Bristol hick who perjured himself before a state mobile home board? That ain't gonna get you transferred outta here."

"Are you representing Hawkins, too?"

"No. I'm afraid that might be a conflict of interest."

Luciano chuckled. "I didn't realize that would stop you."

"Besides," Harvey said, "Mr. Hawkins has a lawyer."

"Oh yeah? Who?"

"Mr. Lovelace."

"Classic," Luciano laughed again. "That figures. Are you nuts, Bing?"

"Yes. But that's got nothing to do with it," he said. "Look, federal cop, you give us five minutes alone with Bubba Hawkins and I'll have something that'll make you a big man at headquarters."

Luciano thought it over. Deep down he liked the shyster's idea, but if anyone found out he put the conspirators in the same room they'd run him out of the Bureau.

"Come on, Luciano. Five minutes. What have you got to lose?"

Luciano turned and walked away slowly. Bing had given it his best shot. It looked like a miss. The lawyer sat outside trying to think of what to tell Lovelace. There was plenty of news, bad and worse.

"Five minutes." he heard a voice from around the corner. Luciano caught up with it. Bubba Hawkins was with him. "Then I'm gagging both of them and throwing your sorry butt in the street, Bing. Your time starts now."

****

Piper sat in the same chair the agents used on their suspects. That was as guilty as they made him feel. A handsomely put together woman poured a Coke over ice and asked if he needed anything else. He asked her if she wouldn't mind moving the light out of his eyes. She smiled and it was done.

Sean studied the tall figure in the corner. The suit hung on him like he was born wearing it. He looked nothing like the men who tackled him in the alley a few minutes earlier, more polished as if he might be able to make a compelling case without resorting to violence.

"I know you from somewhere," Piper said.

"You do," the agent codenamed Mason said.

"You're a lawyer. I've seen you around the courthouse. You work for a big firm out in town, right?"

"Not anymore," Soard said.

"Yeah, yeah. Calhoun and Morgan. That's it. You did a lot of work with Pomerantz. You came before city council the other day."

"I used to work for them. That's all over."

Soard told Piper about Operation Diamond Dog, how he'd been recruited to work for the Attorney General's White Collar Crime Task Force, set up in a mega-firm when Remington Lovelace suddenly left his solo practice, how he'd infiltrated the tax cheat's section working the inside for a year to gain his confidence and enough evidence to take down the centerpiece of corruption in his crooked law firm.

"This is a very interesting cassette, Sean. I'd like for you to listen to it with me and tell us just what this is."

Soard played the tape Piper had listened to with Mary Goolsby and Bristol's Ombuds-person. It was tougher for him to hear it this time. He knew where all the jolts were. There was no shock any more, just helplessness and misery.

"Well?"

"It's Mr. Pomerantz all right," Piper said. "I don't know who the other man is."

"I'm curious about everything on here, but there's one part in particular. Terry," Soard turned to his partner, "cue it up again." Sean's stomach turned.

"Right here," Soard said. "Turn it up."

The killer's voice faded in and out. "Where' on… -un…sends…'is best…"

"Did you catch that?" he asked.

"No," Piper answered. He listened again but it wasn't any plainer.

"What about now?"

"No. I'm sorry," Sean said.

"Terry," Soard handed him the tape. "Take this to the studio. See if they can enhance this part."

"Sure thing, Pete," he said.

Soard continued with Piper's statement. Sean seemed nervous and he asked him why.

"The lady Pomerantz called. The one the answering machine tape belongs to. I know where they are," Sean told him.

"You what?"

"I know where they're staying. Before your guys picked me up—or before they scared the hell out of me in that ambush—I went to her house. She had just returned from the airport. Her grandmother was with me, a lady named Mary Goolsby. Selena and her son had just arrived. There was a man on the front porch. I later found out it was her husband. Guy's name is Eddie Hall. They jumped him. One of them hit him hard across the back of his head. I think he may still be alive."

"One of them?"

"There were two men hiding inside the house," Sean continued. "The grandmother says they were posing as sheriff's investigators. One of them may be. But he's having second thoughts. They cold-cocked her husband and drew their weapons on us. I grabbed Selena and her son and got out of there. They chased us, but I lost them and drove south of here until I was sure of it. Although now I don't know. You found me easy enough."

"Go on, Sean. Where are they now?"

"Hampton Inn. Downtown. Near where you guys started following me."

"What room?"

"Four-nineteen."

"Go get Luc'," Soard told another member of their team. "Hurry."

Luciano was about to break up Bing's meeting when he heard his name. He told them to knock it off, but the man calling looked serious. He let himself in. Piper flinched. He was even nastier looking than he'd remembered.

"The girl's at the Downtown Hampton. Room four-nineteen. She's got her kid and the grandmother with her. Piper says there were two men looking for them. They want the tape. Go get 'em, Luc'."

"Four-nineteen. Right. We're on our way."

Soard pulled up a chair and sat across from Piper.

"You look beat," Sean said. "Almost as tired as I am."

"I started out this morning in London."

"England?"

"That's the one."

"What were you doing there?" Sean asked.

"Forgetting this place," he said. "Then someone decided to kill the D.A. That changed things." Soard rolled his sleeves up and found another gear Piper wished he had. "Okay, Sean. Now tell me the rest."

****

Lovelace hadn't shown anyone his famous cool side for a while. He wasn't sure there was any ice left.

"Bubba, I'm gonna lay this out one more time. Listen carefully. You're screwed. You're screwed in a massive and relentless way. This video's just the warm-up act. I don't know for sure how many counts of perjury this translates to, but it's five years per."

"How'd you get it, Remy? How'd you get a videotape of my driver crashing that trailer into the bridge?"

It was the tape Peaches had given to Soard in Georgetown, the second envelope the lobbyist told him to hand straight to Dunn. The problem was Soard didn't get a sit-down with him. That was the way Morgan wanted it. So when Ethan previewed it in his office he remembered how Lovelace had told him about his commission hearing. This looks like it belongs to you, Morgan told him. You might need it for your hearing…or someday. Ethan was right on time again.

"How did I get it? An old friend of yours had it delivered to me personally. So I could dime your ass out and remove you from the picture while he cleaned up."

"What the hell?"

"You know who I'm talking about. It was Dunn, Bubba. It was your business partner, Warren Dunn."

"You're crazy. Why, I don't—"

"The man who had the D.A. killed. If that didn't work I'm sure you were next. His lawyer brought it to me on a silver platter, Bubba. On a bright, shiny damned silver platter. There was enough room left on it for your head. Now do you want to listen to my proposition or don't you?"

****

Luciano's men swept the hotel's fourth floor. Selena was gone. They found Mary Goolsby and Little Eddie in the game room. Selena thought it would take his mind off his father. When they returned the room was empty. The agent in charge called his partner.

"They got the girl."

Soard was afraid of that. "Say that again, Luc'."

"They got her, Pete. The old lady took the kid to the game room. When they came back Selena was gone."

"Dammit. You in pursuit?"

"Negative. We got nothing."

"Roger. The others okay?"

"Yeah. We're on our way back."

"Okay, Luc'. Keep your eyes open. Looks like whoever's turned in the sheriff's office has friends."

"Yeah," Nick said. Watch out, partner."

"You do the same." Soard dropped the expensive radio and let out a sigh.

Piper heard enough of their conversation to fill in the blanks. "I never should have left them alone," he said.

The technician Soard told to work on Selena's answering machine burst into the room. "I got it, Pete!" he said excitedly. "I know what he's saying. Listen to it now."

He cued up the polished track, leaving no doubt what Pomerantz' killer said right before he pulled the trigger. All that mess, "Where' on... -un...sends...'is best...," was clear now. "Warren Dunn sends his best."

"Dunn," Soard whispered. "But the ordinance passed."

"Warren Dunn?" Piper asked. "Why would he want to kill Michael Pomerantz?"

Soard patted his soundman on the back. "Nice work, Darren. Put yourself down for a commendation."

"Why would he want to kill the D.A.?" Piper asked again.

"I've got to go next door, Sean."

"Pete?"

"When this is all over we're gonna have a long talk about your boss and Calhoun & Morgan," Soard told him.

He left Piper to fill in the missing pieces while he walked across the hall to fetch a big one for himself. He crashed the coup plotters and said, "I'm Agent Soard. Good evening, Remy."

Lovelace scowled at him. "Hello, Pete. I didn't think you'd ever show your face—"

"Not now, Remy," he told his old boss, the tables turned and the junior associate now fully in charge. "My partner wanted to see you, but I can't trust him at the moment. He's got this wild look in his eyes, like he did just before...the incident. I don't think they'd let him kill *two* suspects. Not while they're in custody."

Bing recognized the young man from his ordinance drafting days.

"Oh, my God," Harvey said.

"That's right, you crazy old man. Terry," he turned to his partner. "If he opens his mouth again, close it for him."

"Yes, sir," Terry promised.

"We know all about Warren Dunn," Soard leveled at Bubba.

"So?" Hawkins said.

"And that you're his partner."

"Congratulations," Bubba responded.

"Dunn's got the girl," Soard said. "He's got the girl you've been after."

"I don't know what you're talking about."

"Where'd he take her?"

"How would I know?" Bubba asked.

Soard grabbed him by the lapels. He knocked him chair and all into the wall. Bubba picked himself up and found his place at the table.

"Let me tell you something, you miserable son of a bitch," Soard jammed him enough to make Lovelace proud. "I could arrange for you to hang yourself in your jail cell. And I have a strong feeling that the medical examiner will see it my way. So you may not know where your boss took them, but you sure as hell can guess. And you better get this one right."

Luciano had been a kitten compared to the way Peter Soard conducted an interrogation.

"And I mean on the first try."

****

Skeeter Teal waited on hold until Dunn's secretary gave in.

"I'm sorry," she said. "Now who is this again?"

"This is Joe Poundstone," he tried a fresh approach. "I'm the manager at the Cloud Nine Motel. Mr. Dunn left his American Express card here this afternoon. What does he want me to do with it?"

"Oh, my," Dunn's secretary said. "I don't…I couldn't tell…I'll have to—"

"At least he didn't leave home without it, huh lady?"

"Yes, well, I'll just let you talk to him about it."

Skeeter hung on the line only a moment longer.

"Yes?" the man said.

"Mr. Dunn?"

"Who is this?"

"Are you Warren Dunn?"

"Yes."

"My name's Skeeter Teal. I work for Bubba Hawkins."

"Oh?"

"I just thought you'd like to know they picked him up this afternoon."

Dunn put him on the speaker. "What?"

"Bubba. The cops busted him. I don't know where they took him. I guess he's down at the station by now," Teal said. "I thought you'd like to know that. Maybe you can help get him out. If Bubba sits in jail, none of us get paid."

Dunn wanted to hang up. His phones weren't bugged the last time his people checked, but he didn't know this guy from cold meat. If the sheriff had him, Jennings would be the first to hear about it.

"I appreciate the call," Dunn said. "Goodbye."

He strolled to the window where everything was clear. His men answered to him. They didn't care if Bubba stayed in the picture or not, so long as Dunn paid for their time.

Sorensen stood beside his partner. Jennings had the steel back in his eyes. Dunn turned slowly to see if they were still with him. "You boys get that?"

CHAPTER 40

Bubba shook so hard the agent couldn't work with him.

"Hey," Luciano said. "Relax, okay? They can't fit you for that wire if you don't sit still."

"Gimme a break," Bubba said. "You know what they'll do to me if they find out I'm wearing this."

"All the more reason to keep cool. Look, the hard part's over. You help us tonight and you beat a murder rap. We know Dunn gave the order."

"Yeah. I've got it made, if I come back alive."

"There'll be agents crawling all over that building," Luciano assured him.

"You don't even know if he's there," Bubba said.

Soard answered that one. "He's there. Our spotter saw him through the window just a few minutes ago."

Luciano sat Hawkins down for one more round of instructions.

"Now, we know you don't drop in unannounced very often, Bubba, so make sure Dunn understands you're concerned about the girl. You heard there were others with her and that they got away. You want to make sure everything's still on for your business with him. You've got a lot invested and you want it protected. Understand?"

"Go on."

"Get him talking about Selena, how his men kidnapped her tonight. Ask if he plans to rub her out, like he did with Pomerantz. Don't get too close to him. The microphone's sensitive, so you don't have to smother him. But don't stand far away either."

Bubba was green. If he threw up it would mean a wardrobe change and they were out of time.

"Come on," Luciano tapped his shoulder. "Let's go."

Soard had men stationed in the stairwell, not far from where he stood on the day he called 'Diamond Dog.' They were on the floor beneath Dunn's penthouse, too, and a spotter with night vision goggles on the rooftop across the street. Everyone was patched into Bubba's wire through a command post in a van parked on Pamlico Street.

Bubba drove to the Dunn Plaza garage and the spot his partner had reserved for him as a sign of their lasting relationship. His elevator code still worked, and he held on tight until he reached the top floor. The night help waved him through the outer office. Dunn's suite was open. Bubba walked inside. Someone closed the door behind him before he knew Jennings and Sorensen were there.

"Bubba," Dunn said with a smile he hadn't expected. "Good to see you."

"Good evening, Warren. I didn't think you'd be happy to see me."

Luciano heard that in his earpiece and said, "Putz. He outta just confess to him right now."

Dunn said, "Nonsense. I'm glad you dropped by. Randall and Tommy were just telling me how much they missed you."

"Oh," he turned, surprised to see them.

"Hello, Bubba," Jennings said.

Luciano had confused Hawkins with a code he wanted him to use to identify the number of men he saw in Dunn's office. The spotter could only see anyone who stood by the window. Bubba was too scared to pick up on the system or the harmless sounding terms he was supposed to fit into the small talk. From the conversation they knew there were at least two more besides Dunn.

"What happened to Selena Hall?" Bubba asked. "Did you find her?"

No one answered.

"What about the tape?" he tried instead.

Dunn played dumb. "Tape? I have no idea what you're talking about, Bubba. Have you been drinking?"

"What d'you mean you don't know what I'm talking about? The Hall lady? Did we get her?"

"Randall," Dunn said. "Tommy, do you have any idea what our good friend is referring to?"

"Un-huh," Jennings said.

"No clue," Sorensen followed.

There was a dull thud right after the last man spoke, and a louder one when they couldn't stop Bubba from falling to the floor. No one talked after that. Soard thought the wire had shorted out.

"Talk to me, Luc'," he whispered.

"Nothing, Mason," he slipped back into their sting names. "I got nothing."

"Your call," Soard told the lead agent.

"Dunn didn't say anything. We've got nothing on the tape."

"So what do you want?"

Luciano shrugged his shoulders. The spotter called in that whoever'd been in the window was gone.

Soard confirmed it from his vantage point. "Luc', they may be on the move."

"Roger," Luciano said.

"We're not all mobile," Pete reminded him. They had planned to storm Dunn's penthouse, not get outrun by him in his Mercedes.

"Roll with it, gents," Luciano said. "Let's see where they take him."

The elevator stopped a few paces from Dunn's *Escalade*. Jennings and Sorensen flanked Bubba on either side in the back seat. A third man drove as Warren rode shotgun. They pulled Bubba's tiny microphone off carefully. Jennings wrapped a thick napkin around it and cut the wire.

"This isn't city stuff. Make sure you're not followed," Jennings told the driver.

They drove the speed limit through town, and a little more than that on the frontage road. When they hit the highway the driver floored it like Bristol had an Autobahn.

"I love this car," he said.

"Anyone behind you?" Dunn asked.

The man studied his rearview mirror. "No one who ain't getting smaller."

"Good job," Dunn said.

The FBI chopper kept its distance. The pilot guided the federal convoy as Luciano's men grew farther behind. At the last exit before the road narrowed Piper knew where they were headed.

"He's going to the riverfront," Sean said from the passenger's seat.

"You sure?" Soard asked as he hummed the Mercedes CLS Coupe he borrowed from the boys in narcotics down the off ramp. It was the only car in the motor pool that could keep up with Dunn's men.

"I've been coming this way every week for the last year," Sean said. "There's nothing out this far but the rest of the homes their tearing down for the riverfront project."

Soard grabbed his radio. "Luc', they're heading for the river."

"Way ahead of you, Mason," he said.

Luciano sent the helicopter to scope out the shell buildings on the land beside the Saucostee Reservation. The pilot swooped in low enough to see a truck parked outside the one closest to the Lafayette.

"Lights in the first warehouse," Luciano said.

Soard had him on speaker. "You know how to get there?" he asked Piper.

Sean ran behind the warehouse all the time.

"Yeah, it's near the bike trail," he said.

Soard smiled. "I'm glad I brought you along."

The Escalade circled the industrial park. It slowed at the warehouse Dunn planned to use for storage once he got the green light to build his casino. It was empty now and dark, except for one end where the truck was parked. The helicopter radioed one more transmission before it ducked behind a clump of trees on the other side of the Lafayette.

Luciano told his men to cut the headlights. They crawled along the riverbank to a trailer the foreman used about two hundred yards from the warehouse.

Soard left one agent, Gordon, in the rear to watch Piper. The young lawyer looked able to take care of himself, but Sean was a civilian, at least most of the time, and Pete wasn't losing any more of those tonight.

"Turn your radio up all the way," he said. "And watch your back. We haven't reconned this site. In this light I can't tell what's out here."

"You want me to sit in the car?" Piper asked. "What am I going to do way back here?"

"Stay out of trouble," Pete said. "You've done your job today, Sean. They'd have two more hostages if it weren't for you, or maybe we'd have two more bodies on our hands. You brought us this far, we'll take it from here."

"But—"

"Chuck," he said to Agent Gordon, "sit on him if you have to."

"Sure thing, Pete."

"Toss me those NVGs. It's pitch black out there."

Luciano had his out already, studying the terrain through the night vision goggles from the other side of the parking lot. Soard fitted his and kneeled down for a closer look.

Luciano adjusted his earpiece and slid his microphone in position. Soard did the same and they were back on the net.

"Not a lot of cover, is there?" Luciano asked.

"No," Pete said. "They clear cut the place. Luc', your men in position?"

"Affirmative. There's a hatch on the north side of the building. There are no lights, and I don't see anyone guarding it. If they're at the other end we might be able to crack it open."

"Roger. We're not so lucky," Soard told him. "I can see a silhouette in the doorway on our side. He's definitely watching the vehicles. He shouldn't be able to see past the parking lot, but that's far enough. We'll never make it to the front. We need another way inside."

Luciano spotted something through the infrared binoculars. "Got your toolbox?" he asked.

Luciano guided him to the fire escape and an extension ladder leaning against the west side.

"If you can get to the roof you might be able to come straight down on 'em," he suggested.

"That may take us some time," he said.

Luciano's sniper already had a silencer on his rifle, and Dunn's car in his sights.

"Okay, but hurry up. Sanchez has a bead on the *Cadillac.* If they try to leave they won't get very far without any tires."

Agent Driscoll crawled up beside his team leader. Soard signaled the route. "Let's go, Ron," he whispered.

Soard and Driscoll sprinted through the undeveloped lot, hurdling debris in the huge construction site. They dropped and then low-crawled the last fifty feet to the corner of the warehouse, shielding themselves behind a moving pallet until they reached the ladder. They shimmied up single file. Soard poked his head above the roofline and the coast was clear. They tiptoed past the HVAC unit and a door that gave the fifty thousand square foot building access at its southern end.

"Can you do anything about that lock?" Soard asked him.

The agent eyeballed the steel door and its complicated latch.

"Yes," Driscoll answered. He reached in his jacket and took out a kit that had more tools than a hardware store. "Question is, will they hear it?"

Luciano made it inside without resistance, stopping at a rally point to get their bearings. There were four men in his team, none more reliable than Agent Reni Sanchez.

"Reni," Luciano whispered. He gave a fast hand and arm signal and Sanchez knew what to do. He crept along the darkened hallway and then low-crawled as close as he could get to Dunn. Luciano kept in contact with him on the wire.

"Watch out for the exits. I don't know where that fire escape comes out."

Soard broke in, "Right above them. We're on top of them now, Luc'," Pete said softly. Driscoll had done a safe cracker's job on the lock.

"How many are there?" Luciano asked.

"I see seven counting Dunn."

"That sounds about right," Luciano said. "They kept coming out of the Escalade like it was a circus act. Where's Hawkins?"

"Just sitting there" Pete said.

"And the girl?"

"Tied up right beside Bubba."

Piper listened over the car radio as they planned their next move. "Seven?" he said as Agent Gordon stared into the night. "They're outnumbered. We've gotta help."

Gordon kept his ear to the radio waiting for someone to call for backup.

"Did you hear me?" Sean nudged him. "Let's go."

A sharp metal sound caught them from behind. "Don't move," a man's voice commanded.

Gordon tried to cut off the radio before Dunn's man in the parking lot heard any more of their plans, but all he got for it was a barrel to the side of the head. He slumped over the wheel out cold.

"You wanna get cute, too?" he asked Piper. "That was just a love tap," he told him. "Get out of the car. And bring your buddy, too."

Sean helped Gordon to his feet. They started the long walk to the warehouse. The route was more direct than Soard had taken. The service roads were freshly paved and black as coal. Piper marched beside the shaken agent. Every few steps his knees buckled. He draped Gordon's arm around his neck and dragged him toward the river.

The gunman said, "Ain't that sweet?"

Piper stared straight ahead. The storm drains near the sidewalk were almost impossible to see except for the ones near the streetlights.

"Just helping him along, mister," he said. Sean drifted toward the curb under Gordon's weight. As they passed each lamppost he could see the man's shadow following closely behind them.

Sean whispered into Gordon's ear, "When I squeeze your arm, go completely limp. Can you do it?"

Gordon thought he'd already been doing that. He nodded slightly and Piper said, "Get ready."

"Shut up!" the man yelled. "I ain't telling you that again."

Piper took a long stride directly over the gutter. The gunman didn't see the hazard and stepped between the iron drain. Sean squeezed Gordon's arm and the agent went soft as a feather bed. Sean raked him off his body and threw the dead weight at their captor's feet. The blow jarred the gun from his hand. It bounced on the pavement and rattled down the sewer. Piper jumped on top of him and pummeled the man's head with a series of his own love taps he guaranteed would go unrequited. Sean rolled him on his back, un-looped the man's belt and hog-tied him with it. He was cold meat set out for the next cop who came along, with Gordon to make sure of it.

"I gotta leave you here," Sean told the agent. "You gonna make it?"

"Yeah, Sean. I'll be all right."

"Okay. If this son of a bitch wakes up, kick him in the stomach 'til he's dead."

Gordon leaned against the lamppost to catch his breath. "My pleasure," he said.

Piper moved off the road as far away from the lights as he could get without drowning himself in the Lafayette. He kept low as he neared the side where Soard made his rooftop entrance. He lay face down eyeing the ladder, watching for any movement.

"Get up," a deep voice behind him said. "Slowly."

Piper stood. "I'm unarmed," he promised.

"Good. I won't have to take your gun away then," the man said. "Where the hell's my wife?"

Piper turned slowly and squinted at the huge figure. "Eddie Hall?" he said.

"I asked you a question. Where is she?"

"Thank God. I thought you were dead."

"I'm only going to ask you one more time. Where's Selena?"

"In there," Sean pointed. "At least that's where the FBI thinks she is."

"Are you a cop?"

"No. I work for the City Attorney's Office."

"They got my boy in there, too?"

"No," Piper assured him. "He's safe. Mrs. Goolsby's with him. They're at the federal building. How'd you find me?"

"I saw your car. City logo was staring me in the face, until someone cracked my skull."

"Sylvia," Piper said. There was a massive 'Bristol Pride' logo that covered every square inch of her Ombuds-person car.

"I went to see you downtown, but when I got there everyone was running to the parking lot. I figured you were with them."

"And you tailed us here?"

"Yeah. You and the helicopter. It was like following a parade."

"Oh. Well, can I put my hands down now?" Sean asked.

"Yeah, dummy. I didn't tell you to put them up."

"Thank you."

"You work with my wife's lawyer, the one they killed?"

"Yes. How'd you know he was murdered? Did Sylvia tell you that, too?"

"Was that you whooping up on that dude back there?" Eddie asked admiringly.

"Uh-huh."

"Who's the guy leaning against the pole?"

"He's a federal agent." Piper said. "He's hurt. I told him to watch that fella, but I don't think he's getting up any time soon."

"Yeah. I saw you work him over pretty good. Got any of that left?"

Sean dusted himself off. Adrenalin pumped through his veins and rage leaked from his ears as he felt Pomerantz' killer near.

"Eddie, yesterday somebody put a bullet in my boss' head. I held him as he was dying. Today, they chased me all over town, kidnapped your wife, and tried to kidnap your little boy and his great-grandmother. A man stuck a gun in my back as he marched us to what I'm fairly confident was not the Welcome Wagon. They won't stop until I'm dead. So, yeah," he nodded, "I got some more left."

"All right. Come on then," Eddie said. "And if I were you I'd stick close to me, unless you brought a gun, too."

Sanchez scouted out positions for the rest of Luciano's team. Dunn and his men were in the warehouse manager's office except for the two who guarded the door. They were close enough to hear inside.

"What the hell, Bubba?" Dunn dangled the wire Hawkins had worn, "when did you start recording your conversations with me?"

Bubba jerked like he wasn't going to make it.

"Did you think I wouldn't hear about your little run in with the law?" Dunn asked.

Bubba wrestled against the thick ropes that bound him to the folding chair. He looked just like Selena, except she was beautiful, even tied up and terrified.

"Yeah. Guy named…what was his name, Randall?"

"Skeeter," Jennings said. "Skeeter Teal."

"Yes, that's it. Skeeter phoned just in time to alert me before you showed up this evening, unannounced."

Dunn strolled over and tapped him on the shoulder. "Why, Bubba? You could've had it all."

"Like hell," Bubba said defiantly.

Dunn's eyebrows rose to the ceiling. "You don't believe me?"

"No, Warren. I don't. Just like I didn't believe it when you had the D.A. killed. We never talked about anything like that."

"Circumstances change, Bubba. You know that. I didn't hear any objections from you when I legalized gambling in Bristol. Legitimized all of your high class establishments along the highway. You knew what I was doing. And it would've worked, too. If this beautiful fly in the ointment hadn't come along." He stroked her Selena's high cheekbones. "I still haven't decided what I'm going to do about that."

"Please!" Selena begged. "I don't know anything! I swear it!" She tried to calm herself. "I've been in California the last two weeks. Michael told me nothing about you. I don't even know what's on my answering machine. I still haven't heard the message. Please, just let me go. I don't know where we are now. And I swear I won't try to find out. Please!" she cried. "Just let me go home!"

Soard covered his mouth and whispered into his headset, "Talk to me, Luc'."

"Reni?" Luciano said.

"I can drop one from here," Sanchez said as he crouched in the rafters. "Maybe two."

Not enough, Nick thought. "Cole?"

Agent Cole didn't have a clear shot. He tried crawling to a better spot. His pants leg snagged on a nail that sent a loose board crashing to the ground.

Dunn's men jumped. Luciano's froze.

"Steady," Nick whispered. He opened a lock-blade and held the knife like he was about to carve a frozen turkey.

"Go see what it is," Dunn said.

Luciano made a split decision and it cost the gunman nearest him his life. He covered the guard's mouth and drove the blade into his abdomen, ripping it to his throat as he set the lifeless body at his feet.

Soard saw it and thought he was going to throw up. Before he knew it Sanchez dropped the other man who'd been posted up front with a single round from his silencer.

Luciano counted the live heads. The odds were as even as they were going to get.

"Everybody freeze!" he ordered at the top of his lungs.

Jennings drew his gun. Sorensen pulled his and rested it on Selena Hall's tender shoulder. Someone grabbed Dunn and made sure he wasn't in the line of fire.

"Drop it!" Luciano commanded.

Jennings saw a figure aiming at him from the shadows, and at least one more in the corner. A gunman who'd circled behind them all set Luciano straight.

"No, you drop it," he said.

Sorensen cocked the hammer and held his pistol up to Selena's head.

"Now!" Luciano yelled

Soard dropped from the rafters and knocked Sorensen into the next world. Selena screamed as the unconscious thug landed in her lap.

Sanchez fired a three round burst at the man covering Luciano. He dropped another before the first one hit the ground. Cole covered the rest of the team as they moved closer to the firefight.

Dunn's men opened up with everything they had. The misses ricocheted and echoed off sheet metal to the rafters. Dunn picked up Sorensen's weapon. He snuck over to his old business partner and fired at the helpless man's back. Bubba kicked wildly, and Dunn shot him again for good measure.

Soard wrestled with the man who'd killed Pomerantz. He was outweighed by a hundred pounds, but the Special Agent was holding his own. Dunn lined him up. It was a moving target this time, and he missed badly. He sighted in again as the D.A.'s killer had Pete in a clinch.

"No!" Piper shouted. Dunn squeezed the trigger, and Soard's body jerked wildly. Sean tackled Dunn, and the gun flew out of his hand. Eddie Hall filled Pomerantz' killer with enough lead to block an x-ray. He kicked Sorensen off his wife and picked her up chair and all.

Someone threw his gun down and said he'd had enough.

"On your knees!" Luciano ordered.

Another did the same and was treated to a concrete face plant.

"Pat 'em down," Luciano said. "Sanchez, get a count."

The sniper scurried through the carnage and reported to his boss. "They got Cole, boss."

"Get an ambulance!" Luciano shouted. "Now!" He looked for the thumbs-up from his number two man. It wasn't there. "Where's Mason?"

Sanchez turned him on his side. "Over here, Luc'."

Nick raced over. Sanchez shined a light on the wound. Blood poured from Soard's lower back.

"Pete, can you hear me?" Luciano asked.

"Yeah," Soard managed. "There's nothing wrong with my ears. My back's been better, though," he said.

"Hurry up with that ambulance!" Luciano pleaded. "Hang on, Pete, we'll get you out of here in a second."

"I can't feel my leg, Nick," Soard groaned.

"Forget it," he told Sanchez. "The chopper's in the parking lot. Call the hospital and get clearance for their pad. Move it!"

Eddie cut the ropes that strangled his wife's smooth hands and legs. She threw her arms around him and he almost choked.

"It's over baby," he said. "It's over."

"Where's my son?" Selena sobbed. "What'd they do to my son?"

"Our son," he said. "He's fine. Your grandmother is, too. I'll take you to them."

"Oh, God," Selena cried. "Eddie, I've never been so scared in all my life. I knew they were going to kill me. I just knew it. I thought they'd gotten you this afternoon."

"It's okay, baby. I'm here," he held her close. "It's over, Selena. It's over."

She kissed him. He had to pull away or she'd still be there.

"Eddie, I know when I wake up tomorrow none of this will have happened. I thought the best thing would be for us to go our separate ways. But right now I can't imagine anything worse."

He smiled even as his head throbbed from the concussion. "Oh, yeah? You know I had planned to kick your butt in court. But I'm too tired to do it."

"Some things will have to change," she said.

"I know. Like I could stop getting hit in the head. People could stop shooting at me. That'd be good."

"I mean between us."

"I know what you mean," Eddie said. "I can live with that."

She kissed him again and this time he wasn't getting away. "So can I."

CHAPTER 41

The innkeeper escorted Laura Soard to the only telephone on the floor. No one knew how to find her here, except for Pete and the caller didn't say who it was. It was five-thirty in London, late at night where her husband was.

"Hello," she said.

"Mrs. Soard?"

"Oh, God," she whispered. She'd always heard they broke this kind of news face-to-face, and before the press heard about it.

"Mrs. Soard? Are you there?"

"Yes. I'm here."

"My name is Special Agent Luciano. I've been working with your husband for the past year."

She never knew what he'd been doing for sure, or with whom he did it. Pete just told her to tell everyone he was incredibly dull and too embarrassed to burden her with any of it.

"Yes?"

"There's been an accident."

"Oh, no!" she collapsed. The wall kept her from falling.

"But your husband is alive. He's going to be okay."

Nick heard a pitiful noise long distance, like the sound a dog might make if he stepped on a rusty nail running to a dish filled with prime rib.

"Mrs. Soard?"

"Yes," she cried. "I heard you. My husband's alive. Why isn't he telling me all about it?"

"He's in the recovery room. The surgery went well."

"Surgery? What surgery?"

"Mrs. Soard. I wish I could be there in person to tell you, but Pete wanted me to call you right away."

"He did? He's able to talk?"

"Yes, ma'am. He is."

"Well, what happened?"

"He was shot in the back tonight, in the line of duty."

"Oh, no."

"They patched him up. They won't know for a while, but they think he'll make a full recovery."

"Dear Lord."

"You should have seen him, Mrs. Soard. He was unbelievable. Your husband's a hero. You should be very proud."

"When can I talk to him?"

"Not right now. I asked, but they said he needs to rest. I saw him, Mrs. Soard. I saw him with my own eyes. His voice was strong, and his head was clear. He said, 'Call my wife. Tell her I love her.' So Mrs. Soard, what I got to tell you is this. Your husband loves you."

She let go for good this time. Luciano couldn't stand to hear her sweet whimpers, but somehow he knew she'd be able to tell if he put the phone down. She was a good wife.

"Stand by for his call tomorrow, Mrs. Soard. Next time it will be Pete on the line. Okay?" he said. "Is there anything I can do for you? If you need anything while you're overseas, we can make that happen."

"No," she said. "I'm all right."

"Good."

"Agent Luciano?"

"Yes?"

"The next time they let you in to see my husband, find a part of his body they didn't hurt and then punch him as hard as you can there," she said. "And then tell him his wife's gonna have a baby. And that she loves him more than life itself."

Luciano smiled through the line. "Yes, ma'am," he said. "That's one message I don't mind delivering. So long."

****

The federal indictment against Warren Dunn was thirty-seven pages long. The IRS audit uncovered a string of underreporting or no income disclosure at all dating back to his early years in business. The U.S. Attorney put it all on hold so the state could prosecute him for murdering the local D.A. and Dunn's business partner. The feds could have gone first if they'd wanted, but the state had the death penalty. Everyone who'd ever served under Michael Pomerantz volunteered to work on the case.

With Bubba Hawkins dead and Dunn taking the Fifth Amendment when anyone asked him the time of day, Ethan Morgan found himself a man without a country. An old law school classmate who'd made it to the state supreme court pulled him aside over an easy martini late one day. He told him for the record the Bar would have to look into Calhoun & Morgan, starting with its senior partner. And even though Dunn had his mouth padlocked for now, once sentence was passed he'd likely take as many people down with him as he could. The Justice told Morgan that he shouldn't get into a whizzing contest with a skunk, and Morgan said he made good sense. *Between the two of us, he said, if you take an early retirement I promise to put my laziest people on it.* Ethan told him that was the best idea he'd ever heard. Instead of bringing disciplinary charges against him, the Bar sponsored an oil painting for the founding partner of the state's largest law firm a few weeks after he made his retirement official.

Remington Lovelace gave a two-week deposition to federal prosecutors covering every criminal act he'd ever been involved in, heard about, come across or received bad vibes from, in exchange for two years in a federal jail cell for a state-of-the-art one at an island U.S. Territory. Harvey Bing negotiated the deal, which called for his client to be released even sooner if enough indictments are handed down based on his information. The deposition is under seal and cannot be used against him by any ethics group in the world.

The lawyers Morgan and Lovelace left behind called a shareholders meeting to perform a round of synchronized sword falling. They told their new partners that it was a bad mix, things just never clicked as expected, *that it wasn't them, it was us.* The Calhoun lawyers confirmed that it sure as hell was them, and they gave the Morgan folks less time to pack up than the feds had.

Bristol's flawed gambling ordinance opened the door wide enough to drive the trucks Bubba Hawkins' video poker machines came on to every corner of the state. The legislature took up a bill to undo the damage, but it was too late to stop the boom. Trish McDaniel cut a deal with the remaining members of the Saucostee Preservation Coalition to let them keep the land the city had condemned and to build the swankiest resort east of the Mississippi. As the only ones left on the Coalition were members of the Saucostee Tribe, its sovereign leader took over for the

Coalition's Board as well. Thomas Crazy Bear Walker was demoted to regular council member, where his yearly income, minus expenses, and after all the others in the tribe received their share, was around two million dollars. Chief Navarro took Warren Dunn's place as Chairman of the Board and is now the fifth richest American in the world, Native or not.

As part of the arrangement, McDaniel insisted that the Oakdale school system receive more money than any other under a fee-in-lieu of taxes plan for the casino. Several minorities from her district also became honorary members of the Coalition, and got a yearly stipend to go along with that status. She won reelection in what her national party called the biggest landslide in local election history. She replaced Jake Amsler as the top official in Bristol.

Linda Jaffe was appointed the head of the State Consumer Affairs Commission. She holds weekly meetings on procedure and accountability. After Trish McDaniel, she is the most feared woman in the state.

The Marines tracked down Lieutenant Piper in Virginia. His Platoon Commander yanked him off the rifle range to talk to some guy who wanted to send him a reward for saving his wife. Sean said if it wasn't enough to buy him out of his deal with the Marine Corps he could forget it. He didn't think they'd take anything. Sean asked the man how he felt about starting a scholarship for single moms. Eddie Hall said he'd take care of it.

As Special Agent Luciano predicted, Peter Soard made a full recovery from his gunshot wound. An inch to the left and he wouldn't have been so lucky. He was last seen somewhere in Paris, speaking fluent French and interviewing for a position with that country's leading investment firm. The hiring partner liked what he saw, but he did find it odd that there were so many gaps in his résumé.

When the Island Inn manager heard what Sean Piper had done, he invited him and Anne back to Ocracoke for a free week in his best condo. They didn't even mind that it was the height of the off-season.

"Sean," Anne nudged him.

His eyes were closed as the breeze crossed the weathered deck on the third floor and the salt air rose to meet them.

"Hmmm."

"Look at that sunset," she said. "Why can't everything be like that? So simple, and yet so beautiful. Sean, are you listening?"

He pulled her close and stole a kiss. He liked the way her hair smelled. The aloe from the tanning lotion brought forth memories of past vacations and good times.

She ran her fingers over his warm face. It was the roughest beard he'd ever permitted.

"It's not going to be easy, you know?" he said.

"What?"

"The Basic School."

"Who you telling? I'm the one you kept waiting every night while you ran marathons with your backpack. I know how much you've put into this."

"No," he said. "I mean it won't be easy on you, either."

"I know that. But what in life worth having is easy?"

He considered that for a moment as the sun sank on the intracoastal side.

"This," he said, holding her tight.

"Yeah," she remembered. "I guess I did say the sunset was simple, didn't I?"

"I'm not talking about the sunset," he said. "I'm talking about us. This feels so easy. Do you think we'll be able to keep it that way?"

She held him as the seagulls made a final pass before dark, and he found in her a caress she'd saved until now.

"No," she said. "But I'm willing to let you take your best shot."

"You're a good woman, Anne."

She nestled beneath his rough cheek and recalled the way he felt when the city sent him to change its landscape forever. She hoped he'd be able to forget every damned bit of it, everything but the times they had in between. She squeezed his hand and prayed for her part in making the rest go away.

"At least one of us thinks so, Sean. That's all it takes."

THE END

ABOUT THE AUTHOR

Brad Farrar is a lawyer and writer in South Carolina, and a judge advocate in the U.S. Marine Corps Reserve.

Made in the USA
Lexington, KY
03 January 2014